THE SATURDAY EVENING POST

Short Stories from the Post

F.Scott Fitzgerald's
GATSBY GIRLS

F. Scott Fitzgerald's
GATSBY GIRLS

Short Stories from the Post

Thank you to The Saturday Evening Post and Curtis Licensing staff.

Published by

BroadLit®
14011 Ventura Blvd.
Suite 206 E
Sherman Oaks, CA 91423

ISBN 978-0-9890200-4-6

Produced in the United States of America.

Visit us online at www.gatsbygirls.com

F.Scott Fitzgerald's
GATSBY GIRLS

Short Stories from the Post

Published By BroadLit

Edited by Carol Monroe

Designed by Caryn Drake

SABELLA DERN ENTERTAINMENT

THE SATURDAY EVENING POST

BroadLit

Table of Contents

Editor's Note

In 1920, *The Saturday Evening Post* began publishing a weekly feature entitled "Who's Who – And Why, frivolous facts about the great and near great."

The page featured short articles about some of the people in the particular issue. This is what Fitzgerald wrote about himself for the September 18, 1920 issue.

Who's Who - And Why
F.Scott Fitzgerald

The history of my life is the history of the struggle between an overwhelming urge to write and a combination of circumstances bent on keeping me from it.

When I lived in St. Paul and was about twelve I wrote all through every class in school in the back of my geography book and first year Latin and on the margins of themes and declensions and mathematic problems. Two years later a family congress decided that the only way to force me to study was to send me to boarding school. This was a mistake. It took my mind off my writing. I decided to play football, to smoke, to go to college, to do all sorts of irrelevant things that had nothing to do with the real business of life, which, of course, was the proper mixture of description and dialogue in the short story.

But in school I went off on a new tack. I saw a musical comedy called "The Quaker Girl," and from that day forth my desk bulged with Gilbert & Sullivan librettos and dozens of notebooks containing the germs of dozens of musical comedies.

Near the end of my last year at school I came across a new musical-comedy score lying on top of the piano. It was a show called "His Honor the Sultan", and the title furnished the information that it had been presented by the Triangle Club of Princeton University. That was enough for me. From then on the university question was settled. I was bound for Princeton.

I spent my entire Freshman year writing an operetta for the Triangle Club. To do this I failed in algebra, trigonometry, coordinate geometry and hygiene. But the Triangle Club accepted my show, and by tutoring all through a stuffy August I managed to come back a Sophomore and act in it as a chorus girl. A little after this came a hiatus. My health broke down and I left college one December to spend the rest of the year recuperating in the West. Almost my final memory before I left was of writing a last lyric on that year's Triangle production while in bed in the infirmary with a high fever.

The next year, 1916-17, found me back in college, but by this time I had decided that poetry was the only thing worth while, so with my head ringing with the meters of Swinburne and the matters of Rupert Brooke I spent the spring doing sonnets, ballads and rondels into the small hours. I had read somewhere that every great poet had written great poetry before he was twenty-one. I had only a year and, besides, war was impending. I must publish a book of startling verse before I was engulfed. By autumn I was in an infantry officers' training camp at Fort Leavenworth, with poetry in the discard and a brand-new ambition— I was writing an immortal novel. Every evening, concealing my pad behind <u>Small Problems for Infantry</u>, I wrote paragraph after paragraph on a somewhat edited history of me and my imagination. The outline of twenty-two chapters, four of them in verse, was made, two chapters were completed; and then I was detected and the game was up. I could write no more during study period. This was a distinct complication. I had only three months to live—in those days all infantry officers thought they had only three months to live—and I had left no mark on the world. But such consuming ambition was not to be thwarted by a mere war. Every Saturday at one o'clock when the week's work was over I hurried to the Officers' Club, and there, in a corner of a roomful of smoke, conversation and rattling newspapers, I wrote a one-hundred and-twenty-thousand-word novel on the consecutive weekends of three months. There was no revising; there was no time for it. As I finished each chapter I sent it to a typist in Princeton.

Meanwhile I lived in its smeary pencil pages. The drills, marches and <u>Small Problems for Infantry</u> were a shadowy dream. My whole heart was concentrated upon my book.

I went to my regiment happy. I had written a novel. The war could now go on. I forgot paragraphs and pentameters, similes and syllogisms. I got to be a first lieutenant, got my orders overseas— and then the publishers wrote me that though The Romantic Egotist was the most original manuscript they had received for years they couldn't publish it. It was crude and reached no conclusion.

It was six months after this that I arrived in New York and presented my card to the office boys of seven city editors asking to be taken on as a reporter. I had just turned twenty-two, the war was over, and I was going to trail murderers by day and do short stories by night. But the newspapers didn't need me. They sent their office boys out to tell me they didn't need me. They decided definitely and irrevocably by the sound of my name on a calling card that I was absolutely unfitted to be a reporter. Instead I became an advertising man at ninety dollars a month, writing the slogans that while away the weary hours in rural trolley cars. After hours I wrote stories— from March to June. There were nineteen altogether; the quickest written in an hour and a half, the slowest in three days. No one bought them, no one sent personal letters. I had one hundred and twenty-two rejection slips pinned in a frieze about my room. I wrote movies. I wrote song lyrics. I wrote complicated advertising schemes. I wrote poems. I wrote sketches. I wrote jokes. Near the end of June I sold one story for thirty dollars.

On the Fourth of July, utterly disgusted with myself and all the editors, I went home to St. Paul and informed family and friends that I had given up my position and had come home to write a novel.

They nodded politely, changed the subject and spoke of me very gently. But this time I knew what I was doing. I had a novel to write at last, and all through two hot months I wrote and revised and compiled and boiled down. On September fifteenth <u>This Side of Paradise</u> was accepted by special delivery.

In the next two months I wrote eight stories and sold nine. The ninth was accepted by the same magazine that had rejected it four months before. Then, in November, I sold my first story to the editors of *The Saturday Evening Post*.

By February I had sold them half a dozen. Then my novel came out. Then I got married. Now I spend my time wondering how it all happened.

In the words of the immortal Julius Caesar: "That's all there is; there isn't any more."

September 18, 1920

PHOTO. BY ELLIE NEWMAN LIGON, MONTGOMERY, ALA.

In two months he wrote nine stories and sold eight.

Editor's Note

The illustrations in this volume are being presented in three ways. Imbedded in the body of the story are the original illustrations from the *Post*. These have been cropped and repositioned to allow for easier reading of the text.

The first Appendix contains reproductions of the actual pages of the *Post*, so that the reader can experience the story in its entirety, as originally published.

Finally, the second Appendix contains larger images of the illustrations themselves, for easier viewing.

F. SCOTT FITZGERALD AND HIS AMERICAN GIRL

By Jeff Nilsson, historian
The Saturday Evening Post

By the time he published <u>The Great Gatsby</u>, F. Scott Fitzgerald was already one of the best-known authors in America. His fame had begun years earlier with the bestselling novel, <u>This Side of Paradise</u>, which sold out in 24 hours and went through 12 reprintings.

But his reputation rested on more than just his novels. By the time Gatsby hit the bookstores, Americans had been reading Fitzgerald's stories in *The Saturday Evening Post* for five years. The magazine had first printed one of his stories, "Head and Shoulders," in its February 21, 1920 issue, and followed it with five more stories before the end of the year.

In later years, Fitzgerald recalled the elation he felt when he learned the *Post* had bought one of his stories. "I'd like to get a thrill like that again but I suppose it's only once in a lifetime."

It was the beginning of a long association between America's most promising young writer and its most popular magazine. In 1920, the *Post* had over 2.5 million subscribers, and could bring Fitzgerald into the living rooms of Americans who might never have encountered his novels. Over 17 years, it published 68 of his short stories, more than twice the number that appeared in any other publication. Fitzgerald began to get the reputation of a *"Post* writer."

This reputation troubled the critics. One of them was already seeing his talent fading in 1920. Fitzgerald's fiction in the *Post*, he said, was "clever enough but that's all. Trouble is that he is likely to begin with the money rolling to think that this is literature." Even Fitzgerald's friends were concerned, as Hemingway tried to talk him out of submitting any more stories to the *Post*. Another friend warned that the magazine would use up Fitzgerald's talent and then discard him, and that it would be known as "The Graveyard of the Genius of F. Scott Fitzgerald." Fitzgerald wasn't worried. The *Post* was putting his writing in front of more Americans than any other magazine could. It published stories that were too long for any other periodical. It paid him quicker and it paid him more. He earned $400 for the first stories—a competitive price—but the *Post* increased their payments over time until, in 1929, he was earning $4,000 per story.

Making good money with short fiction was important to Fitzgerald. Throughout his career, he earned far more with short stories than he ever did from his novels. Frequent and fat checks from the *Post* enabled him to pursue the more creative work. They also helped him live in the style to which he felt he should be accustomed. Like Gatsby, Fitzgerald was determined to live a life of success and affluence. Like Gatsby, he was determined to succeed so he could win the girl of his dreams. In 1918, he met and fell in love with a judge's daughter, Zelda Sayre, and she accepted his proposal of marriage. Five months later, though, she broke off the engagement when she realized he didn't earn enough money for her comfort. As Daisy Buchanan tells Gatsby, "Rich girls don't marry poor boys." So Fitzgerald set out to make as much money as he could as quickly as he could, to win back his love. The stories came easily to him in 1920; Fitzgerald claimed to have written one of them, "The Camel's Back," in just 24 hours. But he never found revising to be light work. Every story he finished had to be rewritten several times over. His bright, energetic prose was, in fact, the product of days of dreary revision. But in 1920, he was fueled by imagination, ambition, and youth. The ideas came easier then, before he had exhausted himself, doubted his talent, and seen the collapse of his marriage and his wife.

Fitzgerald's first *Post* stories appeared as the country was entering a promising new decade. Americans were hoping to leave behind the bitterness of 1919, with its strikes, race riots, and arrests and the mass deportations of political dissidents. They looked forward to a new decade of prosperity and convenience made possible by affordable automobiles and electrical power. Many homes were still being wired for electricity in 1920, and the *Post* issues that year were filled with ads for electric stoves, washing machines, and light fixtures. Readers also saw ads for glamour cars rarely seen in the muddy streets of small towns—the Auburn Beauty Six, the Cole Aero-Eight, the Haynes Speedster, the Jordan Silhouette, and the Paige ("The Most Beautiful Car In America").

Adding to that year's optimism was the belief in prohibition, which had begun in January. At this early stage, most Americans believed the country would be happier, more prosperous, and more productive now that alcohol was illegal.

The U.S. reached another turning point in 1920. Census figures revealed that, for the first time, more Americans lived in cities than in the country. People were leaving farms and small town; there was little future left in the country.

Many young Americans already sensed this, but Fitzgerald's stories confirmed what they suspected. If they lived in the city, they would have more interesting lives, spending their days at parties, dances, and Ivy League schools. There the young people were smart and witty. The men drank freely and the women flirted shamelessly.

To many young women in America, these stories must have been a revelation. Modern girls, they learned, were cutting their hair short instead of keeping it long and pinned up. Modern girls were abandoning the corset. They wore make up. They smoked cigarettes. They danced to jazz bands. Most girls didn't even know what jazz was; their parent's phonographs only played foxtrots and two-steps, and radio was years in the future. Still, it seemed all very wicked and fun.

In story after story, the heroines of Fitzgerald's stories were reckless and frivolous and happy. None of them spent their days being useful around the house, or assuming the quiet modesty that mother expected. They drove cars. They drank liquor. They kissed boys—many of them—and never worried what others might think of it.

How the eyes of a nice, country girl—and Fitzgerald assumed all country girls were nice—must have widened as she read of women saying and doing things she had barely admitted to herself she wanted. Yet there it was, in the pages of Daddy's *Saturday Evening Post*, between articles like "New

Fashions In Investments" and "The Petroleum Problem In The World."

If American girls hadn't seen any of these modern women on the streets of their own provincial towns, they could be glimpsed in the stories' illustrations: elegant, slender figures lounging around a bar or coupé, wearing loose, sleeveless dresses, cloche hats, and dark lipstick that emphasized their carefree smiles.

This modern woman—who, in time, would be called the "flapper"—was no mere creation of fiction. There was a living example, and her wild escapades were often reported in the newspaper. Her name was Zelda Fitzgerald and her impetuous self-indulgence and irresistible charms were captured repeatedly in the stories of her husband. "I married the heroine of my stories," Fitzgerald said. Nobody better represented the impulsive, fashionable, carefree American woman of the 1920s.

If the flapper seems outdated today, it's important to remember how much of an impact she had when she was new. Her defiance of convention may seem tame today, but only because generations of women have followed in her footsteps.

Fitzgerald's modern tales of yearning and ambition shaped today's fiction, but his short stories, and his Gatsby, helped create today's society and the expectations of America's women.

THE SATURDAY EVENING POST

An Illustrated Weekly
Founded A° D° by Benj. Franklin

FEB. 21   1920

5c. THE COPY
10c. in Canada

Story Illustrations by
Charles D. Mitchell

Irvin S. Cobb – Princess Cantacuzène – Ben Ames Williams
Hugh Wiley – Alice Duer Miller – Alonzo Englebert Taylor

Head and Shoulders was the first of the Fitzgerald stories published in *The Saturday Evening Post*. It appeared on February 21, 1920, just weeks prior to the March release of his first novel, This Side of Paradise.

For the story, Fitzgerald received $400, the then standard rate. By 1929, his fee for a *Post* story was $4,000.

While the story appeared in February, 6 months later, on August 6, 1920, Metro (prior to the addition of Goldwyn and Mayer) released a silent film version of Head and Shoulders. The film, entitled The Chorus Girl's Romance, was directed by William Dowlan.

Head And Shoulders

In 1915 Horace Tarbox was thirteen years old. In that year he took the examinations for entrance to Princeton University and received the Grade A—excellent—in Caesar, Cicero, Vergil, Xenophon, Homer, Algebra, Plane Geometry, Solid Geometry and Chemistry.

Two years later, while George M. Cohan was composing "Over There," Horace was leading the sophomore class by several lengths and digging out theses on The Syllogism as an Obsolete Scholastic Form, and during the Battle of Château-Thierry he was sitting at his desk deciding whether or not to wait until his seventeenth birthday before beginning his series of essays on The Pragmatic Bias of the New Realists.

After a while some newsboy told him that the war was over, and he was glad, because it meant that Peat Brothers, Publishers, would get out their new edition of <u>Spinoza's Improvement of the Understanding</u>. Wars were all very well in their way, made young men self-reliant or something, but Horace felt that he could never forgive the President for allowing a brass band to play under his window on the night of the false Armistice, causing him to leave three important sentences out of his thesis on German Idealism.

The next year he went up to Yale to take his degree as Master of Arts.

He was seventeen then, tall and slender, with nearsighted gray eyes and an air of keeping himself utterly detached from the mere words he let drop.

"I never feel as though I'm talking to him," expostulated Professor Dillinger to a sympathetic colleague. "He makes me feel as though I were talking to his representative. I always expect him to say, 'Well, I'll ask myself and find out.'"

And then, just as nonchalantly as though Horace Tarbox had been Mr. Beef the butcher or Mr. Hat the haberdasher, life reached in, seized him, handled him, stretched him and unrolled him like a piece of Irish lace on a Saturday-afternoon bargain counter.

To move in the literary fashion I should say that this was all because when way back in colonial days the hardy pioneers had come to a bald place in Connecticut and asked of each other, "Now what shall we build here?" the hardiest one among 'em had answered, "Let's build a town where theatrical managers can try out musical comedies!" How afterward they founded Yale College there, to try the musical comedies on, is a story everyone knows. At any rate one December, "Home James" opened at the Shubert and all the students encored Marcia Meadow, who sang a song about the Blundering Blimp in the first act and did a shaky, shivery, celebrated dance in the last.

Marcia was nineteen. She didn't have wings, but audiences agreed generally that she didn't need them. She was a blonde by natural pigment and she wore no paint on the streets at high noon. Outside of that she was no better than most women.

It was Charlie Moon who promised her five thousand cigarettes if she would pay a call on Horace Tarbox, prodigy extraordinary. Charlie was a senior in Sheffield and he and Horace were first cousins. They liked and pitied each other.

Horace had been particularly busy that night. The failure of the Frenchman, Laurier, to synchronize the sources of the new realists was preying on his mind. In fact, his only reaction to a low, clear-cut rap at his study was to make him speculate as to whether any rap would have actual existence without an ear there to hear it. He fancied he was verging more and more toward pragmatism. But at that moment, though he did not know it, he was verging with astounding rapidity toward something quite different.

The rap sounded—three seconds leaked by—the rap sounded.

"Come in," muttered Horace automatically.

He heard the door open and then close, but, bent over his book in the big armchair before the fire, he did not look up.

"Leave it on the bed in the other room," he said absently.

"Leave what on the bed in the other room?"

Marcia Meadow had to talk her songs, but her speaking voice was like byplay on a harp.

"The laundry."

"I can't."

Horace stirred impatiently in his chair.

"Why can't you?"

"Why, because I haven't got it."

"H'm!" he replied testily. "Suppose you go back and get it."

Across the fire from Horace was another easy chair. He was accustomed to change to it in the course of an evening by way of exercise and variety. One chair he called Berkeley, the other he called Hume. He suddenly heard a sound as of a rustling, diaphanous form sinking into Hume. He glanced up.

"Well," said Marcia with the sweet smile she used in Act Two—"Oh, so the Duke liked my dancing !"— "Well, Omar Khayyam, here I am beside you singing in the wilderness."

Horace stared at her dazedly. The momentary suspicion came to him that she existed there only as a phantom of his imagination. Women didn't come into men's rooms and sink into men's Humes. Women brought laundry and took your seat in the street car and married you later on when you were old enough to know fetters.

This woman had clearly materialized out of Hume. Why, the very froth of her brown gauzy dress was an emanation from Hume's leather arm there! If he looked long enough he would see Hume right through her and then he would be alone again in the room. He passed his fist across his eyes. He really must take up those trapeze exercises again.

"For Pete's sake don't look so critical!" objected the

emanation pleasantly. "I feel as if you were going to wish me away with that patent dome of yours. And then there wouldn't be anything left of me except my shadow in your eyes."

Horace coughed. Coughing was one of his two gestures. When he talked you forgot he had a body at all. It was like hearing a phonograph record by a singer who had been dead a long time.

"What do you want?" he asked.

"I want them letters," whined Marcia melodramatically—"them letters of mine you bought from my grand-sire in 1881."

Horace considered.

"I haven't got your letters," he said evenly. "I am only seventeen years old. My father was not born until March 3, 1879. You evidently have me confused with someone else."

"You're only seventeen?" repeated Marcia suspiciously.

"Only seventeen."

"I knew a girl," said Marcia reminiscently, "who went on the ten-twenty-thirty when she was sixteen. She was so stuck on herself that she could never say 'sixteen' without putting the 'only' before it. We got to calling her 'Only Jessie.' And she's just where she was when she started—only worse. 'Only' is a bad habit, Omar—it sounds like an alibi."

"My name is not Omar."

"I know," agreed Marcia, nodding—" your name's Horace. I just call you Omar because you remind me of a smoked cigarette."

"And I haven't your letters. I doubt if I've ever met your grandfather. In fact, I think it very improbable that you yourself were alive in 1881."

Marcia stared at him in wonder.

"Me-1881? Why sure! I was second-line stuff when the Florodora Sextette was still in the convent. I was the original nurse to Mrs. Sol Smith's Juliet. Why, Omar, I was a canteen singer during the War of 1812."

Horace's mind made a sudden successful leap and he smiled.

"*I Know,*" *Agreed Marcia, Nodding—*"*Your Name's Horace.*
I Just Call You Omar Because You Remind Me of a Smoked Cigarette"

"Did Charlie Moon put you up to this?"

Marcia regarded him inscrutably.

"Who's Charlie Moon?"

"Small—wide nostrils—big ears."

She grew several inches and sniffed.

"I'm not in the habit of noticing my friends' nostrils."

"Then it was Charlie?"

Marcia bit her lip—and then yawned.

"Oh, let's change the subject, Omar. I'll pull a snooze in this chair in a minute."

"Yes," replied Horace gravely, "Hume has often been considered soporific."

"Who's your friend—and will he die?"

Then of a sudden Horace Tarbox rose slenderly and began to pace the room with his hands in his pockets. This was his other gesture.

"I don't care for this," he said as if he were talking to himself—"at all. Not that I mind your being here—I don't. You're quite a pretty little thing, but I don't like Charlie Moon's sending you up here. Am I a laboratory experiment on which the janitors as well as the chemists can make experiments? Is my intellectual development humorous in any way? Do I look like the pictures of the little Boston boy in the comic magazines? Has that callow ass, Moon, with his eternal tales about his week in Paris, any right to —"

"No!" interrupted Marcia emphatically. "And you're a sweet boy. Come here and kiss me."

Horace stopped quickly in front of her.

"Why do you want me to kiss you?" he asked intently. "Do you just go round kissing people?"

"Why, yes," said Marcia, unruffled. "'At's all life is. Just going round kissing people."

"Well," replied Horace emphatically, "I must say your ideas are horribly garbled! In the first place life isn't just that, and in the second place I won't kiss you. It might get to be a habit and I can't get rid of habits. This year I've got in the habit of lolling in bed until seven-thirty."

Marcia nodded understandingly.

"Do you ever have any fun?" she asked.

"What do you mean by fun?"

"See here," said Marcia sternly, "I like you, Omar, but I wish you'd talk as if you had a line on what you were saying. You sound as if you were gargling a lot of words in your mouth and lost a bet every time you spilled a few. I asked you if you ever had any fun."

Horace shook his head.

"Later perhaps," he answered. "You see I'm a plan. I'm an experiment. I don't say that I don't get tired of it sometimes—I do. Yet—oh, I can't explain! But what you and Charlie Moon call fun wouldn't be fun to me."

"Please explain."

Horace stared at her, started to speak and then changing his mind resumed his walk. After an unsuccessful attempt to determine whether or not he was looking at her Marcia smiled at him.

"Please explain."

Horace turned.

"If I do, will you promise to tell Charlie Moon that I wasn't in?"

"Uh-uh."

"Very well then. Here's my history: I was a 'why' child. I wanted to see the wheels go round. My father was a young economics professor at Princeton. He brought me up on the system of answering every question I asked him to the best of his ability. My response to that gave him the idea of making an experiment in precocity. To aid in the massacre I had ear trouble—seven operations between the ages of nine and twelve. Of course this kept me apart from other boys and made me ripe for forcing. Anyway, while my generation was laboring through Uncle Remus I was honestly enjoying Catullus in the original.

"I passed off my college examinations when I was thirteen because I couldn't help it. My chief associates were professors and I took a tremendous pride in knowing that I had a fine intelligence, for though I was unusually gifted I was not abnormal in other ways. When I was sixteen I got tired of being a freak; I decided that someone had made a bad mistake. Still as I'd gone that far I concluded to finish it up by taking my degree of Master of Arts. My chief interest in life is the study of modern philosophy. I am a realist of the School of Anton Laurier—with Bergsonian trimmings—and I'll be eighteen years old in two months. That's all."

"Whew!" exclaimed Marcia. "That's enough! You do a neat job with the parts of speech."

"Satisfied?"

"No, you haven't kissed me."

"It's not in my program," demurred Horace. "Understand that I don't pretend to be above physical things. They have their place, but—"

"Oh, don't be so darned reasonable!"

"I can't help it."

"I hate these slot-machine people."

"I assure you I —" began Horace.

"Oh, shut up!"

"My own rationality —"

"I didn't say anything about your nationality. You're an Amuricun, ar'n't you?"

"Yes."

"Well, that's 0. K. with me. I got a notion I want to see you do something that isn't in your highbrow program. I want to see if a what-ch-call-em with Brazilian trimmings—that thing you said you were—can be a little human."

Horace shook his head again.

"I won't kiss you."

"My life is blighted," muttered Marcia tragically. "I'm a beaten woman. I'll go through life without ever having a kiss with Brazilian trimmings." She sighed. "Anyways, Omar, will you come and see my show?"

"What show?"

"I'm a wicked actress from "Home James!""

"Light opera?"

"Yes—at a stretch. One of the characters is a Brazilian rice planter. That might interest you."

"I saw "The Bohemian Girl" once," reflected Horace aloud. "I enjoyed it—to some extent."

"Then you'll come?"

"Well, I'm—I'm —"

"Oh, I know—you've got to run down to Brazil for the week-end."

"Not at all. I'd be delighted to come."

Marcia clapped her hands.

"Goody for you! I'll mail you a ticket—Thursday night?"

"Why, I—"

"Good! Thursday night it is."

She stood up and walking close to him laid both hands on his shoulders.

"I like you, Omar. I'm sorry I tried to kid you. I thought you'd be sort of frozen, but you're a nice boy."

He eyed her sardonically.

"I'm several thousand generations older than you are."

"You carry your age well."

They shook hands gravely.

"My name's Marcia Meadow," she said emphatically.

"I Hope I Haven't Given You the Impression That I Consider Kissing Intrinsically Irrational"

"'Member it—Marcia Meadow. And I won't tell Charlie Moon you were in."

An instant later as she was skimming down the last flight of stairs three at a time she heard a voice call over the upper banister, "Oh, say —"

She stopped and looked up—made out a vague form leaning over.

"Oh, say !" called the prodigy again. "Can you hear me?"

"Here's your connection, Omar."

"I hope I haven't given you the impression that I consider kissing intrinsically irrational."

"Impression? Why, you didn't even give me the kiss! Never fret—so long."

Two doors near her opened curiously at the sound of a feminine voice. A tentative cough sounded from above. Gathering her skirts, Marcia dived wildly down the last flight and was swallowed up in the murky Connecticut air outside.

Upstairs Horace paced the floor of his study. From time to time he glanced toward Berkeley waiting there in suave dark- red respectability, an open book lying suggestively on his cushions. And then he found that circuit of the floor was bringing him each time nearer to Hume. There was something about Hume that was strangely and inexpressibly different. The diaphanous form still seemed hovering near and had Horace sat there he would have felt as if he were sitting on a lady's lap. And though Horace couldn't have named the quality of difference, there was such a quality—quite intangible to the speculative mind, but real nevertheless. Hume was radiating something that in all the two hundred years of his influence he had never radiated before. Hume was radiating attar of roses.

II

On Thursday night Horace Tarbox sat in an aisle seat in the fifth row and witnessed "Home James." Oddly enough he found that he was enjoying himself. The cynical students near him were annoyed at his audible appreciation of time-honored jokes in the Hammerstein tradition. But Horace was waiting with anxiety for Marcia Meadow singing her song about a jazz-bound Blundering Blimp. When she did appear, radiant under a floppity flower-faced hat, a warm glow settled over him, and when the song was over he did not join in the storm of applause. He felt somewhat numb.

In the intermission after the second act an usher materialized beside him, demanded to know if he were Mr. Tarbox and then handed him a note written in a round adolescent hand. Horace read it in some confusion, while the usher lingered with withering patience in the aisle.

> *Dear Omar:*
> *After the show I always grow an awful hunger.*
> *If you want to satisfy it for me in the Taft Grill*
> *just communicate your answer to the big-*
> *timber guide that brought this and oblige.*
> *Your friend,   MARCIA MEADOW.*

"Tell her "—he coughed—" tell her that it will be quite all right. I'll meet her in front of the theater."

The big-timber guide smiled arrogantly.

"I gins she meant for you to come roun' t' the stage door."

"Where—where is it?"

"Ou'side. Tunayulef. Down ee alley."

"What?"

"Ou'side. Turn to y'left! Down ee alley!"

The arrogant person withdrew. A freshman behind Horace snickered.

Then half an hour later, sitting in the Taft Grill opposite the hair that was yellow by natural pigment, the prodigy was saying an odd thing.

"Do you have to do that dance in the last act?" he was asking earnestly—"I mean, would they dismiss you if you refused to do it?"

Marcia grinned.

"It's fun to do it. I like to do it."

And then Horace came out with a faux pas.

"I should think you'd detest it," he remarked succinctly. "The people behind me were making remarks about your bosom."

Marcia blushed fiery red.

"I can't help that," she said quickly. "The dance to me is only a sort of acrobatic stunt. Lord, it's hard enough to do! I rub liniment into my shoulders for an hour every night."

"Do you have—fun while you're on the stage?"

"Uh-huh—sure! I got in the habit of having people look at me, Omar, and I like it."

"H'm!' Horace sank into a brownish study.

"How's the Brazilian trimmings?"

"H'm!" repeated Horace, and then after a pause—"Where does the play go from here?"

"New York."

"For how long?"

"All depends. Winter—maybe."

"Oh!"

"Coming up to lay eyes on me, Omar, or aren't you int'rested? Not as nice here, is it, as it was up in your room? I wish we was there now. "

"I feel idiotic in this place," confessed Horace, looking round him nervously.

"Too bad! We got along pretty well."

At this he looked suddenly so melancholy that she changed her tone and reaching over patted his hand.

"Ever take an actress out to supper before?"

"No," said Horace miserably, "and I never will again. I don't know why I came tonight. Here under all these lights and with all these people laughing and chattering I feel completely out of my sphere. I don't know what to talk to you about."

"We'll talk about me. We talked about you last time."

"Very well."

"Well, my name really is Meadow, but my first name isn't Marcia—it's Veronica. I'm nineteen. Question—how did the girl make her leap to the footlights? Answer—she was born in Passaic, New Jersey, and up to a year ago she got the right to breathe by pushing biscuits in Marcel's tea room in Trenton. She started going with a guy named Robbins, a singer in the Trent House cabaret, and he got her to try a song and dance with him one evening. In a month we were filling the supper room every night. Then we went to New York with meet-my-friend letters thick as a pile of napkins.

"In two days we'd landed a job at Divinerries' and I learned to shimmy from a kid at the Palais Royal. We stayed at Divinerries' six months until one night Peter Boyce Wendell, the columnist, ate his milk toast there. Next morning a poem about Marvelous Marcia came out in his newspaper and within two days I had three vaudeville offers and a chance at the Midnight Frolic. I wrote Wendell a thank-you letter and he printed it in his column—said that the style was like Carlyle's, only more rugged, and that I ought to quit dancing and do North American literature. This got me a coupla more vaudeville offers and a chance as an ingénue in a regular show. I took it – and here I am, Omar."

When she finished they sat for a moment in silence, she draping the last skeins of a Welsh rabbit on her fork and waiting for him to speak.

"Let's get out of here," he said suddenly.

Marcia's eyes hardened.

"What's the idea? Am I making you sick?"

"No, but I don't like it here. I don't like to be sitting here with you."

Without another word Marcia signaled.

"What's the check?" she demanded briskly. "My part—the rabbit and the ginger ale."

Horace watched blankly as the waiter figured it.

"See here," he began, "I intended to pay for yours too. You're my guest."

With a half sigh Marcia rose from the table and walked from the room. Horace, his face a document in bewilderment, laid a bill down and followed her out, up the stairs and into the lobby. He overtook her in front of the elevator and they faced each other.

"See here," he repeated, "you're my guest. Have I said something to offend you?"

After an instant of wonder Marcia's eyes softened.

"You're a rude fella," she said slowly. "Don't you know you're rude?"

"I can't help it," said Horace with a directness she found quite disarming. "You know I like you."

"You said you didn't like being with me."

"I didn't like it."

"Why not?"

Fire blazed suddenly from the gray forests of his eyes.

"Because I didn't. I've formed the habit of liking you. I've been thinking of nothing much else for two days."

"Well, if you—"

"Wait a minute," he interrupted. "I've got something to say. It's this: in six weeks I'll be eighteen years old. When I'm eighteen years old I'm coming up to New York to see you. Is there some place in New York where we can go and not have a lot of people in the room?"

"Sure!" smiled Marcia. "You can come up to my 'partment. Sleep on the couch if you want to."

"I can't sleep on couches," he said shortly. "But I want to talk to you."

"Why sure," repeated Marcia—"in my 'partment."

In his excitement Horace put his hands in his pockets.

"All right—just so I can see you alone. I want to talk to you as we talked up in my room."

"Honey boy," cried Marcia Laughing, "is it that you want to kiss me?"

"Yes," Horace almost shouted, "I'll kiss you if you want me to."

"What Do They Expect for a Hundred a Week—Perpetual Motion?" She Grumbled to Herself in the Wings

The elevator man was looking at them reproachfully. Marcia edged toward the grated door.

"I'll drop you a post card," she said.

Horace's eyes were quite wild.

"Send me a post card! I'll come up any time after January first. I'll be eighteen then."

And as she stepped into the elevator he coughed enigmatically, yet with a vague challenge, at the ceiling, and walked quickly away.

III

He was there again. She saw him when she took her first glance at the restless Manhattan audience—down in the front row with his head bent a bit forward and his gray eyes fixed on her. And she knew that to him they were alone together in a world where the high-rouged row of ballet faces and the massed whines of the violins were as imperceivable as powder on a marble Venus. An instinctive defiance rose within her.

"Silly boy!" she said to herself hurriedly and she didn't take her encore.

"What do they expect for a hundred a week—perpetual motion?" she grumbled to herself in the wings.

"What's the trouble, Marcia?"

"Guy I don't like down in front."

During the last act as she waited for her specialty she had an odd attack of stage fright. She had never sent Horace the promised post card. Last night she had pretended not to see him—had hurried from the theater immediately after her dance to pass a sleepless night in her apartment, thinking—as she had so often in the last month— of his pale, rather intent face, his slim, boyish figure, the merciless, unworldly abstraction that made him charming to her.

And now that he had come she felt vaguely sorry—as though an unwonted responsibility was being forced on her.

"Infant prodigy!" she said aloud.

"What?' demanded the Negro comedian standing beside her. "Nothing—just talking about myself."

On the stage she felt better. This was her dance—and she always felt that the way she did it wasn't suggestive any more than to some men every pretty girl is suggestive. She made it a stunt.

Uptown, downtown, jelly on a spoon,
After sundown shiver by the moon.

He was not watching her now. She saw that clearly. He was looking very deliberately at a castle on the back drop, wearing that expression he had worn in the Taft Grill. A wave of exasperation swept over her—he was criticizing her.

That's the vibration that thr-ills me,
Funny how affection fi-ills me,
Uptown, downtown—

Unconquerable revulsion seized her. She was suddenly and horribly conscious of her audience as she had never been since her first appearance. Was that a leer on a pallid face in the front row, a droop of disgust on one young girl's mouth? These shoulders of hers—these shoulders shaking—were they hers? Were they real? Surely shoulders weren't made for this!

Then—you'll—see at a glance
I'll need some funeral ushers with St. Vitus dance
At the end of the world I'll –

The bassoon and two cellos crashed into a final chord. She paused and poised a moment on her toes with every muscle tense, her young face looking out dully at the audience in what one young girl afterward called "such a curious, puzzled look," and then without bowing rushed from the stage. Into the dressing room she sped, kicked out of one dress and into another and caught a taxi outside.

Her apartment was very warm—small, it was, with a row of professional pictures and sets of Kipling and O. Henry which she had bought once from a blue-eyed agent and read occasionally. And there were several chairs which matched, but were none of them comfortable, and a pink-shaded lamp with blackbirds painted on it and an atmosphere of rather-stifled pink throughout. There were nice things in it—nice things unrelentingly hostile to each other, offsprings of a vicarious, impatient taste acting in stray moments.

The worst was typified by a great picture framed in oak bark of Passaic as seen from the Erie Railroad—altogether a frantic, oddly extravagant, oddly penurious attempt to make a cheerful room. Marcia knew it was a failure.

Into this room came the prodigy and took her two hands awkwardly.

"I followed you this time," he said.

"Oh!"

"I want you to marry me," he said.

Her arms went out to him. She kissed his mouth with a sort of passionate wholesomeness.

"There!"

"I love you," he said.

She kissed him again and then with a little sigh flung herself into an armchair and half lay there, shaken with absurd laughter.

"Why, you infant prodigy!" she cried.

"Very well, call me that if you want to. I once told you that I was ten thousand years older than you—I am."

She laughed again.

"I don't like to be disapproved of."

"No one's ever going to disapprove of you again."

"Omar," she asked, "why do you want to marry me?"

The prodigy rose and put his hands in his pockets.

"Because I love you, Marcia Meadow."

And then she stopped calling him Omar.

"Dear boy," she said, "you know I sort of love you. There's something about you—I can't tell what—that just puts my heart through the wringer every time I'm round you. But, honey —" she paused.

"But what?"

"But lots of things. But you're only just eighteen and I'm nearly twenty."

"Nonsense!" he interrupted. "Put it this way—that I'm in my nineteenth year and you're nineteen. That makes us pretty close—without counting that other ten thousand years I mentioned."

Marcia laughed.

"But there are some more 'buts.' Your people —"

"My people!" exclaimed the prodigy ferociously. 'My people tried to make a monstrosity out of me." His face grew quite crimson at the enormity of what he was going to say. "My people can go way back and sit down!"

"My heavens!" cried Marcia in alarm. "All that? On tacks, I suppose."

"Tacks—yes," he agreed wildly— "or anything. The more I think of how they allowed me to become a little dried-up mummy -"

"What makes you think you're that?" asked Marcia quietly—"me? "

"Yes, every person I've met on the streets since I met you has made me jealous because they knew what love was before I did. I used to call it the 'sex impulse.' Heavens!"

"There's more 'buts,'" said Marcia.

"What are they?"

"How could we live?"

"I'll make a living."

"You're in college."

"Do you think I care anything about taking a Master of Arts degree?"

"You want to be Master of Me, hey?"

"Yes! What? I mean, no!"

Marcia laughed, and crossing swiftly over sat in his lap. He put his arm round her wildly and implanted the vestige of a kiss somewhere near her neck.

"There's something white about you," mused Marcia, "but it doesn't sound very logical."

"Oh, don't be so darned reasonable!"

"I can't help it," said Marcia.

"I hate these slot-machine people!"

"But we —"

"Oh, shut up!"

And as Marcia couldn't talk through her ears she had to.

IV

Horace and Marcia were married early in February. The sensation in academic circles both at Yale and Princeton was tremendous. Horace Tarbox, who at fourteen had been played up in the Sunday magazine sections of metropolitan newspapers, was throwing over his career, his chance of being a world authority on American philosophy, by marrying a chorus girl—they made Marcia a chorus girl. But like all modern stories it was a four-and-a half-day wonder.

They took a flat in Harlem. After two weeks' search, during which his idea of the value of academic knowledge faded unmercifully, Horace took a position as clerk with a South American export company—someone had told him that exporting was the coming thing. Marcia was to stay in her show for a few months—anyway until he got on his feet. He was getting a hundred and twenty-five to start with, and though of course they told him it was only a question of months until he would be earning double that, Marcia refused even to consider giving up the hundred and fifty a week that she was getting at the time.

"We'll call ourselves Head and Shoulders, dear," she said softly, "and the shoulders 'll have to keep shaking a little longer until the old head gets started."

"I hate it," he objected gloomily.

"Well," she replied emphatically, "your salary wouldn't keep us in a tenement. Don't think I want to be public—I don't. I want to be yours. But I'd be a half-wit to sit in one room and count the sunflowers on the wall paper while I waited for you. When you pull down three hundred a month I'll quit."

And much as it hurt his pride, Horace had to admit that hers was the wiser course.

March mellowed into April. May read a gorgeous riot act to the parks and waters of Manhattan and they were very happy. Horace, who had no habits whatsoever— he had never had time to form any—proved the most adaptable of husbands, and as Marcia entirely lacked opinions on the subjects that engrossed him there were very few joltings and bumpings. Their minds moved in different spheres. Marcia acted as practical factotum and Horace lived either in his old world of abstract ideas or in a sort of triumphantly earthy worship and adoration of his wife. She was a continual source of astonishment to him—the freshness and originality of her mind, her dynamic, clear-headed energy and her unfailing good humor.

And Marcia's coworkers in the nine-o'clock show, whither she had transferred her talents, were impressed with her tremendous pride in her husband's mental powers. Horace they knew only as a very slim, tight-lipped and immature-looking young man who waited every night to take her home.

"Horace," said Marcia one evening when she met him as usual at eleven, "you looked like a ghost standing there against the street lights. You losing weight?"

He shook his head vaguely.

"I don't know. They raised me to a hundred and thirty-five dollars to-day and —"

"I don't care," said Marcia severely. "You're killing yourself working at night. You read those big books on economy —"

"Economics," corrected Horace.

"Well, you read 'em every night long after I'm asleep. And you're getting all stooped over like you were before we were married."

"But, Marcia, I've got to —"

"No, you haven't, dear. I guess I'm running this shop for the present and I won't let my fella ruin his health and eyes. You got to get some exercise."

"I do. Every morning I —"

"Oh, I know! But those dumb-bells of yours wouldn't give a consumptive two degrees of fever. I mean real exercise. You've got to join a gymnasium. 'Member you told me you were such a trick gymnast once that they tried to get you out for the team in college and they couldn't because you had a standing date with Herb Spencer?"

"I used to enjoy it," mused Horace, "but it would take up too much time now."

"All right," said Marcia. "I'll make a bargain with you. You join a gym and I'll read one of those books from the brown row of 'em."

"Pepys' Diary? Why, that ought to be enjoyable. He's very light."

"Not for me—he isn't. It'll be like digesting plate glass. But you been telling me how much it'd broaden my lookout. Well, you go to a gym three nights a week and I'll take one big dose of Sammy."

Horace hesitated.

"Well —"

"Come on now! You do some giant swings for me and I'll chase some culture for you."

So Horace finally consented and all through a baking summer

he spent three and sometimes four evenings a week experimenting on the trapeze in Skipper's Gymnasium. And in August he admitted to Marcia that it made him capable of more mental work during the day.

"Mens sans in corpore sano," he said.

"Don't believe in it," replied Marcia. "I tried one of those patent medicines once and they're all bunk. You stick to gymnastics."

One night in early September while he was going through one of his contortions on the rings in the nearly deserted room he was addressed by a meditative fat man whom he had noticed watching him for several nights.

"Say, lad, do that stunt you were doin' last night."

Horace grinned at him from his perch.

"I invented it," he said. "I got the idea from the fourth proposition of Euclid."

"What circus he with?"

"He's dead."

"Well, he must of broke his neck doin' that stunt. I set here last night thinkin' sure you was goin' to break yours."

"Like this!" said Horace, and swinging onto the trapeze he did his stunt.

"Don't it kill your neck an' shoulder muscles?"

"It did at first, but inside of a week I wrote the quod erat demonstrandum on it."

"H'm!"

Horace swung idly on the trapeze.

"Ever think of takin' it up professionally?" asked the fat man.

"Not I."

"Good money in it if you're willin' to do stunts like 'at an' can get away with it."

"Here's another," chirped Horace eagerly, and the fat man's mouth dropped suddenly agape as he watched this pinkjerseyed

Prometheus again defy the gods and Isaac Newton.

The night following this encounter Horace got home from work to find a rather pale Marcia stretched out on the sofa waiting for him.

"I fainted twice today," she began without preliminaries.

"What?"

"Yep. You see baby's due in three months now. Doctor says I ought to have quit dancing two weeks ago."

Horace sat down and thought it over.

"I'm glad of course," he said pensively—"I mean glad that we're going to have a baby. But this means a lot of expense."

"I've got two hundred and fifty in the bank," said Marcia hopefully, "and two weeks' pay coming."

Horace computed quickly.

"Including my salary, that'll give us nearly fourteen hundred for the next six months."

Marcia looked blue.

"That all? Course I can get a job singing somewhere this month. And I can go to work again in March."

"Of course, nothing!" said Horace gruffly. "You'll stay right here. Let's see now—there'll be doctor's bills and a nurse, besides the maid. We've got to have some more money."

"Well," said Marcia wearily, "I don't know where it's coming from. It's up to the old Head now. Shoulders is out of business."

Horace rose and pulled on his coat.

"Where are you going?"

"I've got an idea," he answered. "I'll be right back."

Ten minutes later as he headed down the street toward Skipper's Gymnasium he felt a placid wonder quite unmixed with humor at what he was going to do. How he would have gaped at himself a year before! How everyone would have gaped! But when you opened your door at the rap of life you let in many things.

The gymnasium was brightly lit and when his eyes became

accustomed to the glare he found the meditative fat man seated on a pile of canvas mats smoking a big cigar.

"Say," began Horace directly, "were you in earnest last night when you said I could make money on my trapeze stunts?"

"Why, yes," said the fat man in surprise.

"Well, I've been thinking it over and I believe I'd like to try it. I could work at night and on Saturday afternoons—and regularly if the pay is high enough."

The fat man looked at his watch. "Well," he said, "Charlie Paulson's the man to see. He'll book you inside of four days, once he sees you work out. He won't be in now, but I'll get hold of him for tomorrow night."

The fat man was as good as his word. Charlie Paulson arrived next night and put in a wondrous hour watching the prodigy swoop through the air in amazing parabolas and on the night following he brought two large men with him who looked as though they had been born smoking black cigars and talking about money in low passionate voices. Then on the succeeding Saturday Horace Tarbox's torso made its first professional appearance in a gymnastic exhibition at the Coleman Street Gardens. But though the audience numbered nearly five thousand people, Horace felt no nervousness.

From his childhood he had read papers to audiences—learned that trick of detaching himself.

"Marcia," he said cheerfully later that same night, "I think we're out of the woods. Paulson thinks he can get me an opening at the Hippodrome and that means an all winter engagement. The Hippodrome, you know, is a big —"

"Yes, I believe I've heard of it," interrupted Marcia, "but I want to know about this stunt you're doing. It isn't any spectacular suicide, is it?"

"It's nothing," said Horace quietly. "But if you can think of any nicer way of a man killing himself than taking a risk for you why that's the way I want to die."

Marcia reached up and wound both arms tightly round his neck.

"Kiss me," she whispered, "and call me 'dear heart.' I love to hear you say 'dear heart.' And bring me the book to read to-morrow. No more Sam Pepys, but something trick and trashy. I've been wild for something to do all day. I felt like writing letters, but I didn't have anybody to write to."

"Write to me," said Horace. "I'll read them."

"I wish I could," breathed Marcia. "If I knew words enough I could write you the longest love letter in the world—and never get tired."

But after two more months Marcia grew very tired indeed and for a row of nights it was a very anxious, weary-looking young athlete who walked out before the Hippodrome crowd. Then there were two days when his place was taken by a young man who wore pale blue instead of white and got very little applause. But after the two days Horace appeared again, and those who sat close to the stage remarked an expression of beatific happiness on that young acrobat's face, even when he was twisting breathlessly in the air in the middle of his amazing and original shoulder swing. After that performance he laughed at the elevator man and dashed up the stairs to the flat five steps at a time—and then tiptoed very carefully into a quiet room.

"Marcia," he whispered.

"Hello!" She smiled up at him wanly. "Horace, there's something I want you to do. Look in my top bureau drawer and you'll find a big stack of paper. It's a book—sort of—Horace. I wrote it down in these last three months while I've been laid up. I wish you'd take it to that Peter Boyce Wendell, who put my letter in his paper. He could tell you whether it'd be a good book. I wrote it just the way I talk, just the way I wrote that letter to him. It's just a story about a lot of things that happened to me. Will you take it to him, Horace?"

"Yes, darling."

He leaned over the bed until his head was beside her on the pillow and began stroking back her yellow hair.

"Dearest Marcia," he said softly.

"No," she murmured, "call me what I told you to call me."

"Dear heart," he whispered passionately—" dearest, dearest heart."

"What'll we call her?"

They rested a minute in happy drowsy content, while Horace considered.

"We'll call her Marcia Hume Tarbox," he said at length.

"Why the Hume?"

"Because he's the fellow who first introduced us."

"That so?" she murmured, sleepily surprised. "I thought his name was Moon."

Her eyes closed and after a moment the slow, lengthening surge of the bedclothes over her breast showed that she was asleep.

Horace tiptoed over to the bureau and opening the top drawer found a heap of closely scrawled, lead-smeared pages. He looked at the first sheet:

SANDRA PEPYS, SYNCOPATED
BY MARCIA TARBOX

He smiled. So Samuel Pepys had made an impression on her after all. He turned a page and began to read. His smile deepened— he read on. Half an hour passed and he became aware that Marcia had waked and was watching him from the bed.

"Honey," came in a whisper.

"What, Marcia?"

"Do you like it?"

Horace coughed.

"I seem to be reading on. It's bright."

"Take it to Peter Boyce Wendell. Tell him you got the highest marks in Princeton once and that you ought to know when a book's good. Tell him this one's a world beater."

"All right, Marcia," said Horace gently.

Her eyes closed again and Horace crossing over kissed her forehead—stood there for a moment with a look of tender pity. Then he left the room.

All that night the sprawly writing on the pages, the constant mistakes in spelling and grammar and the weird punctuation danced before his eyes. He woke several times in the night, each time full of a welling chaotic sympathy for this desire of Marcia's soul to express itself in words. To him there was something infinitely pathetic about it, and for the first time in months he began to turn over in his mind his own half-forgotten dreams.

He had meant to write a series of books, to popularize the new realism as Schopenhauer had popularized pessimism and William James pragmatism.

But life hadn't come that way. Life took hold of people and forced them into flying rings. He laughed to think of that rap at his door, the diaphanous shadow in Hume, Marcia's threatened kiss.

"And it's still me," he said aloud in wonder as he lay awake in the darkness. "I'm the man who sat in Berkeley with temerity to wonder if that rap would have had actual existence had my ear not been there to hear it. I'm still that man. I could be electrocuted for the crimes he committed.

"Poor gauzy souls trying to express ourselves in something tangible. Marcia with her written book; I with my unwritten ones. Trying to choose our mediums and then taking what we get—and being glad."

V

    <u>Sandra Pepys, Syncopated</u>, with an introduction by Peter Boyce Wendell, the columnist, appeared serially in Jordan's Magazine and came out in book form in March. From its first published installment it attracted attention far and wide. A trite enough subject—a girl from a small New Jersey town coming to New York to go on the stage—treated simply, with a peculiar vividness of phrasing and a haunting undertone of sadness in the very inadequacy of its vocabulary, it made an irresistible appeal.

    Peter Boyce Wendell, who happened at that time to be advocating the enrichment of the American language by the immediate adoption of expressive vernacular words, stood as its sponsor and thundered his endorsement over the placid bromides of the conventional reviewers.

    Marcia received three hundred dollars an installment for the serial publication, which came at an opportune time, for though Horace's monthly salary at the Hippodrome was now more than Marcia's had ever been, young Marcia was emitting shrill cries which they interpreted as a demand for country air. So early April found them installed in a bungalow in Westchester County with a place for a lawn, a place for a garage and a place for everything, including a sound-proof impregnable study in which Marcia faithfully promised Mr. Jordan she would shut herself up when her daughter's demands began to be abated and compose immortally illiterate literature.

    "It's not half bad," thought Horace one night as he was on his way from the station to his house. He was considering several prospects that had opened up, a four months' vaudeville offer in five figures, a chance to go back to Princeton in charge of all gymnasium work. Odd! He had once intended to go back there in charge of all philosophic work, and now he had not even been stirred by the arrival in New York of Anton Laurier, his old idol.

    The gravel crunched raucously under his heel. He saw the

lights of his sitting room gleaming and noticed a big car standing in the drive. Probably Mr. Jordan again, come to persuade Marcia to settle down to work.

She had heard the sound of his approach and her form was silhouetted against the lighted door as she came out to meet him.

"There's some Frenchman here," she whispered nervously. "I can't pronounce his name, but he sounds awful deep. You'll have to jaw with him."

"What Frenchman?"

"You can't prove it by me. He drove up an hour ago with Mr. Jordan and said he wanted to meet Sandra Pepys, and all that sort of thing."

Two men rose from chairs as they went inside.

"Hello, Tarbox," said Jordan. "I've just been bringing together two celebrities. M'sieur Laurier, let me present Mr. Tarbox, Mrs. Tarbox's husband."

"Not Anton Laurier!"

"But, yes. I must come. I have to come. I have read the book of Madame and I have been charmed "—he fumbled in his pocket— "ah, I have read of you too. In this newspaper which I read to-day it has your name."

He finally produced a clipping from a magazine.

"Read it!" he said eagerly. "It has about you too."

Horace's eye skipped down the page.

"A distinct contribution to American dialect literature," it said. "No attempt at literary tone; the book derives its very quality from this fact, as did Huckleberry Finn."

Horace's eyes caught a passage lower down; he became suddenly aghast—read on hurriedly.

"Marcia Tarbox's connection with the stage is not only as a spectator but as the wife of a performer. She was married last year to Horace Tarbox, who every evening delights the children at the Hippodrome with his wondrous flying-ring performance. It is said that the young couple have dubbed themselves Head and Shoulders, referring doubtless to the fact that Mrs. Tarbox supplies the literary and mental qualities while the supple and agile shoulders of her husband contribute their share to the family fortunes.

"Mrs. Tarbox seems to merit that much-abused title—'prodigy.' Only twenty—"

Horace stopped reading and with a very odd expression in his eyes gazed intently at Anton Laurier.

"I want to advise you — " he began hoarsely.

"What?"

"About raps. Don't answer them! Let them alone—have a padded door."

*Story Illustrations by
May Wilson Preston*

DRYCHECK CHARLIE–By George Pattullo

Myra appeared almost concurrently with the publication of This Side of Paradise, on March 20, 1920, and earned $400 for the author.

While not a favorite of Fitzgerald's, the story has been brought to the screen twice. The first time was a mere six months after the story appeared in the *Post*. "Husband Hunters," as the silent film was titled, was released by Fox on September 19, 1920 and directed by Howard Mitchell.

On April 22, 1985, PBS' American Playhouse presented an adaptation entitled "Under the Biltmore Clock" starring Sean Young.

Myra Meets His Family

Probably every boy who has attended an Eastern college in the last ten years has met Myra half a dozen times, for the Myras live on the Eastern colleges, as kittens live on warm milk. When Myra is young, seventeen or so, they call her a "wonderful kid"; in her prime—say, at nineteen—she is tendered the subtle compliment of being referred to by her name alone; and after that she is a "prom trotter" or "the famous coast-to-coast Myra."

You can see her practically any winter afternoon if you stroll through the Biltmore lobby. She will be standing in a group of sophomores just in from Princeton or New Haven, trying to decide whether to dance away the mellow hours at the Club de Vingt or the Plaza Red Room. Afterward one of the sophomores will take her to the theater and ask her down to the February prom—and then dive for a taxi to catch the last train back to college.

Invariably she has a somnolent mother sharing a suite with her on one of the floors above.

When Myra is about twenty-four she thinks over all the nice boys she might have married at one time or other, sighs a little and does the best she can. But no remarks, please! She has given her youth to you; she has blown fragrantly through many ballrooms to the tender tribute of many eyes; she has roused strange surges of romance in a hundred pagan young breasts; and who shall say she hasn't counted?

The particular Myra whom this story concerns will have to have a paragraph of history. I will get it over with as swiftly as possible.

When she was sixteen she lived in a big house in Cleveland and attended Derby School in Connecticut, and it was while she was still there that she started going to prep-school dances and college proms. She decided to spend the war at Smith College, but in January of her freshman year falling violently in love with a young infantry officer she failed all her midyear examinations and retired to Cleveland in disgrace. The young infantry officer arrived about a week later.

Just as she had about decided that she didn't love him after all he was ordered abroad, and in a great revival of sentiment she rushed down to the port of embarkation with her mother to bid him good-by. She wrote him daily for two months, and then weekly for two months, and then once more. This last letter he never got, for a machine-gun bullet ripped through his head one rainy July morning. Perhaps this was just as well, for the letter informed him that it had all been a mistake, and that something told her they would never be happy together, and so on.

The "something" wore boots and silver wings and was tall and dark. Myra was quite sure that it was the real thing at last, but as an engine went through his chest at Kelly Field in mid-August she never had a chance to find out.

Instead she came East again, a little slimmer, with a becoming pallor and new shadows under her eyes, and throughout armistice year she left the ends of cigarettes all over New York on little china trays marked "Midnight Frolic" and "Coconut Grove" and "Palais Royal." She was twenty-one now, and Cleveland people said that her mother ought to take her back home—that New York was spoiling her.

You will have to do your best with that. The story should have started long ago.

It was an afternoon in September when she broke a theater date in order to have tea with young Mrs. Arthur Elkins, once her roommate at school.

"I wish," began Myra as they sat down exquisitely, "that I'd been a señorita or a mademoiselle or something. Good grief! What is there to do over here once you're out, except marry and retire!"

Lilah Elkins had seen this form of ennui before.

"Nothing," she replied coolly; "do it."

"I can't seem to get interested, Lilah," said Myra, bending forward earnestly. "I've played round so much that even while I'm kissing the man I just wonder how soon I'll get tired of him. I never get carried away like I used to."

"How old are you, Myra?"

"Twenty-one last spring."

"Well," said Lilah complacently, "take it from me don't get married unless you're absolutely through playing round. It means giving up an awful lot, you know."

"Through! I'm sick and tired of my whole pointless existence. Funny, Lilah, but I do feel ancient. Up at New Haven last spring men danced with me that seemed like little boys—and once I overheard a girl say in the dressing room, 'There's Myra Harper! She's been coming up here for eight years.' Of course she was about three years off, but it did give me the calendar blues."

"You and I went to our first prom when we were sixteen — five years ago."

"Heavens!" sighed Myra. "And now some men are afraid of me. Isn't that odd? Some of the nicest boys. One man dropped me like a hotcake after coming down from Morristown for three straight week-ends. Some kind friend told him I was husband hunting this year, and he was afraid of getting in too deep."

"Well, you are husband hunting, aren't you?"

"I suppose so—after a fashion." Myra paused and looked about her rather cautiously. "Have you ever met Knowleton Whitney? You know what a wiz he is on looks, and his father's worth a fortune, they say. Well, I noticed that the first time he met me he started when he heard my name and fought shy—and, Lilah darling, I'm not so ancient and homely as all that, am I?"

"You certainly are not!" laughed Lilah. "And here's my

advice: Pick out the best thing in sight—the man who has all the mental, physical, social and financial qualities you want, and then go after him hammer and tongs—the way we used to. After you've got him don't say to yourself 'Well, he can't sing like Billy,' or 'I wish he played better golf.' You can't have everything. Shut your eyes and turn off your sense of humor, and then after you're married it'll he very different and you'll he mighty glad."

"Yes," said Myra absently; "I've had that advice before."

"Drifting into romance is easy when you're eighteen," continued Lilah emphatically; "but after five years of it your capacity for it simply burns out."

"I've had such nice times, sighed Myra, "and such sweet men. To tell you the truth I have decided to go after someone."

"Who?"

"Knowleton Whitney. Believe me, I may be a bit blasé, but I can still get any man I want."

"You really want him?"

"Yes—as much as I'll ever want anyone. He's smart as a whip, and shy—rather sweetly shy—and they say his family have the best-looking place in Westchester County."

Lilah sipped the last of her tea and glanced at her wrist watch.

"I've got to tear, dear."

They rose together and, sauntering out on Park Avenue, hailed taxicabs.

"I'm awfully glad, Myra; and I know you'll be glad too." Myra skipped a little pool of water and, reaching her taxi, balanced on the running board like a ballet dancer."

"By, Lilah. See you soon."

"Good-bye, Myra. Good luck!"

And knowing Myra as she did, Lilah felt that her last remark was distinctly superfluous.

II

That was essentially the reason that one Friday night six weeks later Knowleton Whitney paid a taxi bill of seven dollars and ten cents and with a mixture of emotions paused beside Myra on the Biltmore steps.

The outer surface of his mind was deliriously happy, but just below that was a slowly hardening fright at what he had done. He, protected since his freshman year at Harvard from the snares of fascinating fortune hunters, dragged away from several sweet young things by the acquiescent nape of his neck, had taken advantage of his family's absence in the West to become so enmeshed in the toils that it was hard to say which was toils and which was he.

The afternoon had been like a dream: November twilight along Fifth Avenue after the matinee, and he and Myra looking out at the swarming crowds from the romantic privacy of a hansom cab—quaint device—then tea at the Ritz and her white hand gleaming on the arm of a chair beside him; and suddenly quick broken words. After that had come the trip to the jeweler's and a mad dinner in some little Italian restaurant where he had written "Do you?" on the back of the bill of fare and pushed it over for her to add the ever-miraculous "You know I do!" And now at the day's end they paused on the Biltmore steps.

"Say it," breathed Myra close to his ear.

He said it. Ah, Myra, how many ghosts must have flitted across your memory then!

"You've made me so happy, dear," she said softly.

"No—you've made me happy. Don't you know—Myra— "

"I know."

"For good?"

"For good. I've got this, you see." And she raised the diamond solitaire to her lips. She knew how to do things, did Myra.

"Good night."

"Good night. Good night."

Like a gossamer fairy in shimmering rose she ran up the wide stairs and her cheeks were glowing wildly as she rang the elevator bell.

At the end of a fortnight she got a telegram from him saying that his family had returned from the West and expected her up in Westchester County for a week's visit. Myra wired her train time, bought three new evening dresses and packed her trunk.

It was a cool November evening when she arrived, and stepping from the train in the late twilight she shivered slightly and looked eagerly round for Knowleton. The station platform swarmed for a moment with men returning from the city; there was a shouting medley of wives and chauffeurs, and a great snorting of automobiles as they backed and turned and slid away. Then before she realized it the platform was quite deserted and not a single one of the luxurious cars remained. Knowleton must have expected her on another train.

With an almost inaudible "Damn!" she started toward the Elizabethan station to telephone, when suddenly she was accosted by a very dirty, dilapidated man who touched his ancient cap to her and addressed her in a cracked, querulous voice.

"You Miss Harper?"

"Yes," she confessed, rather startled. Was this unmentionable person by any wild chance the chauffeur?

"The chauffeur's sick," he continued in a high whine. "I'm his son."

Myra gasped.

"You mean Mr. Whitney's chauffeur?"

"Yes; he only keeps just one since the war. Great on economizin'—regelar Hoover." He stamped his feet nervously and smacked enormous gauntlets together. "Well, no use waitin' here gabbin' in the cold. Le's have your grip."

Too amazed for words and not a little dismayed, Myra followed her guide to the edge of the platform, where she looked in vain for a car. But she was not left to wonder long, for the person led her steps to a battered old flivver, wherein was deposited her grip.

"Big car's broke," he explained. "Have to use this or walk."

He opened the front door for her and nodded.

"Step in."

"I b'lieve I'll sit in back if you don't mind."

"Surest thing you know," he cackled, opening the back door. "I thought the trunk bumpin' round back there might make you nervous."

"What trunk?"

"Yourn."

"Oh, didn't Mr. Whitney—can't you make two trips?" He shook his head obstinately.

"Wouldn't allow it. Not since the war. Up to rich people to set 'n example; that's what Mr. Whitney says. Le's have your check, please."

As he disappeared Myra tried in vain to conjure up a picture of the chauffeur if this was his son. After a mysterious argument with the station agent he returned, gasping violently, with the trunk on his back. He deposited it in the rear seat and climbed up in front beside her.

It was quite dark when they swerved out of the road and up a long dusky driveway to the Whitney place, whence lighted windows flung great blots of cheerful, yellow light over the gravel and grass and trees. Even now she could see that it was very beautiful, that its blurred outline was Georgian Colonial and that great shadowy garden parks were flung out at both sides. The car plumped to a full stop before a square stone doorway and the chauffeur's son climbed out after her and pushed open the outer door.

"Just go right in," he cackled; and as she passed the threshold she heard him softly shut the door, closing out himself and the dark.

Myra looked round her. She was in a large somber hall paneled in old English oak and lit by dim shaded lights clinging like luminous yellow turtles at intervals along the wall. Ahead of her was a broad staircase and on both sides there were several doors, but there was no sight or sound of life, and an intense stillness seemed to rise ceaselessly from the deep crimson carpet.

She must have waited there a full minute before she began to have that unmistakable sense of someone looking at her. She forced herself to turn casually round.

A sallow little man, bald and clean shaven, trimly dressed in a frock coat and white spats, was standing a few yards away regarding her quizzically. He must have been fifty at the least, but even before he moved she had noticed a curious alertness about him—something in his pose which promised that it had been instantaneously assumed and would be instantaneously changed in a moment. His tiny hands and feet and the odd twist to his eyebrows gave him a faintly elfish expression, and she had one of those vague transient convictions that she had seen him before, many years ago.

For a minute they stared at each other in silence and then she flushed slightly and discovered a desire to swallow.

"I suppose you're Mr. Whitney." She smiled faintly and advanced a step toward him. "I'm Myra Harper."

For an instant longer he remained silent and motionless, and it flashed across Myra that he might be deaf; then suddenly he jerked into spirited life exactly like a mechanical toy started by the pressure of a button.

"Why, of course—why, naturally. I know—ah!" he exclaimed excitedly in a high-pitched elfin voice. Then raising himself on his toes in a sort of attenuated ecstasy of enthusiasm and smiling a wizened smile, he minced toward her across the dark carpet.

She blushed appropriately.

"That's awfully nice of—"

"Ah!" he went on. "You must be tired; a rickety, cindery, ghastly trip, I know. Tired and hungry and thirsty, no doubt, no doubt!" He looked round him indignantly. "The servants are frightfully inefficient in this house!"

Myra did not know what to say to this, so she made no answer. After an instant's abstraction Mr. Whitney crossed over with his furious energy and pressed a button; then almost as if he were dancing he was by her side again, making thin, disparaging gestures with his hands.

"A little minute," he assured her, "sixty seconds, scarcely more. Here!"

He rushed suddenly to the wall and with some effort lifted a great carved Louis Fourteenth chair and set it down carefully in the geometrical center of the carpet.

"Sit down—won't you? Sit down! I'll go get you something. Sixty seconds at the outside."

She demurred faintly, but he kept on repeating "Sit down!" in such an aggrieved yet hopeful tone that Myra sat down. Instantly her host disappeared.

She sat there for five minutes and a feeling of oppression fell over her. Of all the receptions she had ever received this was decidedly the oddest—for though she had read somewhere that Ludlow Whitney was considered one of the most eccentric figures in the financial world, to find a sallow, elfin little man who, when he walked, danced was rather a blow to her sense of form. Had he gone to get Knowleton? She revolved her thumbs in interminable concentric circles.

Then she started nervously at a quick cough at her elbow. It was Mr. Whitney again. In one hand he held a glass of milk and in the other a blue kitchen bowl full of those hard cubical crackers used in soup. "Hungry from your trip!" he exclaimed compassionately. "Poor girl, poor little girl, starving!" He brought out this last word with such emphasis that some of the milk plopped gently over the side of the glass.

Myra took the refreshments submissively. She was not hungry, but it had taken him ten minutes to get them so it seemed ungracious to refuse. She sipped gingerly at the milk and ate a cracker, wondering vaguely what to say. Mr. Whitney, however, solved the problem for her by disappearing again—this time by way of the wide stairs—four steps at a hop—the back of his bald head gleaming oddly for a moment in the half dark.

Minutes passed. Myra was torn between resentment and bewilderment that she should be sitting on a high comfortless chair in the middle of this big hall munching crackers. By what code was a visiting fiancée ever thus received!

Her heart gave a jump of relief as she heard a familiar whistle on the stairs. It was Knowleton at last, and when he came in sight he gasped with astonishment.

"Myra!"

She carefully placed the bowl and glass on the carpet and rose, smiling.

"Why," he exclaimed, "they didn't tell me you were here!"

"Your father—welcomed me."

"Lordy! He must have gone upstairs and forgotten all about it. Did he insist on your eating this stuff? Why didn't you just tell him you didn't want any?"

"Why—I don't know."

"You mustn't mind father, dear. He's forgetful and a little unconventional in some ways, but you'll get used to him."

He pressed a button and a butler appeared.

"Show Miss Harper to her room and have her bag carried up—and her trunk if it isn't there already." He turned to Myra. "Dear, I'm awfully sorry I didn't know you were here. How long have you been waiting?"

"Oh, only a few minutes."

It had been twenty at the least, but she saw no advantage in stressing it. Nevertheless it had given her an oddly uncomfortable feeling.

Half an hour later as she was hooking the last eye on her dinner dress there was a knock on the door.

"It's Knowleton, Myra; if you're about ready we'll go in and see Mother for a minute before dinner."

She threw a final approving glance at her reflection in the mirror and turning out the light joined him in the hall. He led her down a central passage which crossed to the other wing of the house, and stopping before a closed door he pushed it open and ushered Myra into the weirdest room upon which her young eyes had ever rested.

It was a large luxurious boudoir, paneled, like the lower hall, in dark English oak and bathed by several lamps in a mellow orange glow that blurred its every outline into misty amber. In a great armchair piled high with cushions and draped with a curiously figured cloth of silk reclined a very sturdy old lady with bright white hair, heavy features, and an air about her of having been there for many years. She lay somnolently against the cushions, her eyes half closed, her great bust rising and falling under her black negligee.

But it was something else that made the room remarkable, and Myra's eyes scarcely rested on the woman, so engrossed was she in another feature of her surroundings. On the carpet, on the chairs and sofas, on the great canopied bed and on the soft Angora rug in front of the fire sat and sprawled and slept a great army of white poodle dogs. There must have been almost two dozen of them, with curly hair twisting in front of their wistful eyes and wide yellow bows flaunting from their necks. As Myra and Knowleton entered a stir went over the dogs; they raised one-and-twenty cold black noses in the air and from one-and-twenty little throats went up a great clatter of staccato barks until the room was filled with such an uproar that Myra stepped back in alarm.

But at the din the somnolent fat lady's eyes trembled open and in a low husky voice that was in itself oddly like a bark she snapped out: "Hush that racket!" and the clatter instantly ceased. The two or three poodles round the fire turned their silky eyes on each other reproachfully, and lying down with little sighs faded out on the white Angora rug; the tousled ball on the lady's lap dug his nose into the crook of an elbow and went back to sleep, and except for the patches of white wool scattered about the room Myra would have thought it all a dream.

"Mother," said Knowleton after an instant's pause, "this is Myra."

From the lady's lips flooded one low husky word: "Myra?'

"She's visiting us, I told you."

Mrs. Whitney raised a large arm and passed her hand across her forehead wearily.

"Child!" she said—and Myra started, for again the voice was like a low sort of growl—"you want to marry my son Knowleton?"

Myra felt that this was putting the tonneau before the radiator, but she nodded.

"Yes, Mrs. Whitney."

"How old are you?" This very suddenly.

"I'm twenty-one, Mrs. Whitney."

"Ah —and you're from Cleveland?" This was in what was surely a series of articulate barks.

"Yes, Mrs. Whitney."

"Ah—"

Myra was not certain whether this last ejaculation was conversation or merely a groan, so she did not answer.

"You'll excuse me if I don't appear downstairs," continued Mrs. Whitney; "but when we're in the East I seldom leave this room and my dear little doggies."

Myra nodded and a conventional health question was trembling on her lips when she caught Knowleton's warning glance and checked it.

"Well," said Mrs. Whitney with an air of finality, "you seem like a very nice girl. Come in again."

"Good night, Mother," said Knowleton.

"Night!" harked Mrs. Whitney drowsily, and her eyes sealed gradually up as her head receded back again into the cushions.

Knowleton held open the door and Myra feeling a bit blank left the room. As they walked down the corridor she heard a burst of furious sound behind them; the noise of the closing door had again roused the poodle dogs.

When they went downstairs they found Mr. Whitney already seated at the dinner table.

"Utterly charming, completely delightful!" he exclaimed, beaming nervously. "One big family, and you the jewel of it, my dear."

Myra smiled, Knowleton frowned and Mr. Whitney tittered.

"It's been lonely here," he continued; "desolate, with only us three. We expect you to bring sunlight and warmth, the peculiar radiance and efflorescence of youth. It will be quite delightful. Do you sing?"

"Why—I have. I mean, I do, some."

He clapped his hands enthusiastically.

"Splendid! Magnificent! What do you sing? Opera? Ballads? Popular music?"

"Well, mostly popular music."

"Good; personally I prefer popular music. By the way, there's a dance tonight."

"Father," demanded Knowleton sulkily, "did you go and invite a crowd here?"

"I had Monroe call up a few people—just some of the neighbors," he explained to Myra. "We're all very friendly here-abouts; give informal things continually. Oh, it's quite delightful."

Myra caught Knowleton's eye and gave him a sympathetic glance. It was obvious that he had wanted to be alone with her this first evening and was quite put out.

"I want them to meet Myra," continued his father. "I want them to know this delightful jewel we've added to our little household."

"Father," said Knowleton suddenly, "eventually of course Myra and I will want to live here with you and mother, but for the first two or three years I think an apartment in New York would be more the thing for us."

Crash! Mr. Whitney had raked across the tablecloth with his fingers and swept his silver to a jangling heap on the floor "Nonsense!" he cried furiously, pointing a tiny finger at his son. "Don't talk that utter nonsense! You'll live here, do you understand me? Here! What's a home without children?"

"But, father—"

In his excitement Mr. Whitney rose and a faint unnatural color crept into his sallow face.

"Silence!" he shrieked. "If you expect one bit of help from me you can have it under my roof—nowhere else! Is that clear? As for you, my exquisite young lady," he continued, turning his

"As for You, My Exquisite Young Lady, You'd Better Understand That the Best Thing You Can Do is to Decide to Settle Down Right Here. This is My Home, and I Mean to Keep it So!"

wavering finger on Myra, "you'd better understand that the best thing you can do is to decide to settle down right here. This is my home, and I mean to keep it so!"

He stood then for a moment on his tiptoes, bending furiously indignant glances first on one, then on the other, and then suddenly he turned and skipped from the room.

"Well," gasped Myra, turning to Knowleton in amazement, "what do you know about that!"

III

Some hours later she crept into bed in a great state of restless discontent. One thing she knew—she was not going to live in this house. Knowleton would have to make his father see reason to the extent of giving them an apartment in the city. The sallow little man made her nervous; she was sure Mrs. Whitney's dogs would haunt her dreams; and there was a general casualness in the chauffeur, the butler, the maids and even the guests she had met that night, that did not in the least coincide with her ideas on the conduct of a big estate.

She had lain there an hour perhaps when she was startled from a slow reverie by a sharp cry which seemed to proceed from the adjoining room. She sat up in bed and listened, and in a minute it was repeated. It sounded exactly like the plaint of a weary child stopped summarily by the placing of a hand over its mouth. In the dark silence her bewilderment shaded gradually off into uneasiness. She waited for the cry to recur, but straining her ears she heard only the intense crowded stillness of three o'clock. She wondered where Knowleton slept, remembered that his bedroom was over in the other wing just beyond his mother's. She was alone over here—or was she?

With a little gasp she slid down into bed again and lay listening. Not since childhood had she been afraid of the dark, but the unforeseen presence of someone next door startled her and sent her imagination racing through a host of mystery stories that at one time or another had whiled away a long afternoon.

She heard the clock strike four and found she was very tired. A curtain drifted slowly down in front of her imagination, and changing her position she fell suddenly to sleep.

Next morning, walking with Knowleton under starry frosted bushes in one of the hare gardens, she grew quite light-hearted and wondered at her depression of the night before. Probably all families seemed odd when one visited them for the first time in such an intimate capacity. Yet her determination that she and Knowleton were going to live elsewhere than with the white dogs and the jumpy little man was not abated. And if the near-by Westchester County society was typified by the chilly crowd she had met at the dance—

"The family," said Knowleton, "must seem rather unusual. I've been brought up in an odd atmosphere, I suppose, but mother is really quite normal outside of her penchant for poodles in great quantities, and father in spite of his eccentricities seems to hold a secure position in Wall Street."

"Knowleton,' she demanded suddenly, "who lives in the room next door to me?"

Did he start and flush slightly—or was that her imagination?

"Because, she went on deliberately, "I'm almost sure I heard someone crying in there during the night. It sounded like a child, Knowleton."

"There's no one in there," he said decidedly. "It was either your imagination or something you ate. Or possibly one of the maids was sick."

Seeming to dismiss the matter without effort he changed the subject.

The day passed quickly. At lunch Mr. Whitney seemed to have forgotten his temper of the previous night; he was as nervously enthusiastic as ever; and watching him Myra again had that impression that she had seen him somewhere before. She and Knowleton paid another visit to Mrs. Whitney—and again the poodles stirred uneasily and set up a barking, to be summarily silenced by the harsh throaty voice. The conversation was short and of inquisitional flavor. It was terminated as before by the lady's drowsy eyelids and a paean of farewell from the dogs.

In the evening she found that Mr. Whitney had insisted on organizing an informal neighborhood vaudeville. A stage had been erected in the ballroom and Myra sat beside Knowleton in the front row and watched proceedings curiously. Two slim and haughty ladies sang, a man performed some ancient card tricks, a girl gave impersonations, and then to Myra's astonishment Mr. Whitney appeared and did a rather effective buck-and-wing dance. There was something inexpressibly weird in the motion of the well-known financier flitting solemnly back and forth across the stage on his tiny feet. Yet he danced well, with an effortless grace and an unexpected suppleness, and he was rewarded with a storm of applause.

In the half dark the lady on her left suddenly spoke to her.

"Mr. Whitney is passing the word along that he wants to see you behind the scenes. '

Puzzled, Myra rose and ascended the side flight of stairs that led to the raised platform. Her host was waiting for her anxiously.

"Ah," he chuckled, "splendid!"

He held out his hand, and wonderingly she took it. Before she realized his intention he had half led, half drawn her out on to the stage. The spotlight's glare bathed them, and the ripple of conversation washing the audience ceased. The faces before her were pallid splotches on the gloom and she felt her ears burning as she waited for Mr. Whitney to speak.

"Ladies and gentlemen," he began, "most of you know Miss Myra Harper. You had the honor of meeting her last night. She is a delicious girl, I assure you. I am in a position to know. She intends to become the wife of my son."

He paused and nodded and began clapping his hands. The

audience immediately took up the clapping and Myra stood there in motionless horror, overcome by the most violent confusion of her life.

The piping voice went on: "Miss Harper is not only beautiful but talented. Last night she confided to me that she sang. I asked whether she preferred the opera, the ballad or the popular song, and she confessed that her taste ran to the latter. Miss Harper will now favor us with a popular song."

And then Myra was standing alone on the stage, rigid with embarrassment. She fancied that on the faces in front of her she saw critical expectation, boredom, ironic disapproval. Surely this was the height of bad form—to drop a guest unprepared into such a situation.

In the first hush she considered a word or two explaining that Mr. Whitney had been under a misapprehension—then anger came to her assistance. She tossed her head and those in front saw her lips close together sharply.

Advancing to the platform's edge she said succinctly to the orchestra leader: "Have you got Wave That Wishbone?"

"Lemme see. Yes, we got it."

"All right. Let's go!"

She hurriedly reviewed the words, which she had learned quite by accident at a dull house party the previous summer. It was perhaps not the song she would have chosen for her first public appearance, but it would have to do. She smiled radiantly, nodded at the orchestra leader and began the verse in a light clear alto.

As she sang a spirit of ironic humor slowly took possession of her—a desire to give them all a run for their money. And she did. She injected an East Side snarl into every word of slang; she ragged; she shimmied; she did a tickle-toe step she had learned once in an amateur musical comedy; and in a burst of inspiration finished up in an Al Jolson position, on her knees with her arms stretched out to her audience in syncopated appeal.

Then she rose, bowed and left the stage.

For an instant there was silence, the silence of a cold tomb; then perhaps half a dozen hands joined in a faint, perfunctory applause that in a second had died completely away.

Heavens! thought Myra. Was it as bad as all that? Or did I shock 'em?

Mr. Whitney, however, seemed delighted. He was waiting for her in the wings and seizing her hand shook it enthusiastically.

"Quite wonderful!" he chuckled. "You are a delightful little actress—and you'll be a valuable addition to our little plays. Would you like to give an encore?"

"No!" said Myra shortly, and turned away.

In a shadowy corner she waited until the crowd had filed out, with an angry unwillingness to face them immediately after their rejection of her effort.

When the ballroom was quite empty she walked slowly up the stairs, and there she came upon Knowleton and Mr. Whitney alone in the dark hall, evidently engaged in a heated argument.

They ceased when she appeared and looked toward her eagerly.

"Myra," said Mr. Whitney, "Knowleton wants to talk to you."

"Father," said Knowleton intensely, "I ask you —"

"Silence!" cried his father, his voice ascending testily. "You'll do your duty—now."

Knowleton cast one more appealing glance at him, but Mr. Whitney only shook his head excitedly and, turning, disappeared phantomlike up the stairs.

Knowleton stood silent a moment and finally with a look of dogged determination took her hand and led her toward a room that opened off the hall at the back. The yellow light fell through the door after them and she found herself in a dark wide chamber where she could just distinguish on the walls great square shapes which she took to be frames. Knowleton pressed a button, and immediately forty portraits sprang into life—old gallants from colonial days, ladies with floppity Gainsborough hats, fat women with ruffs and placid clasped hands.

She turned to Knowleton inquiringly, but he led her forward to a row of pictures on the side.

"Myra," he said slowly and painfully, "there's something I have to tell you. These"—he indicated the pictures with his hand—"are family portraits."

There were seven of them, three men and three women, all of them of the period just before the Civil War. The one in the middle, however, was hidden by crimson-velvet curtains.

"Ironic as it may seem," continued Knowleton steadily, "that frame contains a picture of my great-grandmother."

Reaching out, he pulled a little silken cord and the curtains parted, to expose a portrait of a lady dressed as a European but with

"Dearest, Dearest!" He Cried. "I Shouldn't Have Told You! I Shouldn't Have Told You!"

the unmistakable features of a Chinese.

"My great-grandfather, you see, was an Australian tea importer. He met his future wife in Hong-Kong."

Myra's brain was whirling. She had a sudden vision of Mr. Whitney's yellowish face, peculiar eyebrows and tiny hands and feet—she remembered ghastly tales she had heard of reversions to type—of Chinese babies—and then with a final surge of horror she thought of that sudden hushed cry in the night. She gasped, her knees seemed to crumple up and she sank slowly to the floor.

In a second Knowleton's arms were round her.

"Dearest, dearest!" he cried. "I shouldn't have told you! I shouldn't have told you!"

As he said this Myra knew definitely and unmistakably that she could never marry him, and when she realized it she cast at him a wild pitiful look, and for the first time in her life fainted dead away.

IV

When she next recovered full consciousness she was in bed. She imagined a maid had undressed her, for on turning up the reading lamp she saw that her clothes had been neatly put away. For a minute she lay there, listening idly while the hall clock struck two, and then her overwrought nerves jumped in terror as she heard again that child's cry from the room next door. The morning seemed suddenly infinitely far away. There was some shadowy secret near her—her feverish imagination pictured a Chinese child brought up there in the half dark.

In a quick panic she crept into a negligee and, throwing open the door, slipped down the corridor toward Knowleton's room. It was very dark in the other wing, but when she pushed open his door she could see by the faint hall light that his bed was empty and had not been slept in. Her terror increased. What could take him out at this hour of the night? She started for Mrs. Whitney's room, but at the thought of the dogs and her bare ankles she gave a little discouraged cry and passed by the door.

Then she suddenly heard the sound of Knowleton's voice issuing from a faint crack of light far down the corridor, and with a glow of joy she fled toward it. When she was within a foot of the door she found she could see through the crack—and after one glance all thought of entering left her.

Before an open fire, his head bowed in an attitude of great dejection, stood Knowleton, and in the corner, feet perched on the table, sat Mr. Whitney in his shirt sleeves, very quiet and calm, and pulling contentedly on a huge black pipe. Seated on the table was a part of Mrs. Whitney—that is, Mrs. Whitney without any hair. Out of the familiar great bust projected Mrs. Whitney's head, but she was bald; on her cheeks was the faint stubble of a beard, and in her mouth was a large black cigar, which she was puffing with obvious enjoyment.

"A thousand," groaned Knowleton as if in answer to a question. "Say twenty-five hundred and you'll be nearer the truth. I got a bill from the Graham Kennels to-day for those poodle dogs. They're soaking me two hundred and saying that they've got to have 'em back to-morrow."

"Well," said Mrs. Whitney in a low baritone voice, "send 'em back. We're through with 'em."

"That's a mere item," continued Knowleton glumly. "Including your salary, and Appleton's here, and that fellow who did the chauffeur, and seventy supes for two nights, and an orchestra—that's nearly twelve hundred, and then there's the rent on the costumes and that darn Chinese portrait and the bribes to the servants. Lord! There'll probably be bills for one thing or another coming in for the next month."

"Well, then," said Appleton, "for pity's sake pull yourself together and carry it through to the end. Take my word for it, that girl will be out of the house by twelve noon."

Knowleton sank into a chair and covered his face with his hands.

"Oh — "

"Brace up! It's all over. I thought for a minute there in the hall that you were going to balk at that Chinese business."

"It was the vaudeville that knocked the spots out of me," groaned Knowleton. "It was about the meanest trick ever pulled on any girl, and she was so darned game about it!"

"She had to be," said Mrs. Whitney cynically.

"Oh, Kelly, if you could have seen the girl look at me to-night just before she fainted in front of that picture. Lord, I believe she loves me! Oh, if you could have seen her!"

Outside Myra flushed crimson. She leaned closer to the door, biting her lip until she could taste the faintly bitter savor of blood.

"If there was anything I could do now," continued Knowleton—"anything in the world that would smooth it over I believe I'd do it."

Kelly crossed ponderously over, his bald shiny head ludicrous above his feminine negligee, and put his hand on Knowleton's shoulder.

"See here, my boy— your trouble is just nerves. Look at it this way: You undertook somep'n to get yourself out of an awful mess. It's a cinch the girl was after your money—now you've beat her at her own game an' saved yourself an unhappy marriage and your family a lot of suffering. Ain't that so, Appleton?"

"Absolutely!" said Appleton emphatically. "Go through with it."

"Well," said Knowleton with a dismal attempt to be righteous, "if she really loved me she wouldn't have let it all affect her this much. She's not marrying my family."

Appleton laughed.

"I thought we'd tried to make it pretty obvious that she is."

"Oh, shut up!" cried Knowleton miserably.

Myra saw Appleton wink at Kelly.

"That's right," he said; "she's shown she was after your money. Well, now then, there's no reason for not going through with it. See here. On one side you've proved she didn't love you and you're rid of her and free as air. She'll creep away and never say a word about it—and your family never the wiser. On the other side twenty-five hundred thrown to the bow-wows, miserable marriage, girl sure to hate you as soon as she finds out and your family all broken up and probably disownin' you for marryin' her. One big mess, I'll tell the world."

"You're right," admitted Knowleton gloomily. "You're right, I suppose—but oh, the look in that girl's face! She's probably in there now lying awake, listening to the Chinese baby—"

Appleton rose and yawned.

"Well—" he began.

But Myra waited to hear no more. Pulling her silk kimono close about her she sped like lightning down the soft corridor, to dive headlong and breathless into her room.

"My heavens!" she cried, clenching her hands in the darkness. "My heavens!"

V

Just before dawn Myra drowsed into a jumbled dream that seemed to act on through interminable hours. She awoke about seven and lay listlessly with one blue-veined arm hanging over the side of the bed. She who had danced in the dawn at many proms was very tired.

A clock outside her door struck the hour, and with her nervous start something seemed to collapse within her—she turned over and began to weep furiously into her pillow, her tangled hair spreading like a dark aura round her head. To her, Myra Harper, had been done this cheap vulgar trick by a man she had thought shy and kind.

Lacking the courage to come to her and tell her the truth he had gone into the highways and hired men to frighten her.

Between her fevered broken sobs she tried in vain to comprehend the workings of a mind which could have conceived this in all its subtlety. Her pride refused to let her think of it as a deliberate plan of Knowleton's. It was probably an idea fostered by this little actor Appleton or by the fat Kelly with his horrible poodles. But it was all unspeakable—unthinkable. It gave her an intense sense of shame.

But when she emerged from her room at eight o'clock and, disdaining breakfast, walked into the garden she was a very self-possessed young beauty, with dry cool eyes only faintly shadowed. The ground was firm and frosty with the promise of winter, and she found gray sky and dull air vaguely comforting and one with her mood. It was a day for thinking and she needed to think.

And then turning a corner suddenly she saw Knowleton seated on a stone bench, his head in his hands, in an attitude of profound dejection. He wore his clothes of the night before and it was quite evident that he had not been to bed.

He did not hear her until she was quite close to him, and then as a dry twig snapped under her heel he looked up wearily. She saw that the night had played havoc with him—his face was deathly pale and his eyes were pink and puffed and tired. He jumped up with a look that was very like dread.

"Good morning," said Myra quietly.

"Sit down," he began nervously. "Sit down; I want to talk to you! I've got to talk to you."

Myra nodded and taking a seat beside him on the bench clasped her knees with her hands and half closed her eyes.

"Myra, for heaven's sake have pity on me!"

She turned wondering eyes on him. "What do you mean?"

He groaned.

"Myra, I've done a ghastly thing—to you, to me, to us. I

"Myra, I've Done a Ghastly Thing — to You, to Me, to Us. I Haven't a Word to Say in Favor of Myself"

haven't a word to say in favor of myself—I've been just rotten. I think it was a sort of madness that came over me."

"You'll have to give me a clew to what you're talking about."

"Myra—Myra "—like all large bodies his confession seemed difficult to imbue with momentum— "Myra—Mr. Whitney is not my father."

"You mean you were adopted?"

"No; I mean—Ludlow Whitney is my father, but this man you've met isn't Ludlow Whitney."

"I know, ' said Myra coolly. "He's Warren Appleton, the actor."

Knowleton leaped to his feet.

"How on earth—"

"Oh," lied Myra easily, "I recognized him the first night. I saw him five years ago in 'The Swiss Grapefruit'."

At this Knowleton seemed to collapse utterly. He sank down limply on to the bench.

"You knew?"

"Of course! How could I help it? It simply made me wonder what it was all about."

With a great effort he tried to pull himself together.

"I'm going to tell you the whole story, Myra."

"I'm all ears."

"Well, it starts with my mother—my real one, not the woman with those idiotic dogs; she's an invalid and I'm her only child. Her one idea in life has always been for me to make a fitting match, and her idea of a fitting match centers round social position in England. Her greatest disappointment was that I wasn't a girl so I could marry a title; instead she wanted to drag me to England—marry me off to the sister of an earl or the daughter of a duke. Why, before she'd let me stay up here alone this fall she made me promise I wouldn't go to see any girl more than twice. And then I met you."

He paused for a second and continued earnestly: "You were the first girl in my life whom I ever thought of marrying. You intoxicated me, Myra. It was just as though you were making me love you by some invisible force."

"I was," murmured Myra.

"Well, that first intoxication lasted a week, and then one day a letter came from mother saying she was bringing home some wonderful English girl, Lady Helena Something-or-Other. And the same day a man told me that he'd heard I'd been caught by the most famous husband hunter in New York. Well, between these two things I went half crazy. I came into town to see you and call it off—got as far as the Biltmore entrance and didn't dare. I started wandering down Fifth Avenue like a wild man, and then I met Kelly. I told him the whole story—and within an hour we'd hatched up this ghastly plan. It was his plan—all the details. His histrionic instinct got the better of him and he had me thinking it was the kindest way out."

"Finish," commanded Myra crisply.

"Well, it went splendidly, we thought. Everything—the

station meeting, the dinner scene, the scream in the night, the vaudeville—though I thought that was a little too much—until—until — Oh, Myra, when you fainted under that picture and I held you there in my arms, helpless as a baby, I knew I loved you. I was sorry then, Myra."

There was a long pause while she sat motionless, her hands still clasping her knees—then he burst out with a wild plea of passionate sincerity.

"Myra!" he cried. "If by any possible chance you can bring yourself to forgive and forget I'll marry you when you say, let my family go to the devil, and love you all my life."

For a long while she considered, and Knowlton rose and began pacing nervously up and down the aisle of bare bushes, his hands in his pockets, his tired eyes pathetic now, and full of dull appeal. And then she came to a decision.

"You're perfectly sure?" she asked calmly.

"Yes,"

"Very well, I'll marry you to-day."

With her words the atmosphere cleared and his troubles seemed to fall from him like a ragged cloak. An Indian summer sun drifted out from behind the gray clouds and the dry bushes rustled gently in the breeze.

"It was a bad mistake," she continued, "but if you're sure you love me now, that's the main thing. We'll go to town this morning, get a license, and I'll call up my cousin, who's a minister in the First Presbyterian Church. We can go west to-night. "

"Myra!" he cried jubilantly. "You're a marvel and I'm not fit to tie your shoe strings. I'm going to make up to you for this, darling girl."

And taking her supple body in his arms he covered her face with kisses.

The next two hours passed in a whirl. Myra went to the telephone and called her cousin, and then rushed upstairs to pack.

When she came down a shining roadster was waiting miraculously in the drive and by ten o'clock they were bowling happily toward the city.

They stopped for a few minutes at the City Hall and again at the jeweler's, and then they were in the house of the Reverend Walter Gregory on Sixty-Ninth Street, where a sanctimonious gentleman with twinkling eyes and a slight stutter received them cordially and urged them to a breakfast of bacon and eggs before the ceremony.

On the way to the station they stopped only long enough to wire Knowleton's father, and then they were sitting in their compartment on the Broadway Limited.

"Darn!" exclaimed Myra. "I forgot my bag. Left it at Cousin Walter's in the excitement."

"Never mind. We can get a whole new outfit in Chicago."

She glanced at her wrist watch.

"I've got time to telephone him to send it on."

She rose.

"Don't be long, dear."

She leaned down and kissed his forehead. "You know I couldn't. Two minutes, honey."

Outside Myra ran swiftly along the platform and up the steel stairs to the great waiting room, where a man met her — a twinkly-eyed man with a slight stutter.

"How d-did it go, M-myra?"

"Fine! Oh, Walter, you were splendid! I almost wish you'd join the ministry so you could officiate when I do get married."

"Well—I r-rehearsed for half an hour after I g-got your telephone call."

"Wish we'd had more time. I'd have had him lease an apartment and buy furniture."

"H'm," chuckled Walter. "Wonder how far he'll go on his honeymoon."

"Oh, he'll think I'm on the train till he gets to Elizabeth."

She shook her little fist at the great contour of the marble dome. "Oh, he's getting off too easy—far too easy!"

"I haven't f-figured out what the f-fellow did to you, M-myra."

"You never will, I hope."

They had reached the side drive and he hailed her a taxicab.

"You're an angel!" beamed Myra. "And I can't thank you enough."

"Well, any time I can be of use t-to you — By the way, what are you going to do with all the rings?"

Myra looked laughingly at her hand.

"That's the question," she said. "I may send them to Lady Helena Something-or-Other—and—well, I've always had a strong penchant for souvenirs. Tell the driver Biltmore, Walter."

Story Illustrations by
Arthur William Brown

Beginning: HIGH LIFE—By Harrison Rhodes

The *Post* published this story on April 24, 1920, the first to appear after the publication date of <u>This Side of Paradise</u>. Fitzgerald's fee had by now increased to $500.

A filmed version of *The Camel's Back* aired on television in the UK on December 13, 1963, as part of an eight-episode BBC anthology series entitled Teletale. Unfortunately, all episodes have been lost.

The Camel's Back

The restless, wearied eye of the tired magazine reader resting for a critical second on the above title will judge it to be merely metaphorical. Stories about the cup and the lip and the bad penny and the new broom rarely have anything to do with cups and lips and pennies and brooms. This story is the great exception. It has to do with an actual, material, visible and large-as-life camel's back.

Starting from the neck we shall work tailward. Meet Mr. Perry Parkhurst, twenty-eight, lawyer, native of Toledo. Perry has nice teeth, a Harvard education, and parts his hair in the middle. You have met him before—in Cleveland, Portland, St. Paul, Indianapolis, Kansas City and elsewhere. Baker Brothers, New York, pause on their semiannual trip through the West to clothe him; Montmorency & Co. dispatch a young man posthaste every three months to see that he has the correct number of little punctures on his shoes. He has a domestic roadster now, will have a French roadster if he lives long enough, and doubtless a Chinese one if it comes into fashion. He looks like the advertisement of the young man rubbing his sunset-colored chest with liniment, goes East every year to the Harvard reunion —does everything—smokes a little too much — Oh, you've seen him.

Meet his girl. Her name is Betty Medill, and she would take well in the movies. Her father gives her two hundred a month to dress on and she has tawny eyes and hair, and feather fans of three colors. Meet her father, Cyrus Medill. Though he is to all appearances flesh and blood he is, strange to say, commonly known in Toledo as the Aluminum Man. But when he sits in his club window with two or three Iron Men and the White Pine Man and the Brass Man they look very much as you and I do, only more so, if you know what I mean.

Meet the camel's back—or no—don't meet the camel's back yet. Meet the story.

During the Christmas holidays of 1919, the first real Christmas holidays since the war, there took place in Toledo, counting only the people with the italicized *the*, forty-one dinner parties, sixteen dances, six luncheons male and female, eleven luncheons female, twelve teas, four stag dinners, two weddings and thirteen bridge parties. It was the cumulative effect of all this that moved Perry Parkhurst on the twenty-ninth day of December to a desperate decision.

Betty Medill would marry him and she wouldn't marry him. She was having such a good time that she hated to take such a *definite* step. Meanwhile, their secret engagement had got so long that it seemed as if any day it might break off of its own weight. A little man named Warburton, who knew it all, persuaded Perry to superman her, to get a marriage license and go up to the Medill house and tell her she'd have to marry him at once or call it off forever. This is some stunt—but Perry tried it on December the twenty-ninth. He presented self, heart, license and ultimatum, and within five minutes they were in the midst of a violent quarrel, a burst of sporadic open fighting such as occurs near the end of all long wars and engagements. It brought about one of those ghastly lapses in which two people who are in love pull up sharp, look at each other coolly and think it's all been a mistake. Afterward they usually kiss wholesomely and assure the other person it was all their fault. Say it all was my fault! Say it was! I want to hear you say it!

But while reconciliation was trembling in the air, while each was, in a measure, stalling it off, so that they might the more voluptuously and sentimentally enjoy it when it came, they were permanently interrupted by a twenty minute phone call for Betty from a garrulous aunt who lived in the country. At the end of eighteen minutes Perry Parkhurst, torn by pride and suspicion and urged on by injured dignity, put on his long fur coat, picked up his light brown soft hat and stalked out the door.

A Little Man Who Knew it All Persuaded Perry to Superman Her, to Tell Her She'd Have to Marry Him at Once or Call it Off Forever. This is Some Stunt

"It's all over," he muttered brokenly as he tried to jam his car into first. "It's all over—if I have to choke you for an hour, darn you!" This last to the car, which had been standing some time and was quite cold.

He drove downtown—that is, he got into a snow rut that led him downtown.

He sat slouched down very low in his seat, much too dispirited to care where he went. He was living over the next twenty years without Betty.

In front of the Clarendon Hotel he was hailed from the sidewalk by a bad man named Baily, who had big huge teeth and lived at the hotel and had never been in love.

"Perry," said the bad man softly when the roadster drew up beside him at the curb, "I've got six quarts of the dog-gonedest champagne you ever tasted. A third of it's yours, Perry, if you'll come upstairs and help Martin Macy and me drink it."

"Baily," said Perry tensely, "I'll drink your champagne. I'll drink every drop of it. I don't care if it kills me. I don't care if it's fifty-proof wood alcohol."

"Shut up, you nut!" said the bad man gently. "They don't put wood alcohol in champagne. This is the stuff that proves the world is more than six thousand years old. It's so ancient that the cork is petrified. You have to pull it with a stone drill."

"Take me upstairs," said Perry moodily. "If that cork sees my heart it'll fall out from pure mortification." The room upstairs was full of those innocent hotel pictures of little girls eating apples and sitting in swings and talking to dogs. The other decorations were neckties and a pink man reading a pink paper devoted to ladies in pink tights.

"When you have to go into the highways and byways —" said the pink man, looking reproachfully at Baily and Perry.

"Hello, Martin Macy," said Perry shortly, "where's this stone-age champagne?"

"What's the rush? This isn't an operation, understand. This is a party."

Perry sat down dully and looked disapprovingly at all the neckties.

Baily leisurely opened the door of a wardrobe and brought out six wicked-looking bottles and three glasses.

"Take off that darn fur coat!" said Martin Macy to Perry. "Or maybe you'd like to have us open all the windows."

"Give me champagne," said Perry.

"Going to the Townsends' circus ball tonight?"

"Am not!"

"'Vited?"

"Uh-huh."

"Why not go?"

"Oh, I'm sick of parties," exclaimed Perry. "I'm sick of 'em." I've been to so many that I'm sick of 'em."

"Maybe you're going to the Howard Tates' party?"

"No, I tell you; I'm sick of 'em."

"Well," said Macy consolingly, "the Tates' is just for college kids anyways."

"I tell you—"

"I thought you'd be going to one of 'em anyways. I see by the papers you haven't missed a one this Christmas."

"Hm," grunted Perry

He would never go to any more parties. Classical phrases played in his mind—that side of his life was closed, closed. Now when a man says "closed, closed" like that, you can be pretty sure that some woman has double-closed him, so to speak. Perry was also thinking that other classical thought, about how cowardly suicide is. A noble thought that one—warm and uplifting. Think of all the fine men we should lose if suicide were not so cowardly!

An hour later was six o'clock, and Perry had lost all resemblance to the young man in the liniment advertisement. He looked like a rough draft for a riotous cartoon. They were singing— an impromptu song of Baily's improvisation:

One Lump Perry, the parlor snake,
Famous through the city for the way he drinks his tea;
Plays with it, toys with it,
Makes no noise with it,
Balanced on a napkin on his well-trained knee.

"Trouble is," said Perry, who had just banged his hair with Baily's comb and was tying an orange tie round it to get the effect of Julius Caesar, "that you fellas can't sing worth a damn. Soon's I leave th' air an' start singin' tenor you start singin' tenor too."

"I'm a natural tenor," said Macy gravely. "Voice lacks cultivation, that's all. Gotta natural voice, m'aunt used say. Naturally good singer."

"Singers, singers, all good singers," remarked Baily, who was at the telephone. "No, not the cabaret; I want night clerk. I mean refreshment clerk or some dog-gone clerk 'at's got food—food! I want —"

"Julius Caesar," announced Perry, turning round from the mirror. "Man of iron will and stern 'termination."

"Shut up!" yelled Baily. "Say, iss Mr. Baily. Sen' up enormous supper. Use y'own judgment. Right away."

He connected the receiver and the hook with some difficulty, and then with his lips closed and an air of solemn intensity in his eyes went to the lower drawer of his dresser and pulled it open.

"Lookit!" he commanded. In his hands he held a truncated garment of pink gingham.

"Julius Cæsar," Announced Perry, Turning Round From the Mirror.
"Man of Iron Will and Stern 'Termination"

"Pants," he explained gravely. "Lookit!" This was a pink blouse, a red tie and a Buster Brown collar. "Lookit!" he repeated. "Costume for the Townsends' circus ball. I'm li'l' boy carries water for the elephants." Perry was impressed in spite of himself.

"I'm going to be Julius Caesar," he announced after a moment of concentration.

"Thought you weren't going!" said Macy.

"Me? Sure, I'm goin'. Never miss a party. Good for the nerves—like celery."

"Caesar!" scoffed Baily. "Can't be Caesar! He's not about a circus. Caesar's Shakspere. Go as a clown."

Perry shook his head.

"Nope; Cesar."

"Caesar?"

"Sure. Chariot."

Light dawned on Baily.

"That's right. Good idea."

Perry looked round the room searchingly. "You lend me a bathrobe and this tie," he said finally.

Baily considered. "No good."

"Sure, tha's all I need. Caesar was a savage. They can't kick if I come as Caesar if he was a savage."

"No," said Baily, shaking his head slowly. "Get a costume over at a costumer's. Over at Nolak's."

"Closed up."

"Find out."

After a puzzling five minutes at the phone a small, weary voice managed to convince Perry that it was Mr. Nolak speaking, and that they would remain open until eight because of the Townsends' ball. Thus assured, Perry ate a great amount of filet mignon and drank his third of the last bottle of champagne. At eight-fifteen the man in the tall hat who stands in front of the Clarendon found him trying to start his roadster.

"Froze up," said Perry wisely. "The cold froze it. The cold air."

"Froze, eh?"

"Yes. Cold air froze it."

"Can't start it?"

"Nope. Let it stand here till summer. One those hot ole August days'll thaw it out awright."

"Goin' let it stand?"

"Sure. Let 'er stand. Take a hot thief to steal it. Gemme taxi."

The man in the tall hat summoned a taxi.

"Where to, mister?"

"Go to Nolak's—costume fella."

II

Mrs. Nolak was short and ineffectual looking, and on the cessation of the World War had belonged for a while to one of the new nationalities. Owing to the unsettled European conditions she had never since been quite sure what she was. The shop in which she and her husband performed their daily stint was dim and ghostly and peopled with suits of armor and Chinese mandarins and enormous papier-mâché birds suspended from the ceiling. In a vague background many rows of masks glared eyelessly at the visitor, and there were glass cases full of crowns and scepters and jewels and enormous stomachers and paints and powders and crape hair and face creams and wigs of all colors.

When Perry ambled into the shop Mrs. Nolak was folding up the last troubles of a strenuous day, so she thought, in a drawer full of pink silk stockings.

"Something for you?" she queried pessimistically.

"Want costume of Julius Hur, the charioteer."

Mrs. Nolak was sorry, but every stitch of charioteer had been rented long ago. Was it for the Townsends' circus ball?

It was.

"Sorry," she said, "but I don't think there's anything left that's really circus."

This was an obstacle.

"Hm," said Perry. An idea struck him suddenly. "If you've got a piece of canvas I could go's a tent."

"Sorry, but we haven't anything like that. A hardware store is where you'd have to go to. We have some very nice Confederate soldiers."

"No, no soldiers."

"And I have a very handsome king."

He shook his head.

"Several of the gentlemen," she continued hopefully, "are wearing stovepipe hats and swallow-tail coats and going as ringmasters—but we're all out of tall hats. I can let you have some crape hair for a mustache."

"Want somep'm 'stinctive."

"Something—let's see. Well, we have a lion's head, and a goose, and a camel —"

"Camel?" The idea seized Perry's imagination, gripped it fiercely.

"Yes, but it needs two people."

"Camel. That's an idea. Lemme see it."

The camel was produced from his resting place on a top shelf. At first glance he appeared to consist entirely of a very gaunt, cadaverous head and a sizable hump, but on being spread out he was found to possess a dark brown, unwholesome-looking body made of thick, cottony cloth.

"You see it takes two people," explained Mrs. Nolak, holding the camel up in frank admiration. "If you have a friend he could be part of it. You see there's sorta pants for two people. One pair is for the fella in front and the other pair for the fella in back. The fella in front does the lookin' out through these here eyes an' the fella in back he's just gotta stoop over an' folla the front fella round."

"Put it on," commanded Perry.

Obediently Mrs. Nolak put her tabby-cat face inside the camel's head and turned it from side to side ferociously. Perry was fascinated.

"What noise does a camel make?"

"What?" asked Mrs. Nolak as her face emerged, somewhat smudgy. "Oh, what noise? Why, he sorta brays."

"Lemme see it in a mirror."

Before a wide mirror Perry tried on the head and turned from side to side appraisingly. In the dim light the effect was distinctly pleasing. The camel's face was a study in pessimism, decorated with numerous abrasions, and it must be admitted that his coat was in that state of general negligence peculiar to camels—in fact, he needed to be cleaned and pressed—but distinctive he certainly was. He was majestic. He would have attracted attention in any gathering if only by his melancholy cast of feature and the look of pensive hunger lurking round his shadowy eyes.

"You see you have to have two people," said Mrs. Nolak again.

Perry tentatively gathered up the body and legs and wrapped them about him, tying the hind legs as a girdle round his waist. The effect on the whole was bad. It was even irreverent—like one of those medieval pictures of a monk changed into a beast by the ministrations of Satan. At the very best the ensemble resembled a humpbacked cow sitting on her haunches among blankets.

"Don't look like anything at all," objected Perry gloomily.

"No," said Mrs. Nolak; "you see you got to have two people."

A solution flashed upon Perry. "You got a date to-night?'

"Oh, I couldn't possibly—"

"Oh, come on," said Perry encouragingly. "Sure you can! Here! Be a good sport and climb into these hind legs."

With difficulty he located them and extended their yawning

depths ingratiatingly. But Mrs. Nolak seemed loath. She backed perversely away.

"Oh, no—"

"C'mon! Why, you can be the front if you want to. Or we'll flip a coin."

"Oh, no —"

"Make it worth your while."

Mrs. Nolak set her lips firmly together.

"Now you just stop!" she said with no coyness implied. "None of the gentlemen ever acted up this way before. My husband—"

"You got a husband?" demanded Perry. "Where is he?"

"He's home."

"Wha's telephone number?"

After considerable parley he obtained the telephone number pertaining to the Nolak penates and got into communication with that small, weary voice he had heard once before that day. But Mr. Nolak, though taken off his guard and somewhat confused by Perry's brilliant flow of logic, stuck staunchly to his point. He refused firmly but with dignity to help out Mr. Parkhurst in the capacity of back part of a camel.

Having rung off, or rather having been rung off on, Perry sat down on a three-legged stool to think it over. He named over to himself those friends on whom he might call, and then his mind paused as Betty Medill's name hazily and sorrowfully occurred to him. He had a sentimental thought. He would ask her. Their love affair was over, but she could not refuse this last request. Surely it was not much to ask—to help him keep up his end of social obligation for one short night. And if she insisted she could be the front part of the camel and he would go as the back. His magnanimity pleased him. His mind even turned to rosy-colored dreams of a tender reconciliation inside the camel—there hidden away from all the world.

"Now you'd better decide right off."

The bourgeois voice of Mrs. Nolak broke in upon his mellow fancies and roused him to action. He went to the phone and called up the Medill house. Miss Betty was out; had gone out to dinner.

Then, when all seemed lost, the camel's back wandered curiously into the store. He was a dilapidated individual with a cold in his head and a general trend about him of downwardness. His cap was pulled down low on his head, and his chin was pulled down low on his chest, his coat hung down to his shoes, he looked run-down, down at the heels, and—Salvation Army to the contrary—down and out. He said that he was the taxicab driver that the gentleman had hired at the Clarendon Hotel. He had been instructed to wait outside, but he had waited some time and a suspicion had grown upon him that the gentleman had gone out the back way with purpose to defraud him—gentlemen sometimes did—so he had come in. He sank down onto the three-legged stool.

"Wanta go to a party? "demanded Perry sternly.

"I gotta work, " answered the taxi driver lugubriously."I gotta keep my job."

"It's a very good party."

"It's a very good job."

"Come on!" urged A. Perry. "Be a good fella. See — it's pretty!" He held the camel up and the taxi driver looked at it cynically.

"Huh!'

Perry searched feverishly among the folds of the cloth.

"See!" he cried enthusiastically, holding up a selection of folds. "This is your part. You don't even have to talk. All you have to do is to walk—and sit down occasionally. You do all the sitting down. Think of it. I'm on my feet all the time and you can sit down some of the time. The only time I can sit down is when we're lying down, and you can sit down when—oh, any time. See?"

"What's 'at thing?" demanded the individual dubiously. "A shroud?"

"Not at all," said Perry hurriedly. "It's a camel."

"Huh?"

Then Perry mentioned a sum of money, and the conversation left the land of grunts and assumed a practical tinge. Perry and the taxi driver tried on the camel in front of the mirror.

"You can't see it," explained Perry, peering anxiously out through the eyeholes, "but honestly, ole man, you look sim'ly great! Honestly!"

A grunt from the hump acknowledged this somewhat dubious compliment.

"Honestly, you look great!" repeated Perry enthusiastically. "Move round a little."

The hind legs moved forward, giving the effect of a huge cat-camel hunching his back preparatory to a spring.

"No; move sideways."

The camel's hips went neatly out of joint; a hula dancer would have writhed in envy.

"Good, isn't it?" demanded Perry, turning to Mrs. Nolak for approval.

"It looks lovely," agreed Mrs. Nolak.

"We'll take it," said Perry.

The bundle was safely stowed under Perry's arm and they left the shop.

"Go to the party!" he commanded as he took his seat in the back.

"What party?"

"Fanzy-dress party."

"Where'bouts is it?"

This presented a new problem. Perry tried to remember, but the names of all those who had given parties during the holidays danced confusedly before his eyes. He could ask Mrs. Nolak, but on looking out the window he saw that the shop was dark. Mrs. Nolak had already faded out, a little black smudge far down the snowy street.

"Drive uptown," directed Perry with fine confidence. "If you see a party, stop. Otherwise I'll tell you when we get there."

He fell into a hazy daydream and his thoughts wandered again to Betty—he imagined vaguely that they had had a disagreement because she refused to go to the party as the back part of the camel. He was just slipping off into a chilly doze when he was wakened by the taxi driver opening the door and shaking him by the arm.

"Here we are, maybe."

Perry looked out sleepily. A striped awning led from the curb up to a spreading gray stone house, from inside which issued the low drummy whine of expensive jazz. He recognized the Howard Tate house.

"Sure," he said emphatically; "'at's it! Tate's party tonight. Sure, everybody's goin'."

"Say," said the individual anxiously after another look at the awning, "you sure these people ain't gonna romp on me for comin' here?"

Perry drew himself up with dignity. "'F anybody says anything to you, just tell 'em you're part of my costume."

The visualization of himself as a thing rather than a person seemed to reassure the individual.

"All right," he said reluctantly.

Perry stepped out under the shelter of the awning and began unrolling the camel.

"Let's go," he commanded.

Several minutes later a melancholy, hungry-looking camel, emitting clouds of smoke from his mouth and from the tip of his noble hump, might have been seen crossing the threshold of the Howard Tate residence, passing a startled footman without so much as a snort, and heading directly for the main stairs that led up to the ballroom. The beast walked with a peculiar gait which varied between an uncertain lockstep and a stampede—but can best be described by the word "halting." The camel had a halting gait—and as he walked he alternately elongated and contracted like a gigantic concertina.

III

The Howard Tates are, as everyone who lives in Toledo knows, the most formidable people in town. Mrs. Howard Tate was a Chicago Todd before she became a Toledo Tate, and the family generally affect that conscious simplicity which has begun to be the earmark of American aristocracy. The Tates have reached the stage where they talk about pigs and farms and look at you icy-eyed if you are not amused. They have begun to prefer retainers rather than friends as dinner guests, spend a lot of money in a quiet way and, having lost all sense of competition, are in process of growing quite dull.

The dance this evening was for little Millicent Tate, and though there was a scattering of people of all ages present the dancers were mostly from school and college—the younger married crowd was at the Townsends' circus ball up at the Tallyho Club. Mrs. Tate was standing just inside the ballroom, following Millicent round with her eyes and beaming whenever she caught her eye. Beside her were two middle-aged sycophants who were saying what a perfectly exquisite child Millicent was. It was at this moment that Mrs. Tate was grasped firmly by the skirt and her youngest daughter, Emily, aged eleven, hurled herself with an "Oof !" into her mother's arms.

"Why, Emily, what's the trouble?"

"Mamma," said Emily, wild-eyed but voluble, "there's something out on the stairs."

"What?"

"There's a thing out on the stairs, mamma. I think it's a big dog, mamma, but it doesn't look like a dog."

"What do you mean, Emily?"

The sycophants waved their heads and hemmed sympathetically.

"Mamma, it looks like a—like a camel."

Mrs. Tate laughed.

"You saw a mean old shadow; dear, that's all."

"No, I didn't. No, it was some kind of thing, mamma—big. I was going downstairs to see if there were any more people and this dog or something, he was coming upstairs. Kinda funny, mamma, like he was lame. And then he saw me and gave a sort of growl and then he slipped at the top of the landing and I ran."

Mrs. Tate's laugh faded.

"The child must have seen something," she said.

The sycophants agreed that the child must have seen something—and suddenly all three women took an instinctive step away from the door as the sounds of muffled footsteps were audible just outside. And then three startled gasps rang out as a dark brown form rounded the corner and they saw what was apparently a huge beast looking down at them hungrily.

"Oof!" cried Mrs. Tate

"O-o-oh!" cried the ladies in a chorus. The camel suddenly humped his back, and the gasps turned to shrieks.

"Oh—look!"

"What is it?"

The dancing stopped, but the dancers hurrying over got quite a different impression of the invader from that of the ladies by the door; in fact, the young people immediately suspected that it was a stunt, a hired entertainer come to amuse the party. The boys in long trousers looked at it rather disdainfully and sauntered over with their hands in their pockets, feeling that their intelligence was being insulted. But the girls ran over with much handclapping and many little shouts of glee.

"It's a camel!"

"Well, if he isn't the funniest!"

The camel stood there uncertainly, swaying slightly from side to side and seeming to take in the room in a careful, appraising glance; then as if he had come to an abrupt decision he turned and ambled swiftly out the door.

Mr. Howard Tate had just come out of his den on the lower floor and was standing chatting with a good-looking young man in the hall. Suddenly they heard the noise of shouting upstairs and almost immediately a succession of bumping sounds, followed by the precipitous appearance at the foot of the stairway of a large brown beast who seemed to be going somewhere in a great hurry.

"Now what the devil!" said Mr. Tate, starting.

The beast picked itself up with some dignity and affecting an air of extreme nonchalance, as if he had just remembered an important engagement, started at a mixed gait toward the front door. In fact, his front legs began casually to run.

"See here now," said Mr. Tate sternly. "Here! Grab it, Butterfield! Grab it!"

The young man enveloped the rear of the camel in a pair of brawny arms, and evidently realizing that further locomotion was quite impossible the front end submitted to capture and stood resignedly in a state of some agitation. By this time a flood of young people was pouring downstairs, and Mr. Tate, suspecting everything from an ingenious burglar to an escaped lunatic, gave crisp directions to the good-looking young man:

"Hold him! Lead him in here; we'll soon see."

The camel consented to be led into the den, and Mr. Tate, after locking the door, took a revolver from a table drawer and instructed the young man to take the thing's head off. Then he gasped and returned the revolver to its hiding place.

"Well, Perry Parkhurst!" he exclaimed in amazement.

"I'm in the wrong pew," said Perry sheepishly. "Got the wrong party, Mr. Tate. Hope I didn't scare you."

"Well—you gave us a thrill, Perry." Realization dawned on him. "Why, of course; you're bound for the Townsends' circus ball."

"That's the general idea."

"Let me introduce Mr. Butterfield, Mr. Parkhurst. Parkhurst is our most famous young bachelor here." Then turning to Perry: "Butterfield is staying with us for a few days."

"I got a little mixed up," mumbled Perry. "I'm very sorry."

"Heavens, it's perfectly all right; most natural mistake in the world. I've got a clown costume and I'm going down there myself after a while. Silly idea for a man of my age." He turned to Butterfield. "Better change your mind and come down with us."

The good-looking young man demurred. He was going to bed.

"Have a drink, Perry?" suggested Mr. Tate.

"Thanks, I will."

"And, say," continued Tate quickly, " I'd forgotten all about your—friend here." He indicated the rear part of the camel. "I didn't mean to seem discourteous. Is it anyone I know? Bring him out."

"It's not a friend," explained Perry hurriedly. "I just rented him."

"Does he drink?"

"Do you?" demanded Perry, twisting himself tortuously round.

There was a faint sound of assent.

"Sure he does!" said Mr. Tate heartily. "A really efficient camel ought to be able to drink enough so it'd last him three days."

"Tell you, sir," said Perry anxiously, "he isn't exactly dressed up enough to come out. If you give me the bottle I can hand it back to him and he can take his inside."

From under the cloth was audible the enthusiastic smacking sound inspired by this suggestion. When a butler had appeared with bottles, glasses and siphon one of the bottles was handed back, and thereafter the silent partner could he heard imbibing long potations at frequent intervals.

Thus passed a peaceful hour. At ten o'clock Mr. Tate decided that they'd better be starting. He donned his clown's costume; Perry replaced the camel's head with a sigh; and side-by-side they progressed on foot the single block between the Tate house and the Tallyho Club.

The circus ball was in full swing. A great tent fly had been put up inside the ballroom and round the walls had been built rows of booths representing the various attractions of a circus side show, but these were now vacated and on the floor swarmed a shouting, laughing medley of youth and color—clowns, bearded ladies, acrobats, bareback riders, ringmasters, tattooed men and charioteers. The Townsends had determined to assure their party of success, so a great quantity of liquor had been surreptitiously brought over from their house in automobiles and it was flowing freely. A green ribbon ran along the wall completely round the ballroom, with pointing arrows alongside of it and signs which instructed the uninitiated to "Follow the green line!" The green line led down to the bar, where waited pure punch and wicked punch and plain dark-green bottles.

On the wall above the bar was another arrow, red and very wavy, and under it the slogan: "Now follow this!"

But even amid the luxury of costume and high spirits represented there the entrance of the camel created something of a stir, and Perry was immediately surrounded by a curious, laughing crowd who were anxious to penetrate the identity of this beast who stood by the wide doorway eying the dancers with his hungry, melancholy gaze.

And then Perry saw Betty. She was standing in front of a booth talking to a group of clowns, comic policemen and ring-masters. She was dressed in the costume of an Egyptian snake charmer, a costume carried out to the smallest detail. Her tawny hair was braided and drawn through brass rings, the effect crowned with a glittering Oriental tiara. Her fair face was stained to a warm olive glow and on her bare arms and the half moon of her back writhed painted serpents with single eyes of venomous green. Her feet were in sandals and her skirt was slit to the knees, so that when she walked one caught a glimpse of other slim serpents painted just above her bare ankles. Wound about her neck was a huge, glittering, cotton-stuffed cobra, and her bracelets were in the form of tiny garter snakes. Altogether a very charming and beautiful costume—one that made the more nervous among the older women shrink away from her when she passed, and the more troublesome ones to make great talk about "shouldn't be allowed" and "perfectly disgraceful."

But Perry, peering through the uncertain eyes of the camel, saw only her face, radiant, animated and glowing with excitement, and her arms and shoulders, whose mobile, expressive gestures made her always the outstanding figure in any gathering. He was fascinated and his fascination exercised a strangely sobering effect on him. With a growing clarity the events of the day came back—he had lost forever this shimmering princess in emerald green and black. Rage rose within him, and with a half-formed intention of taking her away from the crowd he started toward her—or rather he elongated slightly, for he had neglected to issue the preparatory command necessary to locomotion.

But at this point fickle Kismet, who for a day had played with him bitterly and sardonically, decided to reward him in full for the amusement he had afforded her. Kismet turned the tawny eyes of the snake charmer to the camel. Kismet led her to lean toward the man beside her and say, "Who's that? That camel?"

They all gazed.

"Darned if I know."

But a little man named Warburton, who knew it all, found it necessary to hazard an opinion. "It came in with Mr. Tate. I think it's probably Warren Butterfield, the architect, who's visiting the Tates."

Something stirred in Betty Medill— that age-old interest of the provincial girl in the visiting man.

"Oh," she said casually after a slight pause.

At the end of the next dance Betty and her partner finished up within a few feet of the camel. With the informal audacity that

"You 'Fraid of Me?" Said Betty. "Don't Be. You See I'm a Snake Charmer, But I'm Pretty Good at Camels Too"

was the keynote of the evening she reached out and gently rubbed the camel's nose.

"Hello, old camel."

The camel stirred uneasily.

"You 'fraid of me?" said Betty, lifting her eyebrows in mock reproof. "Don't be. You see I'm a snake charmer, but I'm pretty good at camels too."

The camel bowed very low and the groups round laughed and made the obvious remark about the beauty and the beast.

Mrs. Townsend came bustling up.

"Well, Mr. Butterfield," she beamed, "I wouldn't have recognized you."

Perry bowed again and smiled gleefully behind his mask.

"And who is this with you?" she inquired.

"Oh," said Perry in a disguised voice, muffled by the thick cloth and quite unrecognizable, "he isn't a fellow, Mrs. Townsend. He's just part of my costume."

This seemed to get by, for Mrs. Townsend laughed and

bustled away. Perry turned again to Betty.

So, he thought, this is how much she cares! On the very day of our final rupture she starts a flirtation with another man—an absolute stranger.

On an impulse he gave her a soft nudge with his shoulder and waved his head suggestively toward the hall, making it clear that he desired her to leave her partner and accompany him. Betty seemed quite willing.

"Bye-bye, Bobby," she called laughingly to her partner. "This old camel's got me. Where are we going, Prince of Beasts?"

The noble animal made no rejoinder, but stalked gravely along in the direction of a secluded nook on the side stairs.

There Betty seated herself, and the camel, after some seconds of confusion which included gruff orders and sounds of a heated dispute going on in his interior, placed himself beside her—his hind legs stretching out uncomfortably across two steps.

"Well, camel," said Betty cheerfully, "how do you like our happy party?"

The camel indicated that he liked it by rolling his head ecstatically and executing a gleeful kick with his hoofs.

"This is the first time that I ever had a tete-a-tete with a man's valet round"—she pointed to the hind legs—"or whatever that is."

"Oh," said Perry, "he's deaf and blind. Forget about him."

"That sure is some costume! But I should think you'd feel rather handicapped—you can't very well shimmy, even if you want to."

The camel hung his head lugubriously.

"I wish you'd say something," continued Betty sweetly. "Say you like me, camel. Say you think I'm pretty. Say you'd like to belong to a pretty snake charmer."

The camel would.

"Will you dance with me, camel?"

The camel would try.

Betty devoted half an hour to the camel. She devoted at least half an hour to all visiting men. It was usually sufficient. When she approached a new man the current debutantes were accustomed to scatter right and left like a close column deploying before a machine gun. And so to Perry Parkhurst was awarded the unique privilege of seeing his love as others saw her. He was flirted with violently!

IV

This paradise of frail foundation was broken into by the sound of a general ingress to the ballroom; the cotillion was beginning. Betty and the camel joined the crowd, her brown hand resting lightly on his shoulder, defiantly symbolizing her complete adoption of him.

When they entered, the couples were already seating themselves at tables round the walls, and Mrs. Townsend, resplendent as a super bareback rider with rather too rotund calves, was standing in the center with the ringmaster who was in charge of arrangements. At a signal to the band everyone rose and began to dance.

"Isn't it just slick!" breathed Betty.

"You bet!" said the camel.

"Do you think you can possibly dance?"

Perry nodded enthusiastically. He felt suddenly exuberant. After all, he was here incognito talking to his girl—he felt like winking patronizingly at the world.

"I think it's the best idea," cried Betty, "to give a party like this! I don't see how they ever thought of it. Come on, let's dance!"

So Perry danced the cotillion. I say danced, but that is stretching the word far beyond the wildest dreams of the jazziest terpsichorean. He suffered his partner to put her hands on his helpless shoulders and pull him here and there gently over the floor while he hung his huge head docilely over her shoulder and made futile dummy motions with his feet. His hind legs danced in a manner all their own, chiefly by hopping first on one foot and then on the other. Never being sure whether dancing was going on or not, the hind legs played safe by going through a series of steps whenever the music started playing. So the spectacle was frequently presented of the front part of the camel standing at ease and the rear keeping up a constant energetic motion calculated to rouse a sympathetic perspiration in any soft-hearted observer.

He was frequently favored. He danced first with a tall lady covered with straw who announced jovially that she was a bale of hay and coyly begged him not to eat her.

"I'd like to; you're so sweet," said the camel gallantly.

Each time the ringmaster shouted his call of "Men up!" he lumbered ferociously for Betty with the cardboard wienerwurst or the photograph of the bearded lady or whatever the favor chanced to be. Sometimes he reached her first, but usually his rushes were unsuccessful and resulted in intense interior arguments.

"For heaven's sake," Perry would snarl fiercely between his clenched teeth, "get a little pep! I could have gotten her that time if you'd picked your feet up."

"Well, gimme a little warnin'!"

"I did, darn you."

"I can't see a dog-gone thing in here."

"All you have to do is follow me. It's just like dragging a load of sand round to walk with you."

"Maybe you wanta try back here."

"You shut up! If these people found you in this room they'd give you the worst beating you ever had. They'd take your taxi license away from you!"

Perry surprised himself by the ease with which he made this monstrous threat, but it seemed to have a soporific, influence on his companion, for he muttered an "aw gwan" and subsided into abashed silence.

The ringmaster mounted to the top of the piano and waved his hand for silence.

"Prizes!" he cried. "Gather round!"

"Yea! Prizes!"

Self-consciously the circle swayed forward. The rather pretty girl who had mustered the nerve to come as a bearded lady trembled with excitement, hoping to be rewarded for an evening's hideousness. The man who had spent the afternoon having tattoo marks painted on him by a sign painter skulked on the edge of the crowd, blushing furiously when anyone told him he was sure to get it.

"Lady and gent performers of the circus," announced the ringmaster jovially, "I am sure we will all agree that a good time has been had by all. We will now bestow honor where honor is due by bestowing the prizes. Mrs. Townsend has asked me to bestow the prizes. Now, fellow performers, the first prize is for that lady who has displayed this evening the most striking, becoming"—at this point the bearded lady sighed resignedly—"and original costume." Here the bale of hay pricked up her ears. "Now I am sure that the decision which has been decided upon will be unanimous with all here present. The first prize goes to Miss Betty Medill, the charming Egyptian snake charmer."

There was a great burst of applause, chiefly masculine, and Miss Betty Medill, blushing beautifully through her olive paint, was passed up to receive her award. With a tender glance the ringmaster handed down to her a huge bouquet of orchids.

"And now," he continued, looking round him, "the other prize is for that man who has the most amusing and original costume. This prize goes without dispute to a guest in our midst, a gentleman who is visiting here but whose stay we all hope will be long and merry—in short to the noble camel who has entertained us all by his hungry look and his brilliant dancing throughout the evening."

He ceased and there was a hearty burst of applause, for it was a popular choice.

The prize, a huge box of cigars, was put aside for the camel, as he was anatomically unable to accept it in person.

"And now," continued the ringmaster, "we will wind up the cotillion with the marriage of Mirth to Folly!"

"Form for the grand wedding march, the beautiful snake charmer and the noble camel in front!"

Betty skipped forward cheerily and wound an olive arm round the camel's neck. Behind them formed the procession of little boys, little girls, country fakes, policemen, fat ladies, thin men, sword swallowers, wild men of Borneo, armless wonders and charioteers, some of them well in their cups, all of them excited and happy and dazzled by the flow of light and color round them and by the familiar faces strangely unfamiliar under bizarre wigs and barbaric paint. The voluminous chords of the wedding march done in mad syncopation issued in a delirious blend from the saxophones and trombones—and the march began.

"Aren't you glad, camel?" demanded Betty sweetly as they stepped off. "Aren't you glad we're going to he married and you're going to belong to the nice snake charmer ever afterward?"

The camel's front legs pranced, expressing exceeding joy.

Minister, minister! Where's the minister?" cried voices out of the revel. "Who's going to be the clergyman?"

The head of Jumbo, rotund Negro waiter at the Tallyho Club for many years, appeared rashly through a half-opened pantry door.

"Oh, Jumbo!"

"Get old Jumbo."

"He's the fella!"

"Come on, Jumbo."

"How 'bout marrying us a couple?"

"Yea!"

Jumbo despite his protestations was seized by four brawny clowns, stripped of his apron and escorted to a raised dais at the head of the ball. There his collar was removed and replaced back side forward to give him a sanctimonious effect. He stood there grinning from ear to ear, evidently not a little pleased, while the parade separated into two lines leaving an aisle for the bride and groom.

"Lawdy, man," chuckled Jumbo, "Ah got ole Bible 'n' ev'ythin', sho nuff."

He produced a battered Bible from a mysterious interior pocket.

"Yea! Old Jumbo's got a Bible!"

"Razor, too, I'll bet!"

"Marry 'em off, Jumbo!"

Together the snake charmer and the camel ascended the cheering aisle and stopped in front of Jumbo, who adopted a grave pontifical air.

"Where's your license, camel?"

"Make it legal, camel."

A man near by prodded Perry.

"Give him a piece of paper, camel. Anything'll do."

Perry fumbled confusedly in his pocket, found a folded paper and pushed it out through the camel's mouth. Holding it upside down Jumbo pretended to scan it earnestly.

"Dis yeah's a special camel's license," he said. "Get you ring ready, camel."

Inside the camel Perry turned round and addressed his worse half.

"Gimme a ring, for Pete's sake!"

"I ain't got none," protested a weary voice.

"You have. I saw it."

"I ain't goin' to take it offen my hand."

"If you don't I'll kill you."

There was a gasp and Perry felt a huge affair of rhinestone and brass inserted into his hand.

Again he was nudged from the outside. "Speak up!"

"I do!" cried Perry quickly.

He heard Betty's responses given in a laughing debonair

tone, and the sound of them even in this burlesque thrilled him.

If it was only real, he thought. If it only was!

Then he had pushed the rhinestone through a tear in the camel's coat and was slipping it on her finger, muttering ancient and historic words after Jumbo. He didn't want anyone to know about this ever. His one idea was to slip away without having to disclose his identity, for Mr. Tate had so far kept his secret well. A dignified young man, Perry—and this might injure his infant law practice.

"Kiss her, camel!"

"Embrace the bride!"

"Unmask, camel, and kiss her!"

Instinctively his heart beat high as Betty turned to him laughingly and began playfully to stroke the cardboard muzzle. He felt his self-control giving away, he longed to seize her in his arms and declare his identity and kiss those scarlet lips that smiled teasingly at him from only a foot away—when suddenly the laughter and applause round them died away and a curious hush fell over the hall. Perry and Betty looked up in surprise. Jumbo had given vent to a huge "Hello!" in such a startled and amazed voice that all eyes were bent on him.

"Hello!" he said again. He had turned round the camel's marriage license, which he had been holding upside down, produced spectacles and was studying it intently.

"Why," he exclaimed, and in the pervading silence his words were heard plainly by everyone in the room, "this yeah's a sho-nuff marriage permit."

"What?"

"Huh?"

"Say it again, Jumbo!"

"Sure you can read?"

Jumbo waved them to silence and Perry's blood burned to fire in his veins as he realized the break he had made.

"Yassuh!" repeated Jumbo. "This yeah's a sho-nuff license,

and the pa'ties concerned one of 'em is dis yeah young lady, Miz Betty Medill, and th' other's Mistah Perry Pa'khurst."

There was a general gasp, and a low rumble broke out as all eyes fell on the camel. Betty shrank away from him quickly, her tawny eyes giving out sparks of fury.

"Is you Mistah Pa'khurst, you camel?"

Perry made no answer. The crowd pressed up closer and stared at him as he stood frozen rigid with embarrassment, his cardboard face still hungry and sardonic, regarding the ominous Jumbo.

"You-all bettah speak up!" said Jumbo slowly, "this yeah's a mighty serous mattah. Outside mah duties at this club ah happens to be a sho-nuff minister in the Firs' Cullud Baptis' Church. It done look to me as though you-all is gone an' got married."

V

The scene that followed will go down forever in the annals of the Tallyho Club. Stout matrons fainted, strong men swore, wild-eyed débutantes babbled in lightning groups instantly formed and instantly dissolved, and a great buzz of chatter, virulent yet oddly subdued, hummed through the chaotic ballroom. Feverish youths swore they would kill Perry or Jumbo or themselves or someone and the Baptis' preacheh was besieged by a tempestuous covey, of clamorous amateur lawyers, asking questions, making threats, demanding precedents, ordering the bonds annulled, and especially trying to ferret out any hint or suspicion of prearrangement in what had occurred.

In the corner Mrs. Townsend was crying softly on the shoulder of Mr. Howard Tate, who was trying vainly to comfort her; they were exchanging "all my fault's" volubly and voluminously. Outside on a snow covered walk Mr. Cyrus Medill, the Aluminum Man, was being paced slowly up and down between two brawny charioteers, giving vent now to a grunt, now to a string of unrepeatables, now to wild pleadings that they'd just let him get at Jumbo. He was facetiously attired for the evening as a wild man of Borneo, and the most exacting stage manager after one look at his face would have acknowledged that any improvement in casting the part would have been quite impossible.

Meanwhile the two principals held the real center of the stage. Betty Medill—or was it Betty Parkhurst? —weeping furiously, was surrounded by the plainer girls—the prettier ones were too busy talking about her to pay much attention to her—and over on the other side of the hall stood the camel, still intact except for his headpiece, which dangled pathetically on his chest. Perry was earnestly engaged in making protestations of his innocence to a ring of angry, puzzled men. Every few minutes just as he had apparently proved his ease someone would mention the marriage certificate, and the inquisition would begin again.

A girl named Marion Cloud, considered the second best belle of Toledo, changed the gist of the situation by a remark she made to Betty.

"Well," she said maliciously, "it'll all blow over, dear. The courts will annul it without question."

Betty's tears dried miraculously in her eyes, her lips shut tightly together, and she flashed a withering glance at Marion. Then she rose and scattering her sympathizers right and left walked directly across the room to Perry, who also rose and stood looking at her in terror. Again silence crept down upon the room.

"Will you have the decency," she said, "to grant me five minutes' conversation—or wasn't that included in your plans?"

He nodded, his mouth unable to form words.

Indicating coldly that he was to follow her she walked out into the hall with her chin uptilted and headed for the privacy of one of the little card rooms.

Perry started after her, but was brought to a jerky halt by the failure of his hind legs to function.

"You stay here!" he commanded savagely.

"I can't," whined a voice from the hump, "unless you get out first and let me get out."

Perry hesitated, but the curious crowd was unbearable, and unable any longer to tolerate eyes he muttered a command and with as much dignity as possible the camel moved carefully out on its four legs.

Betty was waiting for him.

"Well," she began furiously, "you see what you've done! You and that crazy license! I told you you shouldn't have gotten it! I told you!"

"My dear girl, I—"

"Don't dear-girl me! Save that for your real wife if you ever get one after this disgraceful performance. And don't try to pretend it wasn't all arranged. You know you gave that colored waiter money! You know you did! Do you mean to say you didn't try to marry me?"

"No—I mean, yes—of course —"

"Yes, you'd better admit it! You tried it, what are you going to do? Do you know my father's nearly crazy? It'll serve you right if he tries to kill you. He'll take his gun and put some cold steel in you. O-o-oh! Even if this marr —this thing can be annulled it'll hang over me all the rest of my life!"

Perry could not resist quoting softly: "'Oh, camel, wouldn't you like to belong to the pretty snake charmer for all your —' "

"Shut up!" cried Betty.

There was a pause.

"Betty," said Perry finally with a very faint hopefulness, "there's only one thing to do that will really get us out clear. That's for you to marry me."

"Marry you!"

"Yes. Really it's the only—"

"You shut up! I wouldn't marry you if—if—"

"I know. If I were the last man on earth. But if you care anything about your reputation —"

"Reputation!" she cried. "You're a nice one to think about my reputation now. Why didn't you think about my reputation before you hired that horrible Jumbo to—to—"

Perry tossed up his hands hopelessly. "Very well. I'll do anything you want. Lord knows I renounce all claims!"

"But," said a new voice, "I don't."

Perry and Betty started, and she put her hand to her heart.

"For heaven's sake, what was that?"

"It's me," said the camel's back.

In a minute Perry had whipped off the camel's skin, and a lax, limp object, his clothes hanging on him damply, his hand clenched tightly on an almost empty bottle, stood defiantly before them.

"Oh," cried Betty, tears starting again to her eyes, "you brought that object in here to frighten me! You told me he was deaf—that awful person!"

The ex-camel's back sat down on a chair with a sigh of satisfaction.

"Don't talk 'at way about me, lady. I ain't no person. I'm your husband."

"Husband!"

The cry was wrung simultaneously from Betty and Perry.

"Why, sure. I'm as much your husband as that gink is. The smoke didn't marry you to the camel's front. He married you to the whole camel. Why, that's my ring you got on your finger!"

With a little cry she snatched the ring from her finger and flung it passionately at the floor.

"What's all this?" demanded Perry dazedly.

"Jes' that you better fix me an' fix me right. If you don't I'm a-gonna have the same claim you got to bein' married to her!"

"That's bigamy," said Perry, turning gravely to Betty.

Then came the supreme moment of Perry's early life, the

ultimate chance on which he risked his fortunes. He rose and looked first at Betty, where she sat weakly, her face aghast at this new complication, and then at the individual who swayed from side to side on his chair, uncertainly yet menacingly.

"Very well," said Perry slowly to the individual, "you can have her. Betty, I'm going to prove to you that as far as I'm concerned our marriage was entirely accidental. I'm going to renounce utterly my rights to have you as my wife, and give you to—to the man whose ring you wear—your lawful husband."

There was a pause and four horrorstricken eyes were turned on him.

"Good-by, Betty," he said brokenly. "Don't forget me in your new-found happiness. I'm going to leave for the far west on the morning train. Think of me kindly, Betty."

With a last glance at them he turned on his heel and his head bowed on his chest as his hand touched the door knob.

"Good-by," he repeated. He turned the door knob.

But at these words a flying bundle of snakes and silk and tawny hair hurled itself at him.

"Oh, Perry, don't leave me! I can't face it alone! Perry, Perry, take me with you!"

Her tears rained down in a torrent and flowed damply on his neck. Calmly he folded his arms about her.

"I don't care," she cried tearfully. "I love you and if you can wake up a minister at this hour and have it done over again I'll go West with you."

Over her shoulder the front part of the camel looked at the back part of the camel—and they exchanged a particularly subtle, esoteric sort of wink that only true camels can understand.

Story Illustrations b...
May Wilson Presto...

"Bernice Bobs Her Hair" was first time that *The Saturday Evening Post* used an illustration from a Fitzgerald story for their cover. It was an auspicious debut – the illustrator was Norman Rockwell. The story was published May 1, 1920 and Fitzgerald's fee was $500.

To date, Bernice has been filmed twice. The first production aired on live television, May 17, 1951. It was part of a CBS anthology series, Starlight Theatre, and starred a very young Julie Harris as Bernice.

Bernice came to television a second time on October 6, 1976, as part of the American Short Story Collection on PBS. Directed by Joan Micklin Silver, it starred Shelley Duvall and Veronica Cartwright.

Two stage versions exist -- a one-act written by D. D. Brooke, intended for junior high audiences, and a full-length musical version, created by Adam Gwon and Julia Jordan.

Bernice Bobs Her Hair

After dark on Saturday night one could stand on the first tee of the golf course and see the country club windows as a yellow expanse over a very black and wavy ocean. The waves of this ocean, so to speak, were the heads of many curious caddies, a few of the more ingenious chauffeurs, the golf professional's deaf sister—and there were usually several stray, diffident waves who might have rolled inside had they so desired. This was the gallery.

The balcony was inside. It consisted of the circle of wicker chairs that lined the wall of the combination clubroom and ballroom. At these Saturday-night dances it was largely feminine; a great babel of middle- aged ladies with sharp eyes and icy hearts behind lorgnettes and large bosoms. The main function of the balcony was critical. It occasionally showed grudging admiration, but never approval, for it is well known among ladies over thirty-five that when the younger set dance in the summer time it is with the very worst intentions in the world, and if they are not bombarded with stony eyes stray couples will dance weird barbaric interludes in the corners, and the more popular, more dangerous girls will sometimes be kissed in the parked limousine of unsuspecting dowagers.

But after all, this critical circle is not close enough to the stage to see the actors' faces and catch the subtler byplay. It can only frown and lean, ask questions and make satisfactory deductions from its set of postulates, such as the one which states that every young man with a large income leads the life of a hunted partridge. It never really appreciates the drama of the shifting, semi-cruel world of adolescence. No; boxes, orchestra circle, principals and chorus are represented by the medley of faces and voices that sway to the plaintive African rhythm of Dyer's dance orchestra.

From sixteen-year-old Otis Ormonde, who has two more years at Hill School, to G. Reece Stoddard, over whose bureau at home hangs a Harvard law diploma; from little Madeleine Hogue, whose hair still feels strange and uncomfortable on top of her head, to Bessie MacRae, who has been the life of the party a little too long—more than ten years—the medley is not only the center of the stage but contains the only people capable of getting an unobstructed view of it.

With a flourish and a bang the music stops. The couples exchange artificial, effortless smiles, facetiously repeat "*la*-de-*da*-dadum-*dum*," and then the clatter of young feminine voices soars over the burst of clapping.

A few disappointed stags caught in mid-floor as they had been about to cut in subsided listlessly back to the walls, because this was not like the riotous Christmas dances. These summer hops were considered just pleasantly warm and exciting, where even the younger marrieds rose and performed ancient waltzes and terrifying fox trots to the tolerant amusement of their younger brothers and sisters.

Warren McIntyre, who casually attended Yale, being one of the unfortunate stags, felt in his dinner-coat pocket for a cigarette and strolled out onto the wide, semi-dark veranda, where couples were scattered at tables, filling the lantern-hung night with vague words and hazy laughter. He nodded here and there at the less absorbed and as he passed each couple some half-forgotten fragment of a story played in his mind, for it was not a large city and everyone was Who's Who to everyone else's past. There, for example, were Jim Strain and Ethel Demorest, who had been privately engaged for three years. Everyone knew that as soon as Jim managed to hold a job for more than two months she would marry him. Yet how bored they both looked and how wearily Ethel regarded Jim sometimes, as if she wondered why she had trained the vines of her affection on such a wind-shaken poplar.

Warren was nineteen and rather pitying with those of his friends who hadn't gone East to college. But like most boys he bragged tremendously about the girls of his city when he was away from it. There was Genevieve Ormonde, who regularly made the rounds of dances, house parties and football games at Princeton, Yale, Williams and Cornell; there was black-eyed Roberta Dillon, who was quite as famous to her own generation as Hiram Johnson or Ty Cobb; and, of course, there was Marjorie Harvey, who besides having a fairylike face and a dazzling, bewildering tongue was already justly celebrated for having turned five cart wheels in succession during the last pump-and-slipper dance at New Haven.

Warren, who had grown up across the street from Marjorie, had long been wildly in love with her. Sometimes she seemed to reciprocate his feelings with a faint gratitude, but she had tried him by her infallible test and informed him gravely that she did not love him. Her test was that when she was away from him she forgot him and had affairs with other boys. Warren found this discouraging, especially as Marjorie had been making little trips all summer, and for the first two or three days after each arrival home he saw great heaps of mail on the Harveys' hall table addressed to her in various masculine handwritings. To make matters worse, all during the month of August she had been visited by her cousin Bernice from Eau Claire, and it seemed impossible to see her alone. It was always necessary to hunt round and find someone to take care of Bernice. As August waned this was becoming more and more difficult.

Much as Warren loved Marjorie, he had to admit that Cousin Bernice was sorta hopeless. She was pretty, with dark hair and high color, but she was no fun on a party.

Every Sunday night he danced a long arduous duty dance with her to please Marjorie, but he had never been anything but bored in her company. "Warren"—a soft voice at his elbow broke in upon his thoughts, and he turned to see Marjorie, flushed and radiant as usual. She laid a hand on his shoulder and a glow settled almost imperceptibly over him.

"Warren," she whispered, "do something for me— dance with Bernice. She's been stuck with little Otis Ormonde for almost an hour."

Warren's glow faded.

"Why—sure," he answered half-heartedly.

"You don't mind, do you? I'll see that you don't get stuck."

"'S'all right."

Marjorie smiled—that smile that was thanks enough. "You're an angel, and I'm obliged loads."

With a sigh the angel glanced round the veranda, but Bernice and Otis were not in sight. He wandered back inside, and there in front of the women's dressing room he found Otis in the center of a group of young men who were convulsed with laughter. Otis was brandishing a piece of timber he had picked up, and discoursing volubly wildly.

"She's gone in to fix her hair," he announced wildly. "I'm waiting to dance another hour with her."

Their laughter was renewed.

"Why don't some of you cut in?" cried Otis resentfully. "She likes more variety."

"Why, Otis," suggested a friend, "you've just barely got used to her."

"Why the two-by-four, Otis?" inquired Warren, smiling.

"The two-by-four? Oh, this? This is a club. When she comes out I'll hit her on the head and knock her in again."

Warren collapsed on a settee and howled with glee.

"Never mind, Otis," he articulated finally "I'm relieving you this time."

Otis simulated a sudden fainting attack and handed the stick to Warren.

"If you need it, old man," he said hoarsely.

No matter how beautiful or brilliant a girl may be, the reputation of not being frequently cut in on makes her position at a dance unfortunate. Perhaps boys prefer her company to that of the butterflies with whom they dance a dozen times an evening, but youth in this jazz-nourished generation is temperamentally restless, fox trotting more than one full fox trot with the same girl is distasteful, not to say odious. When it comes to several dances and the intermissions between she can be quite sure that a young man, once relieved, will never tread on her wayward toes again.

Warren danced the next full dance with Bernice, and finally, thankful for the intermission, he led her to a table on the veranda. There was a moment's silence while she did unimpressive things with her fan.

"It's hotter here than in Eau Claire," she said

Warren stifled a sign and nodded. It might be for all he knew or cared. He wondered idly whether she was a poor conversationalist because she got no attention or got no attention because she was a poor conversationalist.

"You going to be here much longer?" he asked, and then

He Wondered Idly Whether She Was a Poor Conversationalist Because She Got No Attention or Got No Attention Because She Was a Poor Conversationalist

turned rather red. She might suspect his reasons for asking.

"Another week," she answered, and stared at him as if to lunge at his next remark when it left his lips.

Warrant fidgeted. Then with a sudden charitable impulse he decided to try part of his line on her. He turned and looked at her eyes.

"You've got an awfully kissable mouth," he began quietly.

This was a remark that he sometimes made to girls at college proms when they were talking in just such half dark as this. Bernice distinctly jumped. She turned an ungraceful red and became clumsy with her fan. No one had ever made such a remark to her before.

"Fresh!"—the word had slipped out before she realized it, and she bit her lip. Too late she decided to be amused, and offered him a flustered smile.

Warren was annoyed. Though not accustomed to have that remark taken seriously, still it usually provoked a laugh or a paragraph of sentimental banter. And he hated to be called fresh, except in a joking way. His charitable impulse died and he switched the topic.

"Jim Strain and Ethel Demorest sitting out as usual," he commented.

This was more in Bernice's line, but a faint regret mingled with her relief as the subject changed. Men did not talk to her about kissable mouths, but she knew that they talked in some such way to other girls.

"Oh, yes," she said, and laughed. "I hear they've been mooning round for years without a red penny. Isn't it silly?"

Warren's disgust increased. Jim Strain was a close friend of his brother's, and anyway he considered it bad form to sneer at people for not having money. But Bernice had had no intention of sneering. She was merely nervous.

II

When Marjorie and Bernice reached home at half after midnight they said good night at the top of the stairs. Though cousins, they were not intimates. As a matter of fact Marjorie had no female intimates—she considered girls stupid. Bernice on the contrary all through this parent-arranged visit had rather longed to exchange those confidences flavored with giggles and tears that she considered an indispensable factor in all feminine intercourse. But in this respect she found Marjorie rather cold; felt somehow the same difficulty in talking to her that she had in talking to men. Marjorie never giggled, was never frightened, seldom embarrassed, and in fact had very few of the qualities which Bernice considered appropriately and blessedly feminine.

As Bernice busied herself with toothbrush and paste this night she wondered for the hundredth time why she never had any attention when she was away from home. That her family were the wealthiest in Eau Claire; that her mother entertained tremendously, gave little dinners for her daughter before all dances and bought her a car of her own to drive round in never occurred to her as factors in her home-town social success. Like most girls she had been brought up on the warm milk prepared by Annie Fellows Johnston and on novels in which the female was beloved because of certain mysterious womanly qualities, always mentioned but never displayed.

Bernice felt a vague pain that she was not at present engaged in being popular. She did not know that had it not been for Marjorie's campaigning she would have danced the entire evening with one man; but she knew that even in Eau Claire other girls with less position and less pulchritude were given a much bigger rush. She attributed this to something subtly unscrupulous in those girls. It had never worried her, and if it had her mother would have assured her that the other girls cheapened themselves and that men really respected girls like Bernice.

She turned out the light in her bathroom, and on an impulse decided to go in and chat for a moment with her Aunt Josephine, whose light was still on. Her soft slippers bore her noiselessly down the carpeted hall, but hearing voices inside she stopped near the partly opened door. Then she caught her own name, and without any definite intention of eavesdropping she lingered—and the thread of the conversation going on inside pierced her consciousness sharply as if it had been drawn through with a needle.

"She's absolutely hopeless!" It was Marjorie's voice. "Oh, I know what you're going to say! So many people have told you how pretty and sweet she is, and how she can cook! What of it? She has a bum time. Men don't like her."

"What's a little cheap popularity?"

Mrs. Harvey sounded annoyed.

"It's everything when you're eighteen," said Marjorie emphatically. "I've done my best. I've been polite and I've made men dance with her, but they just won't stand being bored. When I think of that gorgeous coloring wasted on such a ninny, and think what Martha Carey could do with it—oh!"

"There's no courtesy these days."

Mrs. Harvey's voice implied that modern situations were too much for her. When she was a girl all young ladies who belonged to nice families had glorious times.

"Well," said Marjorie, "no girl can permanently bolster up a lame-duck visitor, because these days it's every girl for herself. I've even tried to drop her hints about clothes and things, and she's been furious—given me the funniest looks. She's sensitive enough to know she's not getting away with much, but I'll bet she consoles herself by thinking that she's very virtuous and that I'm too gay and fickle and will come to a bad end. All unpopular girls think that way. Sour grapes! Sarah Hopkins refers to Genevieve and Roberta and me as gardenia girls! I'll bet she'd give ten years of her life and her European education to be a gardenia girl and have three or four

"Well," said Marjorie, "No Girl Can Permanently Bolster Up a Lame-Duck Visitor, Because These Days it's Every Girl for Herself"

men in love with her and be cut in on every few feet at dances."

"It seems to me," interrupted Mrs. Harvey rather wearily, "that you ought to be able to do something for Bernice. I know she's not very vivacious."

Marjorie groaned.

"Vivacious! Good grief! I've never heard her say anything to a boy except that it's hot or the floor's crowded or that she's going to school in New York next year. Sometimes she asks them what kind of car they have and tells them the kind she has. Thrilling!"

There was a short silence, and then Mrs. Harvey took up her refrain. "All I know is that other girls not half so sweet and attractive get partners. Martha Carey, for instance, is stout and loud, and her mother is distinctly common. Roberta Dillon is so thin this year that she looks as though Arizona were the place for her. She's dancing herself to death."

"But, mother," objected Marjorie impatiently, "Martha is cheerful and awfully witty and an awfully slick girl, and Roberta's a marvelous dancer. She's been popular for ages!"

Mrs. Harvey yawned.

"I think it's that crazy Indian blood in Bernice," continued Marjorie. "Maybe she's a reversion to type. Indian women all just sat round and never said anything."

"Go to bed, you silly child," laughed Mrs. Harvey. "I wouldn't have told you that if I'd thought you were going to remember it. And I think most of your ideas are perfectly idiotic," she finished sleepily.

There was another silence, while Marjorie considered whether or not convincing her mother was worth the trouble. People over forty can seldom be permanently convinced of anything. At eighteen our convictions are hills from which we look; at forty-five they are caves in which we hide.

Having decided this, Marjorie said good night. When she came out into the hall it was quite empty.

III

While Marjorie was breakfasting late next day Bernice came into the room with a rather formal good morning, sat down opposite, stared intently over and slightly moistened her lips.

"What's on your mind?" inquired Marjorie, rather puzzled.

Bernice paused before she threw her hand grenade.

"I heard what you said about me to your mother last night."

Marjorie was startled, but she showed only a faintly heightened color and her voice was quite even when she spoke.

"Where were you?"

"In the hall. I didn't mean to listen—at first."

After an involuntary look of contempt Marjorie dropped her eyes and became very interested in balancing a stray corn flake on her finger.

"I guess I'd better go back to Eau Claire—if I'm such a nuisance." Bernice's lower lip was trembling violently and she continued on a wavering note. "I've tried to be nice, and—and I've been first neglected and then insulted. No one ever visited me and got such treatment."

Marjorie was silent.

"But I'm in the way, I see. I'm a drag on you. Your friends don't like me." She paused, and then remembered another one of her grievances. "Of course I was furious last week when you tried to hint to me that that dress was unbecoming. Don't you think I know how to dress myself?"

"No," murmured Marjorie less than half aloud.

"What?"

"I didn't hint anything," said Marjorie succinctly. "I said, as I remember, that it was better to wear a becoming dress three times straight than to alternate it with two frights."

"Do you think that was a very nice thing to say?"

"I wasn't trying to be nice." Then after a pause: "When do you want to go?"

Bernice drew in her breath sharply. "Oh!" It was a little half cry.

Marjorie looked up in surprise. "Didn't you say you were going?"

"Yes, but—"

"Oh, you were only bluffing!"

They stared at each other across the breakfast table for a moment. Misty waves were passing before Bernice's eyes, while Marjorie's face wore that rather hard expression that she used when slightly intoxicated undergraduates were making love to her.

"So you were bluffing," she repeated as if it were what she might have expected.

Bernice admitted it by bursting into tears. Marjorie's eyes showed boredom.

"You're my cousin," sobbed Bernice. "I'm v-v-visiting you. I was to stay a month, and if I go home my mother will know and she'll wah-wonder —"

Marjorie waited until the shower of broken words collapsed into little sniffles.

"I'll give you my month's allowance," she said coldly, "and you can spend this last week anywhere you want. There's a very nice hotel —"

Bernice's sobs rose to a flute note, and rising of a sudden she fled from the room.

An hour later, while Marjorie was in the library absorbed in composing one of those noncommittal, marvelously elusive letters that only a young girl can write, Bernice reappeared, very red-eyed and consciously calm. She cast no glance at Marjorie but took a book at random from the shelf and sat down as if to read. Marjorie seemed absorbed in her letter and continued writing. When the clock showed noon Bernice closed her book with a snap.

"I suppose I'd better get my ticket."

This was not the beginning of the speech she had rehearsed upstairs, but as Marjorie was not getting her cues—wasn't urging her to be reasonable; it's all a mistake—it was the best opening she could muster.

"Just wait till I finish this letter," said Marjorie without looking round. "I want to get it off in the next mail."

After another minute, during which her pen scratched busily, she turned round and relaxed with an air of "at your service." Again Bernice had to speak.

"Do you want me to go home?"

"Well," said Marjorie, considering, "I suppose if you're not having a good time you'd better go. No use being miserable."

"Don't you think common kindness—"

"Oh, please don't quote Little Women!" cried Marjorie impatiently. "That's out of style."

"You think so?"

"Heavens, yes! What modern girl could live like those inane females?"

"They were the models for our mothers."

Marjorie laughed.

"Yes, they were—not! Besides our mothers were all very well in their way, but they know very little about their daughters' problems."

Bernice drew herself up.

"Please don't talk about my mother."

Marjorie laughed.

"I don't think I mentioned her." Bernice felt that she was being led away from her subject.

"Do you think you've treated me very well?"

"I've done my best. You're rather hard material to work with."

The lids of Bernice's eyes reddened.

"I think you're hard and selfish, and you haven't a feminine quality in you."

"Oh, my Lord!" cried Marjorie in desperation. "You little nut! Girls like you are responsible for all the tiresome colorless marriages; all those ghastly inefficiencies that pass as feminine qualities. What a blow it must be when a man with imagination marries the beautiful bundle of clothes that he's been building ideals round, and finds that she's just a weak, whining, cowardly mass of affectations!"

Bernice's mouth had slipped half open.

"The womanly woman!" continued Marjorie. "Her whole early life is occupied in whining criticisms of girls like me who really do have a good time."

Bernice's jaw descended further as Marjorie's voice rose.

"There's some excuse for an ugly girl whining. If I'd been irretrievably ugly I'd never have forgiven my parents for bringing me into the world. But you're starting life without any handicap—" Marjorie's little fist clenched. "If you expect me to weep with you you'll be disappointed. Go or stay, just as you like." And picking up her letters she left the room.

Bernice claimed a headache and failed to appear at luncheon. They had a matinee date for the afternoon, but the headache persisting, Marjorie made explanations to a not very downcast boy. But when she returned late in the afternoon she found Bernice with a strangely set face waiting for her in her bedroom.

"I've decided," began Bernice without preliminaries, "that maybe you're right about things—possibly not. But if you'll tell me why your friends aren't—aren't interested in me I'll see if I can do what you want me to."

Marjorie was at the mirror shaking down her hair.

"Do you mean it?"

"Yes."

"Without reservations? Will you do exactly what I say?"

"Well, I — "

"Well nothing! Will you do exactly as I say?"

"If they're sensible things."

"They're not! You're no case for sensible things."

"Are you going to make—to recommend — "

"Yes, everything. If I tell you to take boxing lessons you'll have to do it. Write home and tell your mother you're going to stay another two weeks."

"If you'll tell me — "

"All right—I'll just give you a few examples now. First, you have no ease of manner. Why? Because you're never sure about your personal appearance. When a girl feels that she's perfectly groomed and dressed she can forget that part of her. That's charm. The more parts of yourself you can afford to forget the more charm you have."

"Don't I look all right?"

"No; for instance, you never take care of your eyebrows. They're black and lustrous, but by leaving them straggly they're a blemish. They'd be beautiful if you'd take care of them in one-tenth the time you take doing nothing. You're going to brush them so that they'll grow straight."

Bernice raised the brows in question.

"Do you mean to say that men notice eyebrows?"

"Yes—subconsciously. And when you go home you ought to have your teeth straightened a little. It's almost imperceptible, still —"

"But I thought," interrupted Bernice in bewilderment, "that you despised little dainty feminine things like that."

"I hate dainty minds," answered Marjorie. "But a girl has to be dainty in person. If she looks like a million dollars she can talk about Russia, ping-pong or the League of Nations and get away with it."

"What else?"

"Oh, I'm just beginning! There's your dancing."

"Don't I dance all right?"

"No, you don't—you lean on a man; yes, you do—ever so slightly. I noticed it when we were dancing together yesterday. And you dance standing up straight instead of bending over a little. Probably some old lady on the side line once told you that you looked so dignified that way. But except with a very small girl it's much harder on the man, and he's the one that counts."

"Go on." Bernice's brain was reeling.

"Well, you've got to learn to be nice to men who are sad birds. You look as if you'd been insulted whenever you're thrown with any except the most popular boys. Why, Bernice, I'm cut in on every few feet—and who does most of it? Why, those very sad birds. No girl can afford to neglect them. They're the big part of any crowd. Young boys too shy to talk are the very best conversational practice. Clumsy boys are the best dancing practice. If you can follow them and yet look graceful you can follow a baby tank across a barb-wire skyscraper."

Bernice sighed profoundly but Marjorie was not through.

"If you go to a dance and really amuse, say, three sad birds that dance with you; if you talk so well to them that they forget they're stuck with you you've done something. They'll come back next time, and gradually so many sad birds will dance with you that the attractive boys will see there's no danger of being stuck—then they'll dance with you."

"Yes," agreed Bernice faintly. "I think I begin to see."

"And finally," concluded Marjorie, "poise and charm will just come. You'll wake up some morning knowing you've attained it, and men will know it too."

Bernice rose.

"It's been awfully kind of you—but nobody's ever talked to me like this before, and I feel sort of startled."

Marjorie made no answer but gazed pensively at her own image in the mirror.

"You're a peach to help me," continued Bernice.

Still Marjorie did not answer, and Bernice thought she had seemed too grateful.

"I know you don't like sentiment," she said timidly.

Marjorie turned to her quickly.

"Oh, I wasn't thinking about that. I was considering whether we hadn't better bob your hair."

Bernice collapsed backward upon the bed.

IV

On the following Wednesday evening there was a dinner dance at the country club. When the guests strolled in Bernice found her place card with a light feeling of irritation. Though at her right sat G. Reece Stoddard, a most desirable and distinguished young bachelor, the all-important left held only Charley Paulson. Charley lacked height, beauty and social shrewdness, and in her new enlightenment Bernice decided that his only qualification to be her partner was that he had never been stuck with her. But this feeling of irritation left with the last of the soup plates, and Marjorie's specific instruction came to her. Swallowing her pride she turned to Charley Paulson and plunged.

"Do you think I ought to bob my hair, Mr. Charley Paulson?"

Charley looked up in surprise.

"Why?"

"Because I'm considering it. It's such a sure and easy way of attracting attention."

Charley smiled pleasantly. He could not know this had been rehearsed. He replied that he didn't know much about bobbed hair. But Bernice was there to tell him.

"I want to be a society vampire, you see," she announced coolly, and went on to inform him that bobbed hair was the necessary prelude. She added that she wanted to ask his advice, because she had heard he was so critical about girls.

Charley, who knew as much about the psychology of women as he did of the mental states of Buddhist contemplatives, felt vaguely flattered.

"So I've decided," she continued, her voice rising slightly, "that early next week I'm going down to the Sevier Hotel barber shop, sit in the first chair and get my hair bobbed." She faltered, noticing that the people near her had paused in their conversation and were listening; but after a confused second Marjorie's coaching told, and she finished her paragraph to the vicinity at large. "Of course I'm charging admission, but if you'll all come down and encourage me I'll issue passes for the inside seats."

There was a ripple of appreciative laughter, and under cover of it G. Reece Stoddard leaned over quickly and said close to her ear: "I'll take a box right now."

She met his eyes and smiled as if he had said something surpassingly brilliant.

"Do you believe in bobbed hair?" asked G.Reece in the same undertone.

"I think it's unmoral," affirmed Bernice gravely. "But, of course, you've either got to amuse people or feed 'em or shock 'em." Marjorie had culled this from Oscar Wilde. It was greeted with a ripple of laughter from the men and a series of quick, intent looks from the girls. And then as though she had said nothing of wit or moment Bernice turned again to Charley and spoke confidentially in his ear.

"I want to ask you your opinion of several people. I imagine you're a wonderful judge of character."

Charley thrilled faintly—paid her a subtle compliment by overturning her water.

Two hours later, while Warren McIntyre was standing passively in the stag line abstractedly watching the dancers and wondering whither and with whom Marjorie had disappeared, an unrelated perception began to creep slowly upon him—a perception that Bernice, cousin to Marjorie, had been cut in on several times in the past five minutes. He closed his eyes, opened them and looked again. Several minutes back she had been dancing with a visiting boy, a matter easily accounted for; a visiting boy would know no better. But now she was dancing with someone else, and there was Charley Paulson headed for her with enthusiastic determination in his eye. Funny—Charley seldom danced with more than three girls an evening.

Warren was distinctly surprised when—the exchange having been affected—the man relieved proved to be none other than G. Reece Stoddard himself. And G. Reece seemed not at all jubilant at being relieved. Next time Bernice danced near, Warren regarded her intently. Yes, she was pretty, distinctly pretty; and tonight her face seemed really vivacious. She had that look that no woman, however histrionically proficient, can successfully counterfeit—she looked as if she were having a good time. He liked the way she had her hair arranged, wondered if it was brilliantine that made it glisten so. And that dress was becoming—a dark red that set off her shadowy eyes and high coloring. He remembered that he had thought her pretty when she first came to town, before he had realized that she was dull. Too bad she was dull—dull girls unbearable—certainly pretty though.

His thoughts zigzagged back to Marjorie. This disappearance would be like other disappearances. When she reappeared he would demand where she had been—would be told emphatically that it was none of his business. What a pity she was so sure of him! She basked in the knowledge that no other girl in town interested him; she defied him to fall in love with Genevieve or Roberta.

Warren sighed. The way to Marjorie's affections was a labyrinth indeed. He looked up. Bernice was again dancing with the visiting boy. Half unconsciously he took a step out from the stag line in her direction, and hesitated. Then he said to himself that it was charity. He walked toward her—collided suddenly with G. Reece Stoddard.

"Pardon me," said Warren.

But G. Reece had not stopped to apologize. He had again cut in on Bernice.

That night at one o'clock Marjorie, with one hand on the electric-light switch in the hall, turned to take a last look at Bernice's sparkling eyes.

"So it worked?"

"Oh, Marjorie, yes!" cried Bernice.

"I saw you were having a gay time."

"I did! The only trouble was that about midnight I ran short of talk. I had to repeat myself—with different men of course. I hope they won't compare notes."

"Men don't," said Marjorie, yawning, "and it wouldn't matter if they did—they'd think you were even trickier."

She snapped out the light, and as they started up the stairs Bernice grasped the banister thankfully. For the first time in her life she had been danced tired.

"You see," said Marjorie at the top of the stairs, "one man sees another man cut in and he thinks there must be something there. Well, we'll fix up some new stuff tomorrow. Good night."

"Good night."

As Bernice took down her hair she passed the evening before her in review. She had followed instructions exactly. Even when Charley Paulson cut in for the eighth time she had simulated delight and had apparently been both interested and flattered. She had not talked about the weather or Eau Claire or automobiles or her school, but had confined her conversation to me, you and us.

But a few minutes before she fell asleep a rebellious thought was churning drowsily in her brain—after all, it was she who had done it. Marjorie, to be sure, had given her conversation, but then Marjorie got much of her conversation out of things she read. Bernice had bought the red dress, though she had never valued it highly before—and her own voice had said the words, her own lips had smiled, her own feet had danced. Marjorie nice girl—vain, though — nice evening —nice boys —like Warren — Warren — Warren— what's - his-name— Warren -

She fell asleep.

V

To Bernice the next week was a revelation. With the feeling that people really enjoyed looking at her and listening to her came the foundation of self-confidence. Of course there were numerous mistakes at first. She did not know, for instance, that Draycott Deyo was studying for the ministry; she was unaware that he had cut in on her because he thought she was a quiet, reserved girl. Had she known these things she would not have treated him to the line which began "Hello, Shell Shock!" and continued with the bathtub story—"It takes a frightful lot of energy to fix my hair in the summer—there's so much of it—so I always fix it first and powder my face and put on my hat; then I get into the bathtub, and dress afterward. Don't you think that's the best plan?"

Though Draycott Deyo was in the throes of difficulties concerning baptism by immersion and might possibly have seen a connection, it must be admitted that he did not. He considered feminine bathing an immoral subject, and gave her some of his ideas on the depravity of modern society.

But to offset that unfortunate occurrence Bernice had several signal successes to her credit. Little Otis Ormonde pleaded off from a trip East and elected instead to follow her with a puppy-like devotion, to the amusement of his crowd and to the irritation of G. Reece Stoddard, several of whose afternoon calls Otis completely ruined by the disgusting tenderness of the glances he bent on Bernice. He even told her the story of the two-by-four and the dressing room to show her how frightfully mistaken he and everyone else had been in their first judgment of her. Bernice laughed off that incident with a slight sinking sensation.

Of all Bernice's conversation perhaps the best known and most universally approved was the line about the bobbing of her hair.

"Oh, Bernice, when you goin' to get the hair bobbed?"

"Day after to-morrow maybe," she would reply, laughing. "Will you come and see me? Because I'm counting on you, you know."

"Will we? You know! But you better hurry up."

Bernice, whose tonsorial intentions were strictly dishonorable, would laugh again.

"Pretty soon now. You'd be surprised."

But perhaps the most significant symbol of her success was the gray car of the hypercritical Warren McIntyre, parked daily in front of the Harvey house. At first the parlor maid was distinctly startled when he asked for Bernice instead of Marjorie; after a week of it she told the cook that Miss Bernice had gotta holda Miss Marjorie's best fella.

And Miss Bernice had. Perhaps it began with Warren's desire to rouse jealousy in Marjorie; perhaps it was the familiar though unrecognized strain of Marjorie in Bernice's conversation; perhaps it was both of these and something of sincere attraction besides.

But somehow the collective mind of the younger set knew within a week that Marjorie's most reliable beau had made an amazing face-about and was giving an indisputable rush to Marjorie's guest. The question of the moment was how Marjorie would take it. Warren called Bernice on the phone twice a day, sent her notes, and they were frequently seen together in his roadster, obviously engrossed in one of those tense, significant conversations as to whether or not he was sincere.

Marjorie on being twitted only laughed. She said she was mighty glad that Warren had at last found someone who appreciated him. So the younger set laughed, too, and guessed that Marjorie didn't care and let it go at that.

One afternoon when there were only three days left of her visit Bernice was waiting in the hall for Warren, with whom she was going to a bridge party. She was in rather a blissful mood, and when Marjorie—also bound for the party—appeared beside her and began casually to adjust her hat in the mirror Bernice was utterly unprepared for anything in the nature of a clash. Marjorie did her work very coldly and succinctly in three sentences.

"You may as well get Warren out of your head," she said coldly.

"What?" Bernice was utterly astounded.

"You may as well stop making a fool of yourself over Warren McIntyre. He doesn't care a snap of his fingers about you."

For a tense moment they regarded each other—Marjorie scornfully aloof; Bernice astounded, half angry, half afraid. Then two cars drove up in front or the house and there was a riotous honking. Both of them gasped faintly, turned, and side by side hurried out.

All through the bridge party Bernice strove in vain to master a rising uneasiness. She had offended Marjorie, the sphinx of sphinxes. With the most wholesome and innocent intentions in the world she had stolen Marjorie's property. She felt suddenly and horribly guilty. After the bridge game, when they sat in an informal circle and the conversation became general, the storm gradually broke. Little Otis Ormonde inadvertently precipitated it.

"When you going back to kindergarten, Otis?" someone had asked.

"Me? Day Bernice gets her hair bobbed."

"Then your education's over," said Marjorie quickly. "That's only a bluff of hers. I should think you'd have realized."

"That a fact?" demanded Otis, giving Bernice a reproachful glance.

Bernice's ears burned as she tried to think up an effectual come-back. In the face of this direct attack her imagination was paralyzed.

"There's a lot of bluffs in the world," continued Marjorie quite pleasantly. "I should think you'd be young enough to know that, Otis."

"Well," said Otis, "maybe so. But gee! With a line like Bernice's—"

"Really?" yawned Marjorie. "What's her latest bon mot?"

No one seemed to know. In fact, Bernice, having trifled with her muse's beau, had said nothing memorable of late.

"Was that really all a line?" asked Roberta curiously.

Bernice hesitated. She felt that wit in some form was demanded of her, but under her cousin's suddenly frigid eyes she was completely incapacitated.

"I don't know," she stalled.

"Splush!" said Marjorie. "Admit it!"

Bernice saw that Warren's eyes had left a ukulele he had been tinkering with and were fixed on her questioningly.

"Oh, I don't know!" she repeated steadily. Her cheeks were glowing.

"Splush!" remarked Marjorie again.

"Come through, Bernice," urged Otis. "Tell her where to get off."

Bernice looked round again—she seemed unable to get away from Warren's eyes.

"I like bobbed hair," she said hurriedly, as if he had asked her a question, "and I intend to bob mine."

"When?" demanded Marjorie.

"Any time."

"No time like the present," suggested Roberta.

Otis jumped to his feet.

"Swell stuff!" he cried. "We'll have a summer bobbing party. Sevier Hotel barber shop, I think you said."

In an instant all were on their feet. Bernice's heart throbbed violently.

"What?" she gasped.

Out of the group came Marjorie's voice, very clear and contemptuous.

"Don't worry—she'll back out!"

"Come on, Bernice!" cried Otis, starting toward the door.

Four eyes—Warren's and Marjorie's— stared at her, challenged her, defied her. For another second she wavered wildly.

"All right," she said swiftly, "I don't care if I do."

An eternity of minutes later, riding down town through the late afternoon beside Warren, the others following in Roberta's car close behind, Bernice had all the sensations of Marie Antoinette bound for the guillotine in a tumbrel. Vaguely she wondered why she did not cry out that it was all a mistake. It was all she could do to keep from clutching her hair with both hands to protect it from the suddenly hostile world. Yet she did neither. Even the thought of her mother was no deterrent now. This was the test supreme of her sportsmanship; her right to walk unchallenged in the starry heaven of popular girls.

Warren was moodily silent, and when they came to the hotel he drew up at the curb and nodded to Bernice to precede him out. Roberta's car emptied a laughing crowd into the shop, which presented two bold plate-glass windows to the street.

Bernice stood on the curb and looked at the sign, Sevier Barber Shop. It was a guillotine indeed, and the hangman was the first barber, who, attired in a white coat and smoking a cigarette, leaned nonchalantly against the first chair. He must have heard of her; he must have been waiting all week, smoking eternal cigarettes beside that portentous, too-often-mentioned first chair. Would they blindfold her? No, but they would tie a white cloth round her neck lest any of her blood—nonsense—hair— should get on her clothes.

"All right, Bernice," said Warren quickly.

With her chin in the air she crossed the sidewalk, pushed open the swinging screen door, and giving not a glance to the up-roarious, riotous row that occupied the waiting bench went up to the first barber.

"I want you to bob my hair."

The first barber's mouth slid somewhat open. His cigarette dropped to the floor.

"Huh?"

"My hair—bob it!"

Bob it!

Refusing further preliminaries, Bernice took her seat on high. A man in the chair next to her turned on his side and gave her a glance, half lather, half amazement. One barber started and spoiled little Willy Schuneman's monthly haircut. Mr. O'Reilly in the last chair grunted and swore musically in ancient Gaelic as a razor bit into his cheek. Two bootblacks became wide-eyed and rushed for her feet. No, Bernice didn't care for a shine.

Outside a passer-by stopped and stared; a couple joined him; half a dozen small boys' noses sprang into life, flattened against the glass; and snatches of conversation borne on the summer breeze drifted in through the screen door.

"Lookada long hair on a kid!"

"Where'd yuh get 'at stuff? 'At's a bearded lady he just finished shavin'."

But Bernice saw nothing, heard nothing. Her only living sense told her that this man in the white coat had removed one tortoiseshell comb and then another; that his fingers were fumbling clumsily with unfamiliar hairpins; that this hair, this wonderful hair of hers, was going—she would never again feel its long voluptuous pull as it hung in a dark-brown glory down her back. For a second she was near breaking down, and then the picture before her swam mechanically into her vision—Marjorie's mouth curling in a faint ironic smile as if to say:

"Give up and get down! You tried to buck me and I called your bluff. You see you haven't got a prayer."

And some last energy rose up in Bernice, for she clenched her hands under the white cloth, and there was a curious narrowing of her eyes that Marjorie remarked on to someone long afterward.

Twenty minutes later the barber swung her round to face the mirror, and she flinched at the full extent of the damage that had been wrought. Her hair was not curly, and now it lay in lank lifeless blocks on both sides of her suddenly pale face. It was ugly as sin— she had known it would be ugly as sin. Her face's chief charm had been a Madonna-like simplicity. Now that was gone and she was—well, frightfully mediocre—not stagy; only ridiculous, like a Greenwich Villager who had left her spectacles at home.

As she climbed down from the chair she tried to smile—failed miserably. She saw two of the girls exchange glances; noticed Marjorie's mouth curved in attenuated mockery—and that Warren's eyes were suddenly very cold.

"You see"—her words fell into an awkward pause—"I've done it."

"Yes, you've—done it," admitted Warren.

"Do you like it?"

There was a half-hearted "Sure" from two or three voices, another awkward pause, and then Marjorie turned swiftly and with serpent like intensity to Warren.

"Would you mind running me down to Derry's shop?" she asked. "I've simply got to get a hat there before supper. Roberta's driving right home and she can take the others."

Warren stared abstractedly at some infinite speck out the window. Then for an instant his eyes rested coldly on Bernice before they turned to Marjorie.

"Be glad to," he said slowly.

VI

Bernice did not fully realize the outrageous trap that had been set for her until she met her aunt's amazed glance just before dinner.

"Why, Bernice!"

"I've bobbed it, Aunt Josephine."

"Why, child!"

"Do you like it?"

"Why, Bernice!"

"I suppose I've shocked you."

"No, but what'll Mrs. Deyo think tomorrow night? Bernice,

you should have waited until after the Deyos' dance—you should
have waited if you wanted to do that."

"It was sudden, Aunt Josephine. Anyway, why does it matter
to Mrs. Deyo particularly?"

"Why, child," cried Mrs. Harvey, "in her paper on The
Foibles of the Younger Generation that she read at the last meeting
of the Thursday Club she devoted fifteen minutes to bobbed hair.
It's her pet abomination. And the dance is for you and Marjorie!"

"I'm sorry."

"Oh, Bernice, what'll your mother say? She'll think I let you
do it."

"I'm sorry."

Dinner was an agony. She had made a hasty attempt with a
curling iron, and burned her finger and much hair. She could see that
her aunt was both worried and grieved, and her uncle kept saying,
"Well, I'll be darned!" over and over in a hurt and faintly hostile
tone. And Marjorie sat very quietly, entrenched behind a faint smile,
a faintly mocking smile.

Somehow she got through the evening. Three boys called;
Marjorie disappeared with one of them, and Bernice made a listless
mechanical attempt to entertain the two others—sighed thankfully
as she climbed the stairs to her room at half past ten. What a day!

When she had undressed for the night the door opened and
Marjorie came in.

"Bernice," she said, "I'm awfully sorry about the Deyo
dance. I'll give you my word of honor I'd forgotten all about it."

"'S'all right," said Bernice shortly. Standing before the
mirror she passed her comb slowly through her short hair.

"I'll take you downtown to-morrow," continued Marjorie,
"and the hairdresser'll fix it so you'll look slick. I didn't imagine
you'd go through with it. I'm really mighty sorry."

"Oh, 'sall right!"

"Still it's your last night, so I suppose it won't matter much."

Then Bernice winced as Marjorie tossed her own hair over her shoulders and began to twist it slowly into two long blond braids until in her cream-colored negligee she looked like a delicate painting of some Saxon princess. Fascinated, Bernice watched the braids grow. Heavy and luxurious they were, moving under the supple fingers like restive snakes—and to Bernice remained this relic and the curling iron and a tomorrow full of eyes. She could see G. Reece Stoddard, who liked her, assuming his Harvard manner and telling his dinner partner that Bernice shouldn't have been allowed to go to the movies so much; she could see Draycott Deyo exchanging glances with his mother and then being conscientiously charitable to her. But then perhaps by to-morrow Mrs. Deyo would have heard the news; would send round an icy little note requesting that she fail to appear—and behind her back they would all laugh and know that Marjorie had made a fool of her; that her chance at beauty had been sacrificed to the jealous whim of a selfish girl. She sat down suddenly before the mirror, biting the inside of her cheek.

"I like it," she said with an effort. "I think it'll be becoming."

Marjorie smiled. "It looks all right. For heaven's sake, don't let it worry you!"

"I won't."

"Good night, Bernice."

But as the door closed something snapped within Bernice. She sprang dynamically to her feet, clenching her hands, then swiftly and noiselessly crossed over to her bed and from underneath it dragged out her suitcase. Into it she tossed toilet articles and a change of clothing. Then she turned to her trunk and quickly dumped in two drawerfuls of lingerie and summer dresses. She moved quietly, but with deadly efficiency, and in three-quarters of an hour her trunk was locked and strapped and she was fully dressed in a becoming new traveling suit that Marjorie had helped her pick out.

Sitting down at her desk she wrote a short note to Mrs.

Harvey, in which she briefly outlined her reasons for going. She sealed it, addressed it and laid it on her pillow. She glanced at her watch. The train left at one, and she knew that if she walked down to the Marlborough Hotel two blocks away she could easily get a taxicab.

Suddenly she drew in her breath sharply and an expression flashed into her eyes that a practiced character reader might have connected vaguely with the set look she had worn in the barber's chair—somehow a development of it. It was quite a new look for Bernice—and it carried consequences.

She went stealthily to the bureau, picked up an article that lay there, and turning out all the lights stood quietly until her eyes became accustomed to the darkness. Softly she pushed open the door to Marjorie's room. She heard the quiet even breathing of an untroubled conscience asleep.

She was by the bedside now, very deliberate and calm. She acted swiftly. Bending over she found one of the braids of Marjorie's hair, followed it up with her hand to the point nearest the head, and then holding it a little slack so that the sleeper would feel no pull she reached down with the shears and severed it. With the pigtail in her hand she held her breath. Marjorie had muttered something in her sleep. Bernice deftly amputated the other braid, paused for an instant, and then flitted swiftly and silently back to her own room.

Downstairs she opened the big front door, closed it carefully behind her, and feeling wildly happy and exuberant stepped off the porch into the moonlight, swinging her heavy grip like a shopping bag. After a minute's brisk walk she discovered that her left hand still held the two blond braids. She laughed unexpectedly—had to shut her mouth hard to keep from emitting an absolute peal. She was passing Warren's house now, and on the impulse she set down her baggage, and swinging the braids like pieces of rope flung them at the wooden porch, where they landed with a slight thud. She laughed again, no longer restraining herself.

"Huh!" she giggled wildly. "Scalp the selfish thing!"

Then picking up her suitcase she set off at a half run down the moonlit street.

THE SATURDAY EVENING POST

An Illustrated Weekly
Founded A.D. 1728 & Franklin

MAY 22, 1920

5c. THE COPY
10c. in Canada

*Story Illustrations by
James H. Crank*

Arthur Stringer—George Pattullo—Wallace Irwin—F. Scott Fitzgerald—Thomas Joyce
Nina Wilcox Putnam—Eleanor Franklin Egan—Donald Wilhelm—Ferdinand Reyher

In this story, Fitzgerald began his exploration of the differences between Southern and Northern culture. It was a theme that he would return to numerous times and variations of its heroine Sally Carrol would appear in a number of other stories, including "The Jelly Bean", "Two For a Cent" and "The Last of the Belles."

"The Ice Palace" made its appearance in the *Post* on May 22, 1920. Fitzgerald was paid $400 for its publication.

The Ice Palace

The sunlight dripped over the house like golden paint over an art jar and the freckling shadows here and there only intensified the rigor of the bath of light. The Butterworth and Larkin houses flanking were entrenched behind great stodgy trees; only the Happer house took the full sun and all day long faced the dusty road-street with a tolerant kindly patience. This was the city of Tarleton in southernmost Georgia—September afternoon.

Up in her bedroom window Sally Carrol Happer rested her nineteen-year-old chin on a fifty-two-year-old sill and watched Clark Darrow's ancient flivver turn the corner. The car was hot—being partly metallic it retained all the heat it absorbed or evolved—and Clark Darrow sitting bolt upright at the wheel wore a pained, strained expression as though he considered himself a spare part and rather likely to break. He laboriously crossed two dust ruts, the wheels squeaking indignantly at the encounter, and then with a terrifying expression he gave the steering gear a final wrench and deposited self and car approximately in front of the Happer steps. There was a plaintive heaving sound, a death rattle, followed by a short silence; and then the air was rent by a startling whistle.

Sally Carrol gazed down sleepily. She started to yawn, but finding this quite impossible unless she raised her chin from the window sill changed her mind and continued silently to regard the car, whose owner sat brilliantly if perfunctorily at attention as he waited for an answer to his signal. After a moment the whistle once more split the dusty air.

"Good mawnin'."

With difficulty Clark twisted his tall body round and bent a distorted glance on the window.

"'Tain't mawnin', Sally Carrol."

"Isn't it, sure enough?"

"What you doin'?"

"Eatin' 'n apple."

"Come on go swimmin'—want to?"

"Reckon so."

"How 'bout hurryin' up?"

"Sure enough."

Sally Carrol sighed voluminously and raised herself with profound inertia from the floor, where she had been occupied in alternately destroying parts of a green apple and painting paper dolls for her younger sister. She approached a mirror, regarded her expression with a pleased and pleasant languor, dabbed two spots of rouge on her lips and a grain of powder on her nose and covered her bobbed corn-colored hair with a rose-littered sunbonnet. Then she kicked over the painting water, said, "Oh, damn!"—but let it lie—and left the room.

"How you, Clark?" she inquired a minute later as she slipped nimbly over the side of the car.

"Mighty fine, Sally Carrol."

"Where we go swimmin'?"

"Out to Walley's Pool. Told Marylyn we'd call by an' get her an' Joe Ewing."

Clark was dark and lean and when on foot was rather inclined to stoop. His eyes were ominous and his expression rather petulant except when startlingly illuminated by one of his frequent smiles. Clark had what was locally called "an income"—just enough to keep himself in ease and his car in gasoline—and he had spent the two years since he graduated from Georgia Tech in dozing round the lazy streets of his home town discussing how he could best invest his capital for an immediate fortune.

Hanging round he found not at all difficult; a crowd of little girls had grown up beautifully, the amazing Sally Carrol foremost among them; and they enjoyed being swum with and danced with and made love to in the flower-filled summery evenings—and they all liked Clark immensely. When feminine company palled there were half a dozen other youths who were always just about to do something and meanwhile were quite willing to join him in a few holes of golf or a game of billiards or the consumption of a quart of "hard yella licker." Every once in a while one of these contemporaries made a farewell round of calls before going up to New York or Philadelphia or Pittsburgh to go into business, but mostly they just stayed round in this languid paradise of dreamy skies and firefly evenings and noisy street fairs—and especially of gracious soft-voiced girls who were brought up on memories instead of money.

The flivver having been excited into a sort of restless resentful life Clark and Sally Carrol rolled and rattled down Valley Avenue into Jefferson Street, where the dust road became a pavement; along opiate Millicent Place, where there were half a dozen prosperous substantial mansions; and on into the downtown section.

Driving was perilous here, for it was shopping time; the population idled casually across the streets and a drove of low-moaning oxen were being urged along in front of a placid street car; even the shops seemed only yawning their doors and blinking their windows in the sunshine before retiring into a state of utter and finite coma.

"Sally Carrol," said Clark suddenly, "it a fact that you're engaged?"

She looked at him quickly. "Where'd you hear that?"

"Sure enough, you engaged?"

"'At's a nice question to ask a girl!"

"Girl told me you were engaged to a Yankee you met up in Asheville last summah."

Sally Carrol sighed. "Never saw such an old town faw rumors."

"Don't marry a Yankee, Sally Carrol. We need you round here."

Sally Carrol was silent 'a moment. "Clark," she demanded suddenly, "who on earth shall I marry?"

"I offah my services."

"Honey, you couldn't suppawt a wife," she answered cheerfully. "Anyway, I know you too well to fall in love with you."

"'At doesn't mean you ought to marry a Yankee."

"S'pose I love him?"

He shook his head. "You couldn't. He'd be a lot different from us, every way."

He broke off as he halted the car in front of a rambling dilapidated house. Marylyn Wade and Joe Ewing appeared in the doorway.

"'Lo, Sally Carrol."

"Hi!"

"How you-all?"

"Sally Carrol," demanded Marylyn as they started off again, "you engaged?"

"Lawdy, where'd all this start? Can't I look at a man 'thout everybody in town engagin' me to him?"

Clark stared straight in front of him at a bolt on the clattering wind shield. "Sally Carrol," he said with a curious intensity, "don't you like us?"

"What?"

"Us down here?"

"Why, Clark, you know I do. I adore all you boys."

"Then why you gettin' engaged to a Yankee?"

"Clark, I don't know. I'm not sure what I'll do, but—well, I want to go places and see people. I want my mind to grow. I want to live where things happen on a big scale."

"What you mean?"

"Oh, Clark, I love you, and I love Joe here, and Ben Arrot,

and you all, but you'll—you'll —"

"We'll all be failures?"

"Yes. I don't mean only money failures but just sort of—of ineffectual and sad and—oh, how can I tell you?"

"You mean because we stay here in Tarleton?"

"Yes, Clark; and because you like it and never want to change things or think or go ahead."

He nodded and she reached over and pressed his hand.

"Clark," she said softly, "I wouldn't change you for the world. You're sweet the way you are. The things that'll make you fail I'll love always—the living in the past, the lazy days and nights you have, and all your carelessness and generosity."

"But you're goin' away?"

"Yes—because I couldn't ever marry you. You've a place in my heart no one else ever could have, but tied down here I'd get restless. I'd feel I was—wastin' myself. There's two sides to me, you see. There's the sleepy old side you love; an' there's a sawt of energy—the feelin' that makes me do wild things. That's the part of me that may be useful somewhere, that'll last when I'm not beautiful any more."

She broke off with characteristic suddenness and sighed, "Oh, sweet cooky!" as her mood changed.

Half closing her eyes and tipping back her head till it rested on the seat back she let the savory breeze fan her eyes and ripple the fluffy curls of her bobbed hair. They were in the country now, hurrying between tangled growths of bright-green coppice and grass and tall trees that sent sprays of foliage to hang a cool welcome over the road. Here and there they passed a battered Negro cabin, its oldest white-haired inhabitant smoking a corncob pipe beside the door and half a dozen scantily clothed pickaninnies parading tattered dolls on the wild grown grass in front. Farther out were lazy cotton fields, where even the workers seemed intangible shadows lent by the sun to the earth not for toil but to while away some age-old tradition in the golden September fields. And round the drowsy picturesqueness, over the trees and shacks and muddy rivers, flowed the heat, never hostile, only comforting like a great warm nourishing bosom for the infant earth.

"Sally Carrol, we're here!"

"Poor chile's soun' asleep."

"Honey, you dead at last outa sheer laziness?"

"Water, Sally Carrol! Cool water waitin' faw you!"

Her eyes opened sleepily.

"Hi!" she murmured, smiling.

II

In November Harry Bellamy, tall, broad and brisk, came down from his Northern city to spend four days. His intention was to settle a matter that had been hanging fire since he and Sally Carrol had met in Asheville, North Carolina, in midsummer. The settlement took only a quiet afternoon and an evening in front of a glowing open fire, for Harry Bellamy had everything Sally Carrol wanted; and, besides, she loved him—loved him with that side of her she kept especially for loving. Sally Carrol had several rather clearly defined sides.

On his last afternoon they walked, and she found their steps tending half-unconsciously toward one of her favorite haunts, the cemetery. When it came in sight, gray-white and golden-green under the cheerful late sun, she paused irresolute by the iron gate.

"Are you mournful by nature, Harry?" she asked with a faint smile.

"Mournful? Not I."

"Then let's go in here. It depresses some folks, but I like it."

They passed through the gateway and followed a path that led through a wavy valley of graves—dusty-gray and moldy for the fifties; quaintly carved with flowers and jars for the seventies; ornate and hideous for the nineties, with fat marble cherubs lying

They Passed Through the Gateway and Followed a Path That Led Through a Wavy Valley of Graves

in sodden sleep on stone lows and great impossible growths of nameless granite flowers. Occasionally they saw a kneeling figure with tributary flowers, but over most of the graves lay silence and withered leaves with only the fragrance that their own shadowy memories could waken in living minds.

They reached the top of a hill where they were fronted by a tall round headstone, freckled with dark spots of damp and half grown over with vines.

"'Margery Lee,'" she read; "'1844-1873.' Wasn't she nice? She died when she was twenty-nine. Dear Margery Lee," she added softly. "Can't you see her, Harry?"

"Yes, Sally Carrol."

He felt a little hand insert itself into his.

"She was dark, I think; and she always wore her hair with a ribbon in it, and gorgeous hoopskirts of bright blue and old rose."

"Yes."

"Oh, she was sweet, Harry! And she was the sort of girl born to stand on a wide pillared porch and welcome folks in. I think perhaps a lot of men went away to war meanin' to come back to her; but maybe none of 'em ever did."

He stooped down close to the stone, hunting for any record of marriage.

"There's nothing here to show."

"Of course not. How could there be anything there better than just 'Margery Lee,' and that eloquent date?" She drew close to him and an unexpected lump came into his throat as her yellow hair brushed his cheek. "You see how she was, don't you, Harry?"

"I see," he agreed gently. "I see through your precious eyes. You're beautiful now, so I know she must have been."

Silent and close they stood, and he could feel her shoulders trembling a little. An ambling breeze swept up the hill and stirred the brim of her floppity hat.

"Let's go down there!"

She was pointing to a flat stretch on the other side of the hill where along the green turf were a thousand grayish-white crosses stretching in endless ordered rows like the stacked arms of a battalion.

"Those are the Confederate dead," said Sally Carrol simply.

They walked along and read the inscriptions, always only a name and a date, sometimes quite indecipherable.

"The last row is the saddest—see, 'way over there. Every cross has just a date on it and the word 'Unknown.'"

She looked at him and her eyes brimmed with tears.

"I can't tell you how real it is to me, darling—if you don't know."

"How you feel about it is beautiful to me."

"No, no, it's not me, it's them—that old time that I've tried to have live in me. These were just men, unimportant, evidently, or they wouldn't have been 'unknown'; but they died for the most beautiful thing in the world—the dead South. You see," she continued, her voice still husky, her eyes glistening with tears, "people have these dreams they fasten on to things, and I've always grown up with that dream. It was so easy because it was all dead and there weren't any disillusions comin' to me. I've tried in a way to live up to those past standards of noblesse oblige—there's just the last remnants of it, you know, like the roses of an old garden dying all round us— streaks of strange courtliness and chivalry in some of these boys an' stories I used to hear from a Confederate soldier who lived next door, and a few old darkies. Oh, Harry, there was something, there was something! I couldn't ever make you understand, but it was there."

"I understand," he assured her again quietly.

Sally Carrol smiled and dried her eyes on the tip of a handkerchief protruding from his breast pocket.

"You don't feel depressed, do you, lover? Even when I cry I'm happy here, and I get a sawt of strength from it."

Hand in hand they turned and walked slowly away. Finding soft grass she drew him down to a seat beside her with their backs against the remnants of a low broken wall.

"Wish those three old women would clear out," he complained. "I want to kiss you, Sally Carrol."

"Me, too."

They waited impatiently for the three bent figures to move off, and then she kissed him until the sky seemed to fade out and all her smiles and tears to vanish in an ecstasy of eternal seconds.

Afterward they walked slowly back together, while on the corners twilight played at somnolent black-and-white checkers with the end of day.

"You'll be up about mid-January," he said, "and you've got to stay a month at least. It'll be slick. There's a winter carnival on, and if you've never really seen snow it'll be like fairyland to you. There'll be skating and skiing and tobogganing and sleigh riding and all sorts of torchlight parades on snowshoes. They haven't had one for years, so they're going to make it a knock-out."

"Will it be cold, Harry?" she asked suddenly.

"You certainly won't. You may freeze your nose, but you won't be shivery cold. It's hard and dry, you know."

"I guess I'm a summer child. I don't like any cold I've ever seen."

She broke off and they were both silent for a minute.

"Sally Carrol," he said very slowly, "what do you say to— March?"

"I say I love you."

"March?"

"March, Harry."

III

All night in the Pullman it was very cold. She rang for the porter to ask for another blanket, and when he couldn't give her one she tried vainly, by squeezing down into the bottom of her berth and doubling back the bedclothes, to snatch a few hours' sleep.

Sally Carrol wanted to look her best in the morning.

She rose at six and sliding uncomfortably into her clothes stumbled up to the diner for a cup of coffee. The snow had filtered into the vestibules and covered the floor with a slippery coating. It was intriguing, this cold, it crept in everywhere. Her breath was quite visible and she blew into the air with a naive enjoyment. Seated in the diner she stared out the window at white hills and valleys and scattered pines with each branch a green platter for a cold feast of snow.

Sometimes a solitary farmhouse would fly by, ugly and bleak and lone on the white waste; and with each one she had an instant of chill compassion for the souls shut in there waiting for spring.

As she left the diner and swayed back into the Pullman she experienced a surging rush of energy and wondered if she was feeling the bracing air of which Harry had spoken. This was the North, the North—her land now!

Then blow, ye winds, heigho!
A-roving I will go,

she chanted exultantly to herself.

"What's 'at?" inquired the porter politely.

"I said, `Brush me off.' "

The long wires of the telegraph poles doubled; two tracks ran up beside the train—three—four; came a succession of white-roofed houses, a glimpse of a trolley car with frosted windows, streets—more streets—the city.

She stood for a dazed moment in the frosty station before she saw three fur-bundled figures descending upon her.

"There she is!"

"Oh, Sally Carrol!"

Sally Carrol dropped her bag.

"Hi!"

A faintly familiar icy-cold face kissed her, and then she was in a group of faces all apparently emitting great clouds of heavy smoke; she was shaking hands. There was Gordon, a short, eager man of thirty who looked like an amateur knocked-about model for Harry; and his wife Myra, a listless lady with flaxen hair under a fur automobile cap. Almost immediately Sally Carrol thought of her as vaguely Scandinavian. A cheerful chauffeur adopted her bag and amid ricochets of half phrases, exclamations and perfunctory, listless "my dear's" from Myra they swept each other from the station.

Then they were in a sedan bound through a crooked succession of snowy streets where dozens of little boys were hitching sleds behind grocery wagons and automobiles.

"Oh," cried Sally Carrol, "I want to do that! Can we, Harry?"

"That's for kids. But we might —"

"It looks like such a circus!" she said regretfully.

Home was a rambling frame house set on a white lap of snow, and there she met a big, gray-haired man of whom she approved, and a lady who was like an egg and who kissed her—these were Harry's parents. There was a breathless, indescribable hour crammed full of half sentences, hot water, bacon and eggs and confusion; and after that she was alone with Harry in the library asking him if she dared smoke.

It was a large room with a Madonna over the fireplace and rows upon rows of books in covers of light gold and dark gold and shiny red. All the chairs had little lace squares where one's head should rest, the couch was just comfortable, the books looked as if they had been read—some— and Sally Carrol had an instantaneous vision of the battered old library at home with her father's huge medical books and the oil paintings of her three great-uncles and the old couch that had been mended up for forty-five years and was still luxurious to dream in. This room struck her as being neither attractive nor particularly otherwise. It was simply a room with a lot of fairly expensive things in it that all looked about fifteen years old.

"What do you think of it up here?" demanded Harry eagerly. "Does it surprise you? Is it what you expected, I mean?"

"You are, Harry," she said quietly, and reached out her arms to him. But after a brief kiss he seemed anxious to extort enthusiasm from her.

"The town, I mean. Do you like it? Can you feel the pep in the air?"

"Oh, Harry," she laughed, "you'll have to give me time. You can't just fling questions at me."

She puffed at her cigarette with a sigh of contentment.

"One thing I want to ask you," he began rather apologetically; "you Southerners put quite an emphasis on family and all that—not that it isn't quite all right, but you'll find it a little different here. I mean—you'll notice a lot of things that'll seem to you sort of vulgar display at first, Sally Carrol; but just remember that this is a three-generation town. Everybody has a father and about half of us have grandfathers. Back of that we don't go."

"Of course," she murmured.

"Our grandfathers, you see, founded the place, and a lot of them had to take some pretty queer jobs while they were doing the founding.

"For instance, there's one woman who at present is about the social model for the town; well, her father was the first public ash man—things like that."

"Why," said Sally Carrol, puzzled, "did you s'pose I was goin' to make remarks about people?"

"Not at all," interrupted Harry; "and I'm not apologizing for anyone either. It's just that—well, a Southern girl came up here last summer and said some unfortunate things, and—oh, I just thought I'd tell you."

Sally Carrol felt suddenly indignant—as though she had been unjustly spanked—but Harry evidently considered the subject closed, for he went on with a great surge of enthusiasm.

"It's carnival time, you know. First in ten years. And there's an ice palace they're building now that's the first they've had since Eighty-five. Built out of blocks of the clearest ice they could find—on a tremendous scale."

She rose and walking to the window pushed aside the heavy Turkish portieres and looked out.

"Oh!" she cried suddenly. "There's two little boys makin' a snow man! Harry, do you reckon I can go out an' help 'em?"

"You dream! Come here and kiss me."

She left the window rather reluctantly.

"I don't guess this is a very kissable climate, is it? I mean, it makes you so you don't want to sit round, doesn't it?"

"We're not going to. I've got a vacation for the first week you're here, and there's a dinner dance to-night."

"Oh, Harry," she confessed, subsiding in a heap, half in his lap, half in the pillows, "I sure do feel confused. I haven't got an idea whether I'll like it or not, an' I don't know what people expect or anythin'. You'll have to tell me, honey."

"I'll tell you," he said softly, "if you'll just tell me you're glad to be here."

"Glad—just awful glad!" she whispered, insinuating herself into his arms in her own peculiar way. "Where you are is home for me, Harry."

And as she said this she had the feeling for almost the first time in her life that she was acting a part.

That night, amid the gleaming candles of a dinner party where the men seemed to do most of the talking while the girls sat in a haughty and expensive aloofness, even Harry's presence on her left failed to make her feel at home.

"They're a good-looking crowd, don't you think?" he demanded. "Just look round. There's Spud Hubbard, tackle at Princeton last year, and Junie Morton—he and the red-haired fellow next to him were both Yale hockey captains; Junie was in my class. Why, the best athletes in the world come from these states round here. This is a man's country, I tell you. Look at John J. Fishburn!"

"Who's he?" asked Sally Carrol innocently.

"Don't you know?"

"I've heard the name."

"Greatest wheat man in the Northwest, and one of the greatest financiers in the country."

She turned suddenly to a voice on her right.

"I guess they forgot to introduce us. My name's Roger Patton."

"My name is Sally Carrol Happer," she said graciously.

"Yes, I know. Harry told me you were coming."

"You a relative?"

"No, I'm a professor."

"Oh," she laughed.

"At the university. You're from the South, aren't you?"

"Yes; Tarleton, Georgia."

She liked him immediately—a reddish-brown mustache under watery blue eyes that had something in them that these other eyes lacked, some quality of appreciation. They exchanged stray sentences through dinner and she made up her mind to see him again.

After coffee she was introduced to numerous good-looking young men who danced with conscious precision and seemed to take it for granted that she wanted to talk about nothing except Harry.

"Heavens," she thought, "they talk as if my being engaged made me older than they are—as if I'd tell their mothers on them!"

In the South an engaged girl, even a young married woman, expected the same amount of half-affectionate badinage and flattery that would be accorded a debutante, but here all that seemed banned. One young man, after getting well started on the subject of Sally Carrol's eyes and how they had allured him ever since she entered the room, went into a violent confusion when he found she was visiting the Bellamys—was Harry's fiancée. He seemed to feel as though he had made some risque and inexcusable blunder, became immediately formal and left her at the first opportunity.

She was rather glad when Roger Patton cut in on her, and suggested that they sit out a while.

"Well," he inquired, blinking cheerily, "how's Carmen from the South?"

"Mighty fine. How's—how's Dangerous Dan McGrew? Sorry, but he's the only Northerner I know much about."

He seemed to enjoy that.

"Of course," he confessed, "as a professor of literature I'm not supposed to have read Dangerous Dan McGrew."

"Are you a native?"

"No, I'm a Philadelphian. Imported from Harvard to teach

seventeenth-century French. But I've been here ten years."

"Nine years, three hundred an' sixty-four days longer than me."

"Like it here?"

"Uh-huh. Sure do!"

"Really?"

"Well, why not? Don't I look as if I were havin' a good time?"

"I saw you look out the window a minute ago—and shiver."

"Just my imagination," laughed Sally Carrol. "I'm used to havin' everythin' quiet outside, an' sometimes I look out an' see a flurry of snow, an' it's just as if somethin' dead was movin'."

He nodded appreciatively.

"Ever been North before?"

"Spent two Julys in Asheville, North Carolina."

"Nice-looking crowd, aren't they?" suggested Patton, indicating the swirling floor.

Sally Carrol started. This had been Harry's remark.

"Sure are! They're—canine."

"What?"

She flushed.

"I'm sorry; that sounded worse than I meant it. You see I always think of people as feline or canine, irrespective of sex."

"Which are you?"

"I'm feline. So are you. So are most Southern men an' most of these girls here."

"What's Harry?"

"Harry's canine, distinctly. All the men I've met to-night seem to be canine."

"What does "canine' imply? A certain conscious masculinity as opposed to subtlety?"

"Reckon so. I never analyzed it—only I just look at people an' say 'canine' or 'feline' right off. It's right absurd, I guess."

"Not at all. I'm interested. I used to have a theory about these people. I think they're freezing up."

"What?"

"I think they're growing like Swedes— Ibsenesque, you know. Very gradually getting gloomy and melancholy. It's these long winters. Ever read any Ibsen?"

She shook her head.

"Well, you find in his characters a certain brooding rigidity. They're righteous, narrow and cheerless, without infinite possibilities for great sorrow or joy."

"Without smiles or tears?"

"Exactly. That's my theory. You see there are thousands of Swedes up here. They come, I imagine, because the climate is very much like their own, and there's been a gradual mingling. They're probably not half a dozen here to-night, but—we've had four Swedish governors. Am I boring you?"

"I'm mighty interested."

"Your future sister-in-law is half Swedish. Personally I like her, but my theory is that Swedes react rather badly on us as a whole. Scandinavians, you know, have the largest suicide rate in the world."

"Why do you live here if it's so depressing?'

"Oh, it doesn't get me. I'm pretty well cloistered, and I suppose books mean more than people to me anyway."

"But writers all speak about the South being tragic. You know—Spanish senoritas, black hair and daggers an' hauntin' music."

He shook his head.

"No, the Northern races are the tragic races—they don't indulge in the cheering luxury of tears."

Sally Carrol thought of her graveyard. She supposed that that was vaguely what she had meant when she said it didn't depress her.

"The Italians are about the gayest people in the world—but

it's a dull subject," he broke off. "Anyway, I want to tell you you're marrying a pretty fine man."

Sally Carrol was moved by an impulse of confidence.

"I know. I'm the sort of person who wants to be taken care of after a certain point, and I feel sure I will be."

"Shall we dance? You know," he continued as they rose, "it's encouraging to find a girl who knows what she's marrying for. Nine-tenths of them think of it as a sort of walking into a moving-picture sunset."

She laughed, and liked him immensely. Two hours later on the way home she nestled near Harry in the back seat.

"Oh, Harry," she whispered, "it's so co-old!"

"But it's warm in here, darling girl."

"But outside it's cold; and oh, that howling wind!"

She buried her face deep in his fur coat and trembled involuntarily as his cold lips kissed the tip of her ear.

IV

The first week of her visit passed in a whirl. She had her promised toboggan ride at the back of an automobile through a chill January twilight. Swathed in furs she put in a morning tobogganing on the country-club hill; even tried skiing, to sail through the air for a glorious moment and then land in a tangled, laughing bundle on a soft snowdrift. She liked all the winter sports, except an afternoon spent snow-shoeing over a glaring plain under pale yellow sunshine; but she soon realized that these things were for children—that she was being humored and that the enjoyment round her was only a reflection of her own.

At first the Bellamy family puzzled her. The men were reliable and she liked them; to Mr. Bellamy especially, with his iron-gray hair and energetic dignity, she took an immediate fancy once she found that he was born in Kentucky; this made of him a link between the old life and the new. But toward the women she felt a definite hostility. Myra, her future sister-in-law, seemed the essence of spiritless conventionality. Her conversation was so utterly devoid of personality that Sally Carrol, who came from a country where a certain amount of charm and assurance could be taken for granted in the women, was inclined to despise her.

Swathed in Furs Sally Carrol Put in a Morning Tobogganing on the Country-Club Hill

"If those women aren't beautiful," she thought, "they're nothing. They just fade out when you look at them. They're glorified domestics. Men are the center of every mixed group."

Lastly there was Mrs. Bellamy, whom Sally Carrol detested. The first day's impression of an egg had been confirmed—an egg with a cracked, veiny voice and such an ungracious dumpiness of carriage that Sally Carrol felt that if she once fell she would surely scramble. In addition, Mrs. Bellamy seemed to typify the town in being innately hostile to strangers. She called Sally Carrol "Sally," and could not be persuaded that the double name was anything more than a tedious, ridiculous nickname. To Sally Carrol this shortening of her name was like presenting her to the public half clothed. She loved "Sally Carrol"; she loathed "Sally." She knew also that Harry's mother disapproved of her bobbed hair; and she had never dared smoke downstairs after that first day when Mrs. Bellamy had come into the library sniffing violently.

Of all the men she met she preferred Roger Patton, who was a frequent visitor at the house. He never again alluded to the Ibsenesque tendency of the populace, but when he came in one day and found her curled up on the sofa bent over Peer Gynt he laughed and told her to forget what he'd said—that it was all rot.

And then one afternoon in her second week she and Harry hovered on the edge of a dangerously steep quarrel. She considered that he precipitated it entirely, though the Serbia in the case was an unknown man who had not had his trousers pressed.

They had been walking homeward between mounds of high-piled snow and under a sun which Sally Carrol scarcely recognized. They passed a little girl done up in gray wool until she resembled a small Teddy bear, and Sally Carrol could not resist a gasp of maternal appreciation.

"Look! Harry!"

"What?"

"That little girl—did you see her face?"

"Yes, why?"

"It was red as a little strawberry. Oh, she was cute!"

"Why, your own face is almost as red as that already! Everybody's healthy here. We're out in the cold as soon as we're old enough to walk. Wonderful climate!"

She looked at him and had to agree. He was mighty healthy looking; so was his brother.

And she had noticed the new red in her own cheeks that very morning.

Suddenly their glances were caught and held and they stared for a moment at the street corner ahead of them. A man was standing there, his knees bent, his eyes gazing upward with a tense expression as though he were about to make a leap toward the chilly sky. And then they both exploded into a shout of laughter, for coming closer they discovered it had been a ludicrous momentary illusion produced by the extreme bagginess of the man's trousers.

"Reckon that's one on us," she laughed.

"He must be a Southerner, judging by those trousers," suggested Harry mischievously.

"Why, Harry!"

Her surprised look must have irritated him.

"Those damn Southerners!"

Sally Carrol's eyes flashed.

"Don't call 'em that!"

"I'm sorry, dear," said Harry, malignantly apologetic, "but you know what I think of them. They're sort of—sort of degenerates—not at all like the old Southerners. They've lived so long down there with all the colored people that they've gotten lazy and shiftless."

"Hush your mouth, Harry!" she cried angrily. "They're not! They may be lazy—anybody would be in that climate—but they're my best friends, an' I don't want to hear 'em criticized in any such sweepin' way. Some of 'em are the finest men in the world."

"Oh, I know. They're all right when they come North to college, but of all the hangdog, ill-dressed, slovenly lot I ever saw a bunch of small-town Southerners are the worst!"

Sally Carrol was clenching her gloved hands and biting her lip furiously.

"Why," continued Harry, "there was one in my class at New Haven and we all thought that at last we'd found the true type of Southern aristocrat, but it turned out that he wasn't an aristocrat at all—just the son of a Northern carpetbagger who owned about all the cotton round Birmingham."

"A Southerner wouldn't talk the way you're talking now," she said evenly.

"They haven't the energy!"

"Or the somethin' else."

"I'm sorry, Sally Carrol, but I've heard you say yourself that you'd never marry —"

"That's quite different. I told you I wouldn't want to tie my life to any of the boys that are round Tarleton now, but I never made any sweepin' generalities."

They walked along in silence.

"I probably spread it on a bit thick, Sally Carrol. I'm sorry."

She nodded, but made no answer. Five minutes later as they stood in the hallway she suddenly threw her arms round him.

"Oh, Harry," she cried, her eyes full of tears, "let's get married next week. I'm afraid of having fusses like that. I'm afraid, Harry. It wouldn't be that way if we were married."

But Harry being in the wrong was still irritated.

"That'd be idiotic. We decided on March."

The tears in Sally Carrol's eyes faded; her expression hardened slightly.

"Very well—I suppose I shouldn't have said that."

Harry melted.

"Dear little nut!" he cried. "Come and kiss me and let's

"I Told You I Wouldn't Want to Tie My Life to Any of the Boys That are Round Tarleton Now, But I Never Made Any Sweepin' Generalities"

forget."

That very night at the end of a vaudeville performance the orchestra played Dixie, and Sally Carrol felt something stronger and more enduring than her tears and smiles of the day brim up inside her. She leaned forward, gripping the arms of her chair until her face grew crimson.

"Sort of get you, dear?" whispered Harry.

But she did not hear him. To the spirited throb of the violins and the inspiring beat of the kettledrums her own old ghosts were marching by and on into the darkness, and as fifes whistled and sighed in the low encore they seemed so nearly out of sight that she could have waved good-by.

Away, away, away down South in Dixie!
Away, away, away down South in Dixie!

V

It was a particularly cold night. A sudden thaw had nearly cleared the streets the day before, but now they were traversed again with a powdery wraith of loose snow that traveled in wavy lines before the feet of the wind and filled the lower air with a fine-particled mist. There was no sky—only a dark, ominous tent that draped in the tops of the streets and was in reality a vast approaching army of snowflakes—while over it all, chilling away the comfort from the brown-and-green glow of lighted windows and muffling the steady trot of the horse pulling their sleigh, interminably washed the north wind. It was a dismal town after all, she thought—dismal.

Sometimes at night it had seemed to her as though no one lived here—they had all gone long ago, leaving lighted houses to be covered in time by tombing heaps of sleet. Oh, if there should be snow on her grave! To be beneath great piles of it all winter long, where even her headstone would be a light shadow against light shadows. Her grave—a grave that should be flower-strewn and washed with sun and rain.

She thought again of those isolated country houses that her train had passed, and of the life there the long winter through—the ceaseless glare through the windows, the crust forming on the soft drifts of snow, finally the slow, cheerless melting and the harsh spring of which Roger Patton had told her. Her spring—to lose it forever—with its lilacs and the lazy sweetness it stirred in her heart. She was laying away that spring—afterward she would lay away that sweetness.

With a gradual insistence the storm broke. Sally Carrol felt a film of flakes melt quickly on her eyelashes and Harry reached over a furry arm and drew down her complicated flannel cap. Then the small flakes came in skirmish line and the horse bent his neck patiently as a transparency of white appeared momentarily on his coat.

"Oh, he's cold, Harry," she said quickly.

"Who? The horse? Oh, no, he isn't. He likes it!"

After another ten minutes they turned a corner and came in sight of their destination. On a tall hill outlined in vivid glaring green against the wintry sky stood the ice palace. It was three stories in the air, with battlements and embrasures and narrow icicled windows, and the innumerable electric lights inside made a gorgeous transparency of the great central hall. Sally Carrol clutched Harry's hand under the fur robe.

"It's beautiful !" he cried excitedly. "My golly, it's beautiful, isn't it? They haven't had one here since eighty-five!"

Somehow the notion of there not having been one since eighty-five oppressed her. Ice was a ghost, and this mansion of it was surely peopled by those shades of the eighties, with pale faces and blurred snow-filled hair.

"Come on, dear," said Harry.

She followed him out of the sleigh and waited while he hitched the horse. A party of four—Gordon, Myra, Roger Patton and another girl — drew up beside them with a mighty jingle of bells. There was quite a crowd already, bundled in fur or sheepskin, shouting and calling to each other as they moved through the snow, which was now so thick that people could scarcely be distinguished a few yards away.

"It's a hundred and seventy feet tall," Harry was saying to a muffled figure beside him as they trudged toward the entrance; "covers six thousand square yards."

She caught snatches of conversation: "One main hall"—"walls twenty to forty inches thick"—"and the ice cave has almost a mile of"—"This Canuck who built it—"

They found their way inside, and dazed by the magic of the great crystal walls Sally Carrol found herself repeating over and over two lines from Kubla Khan:

It was a miracle of rare device,
A sunny pleasure-dome with caves of ice!

In the great glittering cavern with the dark shut out she took a seat on a wooden bench, and the evening's oppression lifted. Harry was right—it was beautiful; and her gaze traveled the smooth surface of the walls, the blocks for which had been selected for their purity and clearness to obtain this opalescent, translucent effect.

"Look! Here we go—oh, boy!" cried Harry.

A band in a far corner struck up "Hail, Hail, the Gang's All Here!" which echoed over to them in wild muddled acoustics, and then the lights suddenly went out; silence seemed to flow down the icy sides and sweep over them. Sally Carrol could still see her white breath in the darkness, and a dim row of pale faces over on the other side.

The music eased to a sighing complaint, and from outside drifted in the full-throated resonant chant of the marching clubs. It grew louder like some paean of a Viking tribe traversing an ancient wild; it swelled—they were coming nearer; then a row of torches appeared, and another and another, and keeping time with their moccasined feet a long column of gray-mackinawed figures swept in, snowshoes slung at their shoulders, torches soaring and flickering as their voices rose along the great walls.

The gray column ended and another followed, the light streaming luridly this time over red toboggan caps and flaming crimson mackinaws, and as it entered it took up the refrain; then came a long platoon of blue and white, of green, of white, of brown and yellow.

"Those white ones are the Wacouta Club," whispered Harry eagerly. "Those are the men you've met round at dances."

The volume of the voices grew; the great cavern was a phantasmagoria of torches waving in great banks of fire, of colors and the rhythm of soft leather steps. The leading column turned and halted, platoon deployed in front of platoon until the whole procession made a solid flag of flame, and then from thousands of voices burst a mighty shout that filled the air like a crash of thunder and sent the torches wavering. It was magnificent, it was tremendous! To Sally Carrol it was the North offering sacrifice on some mighty altar to the gray pagan God of Snow.

As the shout died the band struck up again and there came more singing, and then long reverberating cheers by each club. She sat very quiet listening while the staccato cries rent the stillness; and then she started, for there was a volley of explosion, and great clouds of smoke went up here and there through the cavern—the flashlight photographers at work—and the council was over. With the band at their head the clubs formed in column once more, took up their chant and began to march out.

"Come on!" shouted Harry. "We want to see the labyrinths downstairs before they turn the lights off!"

They all rose and started toward the chute—Harry and Sally Carrol in the lead, her little glove buried in his big fur gauntlet. At the bottom of the chute was a long empty room of ice with the ceiling so low that they had to stoop—and their hands were parted. Before she realized what he intended Harry had darted down one of the half dozen glittering passages that opened into the room, and was only a vague receding blot against the green shimmer.

"Harry!" she called.

"Come on!" he cried back.

She looked round the empty chamber; the rest of the party had evidently decided to go home, were already outside somewhere in the blundering snow. She hesitated and then darted in after Harry.

"Harry!" she shouted.

She had reached a turning point thirty feet down; she heard a faint muffled answer far to the left, and with a touch of panic fled toward it. She passed another turning, two more yawning alleys.

"Harry!"

No answer. She started to run straight forward, and then turned like lightning and sped back the way she had come, enveloped in a sudden ice terror.

She reached a turn—was it here?—took the left and came to what should have been the outlet into the long low room, but it was only another glittering passage with darkness at the end. She called again, but the walls gave back a flat lifeless echo with no reverberations. Retracing her steps she turned another corner, this time following a wide passage. It was like the green lane between the parted waters of the Red Sea, like a damp vault connecting empty tombs. She slipped a little now as she walked, for ice had formed on the bottom of her overshoes; she had to run her gloves along the half-slippery, half-sticky walls to keep her balance.

"Harry!"

Still no answer. The sound she made bounced mockingly down to the end of the passage.

Then in an instant the lights went out and she was in complete darkness. She gave a small frightened cry and sank down into a cold little heap on the ice. She felt her left knee do something as she fell, but she scarcely noticed it as some deep terror far greater than any fear of being lost settled upon her. She was alone with this presence that came out of the North, the dreary loneliness that rose from ice-bound whalers in the Arctic seas, from smokeless trackless wastes where were strewn the whitened bones of adventure. It was an icy breath of death; it was rolling down low across the land to clutch at her.

With a furious despairing energy she rose again and started blindly down the darkness. She must get out. She might be lost in here for days, freeze to death and lie embedded in the ice like corpses she had read of, kept perfectly preserved until the melting of a glacier. Harry probably thought she had left with the others—he had gone by now; no one would know until late next day. She reached pitifully for the wall. Forty inches thick they had said—forty inches thick!

"Oh!"

On both sides of her along the walls she felt things creeping, damp souls that haunted this palace, this town, this North.

"Oh, send somebody—send somebody!" she cried aloud.

Clark Darrow—he would understand; or Joe Ewing; she couldn't be left here to wander forever—to be frozen, heart, body and soul. This her—this Sally Carrol! Why, she was a happy thing. She was a happy little girl. She liked warmth and summer and Dixie. These things were foreign—foreign.

"You're not crying," something said aloud. "You'll never cry any more. Your tears would just freeze; all tears freeze up here!"

She sprawled full length on the ice.

"O God!" she faltered.

A long single file of minutes went by, and with a great weariness she felt her eyes closing. Then someone seemed to sit down near her and take her face in warm soft hands. She looked up gratefully.

"Why, it's Margery Lee," she crooned softly to herself. "I knew you'd come." It really was Margery Lee, and she was just as Sally Carrol had known she would be, with a young white brow and wide welcoming eyes and a hoop skirt of some soft material that was quite comforting to rest on.

"Margery Lee."

It was getting darker now and darker—all those tombstones ought to he repainted, sure enough, only that would spoil 'em of course. Still, you ought to be able to see 'em.

Then after a succession of moments that went fast and then slow, but seemed to be ultimately resolving themselves into a multitude of blurred rays converging toward a pale yellow sun, she heard a great cracking noise break her new-found stillness.

It was the sun, it was a light; a torch, and a torch beyond that, and another one, and voices; a face took flesh below the torch, heavy arms raised her and she felt something on her cheek, it felt wet. Someone had seized her and was rubbing her face with snow. How ridiculous—with snow!

"Sally Carrol! Sally Carrol!"

It was Dangerous Dan McGrew; and two other faces she didn't know.

"Child, child! We've been looking for you two hours. Harry's half crazy!"

Things came rushing back into place—the singing, the torches, the great shout of the marching clubs. She squirmed in Patton's arms and gave a long low cry.

"Oh, I want to get out of here! I'm going back home. Take me home "—her voice rose to a scream that sent a chill to Harry's heart as he came racing down the next passage—" Tomorrow!" she cried with delirious, unrestrained passion—" Tomorrow! Tomorrow! To-morrow!"

VI

The wealth of golden sunlight poured a quite enervating yet oddly comforting heat over the house where day long it faced the dusty stretch of road. Two birds were making a great to-do in a cool spot found among the branches of a tree next door, and down the street a colored woman was announcing herself melodiously as a purveyor of strawberries. It was an April afternoon.

Sally Carrol Happer, resting her chin on her arm and her arm on an old window seat, gazed sleepily down over the spangled dust whence the heat waves were rising for the first time this spring. She was watching a very ancient flivver turn a perilous corner and rattle and groan to a jolting stop at the end of the walk. She made no sound, and in a minute a strident familiar whistle rent the air. Sally Carrol smiled and blinked.

"Good mawnin'."

A head appeared tortuously from under the car top below.

"'Taint mawnin', Sally Carrol."

"Sure enough," she said in affected surprise. "I guess maybe not."

"What you doin'?"

"Eatin' green peach. 'Spect to die any minute."

Clark twisted himself a last impossible notch to get a view of her face.

"Water's warm as a kettla steam, Sally Carrol. Wanta go swimmin'?"

"Hate to move," sighed Sally Carrol lazily, "but I reckon so."

Story Illustrations by
Leslie L. Benson

THE SATURDAY EVENING POST

An Ill...
Fo...ded

MAY 29, 1920

5c. THE COPY

Charles Brackett—Kenneth L. Roberts—F. Scott Fitzgerald—Sinclair Lewis
George Pattullo—Elizabeth Frazer—Ferdinand Reyher—Maryse Rutledge

Fitzgerald's first six stories for the *Post* were published over a 13 week period in the late-Winter and Spring of 1920, coinciding with the release of his first novel. Following the May 29, 1920 publication of this story, it would be eighteen months before Fitzgerald's next appearance in the *Post*.

"The Offshore Pirate" deals with a theme that is seen repeatedly in Fitzgerald's early stories – a young man "tricks" a young woman into falling in love with him or marrying him or, in the case of Myra Meets His Family, not marrying him. In Pirate, Fitzgerald allows his heroine, Ardita, a great deal of time to explain her philosophy of love and life. It's an in-depth character analysis of what would become one of his prototypical characters – the self-determined young "femme fatale."

Eight months after this story appeared in the *Post*, Metro released a silent film version, January 31, 1921.

The Offshore Pirate

This unlikely story begins on a sea that was a blue dream, as colorful as blue silk stockings, and beneath a sky as blue as the irises of children's eyes. From the western half of the sky the sun was shying little golden disks at the sea—if you gazed intently enough you could see them skip from wave tip to wave tip until they joined a broad collar of golden coin that was collecting half a mile out and would eventually be a dazzling sunset. About halfway between the Florida shore and the golden collar a white steam yacht, very young and graceful, was riding at anchor and under a blue-and-white awning aft a yellow-haired girl reclined in a wicker settee reading The Revolt of the Angels, by Anatole France.

She was about nineteen, slender and supple, with a spoiled, alluring mouth and quick gray eyes full of a radiant curiosity. Her feet, stockingless, and adorned rather than clad in blue satin slippers which swung nonchalantly from her toes, were perched on the arm of a settee adjoining the one she occupied. And as she read she intermittently regaled herself by a faint application to her tongue of a half lemon that she held in her hand. The other half, sucked dry, lay on the deck at her feet and rocked very gently to and fro at the almost imperceptible motion of the tide.

The second half lemon was well-nigh pulpless and the golden collar had grown astonishing in width when suddenly the drowsy silence which enveloped the yacht was broken by the sound of heavy footsteps and an elderly man topped with orderly gray hair and clad in a white flannel suit appeared at the head of the companionway. There he paused for a moment until his eyes became accustomed to the sun, and then seeing the girl under the awning he uttered a long, even grunt of disapproval.

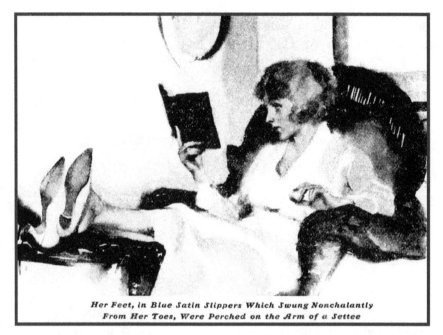

Her Feet, in Blue Satin Slippers Which Swung Nonchalantly
From Her Toes, Were Perched on the Arm of a Settee

If he had intended thereby to obtain a rise of any sort he was doomed to disappointment. The girl calmly turned over two pages, turned back one, raised the lemon mechanically and then faintly but quite unmistakably yawned.

"Ardita!" said the gray-haired man sternly.

Ardita uttered a small sound indicating nothing.

"Ardita!" he repeated. "Ardita!"

Ardita raised the lemon languidly, allowing three words to slip out before it reached her tongue.

"Oh, shut up."

"Ardita!"

"What?"

"Will you listen to me—or will I have to get a servant to hold you while I talk to you?"

The lemon descended slowly and scornfully.

"Put it in writing."

"Will you have the decency to close that abominable book

and discard that damn lemon for two minutes?"

"Oh, can't you lemme alone for a second?"

"Ardita, I have just received a telephone message from the shore—"

"Telephone?" She showed for the first time a faint interest.

"Yes, it was —"

"Do you mean to say," she interrupted wonderingly, "'at they let you run a wire out here?"

"Yes, and just now —"

"Won't other boats bump into it?"

"No. It's too low. It's run along the bottom. Five min —"

"Well, I'll be darned! Gosh! Science is golden or something—isn't it?"

"Will you let me say what I started to?"

"Shoot !"

"Well, it seems—well, I am up here —" He paused and swallowed several times distractedly. "Oh, yes. Young woman, Colonel Moreland has called up again to ask me to be sure to bring you in to dinner. His son Toby has come all the way from New York to meet you and he's invited several other young people. For the last time, will you —"

"No," said Ardita shortly, "I won't. I came along on this darn cruise with the one idea of going to Palm Beach, and you knew it, and I absolutely refuse to meet any darn old colonel or any darn young Toby or any darn old young people or to set foot in any other darn old town in this crazy state. So you either take me to Palm Beach or else shut up and go away."

"Very well. This is the last straw. In your infatuation for this man—a man who is notorious for his excesses, a man your father would not have allowed so much as to mention your name—you have reflected the demi-monde rather than the circles in which you have presumably grown up. From now on —"

"I know," interrupted Ardita ironically, "from now on you

go your way and I go mine. I've heard that story before. You know I'd like nothing better."

"From now on," he announced grandiloquently, "you are no niece of mine. I —"

"O-o-o-oh!" The cry was wrung from Ardita with the agony of a lost soul. "Will you stop boring me! Will you go way! Will you jump overboard and drown! Do you want me to throw this book at you!"

"If you dare do any —"

Smack !

The Revolt of the Angels sailed through the air, missed its target by the length of a short nose and bumped cheerfully down the companionway.

The gray-haired man made an instinctive step backward and then two cautious steps forward. Ardita jumped to her five feet four and stared at him defiantly, her gray eyes blazing.

"Keep off!"

"How dare you!" he cried.

"Because I darn please!"

"You've grown unbearable! Your disposition —"

"You've made me that way! No child ever has a bad disposition unless it's her family's fault! Whatever I am, you did it."

Muttering something under his breath her uncle turned and, walking forward, called in a loud voice for the launch. Then he returned to the awning, where Ardita had again seated herself and resumed her attention to the lemon.

"I am going ashore," he said slowly. "I will be out again at nine o'clock to-night. When I return we will start back to New York, where I shall turn you over to your aunt for the rest of your natural, or rather unnatural, life."

He paused and looked at her, and then all at once something in the utter childishness of her beauty seemed to puncture his anger

like an inflated tire and render him helpless, uncertain, utterly
fatuous.

"Ardita," he said not unkindly, "I'm no fool. I've been
round. I know men. And, child, confirmed libertines don't reform
until they're tired—and then they're not themselves—they're
husks of themselves." He looked at her as if expecting agreement,
but receiving no sight or sound of it he continued. "Perhaps the
man loves you—that's possible. He's loved many women and
he'll love many more. Less than a month ago, one month, Ardita,
he was involved in a notorious affair with that red-haired Mimi
Merril; promised to give her the diamond bracelet that the Czar of
Russia gave his mother. You know—you read the papers."

"Thrilling scandals by an anxious uncle," yawned Ardita.
"Have it filmed. Wicked clubman making eyes at virtuous flapper.
Virtuous flapper conclusively vamped by his lurid past. Plans to
meet him at Palm Beach. Foiled by anxious uncle."

"Will you tell me why the devil you want to marry him?"

"I'm sure I couldn't say," said Ardita shortly. "Maybe
because he's the only man I know, good or bad, who has an
imagination and the courage of his convictions. Maybe it's to get
away from the young fools that spend their vacuous hours pursuing
me round the country. But as for the famous Russian bracelet, you
can set your mind at rest on that score. He's going to give it to me
at Palm Beach—if you'll have a little sense."

"How about the—red-haired woman?"

"He hasn't seen her for six months," she said angrily. "I
have enough pride to see to that. Don't you know that I can do any
darn thing with any darn man I want to?"

She put her chin in the air like the statue of France Aroused,
and then spoiled the pose somewhat by raising the lemon for
action.

"Is it the Russian bracelet that fascinates you?"

"No, I'm merely trying to give you the sort of argument

that would appeal to your intelligence. And I wish you'd go way," she said, her temper rising again. "You know I never change my mind. You've been boring me for three days until I'm about to go crazy. I won't go ashore! Won't! Do you hear? Won't!"

"Very well," he said, "and you won't go to Palm Beach either. Of all the selfish, spoiled, uncontrolled, disagreeable, impossible girls I have —"

Splush! The half lemon caught him in the neck. Simultaneously came a hail from over the side.

"The launch is ready, Mr. Farnam."

Too full of words and rage to speak, Mr. Farnam cast one utterly condemning glance at his niece and, turning, ran swiftly down the ladder.

II

Five o'clock rolled down from the sun and plumped soundlessly into the sea. The golden collar widened into a glittering island; and a faint breeze that had been playing with the edges of the awning and swaying one of the dangling blue slippers became suddenly freighted with song. It was a chorus of men in close harmony and in perfect rhythm to an accompanying sound of oars cleaving the blue waters. Ardita lifted her head and listened:

> *Carrots and peas,*
> *Beans on their knees,*
> *Pigs in the seas,*
> *Lucky fellows!*
> *Blow us a breeze,*
> *Blow us a breeze,*
> *Blow us a breeze,*
> *With your bellows.*

Ardita's brow wrinkled in astonishment. Sitting very still she listened eagerly as the chorus took up a second verse:

> *Onions and beans,*
> *Marshalls and Deans,*
> *Goldbergs and Greens*
> *And Costellos.*
> *Blow us a breeze,*
> *Blow us a breeze,*
> *Blow us a breeze,*
> *With your bellows*

With an exclamation she tossed her book to the deck, where it sprawled at a straddle, and hurried to the rail. Fifty feet away a large rowboat was approaching containing seven men, six of them rowing and one standing up in the stern keeping time to their song with an orchestra leader's baton:

> *Oysters and rocks,*
> *Sawdust and socks,*
> *Who could make clocks*
> *Out of cellos?*

The leader's eyes suddenly rested on Ardita, who was leaning over the rail spellbound with curiosity. He made a quick movement with his baton and the singing instantly ceased. She saw that he was the only white man in the boat—the six rowers were Negroes.

"Narcissus ahoy!" he called politely.

"What's the idea of all the discord?" demanded Ardita cheerfully. "Is this the varsity crew from the county nut farm?"

By this time the boat was scraping the side of the yacht and a great hulking Negro in the bow turned round and grasped the ladder. Thereupon the leader left his position in the stern and before Ardita had realized his intention he ran up the ladder and stood breathless before her on the deck.

"The women and children will be spared!" he said briskly. "All crying babies will be immediately drowned and all males put in double irons!"

Digging her hands excitedly down into the pockets of her dress Ardita stared at him, speechless with astonishment.

He was a young man with a scornful mouth and the bright blue eyes of a healthy baby set in a dark, sensitive face. His hair was pitch black, damp and curly—the hair of a Grecian statue gone brunet. He was trimly built, trimly dressed and graceful as an agile quarterback.

"Well, I'll be a son of a gun!" she said dazedly.

They eyed each other coolly.

"Do you surrender the ship?"

"Is this an outburst of wit?" demanded Ardita. "Are you an idiot—or just being initiated to some fraternity?"

"I asked you if you surrendered the ship."

"I thought the country was dry," said Ardita disdainfully. "Have you been drinking finger-nail enamel? You better get off this yacht!"

"What?" The young man's voice expressed incredulity.

"Get off the yacht! You heard me!"

He looked at her for a moment as if considering what she had said.

"No," said his scornful mouth slowly; "no, I won't get off the yacht. You can get off if you wish."

Going to the rail he gave a curt command and immediately the crew of the rowboat scrambled up the ladder and ranged themselves in line before him, a coal black and burly darky at one end and a miniature mulatto of four feet nine at the other. They seemed to be uniformly dressed in some sort of blue costume ornamented with dust, mud and tatters; over the shoulder of each was slung a small, heavy-looking white sack, and under their arms they carried large black cases apparently containing musical instruments.

"'Ten-*shun*!" commanded the young man, snapping his own heels together crisply. "Right *driss*! Front! Step out here, Babe!"

The smallest Negro took a quick step forward and saluted. "Yas-suh!"

"Take command; go down below, catch the crew and tie 'em up—all except the engineer. Bring him up to me. Oh, and pile those bags by the rail there."

"Yas-suh!"

He saluted again and, wheeling about, motioned for the five others to gather about him. Then after a short whispered consultation they all filed noiselessly down the companionway.

"Now," said the young man cheerfully to Ardita, who had witnessed this last scene in withering silence, "if you will swear on your honor as a flapper—which probably isn't worth much—that you'll keep that spoiled little mouth of yours tight shut for forty-eight hours you can row yourself ashore in our rowboat."

"Otherwise what?"

"Otherwise you're going to sea in a ship."

With a little sigh as for a crisis well passed the young man sank into the settee Ardita had lately vacated, and stretched his arms lazily. The corners of his mouth relaxed appreciatively as he looked round at the rich striped awning, the polished brass and the luxurious fittings of the deck. His eye fell on the book and then on the exhausted lemon.

"Hm," he said, "Stonewall Jackson claimed that lemon juice cleared his head. Your head feel pretty clear?"

Ardita disdained to answer.

"Because inside of five minutes you'll have to make a clear decision whether it's go or stay."

He picked up the book and opened it curiously.

"The Revolt of the Angels. Sounds pretty good. French, eh?" He stared at her with new interest. "You French?"

"No."

"What's your name?"

"Farnam."

"Farnam what?"

"Ardita Farnam."

"Well, Ardita, no use standing up there and chewing out the insides of your mouth. You ought to break those nervous habits while you're young. Come over here and sit down."

Ardita took a carved jade case from her pocket, extracted a cigarette and lit it with a conscious coolness, though she knew her hand was trembling a little; then she crossed over with her supple, swinging walk and sitting down in the other settee blew a mouthful of smoke at the awning.

"You can't get me off this yacht," she said steadily; "and you haven't got very much sense if you think you'll get far with it. My uncle'll have wirelesses zigzagging all over this ocean by half past six."

"Hm."

She looked quickly at his face, caught anxiety stamped there plainly in the faintest depression of the mouth's corners.

"It's all the same to me," she said, shrugging her shoulders. "'Tisn't my yacht. I don't mind going for a coupla hours' cruise. I'll even lend you that book so you'll have something to read on the revenue boat that takes you up to Sing Sing."

He laughed scornfully.

"If that's advice you needn't bother. This is part of a plan arranged before I ever knew this yacht existed. If it hadn't been this one it'd have been the next one we passed anchored along the coast."

"Who are you?" demanded Ardita suddenly. "And what are you?"

"You've decided not to go ashore?"

"I never even faintly considered it."

"We're generally known," he said, "all seven of us, as Curtis Carlyle and his Six Black Buddies, late of the Winter Garden and the Midnight Frolic."

"You're singers?"

"We were until to-day. At present, due to those white bags you see there, we're fugitives from justice, and if the reward offered for our capture hasn't by this time reached twenty thousand dollars I miss my guess."

"What's in the bags?" asked Ardita curiously.

"Well," he said, "for the present we'll call it—mud—Florida mud."

III

Within ten minutes after Curtis Carlyle's interview with a very frightened engineer the yacht Narcissus was under way, steaming south through a balmy tropical twilight. The little mulatto, Babe, who seemed to have Carlyle's implicit confidence, took full command of the situation. Mr. Farnam's valet and the chef, the only members of the crew on board except the engineer, having shown fight, were now reconsidering, strapped securely to their bunks below. Trombone Mose, the biggest Negro, was set busy with a can of paint obliterating the name Narcissus from the bow and substituting the name Hula Hula, and the others congregated aft and became intently involved in a game of craps.

Having given orders for a meal to be prepared and served on deck at seven-thirty Carlyle rejoined Ardita and, sinking back into his settee, half closed his eyes and fell into a state of profound abstraction.

Ardita scrutinized him carefully—and classed him immediately as a romantic figure. He gave the effect of towering self-confidence erected on a slight foundation; just under the surface of each of his decisions she discerned a hesitancy that was in decided contrast to the arrogant curl of his lips.

"He's not like me," she thought. "There's a difference somewhere."

Being a supreme egotist Ardita frequently thought about herself; never having had her egotism disputed she did it entirely naturally and with no distraction from her unquestioned charm. Though she was nineteen she gave the effect of a high-spirited precocious child, and in the present glow of her youth and beauty all the men and women she had known were but driftwood on the ripples of her temperament. She had met other egotists; in fact, she found that selfish people bored her rather less than unselfish people—but as yet there had not been one she had not eventually defeated and brought to her feet.

But though she recognized an egotist in the settee next to her she felt none of that usual shutting of doors in her mind which meant clearing ship for action; on the contrary her instinct told her that this man was somehow completely pregnable and quite defenseless. When Ardita defied convention—and of late it had been her chief amusement—it was from an intense desire to be herself, and she felt that this man on the contrary was preoccupied with his own defiance.

She was much more interested in him than she was in her own situation, which affected her as the prospect of a matinee might affect a ten-year-old child. She had implicit confidence in her ability to take care of herself under any and all circumstances.

The night deepened. A pale new moon smiled misty-eyed upon the sea, and as the shore faded dimly out and dark clouds were blown like leaves along the far horizon a great haze of moonshine suddenly bathed the yacht and spread an avenue of glittering mail in her swift path. From time to time there was the bright flare of a match as one of them lighted a cigarette, but except for the low undertone of the throbbing engines and the even

wash of the waves about the stern the yacht was quiet as a dream
boat star-bound through the heavens. Round them flowed the
smell of the night sea, bringing with it an infinite languor.

Carlyle broke the silence at last.

"Lucky girl," he sighed, "I've always wanted to be rich—
and buy all this beauty."

Ardita yawned.

"I'd rather be you," she said frankly.

"You would—for about a day. But you do seem to possess
a lot of nerve for a flapper."

"I wish you wouldn't call me that."

"Beg your pardon."

"As to nerve," she continued slowly, "it's my one
redeeming feature. I'm not afraid of anything in heaven or earth."

"Hm, I am."

"To be afraid," said Ardita, "a person has either to be very
great and strong—or else a coward. I'm neither." She paused for a
moment, and eagerness crept into her tone.

"But I want to talk about you. What on earth have you
done—and how did you do it?"

"Why?" he demanded cynically. "Going to write a movie
about me?"

"Go on," she urged. "Lie to me by the moonlight. Do a
fabulous story."

A Negro appeared, switched on a string of small lights
under the awning and began setting the wicker table for supper.
And while they ate cold sliced chicken, salad, artichokes and
strawberry jam from the plentiful larder below, Carlyle began to
talk, hesitatingly at first, but eagerly as he saw she was interested.
Ardita scarcely touched her food as she watched his dark young
face—handsome, ironic, faintly ineffectual.

He began life as a poor kid in a Tennessee town, he said,
so poor that his people were the only white family in their street.

"Go on," she Urged. "Lie to Me by the Moonlight. Do a Fabulous Story"

He never remembered any white children—but there were always a dozen pickaninnies streaming in his trail, passionate admirers whom he kept in tow by the vividness of his imagination and the amount of trouble he was always getting them in and out of. And it seemed that this association diverted a rather unusual musical gift into a strange channel.

There had been a colored woman named Belle Pope Calhoun who played the piano at parties given for white children— nice white children that would have passed Curtis Carlyle with a sniff. But the ragged little "po' white" used to sit beside her piano by the hour and try to get in an alto with one of those kazoos that boys hum through. Before he was thirteen he was picking up a living teasing ragtime out of a battered violin in little cafes round Nashville. Eight years later the ragtime craze hit the country and he took six darkies on the Orpheum circuit. Five of them were boys he had grown up with; the other was the little mulatto, Babe Divine, who was a wharf nigger round New York and long before that a plantation hand in Bermuda, until he stuck an eight-inch stiletto in his master's back. Almost before Carlyle realized his good fortune he was on Broadway, with offers of engagements on all sides, and more money than he had ever dreamed of.

It was about then that a change began in his whole attitude, a rather curious, embittering change. It was when he realized that he was spending the golden years of his life gibbering round a stage with a lot of black men. His act was good of its kind—three trombones, three saxophones and Carlyle's flute—and it was his own peculiar sense of rhythm that made all the difference; but he began to grow strangely sensitive about it, began to hate the thought of appearing, dreaded it from day to day.

They were making money—each contract he signed called for more—but when he went to managers and told them that he wanted to separate from his sextet and go on as a regular pianist they laughed at him and told him he was crazy—it would be an artistic suicide. He used to laugh afterward at the phrase "artistic suicide." They all used it.

Half a dozen times they played at private dances at three thousand dollars a night, and it seemed as if these crystallized all his distaste for his mode of livelihood. They took place in clubs and houses that he couldn't have gone into in the daytime. After all, he was merely playing the role of the eternal monkey, a sort of sublimated chorus man. He was sick of the very smell of the theater, of powder and rouge and the chatter of the green room and the patronizing approval of the boxes. He couldn't put his heart into it any more. The idea of a slow approach to the luxury of leisure drove him wild. He was, of course, progressing toward it but, like a child, eating his ice cream so slowly that he couldn't taste it at all.

He wanted to have a lot of money, and time and opportunity

to read and play, and the sort of men and women round him that he could never have—the kind who, if they thought of him at all, would have considered him rather contemptible; in short he wanted all those things which he was beginning to lump under the general head of aristocracy, an aristocracy which it seemed almost any money could buy except money made as he was making it. He was twenty-five then, without family or education or any promise that he would succeed in a business career. He began speculating wildly, and within three weeks he had lost every cent he had saved.

Then the war came. He went to Plattsburg, and even there his profession followed him. A brigadier general called him up to headquarters and told him he could serve the country better as a band leader—so he spent the war entertaining celebrities behind the line with a headquarters band. It was not so bad—except that when the infantry came limping back from the trenches he wanted to be one of them. The sweat and mud they wore seemed only one of those ineffable symbols of aristocracy that were forever eluding him.

"It was the private dances that did it. After I came back from the war the old routine started. We had an offer from a syndicate of Florida hotels. It was only a question of time then."

He broke off and Ardita looked at him expectantly, but he shook his head.

"No," he said, "I'm not going to tell you about it. I'm enjoying it too much, and I'm afraid I'd lose a little of that enjoyment if I shared it with anyone else. I want to hang on to those few breathless, heroic moments when I stood out before them all and let them know I was more than a damn bobbing, squawking clown."

From up forward came suddenly the low sound of singing. The Negroes had gathered together on the deck and their voices rose together in a haunting melody that soared in poignant harmonics toward the moon. And Ardita listened in enchantment:

Oh down—
Oh down,
Mammy wanna take me downa milky way,
Oh down—
Oh down,
Pappy say to-morra-a-a-ah!
But mammy say to-day,
Yes—mammy say to-day!

Carlyle sighed and was silent for a moment, looking up at the gathered host of stars blinking like arc lights in the warm sky. The Negroes' song had died away to a plaintive humming and it seemed as if minute by minute the brightness and the great silence were increasing until he could almost hear the midnight toilet of the mermaids as they combed their silver-dripping curls under the moon and gossiped to each other of the fine wrecks they lived in on the green opalescent avenues below.

"You see," said Carlyle softly, "this is the beauty I want. Beauty has got to be astonishing, astounding—it's got to burst in on you like a dream, like the exquisite eyes of a girl."

He turned to her, but she was silent.

"You see, don't you, Anita—I mean, Ardita?"

Again she made no answer. She had been sound asleep for some time.

IV

In the dense sun-flooded noon of next day a spot in the sea before them resolved casually into a green-and-gray islet, apparently composed of a great granite cliff at its northern end which slanted south through a mile of vivid coppice and grass to a sandy beach melting lazily into the surf. When Ardita, reading in her favorite seat, came to the last page of The Revolt of the Angels and slamming the book shut looked up and saw it, she gave a little cry of delight and called to Carlyle, who was standing moodily by the rail.

"Is this it? Is this where you're going?"

Carlyle shrugged his shoulders carelessly.

"You've got me." He raised his voice and called up to the acting skipper. "Oh, Babe, is this your island?"

The mulatto's miniature head appeared from round the corner of the deckhouse.

"Yas-suh! This yeah's it."

Carlyle joined Ardita.

"Looks sort of sporting, doesn't it?"

"Yes," she agreed; "but it doesn't look big enough to be much of a hiding place."

"You still putting your faith in those wirelesses your uncle was going to have zigzagging round?"

"No," said Ardita frankly. "I'm all for you. I'd really like to see you make a get-away."

He laughed.

"You're our Lady Luck. Guess we'll have to keep you with us as a mascot—for the present anyway."

"You couldn't very well ask me to swim back," she said coolly. "If you do I'm going to start writing dime novels founded on that interminable history of your life you gave me last night."

He flushed and stiffened slightly.

"I'm very sorry I bored you."

"Oh, you didn't—until just at the end with some story about how furious you were because you couldn't dance with the ladies you played music for."

He rose angrily.

"You have got a darn mean little tongue."

"Excuse me," she said, melting into laughter, "but I'm not used to having men regale me with the story of their life ambitions—especially if they've lived such deathly platonic lives."

"Why? What do men usually regale you with?"

"Oh, they talk about me," she yawned. "They tell me I'm the spirit of youth and beauty."

"What do you tell them?"

"Oh, I agree quietly."

"Does every man you meet tell you he loves you?" Ardita nodded.

"Why shouldn't he? All life is just a progression toward and then a recession from one phrase— 'I love you.'"

Carlyle laughed and sat down.

"That's very true. That's—that's not bad. Did you make that up?"

"Yes—or rather I found it out. It doesn't mean anything especially. It's just clever."

"It's the sort of remark," he said gravely, "that's typical of your class."

"Oh," she interrupted impatiently, "don't start that lecture on aristocracy again! I distrust people who can be intense at this hour in the morning. It's a mild form of insanity—a sort of breakfast-food jag. Morning's the time to sleep, swim and be careless."

Ten minutes later they had swung round in a wide circle as if to approach the island from the north.

"There's a trick somewhere," commented Ardita thoughtfully. "He can't mean just to anchor up against this cliff."

They were heading straight in now toward the solid rock, which must have been well over a hundred feet tall, and not until they were within fifty yards of it did Ardita see their objective. Then she clapped her hands in delight.

There was a break in the cliff entirely hidden by a curious overlapping of rock and through this break the yacht entered and very slowly traversed a narrow channel of crystal-clear water between high gray walls. Then they were riding at anchor in a miniature world of green and gold, a gilded bay smooth as glass and set round with tiny palms, the whole resembling the mirror lakes and twig trees that children set up in sand piles.

"Not so darned bad!" cried Carlyle excitedly. "I guess that little coon knows his way round this corner of the Atlantic."

His exuberance was contagious and Ardita became quite jubilant.

"It's an absolutely sure-fire hiding place!"

"Lordy, yes! It's the sort of island you read about."

The rowboat was lowered into the golden lake and they pulled ashore.

"Come on," said Carlyle as they landed in the slushy sand; "we'll go exploring."

The fringe of palms was in turn ringed in by a round mile of flat sandy country. They followed it south and, brushing through a farther rim of tropical vegetation, came out on a pearl-gray virgin beach where Ardita kicked off her brown golf shoes—she seemed to have permanently abandoned stockings and went wading. Then they sauntered back to the yacht, where the indefatigable Babe had luncheon ready for them. He had posted a lookout on the high cliff to the north to watch the sea on both sides, though he doubted if the entrance to the cliff was generally known—he had never seen a map on which the island was even marked.

"What's its name," asked Ardita—"the island, I mean?"

"No name 'tall," chuckled Babe. "Reckin she jus' island, 'at's all."

Ardita thought for a moment.

"I'll name it," she said. "It'll be the Isle of Illusion."

"Or of Disillusion," murmured Carlyle. "Disillusion, if more people know about it than Babe seems to think."

In the late afternoon they sat with their backs against great boulders on the highest part of the cliff and Carlyle sketched for her his vague plans. He was sure they were hot after him by this time. The total proceeds of the coup he had pulled off, and concerning which he still refused to enlighten her, he estimated as just under a million dollars. He counted on lying up here several weeks and then setting off southward, keeping well outside the usual channels of travel, rounding the Horn and heading for Callao, in Peru. The details of coaling and provisioning he was leaving entirely to Babe, who, it seemed, had sailed these seas in every capacity from cabin boy aboard a coffee trader to virtual first mate on a Brazilian pirate craft, whose skipper had long since been hung.

"If he'd been white he'd have been king of South America long ago," said Carlyle emphatically. "When it comes to intelligence he makes Booker T. Washington look like a moron. He's got the guile of every race and nationality whose blood is in his veins, and that's half a dozen or I'm a liar. He worships me because I'm the only man in the world who can play better ragtime than he can. We used to sit together on the wharves down on the New York water front, he with a bassoon and I with an oboe, and we'd blend minor keys in African harmonics a thousand years old until the rats would crawl up the posts and sit round groaning and squeaking like dogs will in front of a phonograph."

Ardita roared.

"How you can tell 'em!"

Carlyle grinned.

"I swear that's the gos—"

"What you going to do when you get to Callao?" she interrupted.

"Take ship for India. I want to be a rajah. I mean it. My idea is to go up into Afghanistan somewhere, buy up a palace and a reputation, and then after about five years appear in England with a foreign accent and a mysterious past. But India first. Do you know, they say that all the gold in the world drifts very gradually back to India! Something fascinating about that to me. And I want leisure to read—an immense amount."

"How about after that?"

"Then," he answered defiantly, "comes aristocracy. Laugh if you want to—but at least you'll have to admit that I know what I want—which I imagine is more than you do."

"On the contrary," contradicted Ardita, reaching in her pocket for her cigarette case, "when I met you I was in the midst of a great uproar of all my friends and relatives because I did know what I wanted."

"What was it?"

"A man."

He started.

"You mean you were engaged?"

"After a fashion. If you hadn't come aboard I had every intention of slipping ashore yesterday evening—how long ago it seems—and meeting him in Palm Beach. He's waiting there for me with a bracelet that once belonged to Catharine of Russia. Now don't mutter anything about aristocracy," she put in quickly. "I liked him simply because he had an imagination and the utter courage of his convictions."

"But your family disapproved, eh?"

"What there is of it—only a silly uncle and a sillier aunt. It seems he got into some scandal with a red-haired woman named Mimi something—it was frightfully exaggerated, he said, and men don't lie to me—and anyway I didn't care what he'd done; it was the future that counted. And I'd see to that. When a man's in love with me he doesn't care for other amusements. I told him to drop her like a hot cake, and he did."

"I feel rather jealous," said Carlyle, frowning—and then he laughed. "I guess I'll just keep you along with us until we get to Callao. Then I'll lend you enough money to get back to the States. By that time you'll have had a chance to think that gentleman over a little more."

"Don't talk to me like that!" fired up Ardita. "I won't tolerate the parental attitude from anybody! Do you understand me?"

He chuckled and then stopped, rather abashed, as her cold anger seemed to fold him about and chill him.

"I'm sorry," he offered uncertainly.

"Oh, don't apologize! I can't stand men who say 'I'm sorry' in that manly, reserved tone. Just shut up!"

A pause ensued, a pause which Carlyle found rather awkward, but which Ardita seemed not to notice at all as she sat contentedly enjoying her cigarette and gazing out at the shining sea. After a minute she crawled out on the rock and lay with her face over the edge, looking down. Carlyle, watching her, reflected how it seemed impossible for her to assume an ungraceful attitude.

"Oh, look !" she cried. "There's a lot of sort of ledges down there. Wide ones of all different heights."

He joined her and together they gazed down the dizzy height.

"We'll go swimming to-night!" she said excitedly. "By moonlight."

"Wouldn't you rather go in at the beach on the other end?"

"Not a chance. I like to dive. You can use my uncle's bathing suit, only it'll fit you like a gunny sack, because he's a very flabby man. I've got a one-piece affair that's shocked the natives all along the Atlantic coast from Biddeford Pool to St. Augustine."

"I suppose you're a shark."

"Yes, I'm pretty good. And I look cute too. A sculptor last summer told me my calves were worth five hundred dollars."

There didn't seem to be any answer to this, so Carlyle was silent, permitting himself only a discreet interior smile.

V

When the night crept down in shadowy blue and silver they threaded the shimmering channel in the rowboat and tying it to a jutting rock began climbing the cliff together. The first shelf was ten feet up, wide and furnishing a natural diving platform. There they sat down in the bright moonlight and watched the faint incessant surge of the waters, almost stilled now as the tide set seaward.

"Are you happy?" he asked suddenly.

She nodded.

"Always happy near the sea. You know," she went on, "I've been thinking all day that you and I are somewhat alike. We're both rebels—only for different reasons. One year ago, when I was just eighteen, and you were —"

"Twenty-five."

"—Well, we were both conventional successes. I was an utterly devastating debutante and you were a prosperous musician just commissioned in the army —"

"Gentleman by act of Congress," he put in ironically.

"Well, at any rate, we both fitted. If our corners were not rubbed off they were at least pulled in. But deep in us both was something that made us require more for happiness. I didn't know what I wanted. I went from man to man, restless, impatient, month by month getting less acquiescent and more dissatisfied. I used to sit sometimes chewing at the insides of my mouth and thinking I was going crazy—I had a frightful sense of transiency. I wanted things now—now—now! Here I was—beautiful — I am, aren't I?"

"Yes," agreed Carlyle tentatively.

Ardita rose suddenly.

"Wait a second. I want to try this delightful-looking sea."

She walked to the end of the ledge and shot out over the water, doubling up in midair and then straightening out and entering the water straight as a blade in a perfect jackknife dive. In a minute her voice floated up to him. "You see, I used to read all day and most of the night. I began to resent society—"

"Come on up here," he interrupted. "What on earth are you doing?"

"Just floating round on my back. I'll be up in a minute. Let me tell you. The only thing I enjoyed was shocking people; wearing something quite impossible and quite charming to fancy-dress parties, going round with the fastest men in New York and getting into some of the most hellish scrapes imaginable."

The sounds of splashing mingled with her words, and then he heard her hurried breathing as she began climbing up the side to the ledge.

"Go on in!" she called.

Obediently he rose and dived. When he emerged, dripping, and made the climb he found that she was no longer on the ledge, but after a frightened second he heard her light laughter from another shelf ten feet up. There he joined her and they both sat quietly for a moment, their arms clasped round their knees, panting a little from the climb.

"The family were wild," she said suddenly. "They tried to marry me off. And then when I'd begun to feel that after all life was scarcely worth living I found something"—her eyes went skyward exultantly—"I found something!"

Carlyle waited and her words came with a rush.

"Courage—just that; courage as a rule of life and something to cling to always. I began to build up this enormous faith in myself. I began to see that in all my idols in the past some manifestation of courage had unconsciously been the thing that attracted me. I began separating courage from the other things of life. All sorts of courage—the beaten, bloody prize fighter coming up for more—I used to make men take me to prize fights; the *declassee* woman sailing through a nest of cats and looking at them as if they were mud under her feet; the liking what you like always; the utter disregard for other people's opinions—just to live as I liked always and to die in my own way. Did you bring up the cigarettes?"

He handed one over and held a match for her silently.

"Still," Ardita continued, "the men kept gathering—old men and young men, my mental and physical inferiors, most of them, but all intensely desiring to have me—to own this rather magnificent proud tradition I'd built up round me. Do you see?"

"Sort of. You never were beaten and you never apologized."

"Never!"

She sprang to the edge, poised for a moment like a crucified figure against the sky; then describing a dark parabola plunked without a splash between two silver ripples twenty feet below.

Her voice floated up to him again.

"And courage to me meant plowing through that dull gray mist that comes down on life—not only overriding people and circumstances but overriding the bleakness of living. A sort of insistence on the value of life and the worth of transient things."

She was climbing up now, and at her last words her head, with the damp yellow hair slicked symmetrically back, appeared on his level.

"All very well," objected Carlyle. "You can call it courage, but your courage is really built, after all, on a pride of birth. You were bred to that defiant attitude. On my gray days even courage is one of the things that's gray and lifeless."

She was sitting near the edge, hugging her knees and gazing abstractedly at the white moon; he was farther back, crammed like a grotesque god into a niche in the rock.

"I don't want to sound like Pollyanna," she began, "but you haven't grasped me yet. My courage is faith—faith in the eternal resilience of me—that joy'll come back, and hope and spontaneity.

And I feel that till it does I've got to keep my lips shut and my chin high and my eyes wide—not necessarily any silly smiling. Oh, I've been through hell without a whine quite often—and the female hell is deadlier than the male."

"But supposing," suggested Carlyle, "that before joy and hope and all that came back the curtain was drawn on you for good?"

Ardita rose, and going to the wall climbed with some difficulty to the next ledge, another ten or fifteen feet above.

"Why," she called back, "then I'd have won!"

He edged out till he could see her.

"Better not dive from there! You'll break your back," he said quickly.

She laughed.

"Not I!"

Slowly she spread her arms and stood there swanlike, radiating a pride in the young life within her that lit a warm glow in Carlyle's heart.

"We're going through the black air with our arms wide," she called, "and our feet straight out behind like a dolphin's tail, and we're going to think we'll never hit the silver down there till suddenly it'll be all warm round us and full of little kissing, caressing waves."

Then she was in the air and Carlyle involuntarily held his breath. He had not realized that the dive was nearly forty feet. It seemed an eternity before he heard the swift compact sound as she reached the sea.

And it was with his glad sigh of relief when her light watery laughter curled up the side of the cliff and into his anxious ears that he knew he loved her.

VI

Time, having no ax to grind, showered down upon them three days of afternoons. When the sun cleared the porthole of Ardita's cabin an hour after dawn she rose cheerily, donned her bathing suit and went up on deck. The Negroes would leave their work when they saw her, and crowd, chuckling and chattering, to the rail as she floated, an agile minnow, on and under the surface of the clear water. Again in the cool of the afternoon she would swim—and loll and smoke with Carlyle upon the cliff; or else they would lie on their sides in the sands of the southern beach, talking little, but watching the day fade colorfully and tragically into the infinite languor of a tropical evening.

And with the long sunny hours Ardita's idea of the episode as incidental, madcap, a sprig of romance in a desert of reality, gradually left her. She dreaded the time when he would strike off southward; she dreaded all the eventualities that presented themselves to her; thoughts were suddenly troublesome and decisions odious. Had prayers found place in the pagan rituals of her soul she would have asked of life only to be unmolested for a while, lazily acquiescent to the ready, untutored flow of Carlyle's ideas, his vivid boyish imagination and the vein of monomania that seemed to run crosswise through his temperament and colored his every action.

But this is not a story of two on an island nor concerned primarily with love bred of isolation. It is merely the presentation of two personalities, and its idyllic setting among the palms of the Gulf Stream is quite incidental. Most of us are content to exist and breed, and fight for the right to do both, and the dominant idea, the foredoomed attempt to control one's destiny, is reserved for the fortunate or unfortunate few. To me the interesting thing about Ardita is the courage that will tarnish with her beauty and youth.

"Take me with you," said Ardita late one night as they sat lazily in the grass under the shadowy spreading palms. The

"Is it a Proposal of Marriage? Extra! Ardita Farnam Becomes Pirate's Bride. Society Girl Kidnaped by Ragtime Bank Robber"

Negroes had brought ashore their instruments and the sound of weird ragtime was drifting over softly on the warm breath of the night. "I'd love to reappear in ten years as a fabulously wealthy high-caste Indian lady," she continued.

Carlyle looked at her quickly.

"You can, you know."

She laughed.

"Is it a proposal of marriage? Extra! Ardita Farnam becomes pirate's bride. Society girl kidnapped by ragtime bank robber."

"It wasn't a bank."

"What was it? Why won't you tell me?"

"I don't want to break down your illusions."

"My dear man, I have no illusions about you."

"I mean your illusions about yourself." She looked up in surprise.

"About myself! What on earth have I got to do with

whatever stray felonies you've committed?"

"That remains to be seen."

She reached over and patted his hand. "Dear Mr. Curtis Carlyle," she said softly, "are you in love with me?"

"As if it mattered."

"But it does—because I think I'm in love with you."

He looked at her ironically.

"Thus swelling your January total to half a dozen," he suggested. "Suppose I call your bluff and ask you to come to India with me?"

"Shall I?"

He shrugged his shoulders.

"We can get married in Callao."

"What sort of life can you offer me? I don't mean that unkindly, but seriously; what would become of me if the people who want that twenty-thousand-dollar reward ever catch up with you?"

"I thought you weren't afraid."

"I never am—but I won't throw my life away just to show one man I'm not."

"I wish you'd been poor. Just a little poor girl dreaming over a fence in a warm cow country."

"Wouldn't it have been nice?"

"I'd have enjoyed astonishing you—watching your eyes open on things. If you only wanted things! Don't you see?"

"I know—like girls who stare into the windows of jewelry stores."

"Yes—and want the big oblong watch that's platinum and has diamonds all round the edge. Only you'd decide it was too expensive and choose one of white gold for a hundred dollars. Then I'd say, 'Expensive? I should say not!' And we'd go into the store and pretty soon the platinum one would be gleaming on your wrist."

"That sounds so nice and vulgar—and fun, doesn't it?" murmured Ardita.

"Doesn't it? Can't you see us traveling round and spending money right and left and being worshiped by bell boys and waiters? Oh, blessed are the simple rich, for they inherit the earth!"

"I honestly wish we were that way."

"I love you, Ardita," he said gently.

Her face lost its childish look for a moment and became oddly grave.

"I love to be with you," she said, "more than with any man I've ever met. And I like your looks and your dark old hair and the way you go over the side of the rail when we come ashore. In fact, Curtis Carlyle, I like all the things you do when you're perfectly natural. I think you've got nerve, and you know how I feel about that. Sometimes when you're round I've been tempted to kiss you suddenly and tell you that you were just an idealistic boy with a lot of caste nonsense in his head. Perhaps if I were just a little bit older and a little more bored I'd go with you. As it is, I think I'll go back and marry—that other man."

Over across the silver lake the figures of the Negroes writhed and squirmed in the moonlight, like acrobats who, having been too long inactive, must go through their tricks from sheer surplus energy. In single file they marched, weaving in concentric circles, now with their heads thrown back, now bent over their instruments like piping fauns. And from trombone and saxophone ceaselessly whined a blended melody, sometimes riotous and jubilant, sometimes haunting and plaintive as a death dance from the Congo's heart.

"Let's dance!" cried Ardita. "I can't sit still with that perfect jazz going on."

Taking her hand, he led her out into a broad stretch of hard sandy soil that the moon flooded with great splendor. They floated out like drifting moths under the rich hazy light, and as the fantastic symphony wept and exulted and wavered and despaired Ardita's last sense of reality dropped away and she abandoned her imagination to the dreamy summer scents of tropical flowers and the infinite starry spaces overhead, feeling that if she opened her eyes it would be to find herself dancing with a ghost in a land created by her own fancy.

"This is what I should call an exclusive private dance," he whispered.

"I feel quite mad — but delightfully mad!"

"We're enchanted. The shades of unnumbered generations of cannibals are watching us from high up on the side of the cliff there."

"And I'll bet the cannibal women are saying that we dance too close and that it was immodest of me to come without my nose ring."

They both laughed softly—and then their laughter died as over across the lake they heard the trombones stop in the middle of a bar and the saxophones give a startled moan and fade out.

"What's the matter?" called Carlyle.

After a moment's silence they made out the dark figure of a man rounding the silver lake at a run. As he came closer they saw it was Babe in a state of unusual excitement. He drew up before them and gasped out his news in a breath.

"Ship stan'in' off sho' 'bout half a mile, suh. Mose, he uz on watch, he say look's if she's done ancho'd."

"A ship—what kind of a ship?" demanded Carlyle anxiously.

Dismay was in his voice and Ardita's heart gave a sudden wrench as she saw his whole face suddenly droop.

"He say he don't know, suh."

"Are they landing a boat?"

"No, suh."

"We'll go up," said Carlyle.

They ascended the hill in silence, Ardita's hand still resting in Carlyle's as it had when they finished dancing. She felt it clench nervously from time to time as though he were unaware of the contact, but though he hurt her she made no attempt to remove it. It seemed an hour's climb before they reached the top and crept cautiously across the silhouetted plateau to the edge of the cliff. After one short look Carlyle involuntarily gave a little cry. It was a revenue boat with six-inch guns mounted fore and aft.

"They know!" he said with a short intake of breath. "They know! They picked up the trail somewhere."

"Are you sure they know about the channel? They may be only standing by to take a look at the island in the morning. From where they are they couldn't see the opening in the cliff."

"They could with field glasses," he said hopelessly. He looked at his wrist watch. "It's nearly two now. They won't do anything until dawn, that's certain. Of course there's always the faint possibility that they're waiting for some other ship to join; or for a coaler."

"I suppose we may as well stay right here."

The hours passed and they lay there side by side, very silently, their chins in their hands like dreaming children. In back of them squatted the Negroes, patient, resigned, acquiescent, announcing now and then with sonorous snores that not even the presence of danger could subdue their unconquerable African craving for sleep.

Just before five o'clock Babe approached Carlyle.

There were half a dozen rifles aboard the Narcissus, he said. Had it been decided to offer no resistance? A pretty good fight might be made, he thought, if they worked out some plan.

Carlyle laughed and shook his head.

"That isn't a Spic army out there, Babe. That's a revenue boat. It'd be like a bow and arrow trying to fight a machine gun. If you want to bury those bags somewhere and take a chance on recovering them later, go on do it. But it won't work—they'd dig this island over from one end to another. It's a lost battle all round, Babe."

Babe inclined his head silently and turned away, and Carlyle's voice was husky as he turned to Ardita.

"There's the best friend I ever had. He'd die for me, and be proud to, if I'd let him."

"You've given up?"

"I've no choice. Of course there's always one way out—the sure way—but that can wait. I wouldn't miss my trial for anything—it'll be an interesting experiment in notoriety. `Miss Farnam testifies that the pirate's attitude to her was at all times that of a gentleman.'"

"Don't!" she said. "I'm awfully sorry."

When the color faded from the sky and lusterless blue changed to leaden gray a commotion was visible on the ship's deck and they made out a group of officers clad in white duck, gathered near the rail. They had field glasses in their hands and were attentively examining the islet.

"It's all up," said Carlyle grimly.

"Damn!" whispered Ardita. She felt tears gathering in her eyes.

"We'll go back to the yacht," he said. "I prefer that to being hunted out up here like a 'possum."

Leaving the plateau they descended the hill, and reaching the lake were rowed out to the yacht by the silent Negroes. Then, pale and weary, they sank into the settees and waited.

Half an hour later in the dim gray light the nose of the revenue boat appeared in the channel and stopped, evidently fearing that the bay might be too shallow. From the peaceful look of the yacht, the man and the girl in the settees and the Negroes lounging curiously against the rail, they evidently judged that there would be no resistance.

Two boats were lowered casually over the side, one containing an officer and six bluejackets, and the other, four rowers and in the stern two gray-haired men in yachting flannels. Ardita and Carlyle stood up and half unconsciously started toward each other. Then he paused and putting his hand suddenly into his pocket he pulled out a round glittering object and held it out to her.

"What is it?" she asked wonderingly.

"I'm not positive, but I think from the Russian inscription inside that it's your promised bracelet."

"Where—where on earth —"

"It came out of one of those bags. You see, Curtis Carlyle and his Six Black Buddies, in the middle of their performance in the tea room of the hotel at Palm Beach, suddenly changed their instruments for automatics and held up the crowd. I took this bracelet from a pretty overrouged woman with red hair."

Ardita frowned and then smiled.

"So that's what you did! You have got nerve!"

He bowed.

"A well-known bourgeois quality," he said.

And then dawn slanted dynamically across the deck and flung the shadows reeling into gray corners. The dew rose and turned to golden mist, thin as a dream, enveloping them until they seemed gossamer relics of the late night, infinitely transient and already fading. For a moment sea and sky were breathless and dawn held a pink hand over the young mouth of life—then from out in the lake came the complaint of a rowboat and the swish of oars.

Suddenly against the golden furnace low in the east their two graceful figures melted into one and he was kissing her spoiled young mouth.

"It's a sort of glory," he murmured after a second.

She smiled up at him.

"Happy, are you?"

Her sigh was a benediction—an ecstatic surety that she was youth and beauty now as much as she would ever know. For another instant life was radiant and time a phantom and their strength eternal—then there was a bumping, scraping sound as the rowboat scraped alongside.

Up the ladder scrambled the two gray-haired men, the officer and two of the sailors with their hands on their revolvers. Mr. Farnam folded his arms and stood looking at his niece.

"So," he said, nodding his head slowly.

With a sigh her arms unwound from Carlyle's neck, and her eyes, transfigured and far away, fell upon the boarding party. Her uncle saw her upper lip slowly swell into that arrogant pout he knew so well.

"So," he repeated savagely. "So this is your idea of—of romance. A runaway affair, with a—a high-seas pirate."

Ardita considered him carelessly.

"What an old fool you are!" she said quietly.

"Is that the best you can say for yourself?"

"No," she said as if considering. "No, there's something else. There's that well-known phrase with which I have ended most of our conversations for the past few years—'Shut up!'"

And with that she turned, included the two old men, the officer and the two sailors in a curt glance of contempt, and walked proudly down the companionway.

But had she waited an instant longer she would have heard a sound from her uncle quite unfamiliar in most of their interviews. Her uncle gave vent to a wholehearted amused chuckle, in which the second old man joined.

The latter turned briskly to Carlyle, who had been regarding this scene with an air of cryptic amusement.

"Well, Toby," he said genially, "you incurable, harebrained, romantic chaser of rainbows, did you find that she was the person you wanted?"

Carlyle smiled confidently.

"Why—naturally," he said. "I've been perfectly sure ever since I first heard tell of her wild career. That's why I had Babe send up the rocket last night."

"I'm glad you did," said Colonel Moreland gravely. "We've been keeping pretty close to you in case you should have trouble with those six strange niggers. And we hoped we'd find you two in some such compromising position," he sighed. "Well, set a crank to catch a crank!"

"Your father and I sat up all night hoping for the best—or perhaps it's the worst. Lord knows you're welcome to her, my boy. She's run me crazy. Did you give her the Russian bracelet my detective got from that Mimi woman?"

Carlyle nodded.

"Sh!" he said. "She's coming on deck."

Ardita appeared at the head of the companionway and gave a quick involuntary glance at Carlyle's wrists. A puzzled look came over her face. Back aft the Negroes had begun to sing, and the cool lake, fresh with dawn, echoed serenely to their low voices.

"Ardita," said Carlyle unsteadily.

She swayed a step toward him.

"Ardita," he repeated breathlessly, "I've got to tell you the—the truth. It was all a plant, Ardita. My name isn't Carlyle. It's Moreland, Toby Moreland. The story was invented, Ardita, invented out of thin Florida air."

She stared at him, bewildered amazement, disbelief and anger flowing in quick waves across her face. The three men held their breaths. Moreland, Senior, took a step toward her; Mr. Farnam's mouth dropped a little open as he waited, panic-stricken, for the expected crash.

But it did not come. Ardita's face became suddenly radiant, and with a little laugh she went swiftly to young Moreland and looked up at him without a trace of wrath in her gray eyes.

"Will you swear," she said quietly, "that it was entirely a product of your own brain?"

"I swear," said young Moreland eagerly.

She drew his head down and kissed him gently.

"What an imagination!" she said softly and almost enviously. "I want you to lie to me just as sweetly as you know how for the rest of my life."

The Negroes' voices floated drowsily back, mingled in an air that she had heard them sing before:

> *Time is a thief;*
> *Gladness and grief*
> *Cling to the leaf*
> *As it yellows -*

"What was in the bags?" she asked softly.

"Florida mud," he answered. "That was one of the two true things I told you."

And Ardita being a girl of some perspicacity had no difficulty in guessing the other.

THE SATURDAY EVENING POST

FEB. 11, 1922

5c. THE COPY

Story Illustrations by
Charles D. Mitchell

In This Number: F. Scott Fitzgerald—Kenneth L. Roberts—St. John Ervin
Louise Dutton—Samuel Merwin—Earl Derr Biggers—Harry Leon Wilso

For the first time, the *Post* published one of Fitzgerald's stories in two parts, on February 11 and 18, 1922. It was his highest paid work for the magazine to that point, earning $1,500 for the two pieces.

Once again, the femme fatale will be tamed by a wise young man.

The Popular Girl, Part One

Along about half past ten every Saturday night Yanci Bowman eluded her partner by some graceful subterfuge and from the dancing floor went to point of vantage overlooking the country-club bar. When she saw her father she would either beckon to him, if he chanced to be looking in her direction, or else she would dispatch a waiter to call attention to her impendent presence. If it were no later than half past ten—that is, if he had had no more than an hour of synthetic gin rickeys—he would get up from his chair and suffer himself to be persuaded into the ballroom.

"Ballroom," for want of a better word. It was that room, filled by day with wicker furniture, which was always connotated in the phrase "Let's go in and dance." It was referred to as "inside" or "downstairs." It was that nameless chamber wherein occur the principal transactions of all the country clubs in America.

Yanci knew that if she could keep her father there for an hour, talking, watching her dance, or even on rare occasions dancing himself, she could safely release him at the end of that time. In the period that would elapse before midnight ended the dance he could scarcely become sufficiently stimulated to annoy anyone.

All this entailed considerable exertion on Yanci's part, and it was less for her father's sake than for her own that she went through with it. Several rather unpleasant experiences were scattered through this past summer. One night when she had been detained by the impassioned and impossible-to-interrupt speech of a young man from Chicago her father had appeared swaying gently in the ballroom doorway; in his ruddy handsome face two faded blue eyes were squinted half shut as he tried to focus on them on the dancers, and he was obviously preparing to offer himself to the first dowager who caught his eye. He was ludicrously injured when Yanci insisted upon an immediate withdrawal.

After that night Yanci went through her Fabian maneuver to the minute. Yanci and her father were the handsomest two people in the Middle Western city where they lived. Tom Bowman's complexion was hearty from twenty years spent in the service of good whisky and bad golf. He kept an office downtown, where he was thought to transact some vague real-estate business; but in point of fact his chief concern in life was the exhibition of a handsome profile and an easy well-bred manner at the country club, where he had spent the greater part of the ten years that had elapsed since his wife's death.

Yanci was twenty, with a vague die-away manner which was partly the setting for her languid disposition and partly the effect of a visit she had paid to some Eastern relatives at an impressionable age. She was intelligent, in a flitting way, romantic under the moon and unable to decide whether to marry for sentiment or for comfort, the latter of these two abstractions being well enough personified by one of the most ardent among her admirers. Meanwhile she kept house, not without efficiency, for her father, and tried in a placid unruffled tempo to regulate his constant tippling to the sober side of inebriety.

She admired her father. She admired him for his fine appearance and for his charming manner. He had never quite lost the air of having been a popular Bones man at Yale. This charm of his was a standard by which her susceptible temperament unconsciously judged the men she knew. Nevertheless, father and daughter were far from that sentimental family relationship which is a stock plant in fiction, but in life usually exists in the mind of only the older party to it. Yanci Bowman had decided to leave her home by marriage within the year. She was heartily bored.

Scott Kimberly, who saw her for the first time this November evening at the country club, agreed with the lady whose houseguest he was that Yanci was an exquisite little beauty. With a sort of conscious sensuality surprising in such a young man—Scott was only twenty-five—he avoided an introduction that he might watch her undisturbed for a fanciful hour, and sip the pleasure or the disillusion of her conversation at the drowsy end of the evening.

"She never got over the disappointment of not meeting the Prince of Wales when he was in this country," remarked Mrs. Orrin Rogers, following his gaze. "She said so, anyhow; whether she was serious or not I don't know. I hear that she has her walls simply plastered with pictures of him."

"Who?" asked Scott suddenly.

"Why, the Prince of Wales."

"Who has plaster pictures of him?"

"Why, Yanci Bowman, the girl you said you thought was so pretty."

"After a certain degree of prettiness, one pretty girl is as pretty as another," said Scott argumentatively. "Yes, I suppose so."

Mrs. Rogers' voice drifted off on an indefinite note. She had never in her life compassed a generality until it had fallen familiarly on her ear from constant repetition.

"Let's talk her over," Scott suggested.

With a mock reproachful smile Mrs. Rogers lent herself agreeably to slander. An encore was just beginning. The orchestra trickled a light overflow of music into the pleasant green-latticed room and the two score couples who for the evening comprised the local younger set moved placidly into time with its beat.

Only a few apathetic stags gathered one by one in the doorways, and to a close observer it was apparent that the scene did not attain the gayety which was its aspiration. These girls and men had known each other from childhood; and though there were marriages incipient upon the floor tonight, they were marriages of environment, of resignation, or even of boredom.

Their trappings lacked the sparkle of the seventeen-year-old affairs that took place through the short and radiant holidays. On such occasions as this, thought Scott as his eyes still sought casually for Yanci, occurred the matings of the leftovers, the plainer, the duller, the poorer of the social world; matings actuated by the same urge toward perhaps a more glamorous destiny, yet, for all that, less beautiful and less young. Scott himself was feeling very old.

But there was one face in the crowd to which his generalization did not apply. When his eyes found Yanci Bowman among the dancers he felt much younger. She was the incarnation of all in which the dance failed—graceful youth, arrogant, languid freshness and beauty that was sad and perishable as a memory in a dream. Her partner, a young man with one of those fresh red complexions ribbed with white streaks, as though he had been slapped on a cold day, did not appear to be holding her interest, and her glance fell here and there upon a group, a face, a garment, with a far-away and oblivious melancholy.

"Dark-blue eyes," said Scott to Mrs. Rogers. "I don't know that they mean anything except that they're beautiful, but that nose and upper lip and chin are certainly aristocratic—if there is any such thing," he added apologetically.

"Oh, she's very aristocratic," agreed Mrs. Rogers. "Her grandfather was a senator or governor or something in one of the Southern States. Her father's very aristocratic looking too. Oh, yes, they're very aristocratic; they're aristocratic people."

"She looks lazy."

Scott was watching the yellow gown drift and submerge among the dancers.

"She doesn't like to move. It's a-wonder she dances so well. Is she engaged? Who is the man who keeps cutting in on her, the one who tucks his tie under his collar so rakishly and affects the remarkable slanting pockets?"

He was annoyed at the young man's persistence, and his sarcasm lacked the ring of detachment.

"Oh, that's "—Mrs. Rogers bent forward, the tip of her tongue just visible between her lips—"that's the O'Rourke boy. He's quite devoted, I believe."

"I believe," Scott said suddenly, "that I'll get you to introduce me if she's near when the music stops."

They arose and stood looking for Yanci—Mrs. Rogers, small, stoutening, nervous, and Scott Kimberly, her husband's cousin, dark and just below medium height. Scott was an orphan with half a million of his own, and he was in this city for no more reason than that he had missed a train. They looked for several minutes, and in vain. Yanci, in her yellow dress, no longer moved with slow loveliness among the dancers.

The clock stood at half past ten.

II

Good evening," her father was saying to her at that moment in syllables faintly slurred. "This seems to be getting to be a habit."

They were standing near a side stairs, and over his shoulder through a glass door Yanci could see a party of half a dozen men sitting in familiar joviality about a round table.

"Don't you want to come out and watch for a while?" she suggested, smiling arid affecting a casualness she did not feel.

"Not tonight, thanks."

Her father's dignity was a bit too emphasized to be convincing.

"Just come out and take a look," she urged him. "Everybody's here, and I want to ask you what you think of somebody."

This was not so good, but it was the best that occurred to her.

"I doubt very strongly if I'd find anything to interest me out there," said Tom Bowman emphatically. "I observe that f'some insane reason I'm always taken out and aged on the wood for half an hour as though I was irresponsible."

"I only ask you to stay a little while."

"Very considerate, I'm sure. But tonight I happ'n be interested in a discussion that's taking place in here."

"Come on, father."

Yanci put her arm through his ingratiatingly; but he released it by the simple expedient of raising his own arm and letting hers drop.

"I'm afraid not."

"I'll tell you," she suggested lightly, concealing her annoyance at this unusually protracted argument, "you come in and look, just once, and then if it bores you you can go right back."

He shook his head.

"No, thanks."

Then without another word he turned suddenly and reentered the bar. Yanci went back to the ballroom. She glanced easily at the stag line as she passed, and making a quick selection murmured to a man near her, "Dance with me, will you, Carty? I've lost my partner."

"Glad to," answered Carty truthfully.

"Awfully sweet of you."

"Sweet of me? Of you, you mean."

She looked up at him absently. She was furiously annoyed at her father. Next morning at breakfast she would radiate a consuming chill, but for tonight she could only wait, hoping that if the worst happened he would at least remain in the bar until the dance was over.

Mrs. Rogers, who lived next door to the Bowmans, appeared suddenly at her elbow with a strange young man.

"Yanci," Mrs. Rogers was saying with a social smile. "I want to introduce Mr. Kimberly. Mr. Kimberly's spending the weekend with us, and I particularly wanted him to meet you."

"How perfectly slick!" drawled Yanci with lazy formality.

Mr. Kimberly suggested to Miss Bowman that they dance, to which proposal Miss Bowman dispassionately acquiesced. They mingled their arms in the gesture prevalent and stepped into time with the beat of the drum. Simultaneously it seemed to Scott that the room and the couples who danced up and down upon it converted themselves into a background behind her. The commonplace lamps, the rhythm of the music playing some paraphrase of a paraphrase, the faces of many girls, pretty, undistinguished or absurd, assumed a certain solidity as though they had grouped themselves in a retinue for Yanci's languid eyes and dancing feet.

"I've been watching you," said Scott simply. "You look rather bored this evening."

"Do I?" Her dark-blue eyes exposed a borderland of fragile iris as they opened in a delicate burlesque of interest. "How perfectly killing !" she added.

Scott laughed. She had used the exaggerated phrase without smiling, indeed without any attempt to give it verisimilitude. He had heard the adjectives of the year —" "hectic," "marvelous" and "slick "— delivered casually, but never before without the faintest meaning. In this lackadaisical young beauty it was inexpressibly charming.

The dance ended. Yanci and Scott strolled toward a lounge set against the wall, but before they could take possession there was a shriek of laughter and a brawny damsel dragging an embarrassed boy in her wake skidded by them and plumped down upon it.

"How rude!" observed Yanci.

"I suppose it's her privilege."

"A girl with ankles like that has no privileges."

They seated themselves uncomfortably on two stiff chairs.

"Where do you come from?" she asked of Scott with polite disinterest.

"New York."

This having transpired, Yanci deigned to fix her eyes on him for the best part of ten seconds.

"Who was the gentleman with the invisible tie," Scott asked

"Who Was the Gentleman With the Invisible Tie?" Scott Asked. "Is His Personality as Diverting as His Haberdashery?"

rudely, in order to make her look at him again, "who was giving you such a rush? I found it impossible to keep my eyes off him. Is his personality as diverting as his haberdashery?"

"I don't know," she drawled; "I've only been engaged to him for a week."

"My Lord!" exclaimed Scott, perspiring suddenly under his eyes. "I beg your pardon. I didn't —"

"I was only joking," she interrupted with a sighing laugh. "I thought I'd see what you'd say to that."

Then they both laughed, and Yanci continued, "I'm not engaged to anyone. I'm too horribly unpopular." Still the same key, her languorous voice humorously contradicting the content of her remark. "No one'll ever marry me."

"How pathetic!"

"Really," she murmured; "because I have to have compliments all the time, in order to live, and no one thinks I'm attractive any more, so no one ever gives them to me."

Seldom had Scott been so amused.

"Why, you beautiful child," he cried, "I'll bet you never hear anything else from morning till night !"

"Oh, yes I do," she responded, obviously pleased. "I never get compliments unless I fish for them."

"Everything's the same," she was thinking as she gazed around her in a peculiar mood of pessimism. Same boys sober and same boys tight; same old women sitting by the walls—and one or two girls sitting with them who were dancing this time last year.

Yanci had reached the stage where these country-club dances seemed little more than a display of sheer idiocy. From being an enchanted carnival where jeweled and immaculate maidens rouged to the pinkest propriety displayed themselves to strange and fascinating men, the picture had faded to a medium-sized hall where was an almost indecent display of unclothed motives and obvious failures. So much for several years! And the dance had changed scarcely by a ruffle in the fashions or a new flip in a figure of speech.

Yanci was ready to be married.

Meanwhile the dozen remarks rushing to Scott Kimberly's lips were interrupted by the apologetic appearance of Mrs. Rogers.

"Yanci," the older woman was saying, "the chauffeur's just telephoned to say that the car's broken down. I wonder if you and your father have room for us going home. If it's the slightest inconvenience don't hesitate to tell----"

"I know he'll be terribly glad to. He's got loads of room, because I came out with someone else."

She was wondering if her father would be presentable at twelve.

He could always drive at any rate—and, besides, people who asked for a lift could take what they got.

"That'll be lovely. Thank you so much," said Mrs. Rogers.

Then, as she had just passed the kittenish late thirties when women still think they are persona grata with the young and entered upon the early forties when their children convey to them tactfully that they no longer are, Mrs. Rogers obliterated herself from the scene. At that moment the music started and the unfortunate young man with white streaks in his red complexion appeared in front of Yanci.

Just before the end of the end of the next dance Scott Kimberly cut in on her again.

"I've come back," he began, "to tell you how beautiful you are."

"I'm not, really," she answered. "And, besides, you tell everyone that."

The music gathered gusto for its finale, and they sat dawn upon the comfortable lounge.

"I've told no one that for three years," said Scott.

There was no reason why he should have made it three years, yet somehow it sounded convincing to both of them. Her curiosity was stirred. She began finding out about him. She put him to a lazy questionnaire which began with his relationship to the Rogerses and ended, he knew not by what steps, with a detailed description of his apartment in New York.

"I want to live in New York," she told him; "on Park Avenue, in one of those beautiful white buildings that have twelve big rooms in each apartment and cost a fortune to rent."

"That's what I'd want, too, if I were married. Park Avenue— it's one of the most beautiful streets in the world, I think, perhaps chiefly because it hasn't any leprous park trying to give it an artificial suburbanity."

"Whatever that is," agreed Yanci. "Anyway, father and I go to New York about three times a year. We always go to the Ritz."

This was not precisely true. Once a year she generally pried her father from his placid and not unbeneficent existence that she might spend a week lolling by the Fifth Avenue shop windows, lunching or having tea with some former school friend from Farmover, and occasionally going to dinner and the theater with boys who came up from Yale or Princeton for the occasion. These had been pleasant adventures—not one but was filled to the brim with colorful hours—dancing at Mont Martre, dining at the Ritz, with some movie star or supereminent society woman at the next table, or else dreaming of what she might buy at Hempel's or Waxe's or Thrumble's if her father's income had but one additional naught on the happy side of the decimal. She adored New York with a great impersonal affection—adored it as only a Middle Western or Southern girl can. In its gaudy bazaars she felt her soul transported with turbulent delight, for to her eyes it held nothing ugly, nothing sordid, nothing plain.

She had stayed once at the Ritz—once only. The Manhattan, where they usually registered, had been torn down. She knew that she could never induce her father to afford the Ritz again.

After a moment she borrowed a pencil and paper and scribbled a notification "To Mr. Bowman in the grill" that he was expected to drive Mrs. Rogers and her guest home, "by request "—this last underlined. She hoped that he would be able to do so with dignity. This note she sent by a waiter to her father. Before the next dance began it was returned to her with a scrawled 0. K. and her father's initials.

The remainder of the evening passed quickly. Scott Kimberly cut in on her as often as time permitted, giving her those comforting assurances of her enduring beauty which not without a whimsical pathos she craved. He laughed at her also, and she was not so sure that she liked that. In common with all vague people, she was unaware that she was vague. She did not entirely comprehend when Scott Kimberly told her that her personality would endure long after she was too old to care whether it endured or not.

She liked best to talk about New York, and each of their interrupted conversations gave her a picture or a memory of the metropolis on which she speculated as she looked over the shoulder of Jerry O'Rourke or Carty Braden or some other beau, to whom, as to all of them, she was comfortably anesthetic. At midnight she sent another note to her father, saying that Mrs. Rogers and Mrs. Rogers' guest would meet him immediately on the porch by the main driveway. Then, hoping for the best, she walked out into the starry night and was assisted by Jerry O'Rourke into his roadster.

III

GOOD night, Yanci." With her late escort she was standing on the curbstone in front of the rented stucco house where she lived. Mr. O'Rourke was attempting to put significance into his lingering rendition of her name. For weeks he had been straining to boost their relations almost forcibly onto a sentimental plane; but Yanci, with her vague impassivity, which was a defense against almost anything, had brought to naught his efforts. Jerry O'Rourke was an old story. His family had money; but he—he worked in a brokerage house along with most of the rest of his young generation. He sold bonds—bonds were now the thing; real estate was once the thing—in the days of the boom; then automobiles were the thing. Bonds were the thing now. Young men sold them who had nothing else to go into.

"Don't bother to come up, please." Then as he put his car into gear, "Call me up soon!"

A minute later he turned the corner of the moonlit street and disappeared, his cutout resounding voluminously through the night as it declared that the rest of two dozen weary inhabitants was of no concern to his gay meanderings.

Yanci sat down thoughtfully upon the porch steps. She had no key and must wait for her father's arrival. Five minutes later a roadster turned into the street, and approaching with an exaggerated caution stopped in front of the Rogers' large house next door. Relieved, Yanci arose and strolled slowly down the walk. The door of the car had swung open and Mrs. Rogers, assisted by Scott Kimberly, had alighted safely upon the sidewalk; but to Yanci's surprise Scott Kimberly, after escorting Mrs. Rogers to her steps, returned to the car. Yanci was close enough to notice that he took the driver's seat. As he drew up at the Bowman's curbstone Yanci saw that her father was occupying the far corner, fighting with ludicrous dignity against a sleep that had come upon him. She groaned. The fatal last hour had done its work—Tom Bowman was once more hors de combat.

"Hello," cried Yanci as she reached the curb.

"Yanci," muttered her parent, simulating, unsuccessfully, a brisk welcome. His lips were curved in an ingratiating grin.

"Your father wasn't feeling quite fit, so he let me drive home," explained Scott cheerfully as he got himself out and came up to her.

"Nice little car. Had it long?"

Yanci laughed, but without humor.

"Is he paralyzed?"

"Is who paralyze'?" demanded the figure in the car with an offended sigh.

Scott was standing by the car.

"Can I help you out, sir?"

"I c'n get out. I c'n get out," insisted Mr. Bowman. "Just step a li'l' out my way. Someone must have given me some stremely bad wisk'."

"You mean a lot of people must have given you some," retorted Yanci in cold unsympathy. Mr. Bowman reached the curb with astonishing ease; but this was a deceitful success, for almost immediately he clutched at a handle of air perceptible only to himself, and was saved by Scott's quickly proffered arm. Followed by the two men, Yanci walked toward the house in a furor of embarrassment. Would the young man think that such scenes went on every night? It was chiefly her own presence that made it humiliating for Yanci.

Had her father been carried to bed by two butlers each evening she might even have been proud of the fact that he could afford such dissipation; but to have it thought that she assisted, that she was burdened with the worry and the care! And finally she was annoyed with Scott Kimberly for being there, and for his officiousness in helping to bring her father into the house.

Reaching the low porch of tapestry brick, Yanci searched in Tom Bowman's vest for the key and unlocked the front door. A minute later the master of the house was deposited in an easy chair.

"Thanks very much," he said, recovering for a moment. "Sit down. Like a drink? Yanci, get some crackers and cheese, if there's any, won't you, dear?"

At the unconscious coolness of this Scott and Yanci laughed.

"It's your bedtime, father," she said, her anger struggling with diplomacy.

"Give me my guitar," he suggested, "and I'll play you tune."

Except on such occasions as this, he had not touched his guitar for twenty years. Yanci turned to Scott. "He'll be fine now. Thanks a lot. He'll fall asleep in a minute and when I wake him he'll go to bed like a lamb."

"Well —"

They strolled together out the door. "Sleepy?" he asked.

"No, not a bit."

"Then perhaps you'd better let me stay here with you a few minutes until you see if he's all right. Mrs. Rogers gave me a key so I can get in without disturbing her."

"It's quite all right," protested Yanci. " I don't mind a bit, and he won't be any trouble. He must have taken a glass too much, and this whisky we have out here—you know! This has happened once before—last year," she added.

Her words satisfied her; as an explanation it seemed to have a convincing ring.

"Can I sit down for a moment, anyway?" They sat side by

side upon a wicker porch settee.

"I'm thinking of staying over a few days," Scott said.

"How lovely !" Her voice had resumed its die-away note.

"Cousin Pete Rogers wasn't well today, but to-morrow he's going duck shooting, and he wants me to go with him."

"Oh, how thrilling! I've always been mad to go, and father's always promised to take me, but he never has."

"We're going to be gone about three days, and then I thought I'd come back here and stay over the next week-end —" He broke off suddenly and bent forward in a listening attitude.

"Now what on earth is that?"

The sounds of music were proceeding brokenly from the room they had lately left—a ragged chord on a guitar and half a dozen feeble starts.

"It's father !" cried Yanci.

And now a voice drifted out to them, drunken and murmurous, taking the long notes with attempted melancholy:

> *Sing a song of cities,*
> *Ridin' on a rail,*
> *A niggah's ne'er so happy*
> *As when he's out-a jail.*

"How terrible!" exclaimed Yanci. "He'll wake up everybody in the block."

The chorus ended, the guitar jangled again, then gave out a last harsh spang! and was still. A moment later these disturbances were followed by a low but quite definite snore. Mr. Bowman, having indulged his musical proclivity, had dropped off to sleep.

"Let's go to ride," suggested Yanci impatiently. "This is too hectic for me."

Scott arose with alacrity and they walked down to the car.

"Where'll we go?" she wondered.

"I don't care."

"We might go up half a block to Crest Avenue—that's our show street—and then ride out to the river boulevard."

As they turned into Crest Avenue the new cathedral, immense and unfinished, in imitation of a cathedral left unfinished by accident in some little Flemish town, squatted just across the way like a plump white bulldog on its haunches. The ghosts of four moonlit apostles looked down at them wanly from wall niches still littered with the white, dusty trash of the builders. The cathedral inaugurated Crest Avenue.

After it came the great brownstone mass built by R. R. Comerford, the flour king, followed by a half mile of pretentious stone houses put up in the gloomy 90's. These were adorned with monstrous driveways and porte-cocheres which had once echoed to the hoofs of good horses and with huge circular windows that corseted the second stories.

The continuity of these mausoleums was broken by a small park, a triangle of grass where Nathan Hale stood ten feet tall with his hands bound behind his back by stone cord and stared over a great bluff at the slow Mississippi. Crest Avenue ran along the bluff, but neither faced it nor seemed aware of it, for all the houses fronted inward toward the street. Beyond the first half mile it became newer, essayed ventures in terraced lawns, in concoctions of stucco or in granite mansions which imitated through a variety of gradual refinements the marble contours of the Petit Trianon. The houses of this phase rushed by the roadster for a succession of minutes; then the way turned and the car was headed directly into the moonlight which swept toward it like the lamp of some gigantic motorcycle far up the avenue.

Past the low Corinthian lines of the Christian Science Temple, past a block of dark frame horrors, a deserted row of grim red brick—an unfortunate experiment of the late 90's—then new houses again, bright-red brick now, with trimmings of white, black iron fences and hedges binding flowery lawns. These swept by, faded, passed, enjoying their moment of grandeur; then waiting there in the moonlight to be outmoded as had the frame, cupolaed mansions of lower town and the brownstone piles of older Crest Avenue in their turn.

The roofs lowered suddenly, the lots narrowed, the houses shrank up in size and shaded off into bungalows. These held the street for the last mile, to the bend in the river which terminated the prideful avenue at the statue of Chelsea Arbuthnot. Arbuthnot was the first governor—and almost the last of Anglo-Saxon blood.

All the way thus far Yanci had not spoken, absorbed still in the annoyance of the evening, yet soothed somehow by the fresh air of northern November that rushed by them. She must take her fur coat out of storage next day, she thought.

"Where are we now?"

As they slowed down Scott looked up curiously at the pompous stone figure, clear in the crisp moonlight, with one hand on a book and the forefinger of the other pointing, as though with reproachful symbolism, directly at some construction work going on in the street.

"This is the end of Crest Avenue," said Yanci, turning to him. "This is our show street."

"A museum of American architectural failures."

"What?"

"Nothing," he murmured.

"I should have explained it to you. I forgot. We can go along the river boulevard if you'd like—or are you tired?"

Scott assured her that he was not tired—not in the least.

Entering the boulevard, the cement road twisted under darkling trees.

"The Mississippi—how little it means to you now!" said Scott suddenly.

"What?" Yanci looked around. "Oh, the river."

"I guess it was once pretty important to your ancestors up here."

"My ancestors weren't up here then," said Yanci with some dignity. " My ancestors were from Maryland. My father came out here when he left Yale."

"Oh!" Scott was politely impressed.

"My mother was from here. My father came out here from Baltimore because of his health."

"Oh!"

"Of course we belong here now, I suppose"—this with faint condescension—" as much as anywhere else."

"Of course. "

"Except that I want to live in the East and I can't persuade father to," she finished.

It was after one o'clock and the boulevard was almost deserted. Occasionally two yellow disks would top a rise ahead of them and take shape as a late-returning automobile. Except for that they were alone in a continual rushing dark. The moon had gone down.

"Next time the road goes near the river let's stop and watch it," he suggested.

Yanci smiled inwardly. This remark was obviously what one boy of her acquaintance had named an international petting cue, by which was meant a suggestion that aimed to create naturally a situation for a kiss. She considered the matter. As yet the man had made no particular impression on her. He was good-looking, apparently well to do and from New York. She had begun to like him during the dance, increasingly as the evening had drawn to a close; then the incident of her father's appalling arrival had thrown cold water upon this tentative warmth; and now—it was November, and the night was cold. Still.

"All right," she agreed suddenly.

The road divided; she swerved around and brought the car to

a stop in an open place high above the river.

"Well?" she demanded in the deep quiet that followed the shutting off of the engine.

"Thanks."

"Are you satisfied here?"

"Almost. Not quite."

"Why not?'

"I'll tell you in a minute," he answered. "Why is your name Yanci?"

"It's a family name."

"It's very pretty." He repeated it several times caressingly. "Yanci—it has all the grace of Nancy, and yet it isn't prim."

"What's your name?" she inquired.

"Scott."

"Scott what?"

"Kimberly. Didn't you know?"

"I wasn't sure. Mrs. Rogers introduced you in such a mumble."

There was a slight pause.

"Yanci," he repeated; "beautiful Yanci, with her dark-blue eyes and her lazy soul. Do you know why I'm not quite satisfied, Yanci?"

"Why?"

Imperceptibly she had moved her face nearer until as she waited for an answer with her lips faintly apart he knew that in asking she had granted. Without haste he bent his head forward and touched her lips. He sighed, and both of them felt a sort of relief—relief from the embarrassment of playing up to what conventions of this sort of thing remained.

"Thanks," he said as he had when she first stopped the car.

"Now are you satisfied?"

Her blue eyes regarded him unsmilingly in the darkness.

"After a fashion; of course, you can never say—definitely."

Again he bent toward her, but she stooped and started the motor. It was late and Yanci was beginning to be tired. What purpose there was in the experiment was accomplished. He had had what he asked. If he liked it he would want more, and that put her one move ahead in the game which she felt she was beginning.

"I'm hungry," she complained. "Let's go down and eat."

"Very well," he acquiesced sadly. "Just when I was so enjoying—the Mississippi."

"Do you think I'm beautiful?" she inquired almost plaintively as they backed out.

"What an absurd question!"

"But I like to hear people say so."

"I was just about to—when you started the engine."

Downtown in a deserted all-night lunchroom they ate bacon and eggs. She was pale as ivory now. The night had drawn the lazy vitality and languid color out of her face. She encouraged him to talk to her of New York until he was beginning every sentence with, "Well, now, let's see."

The repast over, they drove home. Scott helped her put the car in the little garage, and just outside the front door she lent him her lips again for the faint brush of a kiss.   Then she went in.

The long living room which ran the width of the small stucco house was reddened by a dying fire which had been high when Yanci left and now was faded to a steady undancing glow. She took a log from the firebox and threw it on the embers, then started as a voice came out of the half darkness at the other end of the room.

"Back so soon?"

It was her father's voice, not yet quite sober, but alert and intelligent.

"Yes. Went riding," she answered shortly, sitting down in a wicker chair before the fire. "Then went down and had something to eat."

"Oh!"

Her father left his place and moved to a chair nearer the fire, where he stretched himself out with a sigh. Glancing at him from the corner of her eye, for she was going to show an appropriate coldness, Yanci was fascinated by his complete recovery of dignity in the space of two hours. His graying hair was scarcely rumpled; his handsome face was ruddy as ever. Only his eyes, crisscrossed with tiny red lines, were evidence of his late dissipation.

"Have a good time?"

"Why should you care?" she answered rudely.

"Why shouldn't I?"

"You didn't seem to care earlier in the evening. I asked you to take two people home for me, and you weren't able to drive your own car."

"The deuce I wasn't!" he protested. "I could have driven in—in a race in an arana, areaena. That Mrs. Rogers insisted that her young admirer should drive, so what could I do?"

"That isn't her young admirer," retorted Yanci crisply. There was no drawl in her voice now. "She's as old as you are. That's her niece—I mean her nephew."

"Excuse me!"

"I think you owe me an apology." She found suddenly that she bore him no resentment. She was rather sorry for him, and it occurred to her that in asking him to take Mrs. Rogers home she had somehow imposed on his liberty. Nevertheless, discipline was necessary—there would be other Saturday nights. "Don't you?" she concluded.

"I apologize, Yanci."

"Very well, I accept your apology," she answered stiffly.

"What's more, I'll make it up to you."

Her blue eyes contracted. She hoped—she hardly dared to hope that he might take her to New York.

"Let's see," he said. "November, isn't it? What date?"

"The twenty-third."

"Well, I'll tell you what I'll do." He knocked the tips of his fingers together tentatively. "I'll give you a present. I've been meaning to let you have a trip all fall, but business has been bad." She almost smiled—as though business was of any consequence in his life. "But then you need a trip. I'll make you a present of it."

He rose again, and crossing over to his desk sat down.

"I've got a little money in a New York bank that's been lying there quite a while," he said as he fumbled in a drawer for a checkbook. "I've been intending to close out the account. Let—me—see. There's just —" His pen scratched. "Where the devil's the blotter? Uh!"

He came back to the fire and a pink oblong paper fluttered into her lap.

"Why, father!"

It was a check for three hundred dollars. "But can you afford this?" she demanded.

"It's all right," he reassured her, nodding. "That can be a Christmas present, too, and you'll probably need a dress or a hat or something before you go."

"Why," she began uncertainly, " I hardly know whether I ought to take this much or not! I've got two hundred of my own downtown, you know. Are you sure —"

"Oh, yes!" He waved his hand with magnificent carelessness. "You need a holiday. You've been talking about New York, and I want you to go down there. Tell some of your friends at Yale and the other colleges and they'll ask you to the prom or something. That'll be nice. You'll have a good time."

He sat down abruptly in his chair and gave vent to a long sigh. Yanci folded up the check and tucked it into the low bosom of her dress.

"Well," she drawled softly with a return to her usual manner, "you're a perfect lamb to be so sweet about it, but I don't want to be horribly extravagant."

Her father did not answer. He gave another little sigh and relaxed sleepily into his chair.

"Of course I do want to go," went on Yanci.

Still her father was silent. She wondered if he were asleep.

"Are you asleep?" she demanded, cheerfully now. She bent toward him; then she stood up and looked at him.

"Father," she said uncertainly.

Her father remained motionless; the ruddy color had melted suddenly out of his face.

"Father!"

It occurred to her—and at the thought she grew cold, and a brassiere of iron clutched at her breast—that she was alone in the room. After a frantic instant she said to herself that her father was dead.

Yanci judged herself with inevitable gentleness—judged herself very much as a mother might judge a wild, spoiled child. She was not hard-minded, nor did she live by any ordered and considered philosophy of her own. To such a catastrophe as the death of her father her immediate reaction was a hysterical self-pity. The first three days were something of a nightmare; but sentimental civilization, being as infallible as Nature in healing the wounds of its more fortunate children, had inspired a certain Mrs. Oral, whom Yanci had always loathed, with a passionate interest in all such crises. To all intents and purposes Mrs. Oral buried Tom Bowman. The morning after his death Yanci had wired her maternal aunt in Chicago, but as yet that undemonstrative and well-to-do lady had sent no answer.

All day long, for four days, Yanci sat in her room upstairs, hearing steps come and go on the porch, and it merely increased her nervousness that the doorbell had been disconnected. This by order of Mrs. Oral ! Doorbells were always disconnected! After the burial of the dead the strain relaxed. Yanci, dressed in her new black, regarded herself in the pier glass, and then wept because she seemed to herself very sad and beautiful. She went downstairs and tried to read a moving-picture magazine, hoping that she would not be alone in the house when the winter dark came down just after four.

This afternoon Mrs. Oral had said carpe diem to the maid, and Yanci was just starting for the kitchen to see whether she had yet gone when the reconnected bell rang suddenly through the house. Yanci started. She waited a minute, then went to the door. It was Scott Kimberly.

"I was just going to inquire for you," he said.

"Oh! I'm much better, thank you," she responded with the quiet dignity that seemed suited to her role.

They stood there in the hall awkwardly, each reconstructing the half-facetious, half-sentimental occasion on which they had last met. It seemed such an irreverent prelude to such a somber disaster. There was no common ground for them now, no gap that could be bridged by a slight reference to their mutual past, and there was no foundation on which he could adequately pretend to share her sorrow.

"Won't you come in?" she said, biting her lip nervously. He followed her to the sitting room and sat beside her on the lounge. In another minute, simply because he was there and alive and friendly, she was crying on his shoulder.

"There, there!" he said, putting his arm behind her and patting her shoulder idiotically. "There, there, there!"

He was wise enough to attribute no ulterior significance to her action. She was overstrained with grief and loneliness and sentiment; almost any shoulder would have done as well. For all the biological thrill to either of them he might have been a hundred years old. In a minute she sat up.

"I beg your pardon," she murmured brokenly. But it's—it's so dismal in this house to-day."

"I know just how you feel, Yanci."

"Did I—did I —get—tears on your coat? "

In tribute to the tenseness of the incident they both laughed hysterically, and with the laughter she momentarily recovered her propriety.

"I don't know why I should have chosen you to collapse on," she wailed. "I really don't just go round doing it indiscriminately on anyone who comes in."

"I consider it a—a compliment," he responded soberly, "and I can understand the state you're in." Then, after a pause, "Have you any plans?"

She shook her head.

She Was Overstrained With Grief and Loneliness; Almost Any Shoulder Would Have Done as Well

"Va-vague ones," she muttered between little gasps. "I thoought I'd go down and stay with my aunt in Chicago a while."

"I should think that'd be best—much the best thing." Then, because he could think of nothing else to say, he added, "Yes, very much the best thing."

"What are you doing—here in town?" she inquired, taking in her breath in minute gasps and dabbing at her eyes with a handkerchief.

"Oh, I'm here with—with the Rogerses. I've been here."

"Hunting?"

"No, I've just been here."

He did not tell her that he had stayed over on her account. She might think it fresh.

"I see," she said. She didn't see.

"I want to know if there's any possible thing I can do for you, Yanci. Perhaps go downtown for you, or do some errands — anything. Maybe you'd like to bundle up and get a bit of air. I could take you out to drive in your car some night, and no one would see you."

He clipped his last word short as the inadvertency of this suggestion dawned on him. They stared at each other with horror in their eyes.

"Oh, no, thank you!" she cried. "I really don't want to drive."

To his relief the outer door opened and an elderly lady came in. It was Mrs. Oral. Scott rose immediately and moved backward toward the door.

"If you're sure there isn't anything I can do."   Yanci introduced him to Mrs. Oral; then leaving the elder woman by the fire walked with him to the door. An idea had suddenly occurred to her.

"Wait a minute." She ran up the front stairs and returned immediately with a slip of pink paper in her hand.

"Here's something I wish you'd do," she said. "Take this to

the First National Bank and have it cashed for me. You can leave the money here for me any time."

Scott took out his wallet and opened it.

"Suppose I cash it for you now," he suggested.

"Oh, there's no hurry."

"But I may as well." He drew out three new one-hundred-dollar bills and gave them to her.

"That's awfully sweet of you," said Yanci.

"Not at all. May I come in and see you next time I come west?"

"I wish you would."

"Then I will. I'm going east to-night."

The door shut him out into the snowy dusk and Yanci returned to Mrs. Oral. Mrs. Oral had come to discuss plans.

"And now, my dear, just what do you plan to do? We ought to have some plan to go by, and I thought I'd find out if you had any definite plan in your mind."

Yanci tried to think. She seemed to herself to be horribly alone in the world.

"I haven't heard from my aunt. I wired her again this morning. She may be in Florida."

"In that case you'd go there?"

"I suppose so."

"Would you close this house?"

"I suppose so."

Mrs. Oral glanced around with placid practicality. It occurred to her that if Yanci gave the house up she might like it for herself.

"And now," she continued, "do you know where you stand financially?"

"All right, I guess," answered Yanci indifferently; and then with a rush of sentiment, "There was enough for t-two; there ought to be enough for o-one."

"I didn't mean that," said Mrs. Oral. "I mean, do you know

the details?"

"No."

" Well, I thought you didn't know the details. And I thought you ought to know all the details—have a detailed account of what and where your money is. So I called up Mr. Haedge, who knew your father very well personally, to come up this afternoon and glance through his papers. He was going to stop in your father's bank, too, by the way, and get all the details there. I don't believe your father left any will."

Details! Details! Details!

"Thank you," said Yanci. "That'll be—nice."

Mrs. Oral gave three or four vigorous nods that were like heavy periods. Then she got up. "And now if Hilma's gone out I'll make you some tea. Would you like some tea?"

"Sort of."

"All right, I'll make you some nice tea."

Tea! Tea! Tea!

Mr. Haedge, who came from one of the best Swedish families in town, arrived to see Yanci at five o'clock. He greeted her funereally; said that he had been several times to inquire for her; had organized the pallbearers and would now find out how she stood in no time. Did she have any idea whether or not there was a will? No? Well, there probably wasn't one.

There was one. He found it almost at once in Mr. Bowman's desk—but he worked there until eleven o'clock that night before he found much else. Next morning he arrived at eight, went down to the bank at ten, then to a certain brokerage firm, and came back to Yanci's house at noon. He had known Tom Bowman for some years, but he was utterly astounded when he discovered the condition in which that handsome gallant had left his affairs.

He consulted Mrs. Oral, and that afternoon he informed a frightened Yanci in measured language that she was practically penniless. In the midst of the conversation a telegram from Chicago told her that her aunt had sailed the week previous for a trip through the Orient and was not expected back until late spring.

The beautiful Yanci, so profuse, so debonair, so careless with her gorgeous adjectives, had no adjectives for this calamity. She crept upstairs like a hurt child and sat before a mirror, brushing her luxurious hair to comfort herself. One hundred and fifty strokes she gave it, as it said in the treatment, and then a hundred and fifty more—she was too distraught to stop the nervous motion. She brushed it until her arm ached, then she changed arms and went on brushing.

The maid found her next morning, asleep, sprawled across the toilet things on the dresser in a room that was heavy and sweet with the scent of spilled perfume.

(to be concluded)

The Maid Found Her Next Morning, Asleep, Sprawled Across the Toilet Things on the Dresser in a Room That Was Heavy and Sweet With the Scent of Spilled Perfume

Story Illustrations by
Charles D. Mitchell

More Than Two Million and a Quarter Weekly

"The Popular Girl" was reportedly a great favorite of the author's and he expressed hopes to his agent that it would be bought by a film studio, but no record exists of such a sale.

It was following "The Popular Girl" that Fitzgerald took time away from short stories and moved to Europe to write The Great Gatsby. More than two years would pass before his next story appeared in the *Post*, "Gretchen's Forty Winks."

The Popular Girl, Part Two

To be precise, as Mr. Haedge was to a depressing degree, Tom Bowman left a bank balance that was more than ample—that is to say, more than ample to supply the post-mortem requirements of his own person. There was also twenty years' worth of furniture, a temperamental roadster with asthmatic cylinders and two one-thousand-dollar bonds of a chain of jewelry stores which yielded 7.5 per cent interest. Unfortunately these were not known in the bond market.

When the car and the furniture had been sold and the stucco bungalow sublet, Yanci contemplated her resources with dismay. She had a bank balance of almost a thousand dollars. If she invested this she would increase her total income to about fifteen dollars a month. This, as Mrs. Oral cheerfully observed, would pay for the boarding-house room she had taken for Yanci as long as Yanci lived. Yanci was so encouraged by this news that she burst into tears.

So she acted as any beautiful girl would have acted in this emergency. With rare decision she told Mr. Haedge that she would leave her thousand dollars in a checking account, and then she walked out of his office and across the street to a beauty parlor to have her hair waved.

This raised her morale astonishingly.

Indeed, she moved that very day out of the boarding house and into a small room at the best hotel in town. If she must sink into poverty she would at least do so in the grand manner. Sewed into the lining of her best mourning hat were the three new one-hundred-dollar bills, her father's last present. What she expected of them, why she kept them in such a way, she did not know, unless perhaps because they had come to her under cheerful auspices and might through some gayety inherent in their crisp and virgin paper buy happier things than solitary meals and narrow hotel beds. They were hope and youth and luck and beauty; they began, somehow, to stand for all the things she had lost in that November night when Tom Bowman, having led her recklessly into space, had plunged off himself, leaving her to find the way back alone.

Yanci remained at the Hiawatha Hotel for three months, and she found that after the first visits of condolence her friends had happier things to do with their time than to spend it in her company. Jerry O'Rourke came to see her one day with a wild Celtic look in his eyes, and demanded that she marry him immediately. When she asked for time to consider he walked out in a rage. She heard later that he had been offered a position in Chicago and had left the same night.

She considered, frightened and uncertain. She had heard of people sinking out of place, out of life. Her father had once told her of a man in his class at college who had become a worker around saloons, polishing brass rails for the price of a can of beer; and she knew also that there were girls in this city with whose mothers her own mother had played as a little girl, but who were poor now and had grown common; who worked in stores and had married into the proletariat. But that such a fate should threaten her—how absurd! Why, she knew everyone! She had been invited everywhere; her great-grandfather had been governor of one of the Southern States!

She had written to her aunt in India and again in China, receiving no answer. She concluded that her aunt's itinerary had changed, and this was confirmed when a post card arrived from Honolulu which showed no knowledge of Tom Bowman's death, but announced that she was going with a party to the east coast of Africa. This was a last straw. The languorous and lackadaisical Yanci was on her own at last.

"Why not go to work for a while?" suggested Mr. Haedge with some irritation. "Lots of nice girls do nowadays, just for something to occupy themselves with. There's Elsie Prendergast, who does society news on the Bulletin, and that Semple girl."

"I can't," said Yanci shortly with a glitter of tears in her eyes. "I'm going east in February."

"East? Oh, you're going to visit someone?"

She nodded.

"Yes, I'm going to visit," she lied, "so it'd hardly be worth while to go to work." She could have wept, but she managed a haughty look. "I'd like to try reporting sometime, though, just for the fun of it."

"Yes, it's quite a lot of fun," agreed Mr. Haedge with some irony. "Still, I suppose there's no hurry about it. You must have plenty of that thousand dollars left."

"Oh, plenty!"

There were a few hundred, she knew.

"Well, then I suppose a good rest, a change of scene would be the best thing for you."

"Yes," answered Yanci. Her lips were trembling and she rose, scarcely able to control herself. Mr. Haedge seemed so impersonally cold. "That's why I'm going. A good rest is what I need."

"I think you're wise."

What Mr. Haedge would have thought had he seen the dozen drafts she wrote that night of a certain letter is problematical. Here are two of the earlier ones. The bracketed words are proposed substitutions:

Dear Scott:

Not having seen you since that day I was such a silly ass and wept on your coat, I thought I'd write and tell you that I'm coming east pretty soon and would like you to have lunch [dinner] with me or something. I have been living in a room [suite] at the Hiawatha Hotel, intending to meet my aunt, with whom I am

going to live [stay], and who is coming back from
China this month [spring]. Meanwhile I have a lot
of invitations to visit, etc., in the east, and I thought I
would do it now. So I'd like to see you —

This draft ended here and went into the wastebasket. After
an hour's work she produced the following:

My dear Mr. Kimberly:
I have often [sometimes] wondered how you've been
since I saw you. I am coming east next month before
going to visit my aunt in Chicago, and you must
come and see me. I have been going out very little,
but my physician advises me that I need a change,
so I expect to shock the proprieties by some very gay
visits in the east –

Finally in despondent abandon she wrote a simple note
without explanation or subterfuge, tore it up and went to bed. Next
morning she identified it in the wastebasket, decided it was the best
one after all and sent him a fair copy. It ran:

Dear Scott:
Just a line to tell you I will be at the Ritz-Carlton
Hotel from February seventh, probably for ten days.
If you'll phone me some rainy afternoon I'll invite
you to tea.
Sincerely,
Yanci Bowman

Yanci was going to the Ritz for no more reason than that she
had once told Scott Kimberly that she always went there. When she
reached New York—a cold New York, a strangely menacing New

York, quite different from the gay city of theaters and hotel corridor rendezvous that she had known—there was exactly two hundred dollars in her purse. It had taken a large part of her bank account to live, and she had at last broken into her sacred three hundred dollars to substitute pretty and delicate quarter-mourning clothes for the heavy black she had laid away.

Walking into the hotel at the moment when its exquisitely dressed patrons were assembling for luncheon, it drained at her confidence to appear bored and at ease. Surely the clerks at the desk knew the contents of her pocketbook. She fancied even that the bellboys were snickering at the foreign labels she had steamed from an old trunk of her father's and pasted on her suitcase. This last thought horrified her. Perhaps the very hotels and steamers so grandly named had long since been out of commission!

As she stood drumming her fingers on the desk she was wondering whether if she were refused admittance she could muster a casual smile and stroll out coolly enough to deceive two richly dressed women standing near. It had not taken long for the confidence of twenty years to evaporate. Three months without security had made an ineffaceable mark on Yanci's soul.

"Twenty-four sixty-two," said the clerk callously.

Her heart settled back into place as she followed the bellboy to the elevator, meanwhile casting a nonchalant glance at the two fashionable women as she passed them. Were their skirts long or short?—longer, she noticed.

She wondered how much the skirt of her new walking suit could he let out.

At luncheon her spirits soared. The headwaiter bowed to her. The light rattle of conversation, the subdued hum of the music soothed her. She ordered supreme of melon, eggs Susette and an artichoke, and signed her room number to the check with scarcely a glance at it as it lay beside her plate. Up in her room, with the telephone directory open on the bed before her, she tried to locate her scattered metropolitan acquaintances. Yet even as the phone numbers, with their supercilious tags, Plaza, Circle and Rhinelander, stared out at her, she could feel a cold wind blow at her unstable confidence. These girls, acquaintances of school, of a summer, of a house party, even of a weekend at a college prom—what claim or attraction could she, poor and friendless, exercise over them? They had their loves, their dates, their week's gayety planned in advance. They would almost resent her inconvenient memory.

Nevertheless, she called four girls. One of them was out, one at Palm Beach, one in California. The only one to whom she talked said in a hearty voice that she was in bed with grippe, but would phone Yanci as soon as she felt well enough to go out.

Then Yanci gave up the girls. She would have to create the illusion of a good time in some other manner. The illusion must be created—that was part of her plan.

She looked at her watch and found that it was three o'clock. Scott Kimberly should have phoned before this, or at least left some word. Still, he was probably busy—at a club, she thought vaguely, or else buying some neckties. He would probably call at four.

Yanci was well aware that she must work quickly. She had figured to a nicety that one hundred and fifty dollars carefully expended would carry her through two weeks, no more. The idea of failure, the fear that at the end of that time she would be friendless and penniless had not begun to bother her.

It was not the first time that for amusement, for a coveted invitation or for curiosity she had deliberately set out to capture a man; but it was the first time she had laid her plans with necessity and desperation pressing in on her.

One of her strongest cards had always been her background, the impression she gave that she was popular and desired and happy. This she must create now, and apparently out of nothing. Scott must somehow be brought to think that a fair portion of New York was at her feet.

At four she went over to Park Avenue, where the sun was out walking and the February day was fresh and odorous of spring and the high apartments of her desire lined the street with radiant whiteness. Here she would live on a gay schedule of pleasure. In these smart not-to-be-entered-without-a-card women's shops she would spend the morning hours acquiring and acquiring, ceaselessly and without thought of expense; in these restaurants she would lunch at noon in company with other fashionable women, orchid-adorned always, and perhaps bearing an absurdly dwarfed Pomeranian in her sleek arms.

In the summer—well, she would go to Tuxedo, perhaps to an immaculate house perched high on a fashionable eminence, where she would emerge to visit a world of teas and balls, of horse shows and polo. Between the halves of the polo game the players would cluster around her in their white suits and helmets, admiringly, and when she swept away, bound for some new delight, she would be followed by the eyes of many envious but intimidated women.

Every other summer they would, of course, go abroad. She began to plan a typical year, distributing a few months here and a few months there until she—and Scott Kimberly, by implication— would become the very auguries of the season, shifting with the slightest stirring of the social barometer from rusticity to urbanity, from palm to pine. She had two weeks, no more, in which to attain to this position. In an ecstasy of determined emotion she lifted up her head toward the tallest of the tall white apartments.   "It will be too marvelous!" she said to herself.

For almost the first time in her life her words were not too exaggerated to express the wonder shining in her eyes.

VIII

About five o'clock she hurried back to the hotel, demanding feverishly at the desk if there had been a telephone message for her. To her profound disappointment there was nothing. A minute after she had entered her room the phone rang.

"This is Scott Kimberly."

At the words a call to battle echoed in her heart. "Oh, how do you do?"

Her tone implied that she had almost forgotten him.

It was not frigid—it was merely casual.

As she answered the inevitable question as to the hour when she had arrived a warm glow spread over her. Now that, from a personification of all the riches and pleasure she craved, he had materialized as merely a male voice over the telephone, her confidence became strengthened. Male voices were male voices. They could be managed; they could be made to intone syllables of which the minds behind them had no approval. Male voices could be made sad or tender or despairing at her will.

She rejoiced. The soft clay was ready to her hand.

"Won't you take dinner with me to-night?" Scott was suggesting.

"Why"—perhaps not, she thought; let him think of her tonight—"I don't believe I'll be able to," she said. "I've got an engagement for dinner and the theater. I'm terribly sorry."

Her voice did not sound sorry—it sounded polite. Then as though a happy thought had occurred to her as to a time and place where she could work him into her list of dates, "I'll tell you: Why don't you come around here this afternoon and have tea with me?"

He would be there immediately. He had been playing squash and as soon as he took a plunge he would arrive. Yanci hung up the phone and turned with a quiet efficiency to the mirror, too tense to smile.

She regarded her lustrous eyes and dusky hair in critical approval. Then she took a lavender tea gown from her trunk and began to dress.

She let him wait seven minutes in the lobby before she appeared; then she approached him with a friendly, lazy smile.

"How do you do?" she murmured. "It's marvelous to see you again. How are you?"

And, with a long sigh, "I'm frightfully tired. I've been on the go ever since I got here this morning; shopping and then tearing off to luncheon and a matinee. I've bought everything I saw. I don't know how I'm going to pay for it all."

She remembered vividly that when they had first met she had told him, without expecting to be believed, how unpopular she was. She could not risk such a remark now, even in jest. He must think that she had been on the go every minute of the day.

They took a table and were served with olive sandwiches and tea. He was so good-looking, she thought, and marvelously dressed. His gray eyes regarded her with interest from under immaculate ash-blond hair. She wondered how he passed his days, how he liked her costume, what he was thinking of at that moment.

"How long will you be here?" he asked.

"Well, two weeks, off and on. I'm going down to Princeton for the February prom and then up to a house party in Westchester County for a few days. Are you shocked at me for going out so soon? Father would have wanted me to, you know. He was very modern in all his ideas."

She had debated this remark on the train. She was not going to a house party. She was not invited to the Princeton prom. Such things, nevertheless, were necessary to create the illusion. That was everything—the illusion.

"And then," she continued, smiling, "two of my old beaus are in town, which makes it nice for me."

She saw Scott blink and she knew that he appreciated the significance of this.

"What are your plans for this winter?" he demanded. "Are you going back west?"

"No. You see, my aunt returns from India this week. She's going to open her Florida house, and we'll stay there until the middle of March. Then we'll come up to Hot Springs and we may go to Europe for the summer."

This was all the sheerest fiction. Her first letter to her aunt, which had given the bare details of Tom Bowman's death, had at last reached its destination. Her aunt had replied with a note of conventional sympathy and the announcement that she would be back in America within two years if she didn't decide to live in Italy.

"But you'll let me see something of you while you're here," urged Scott, after attending to this impressive program. "If you can't take dinner with me tonight, how about Wednesday—that's the day after tomorrow?"

"Wednesday? Let's see." Yanci's brow was knit with imitation thought. "I think I have a date for Wednesday, but I don't know for certain. How about phoning me tomorrow, and I'll let you know? Because I want to go with you, only I think I've made an engagement."

"Very well, I'll phone you."

"Do—about ten."

"Try to be able to—then or any time."

"I'll tell you—if I can't go to dinner with you Wednesday I can go to lunch surely."

"All right," he agreed. "And we'll go to a matinee."

They danced several times. Never by word or sign did Yanci betray more than the most cursory interest in him until just at the end, when she offered him her hand to say good-by.

"Good-by, Scott."

For just the fraction of a second—not long enough for him to be sure it had happened at all, but just enough so that he would be reminded, however faintly, of that night on the Mississippi boulevard—she looked into his eyes. Then she turned quickly and hurried away.

She took her dinner in a little tearoom around the corner. It was an economical dinner which cost a dollar and a half. There was no date concerned in it at all, and no man—except an elderly person in spats who tried to speak to her as she came out the door.

IX

Sitting alone in one of the magnificent moving-picture theaters—a luxury which she thought she could afford—Yanci watched Mae Murray swirl through splendidly imagined vistas, and meanwhile considered the progress of the first day. In retrospect it was a distinct success. She had given the correct impression both as to her material prosperity and as to her attitude toward Scott himself. It seemed best to avoid evening dates. Let him have the evenings to himself, to think of her, to imagine her with other men, even to spend a few lonely hours in his apartment, considering how much more cheerful it might be if — Let time and absence work for her.

Engrossed for a while in the moving picture, she calculated the cost of the apartment in which its heroine endured her movie wrongs. She admired its slender Italian table, occupying only one side of the large dining room and flanked by a long bench which gave it an air of medieval luxury. She rejoiced in the beauty of Mae Murray's clothes and furs, her gorgeous hats, her short-seeming French shoes. Then after a moment her mind returned to her own drama; she wondered if Scott was already engaged, and her heart dipped at the thought. Yet it was unlikely. He had been too quick to phone her on her arrival, too lavish with his time, too responsive that afternoon.

After the picture she returned to the Ritz, where she slept deeply and happily for almost the first time in three months. The atmosphere around her no longer seemed cold. Even the floor clerk had smiled kindly and admiringly when Yanci asked for her key.

Next morning at ten Scott phoned. Yanci, who had been up for hours, pretended to be drowsy from her dissipation of the night before.

No, she could not take dinner with him on Wednesday. She was terribly sorry; she had an engagement, as she had feared. But she could have luncheon and go to a matinee if he would get her back in time for tea.

She spent the day roving the streets. On top of a bus, though not on the front seat, where Scott might possibly spy her, she sailed out Riverside Drive and back along Fifth Avenue just at the winter twilight, and her feeling for New York and its gorgeous splendors deepened and redoubled. Here she must live and be rich, be nodded to by the traffic policemen at the corners as she sat in her limousine—with a small dog—and here she must stroll on Sunday to and from a stylish church, with Scott, handsome in his cutaway and tall hat, walking devotedly at her side.

At luncheon on Wednesday she described for Scott's benefit a fanciful two days. She told of a motoring trip up the Hudson and gave him her opinion of two plays she had seen with—it was implied—adoring gentlemen beside her. She had read up very carefully on the plays in the morning paper and chosen two concerning which she could garner the most information.

"Oh," he said in dismay, "you've seen Duley? I have two seats for it—but you won't want to go again."

"Oh, no, I don't mind," she protested truthfully. "You see, we went late, and anyway I adored it."

But he wouldn't hear of her sitting through it again—besides, he had seen it himself. It was a play Yanci was mad to see, but she was compelled to watch him while he exchanged the tickets for others, and for the poor seats available at the last moment. The game seemed difficult at times.

"By the way," he said afterwards as they drove back to

the hotel in a taxi, "you'll be going down to the Princeton prom tomorrow, won't you?"

She started. She had not realized that it would be so soon or that he would know of it.

"Yes," she answered coolly. "I'm going down to-morrow afternoon."

"On the 2:20, I suppose," Scott commented; and then, "Are you going to meet the boy who's taking you down—at Princeton?"

For an instant she was off her guard. "Yes, he'll meet the train."

"Then I'll take you to the station," proposed Scott. "There'll be a crowd, and you may have trouble getting a porter."

She could think of nothing to say, no valid objection to make. She wished she had said that she was going by automobile, but she could conceive of no graceful and plausible way of amending her first admission.

"That's mighty sweet of you."

"You'll be at the Ritz when you come back?"

"Oh, yes," she answered. "I'm going to keep my rooms."

Her bedroom was the smallest and least expensive in the hotel.

She concluded to let him put her on the train for Princeton; in fact, she saw no alternative. Next day as she packed her suitcase after luncheon the situation had taken such hold of her imagination that she filled it with the very things she would have chosen had she really been going to the prom. Her intention was to get out at the first stop and take the train back to New York.

Scott called for her at half past one and they took a taxi to the Pennsylvania Station. The train was crowded as he had expected, but he found her a seat and stowed her grip in the rack overhead.

"I'll call you Friday to see how you've behaved," he said.

"All right. I'll be good."

Their eyes met and in an instant, with an inexplicable, only half-conscious rush of emotion, they were in perfect communion. When Yanci came back, the glance seemed to say, ah, then —

A voice startled her ear:

"Why, Yanci!"

Yanci looked around. To her horror she recognized a girl named Ellen Harley, one of those to whom she had phoned upon her arrival.

"Well, Yanci Bowman! You're the last person I ever expected to see. How are you?"

Yanci introduced Scott. Her heart was beating violently.

"Are you coming to the prom? How perfectly slick!" cried Ellen. "Can I sit here with you? 'I've been wanting to see you. Who are you going with?"

"No one you know."

"Maybe I do."

Her words, falling like sharp claws on Yanci's sensitive soul, were interrupted by an unintelligible outburst from the conductor. Scott bowed to Ellen, cast at Yanci one level glance and then hurried off.

The train started. As Ellen arranged her grip and threw off her fur coat Yanci looked around her. The car was gay with girls whose excited chatter filled the damp, rubbery air like smoke. Here and there sat a chaperone, a mass of decaying rock in a field of flowers, predicting with a mute and somber fatality the end of all gaiety and all youth. How many times had Yanci herself been one of such a crowd, careless and happy, dreaming of the men she would meet, of the battered hacks waiting at the station, the snow-covered campus, the big open fires in the clubhouses, and the imported orchestra beating out defiant melody against the approach of morning.

And now—she was an intruder, uninvited, undesired. As at the Ritz on the day of her arrival, she felt that at any instant her mask would be torn from her and she would be exposed as a pretender to the gaze of all the car.

"Tell me everything!" Ellen was saying. "Tell me what you've been doing. I didn't see you at any of the football games last fall."

This was by way of letting Yanci know that she had attended them herself.

The conductor was bellowing from the rear of the car, "Manhattan Transfer next stop!"

Yanci's cheeks burned with shame. She wondered what she had best do—meditating a confession, deciding against it, answering Ellen's chatter in frightened monosyllables—then, as with an ominous thunder of brakes the speed of the train began to slacken, she sprang on a despairing impulse to her feet.

"My heavens!" she cried. "I've forgotten my shoes! I've got to go back and get them."

Ellen reacted to this with annoying efficiency.

"I'll take your suitcase," she said quickly, "and you can call for it. I'll be at the Charter Club."

"No!" Yanci almost shrieked. "It's got my dress in it!"

Ignoring the lack of logic in her own remark, she swung the suitcase off the rack with what seemed to her a superhuman effort and went reeling down the aisle, stared at curiously by the arrogant eyes of many girls. When she reached the platform just as the train came to a stop she felt weak and shaken. She stood on the hard cement which marks the quaint old village of Manhattan Transfer and tears were streaming down her cheeks as she watched the unfeeling cars speed off to Princeton with their burden of happy youth.

After half an hour's wait Yanci got on a train and returned to New York. In thirty minutes she had lost the confidence that a week had gained for her. She came back to her little room and lay down quietly upon the bed.

By Friday Yanci's spirits had partly recovered from their chill depression. Scott's voice over the telephone in midmorning was like a tonic, and she told him of the delights of Princeton with convincing enthusiasm, drawing vicariously upon a prom she had attended there two years before. He was anxious to see her, he said. Would she come to dinner and the theater that night? Yanci considered, greatly tempted. Dinner—she had been economizing on meals, and a gorgeous dinner in some extravagant show place followed by a musical comedy appealed to her starved fancy, indeed; but instinct told her that the time was not yet right. Let him wait. Let him dream a little more, a little longer.

"I'm too tired, Scott," she said with an air of extreme frankness; "that's the whole truth of the matter. I've been out every night since I've been here, and I'm really half dead. I'll rest up on this house party over the week-end and then I'll go to dinner with you any day you want me."

There was a minute's silence while she held the phone expectantly.

"Lot of resting up you'll do on a house party," he replied; "and, anyway, next week is so far off. I'm awfully anxious to see you, Yanci."

"So am I, Scott."

She allowed the faintest caress to linger on his name. When she had hung up she felt happy again. Despite her humiliation on the train her plan had been a success. The illusion was still intact; it was nearly complete. And in three meetings and half a dozen telephone calls she had managed to create a tenser atmosphere between them than if he had seen her constantly in the moods and avowals and beguilements of an out-and-out flirtation.

When Monday came she paid her first week's hotel bill. The size of it did not alarm her—she was prepared for that—but the shock of seeing so much money go, of realizing that there remained only one hundred and twenty dollars of her father's present, gave her a peculiar sinking sensation in the pit of her stomach. She decided to bring guile to bear immediately, to tantalize Scott by a carefully planned incident, and then at the end of the week to show him simply and definitely that she loved him.

As a decoy for Scott's tantalization she located by telephone a certain Jimmy Long, a handsome boy with whom she had played as a little girl and who had recently come to New York to work. Jimmy Long was deftly maneuvered into asking her to go to a matinee with him on Wednesday afternoon. He was to meet her in the lobby at two.

On Wednesday she lunched with Scott. His eyes followed her every motion, and knowing this she felt a great rush of tenderness toward him. Desiring at first only what he represented, she had begun half unconsciously to desire him also. Nevertheless, she did not permit herself the slightest relaxation on that account. The time was too short and the odds too great. That she was beginning to love him only fortified her resolve.

"Where are you going this afternoon?" he demanded.

"To a matinee—with an annoying man."

"Why is he annoying?"

"Because he wants me to marry him and I don't believe I want to."

There was just the faintest emphasis on the word "believe." The implication was that she was not sure—that is, not quite.

"Don't marry him."

"I won't—probably."

"Yanci," he said in a low voice, "do you remember a night on that boulevard?

She changed the subject. It was noon and the room was full of sunlight. It was not quite the place, the time. When he spoke she must have every aspect of the situation in control. He must say only what she wanted said; nothing else would do.

"It's five minutes to two," she told him, looking at her wristwatch. " We'd better go. I've got to keep my date."

"Do you want to go?"

"No, she answered simply.

This seemed to satisfy him, and they walked out to the lobby. Then Yanci caught sight of a man waiting there, obviously ill at ease and dressed as no habitué of the Ritz ever was. The man was Jimmy Long, not long since a favored beau of his Western city. And now—his hat was green, actually! His coat, seasons old, was quite evidently the product of a well-known ready-made concern. His shoes, long and narrow, turned up at the toes. From head to foot everything that could possibly he wrong about him was wrong. He was embarrassed by instinct only, unconscious of his gaucherie, an obscene specter, a Nemesis, a horror.

"Hello, Yanci!" he cried, starting toward her with evident relief.

With a heroic effort Yanci turned to Scott, trying to hold his glance to herself. In the very act of turning she noticed the impeccability of Scott's coat, his tie.

"Thanks for luncheon," she said with a radiant smile. "See you to-morrow."

Then she dived rather than ran for Jimmy Long, disposed of his outstretched hand and bundled him bumping through the revolving door with only a quick "Let's hurry!" to appease his somewhat sulky astonishment.

The incident worried her. She consoled herself by remembering that Scott had had only a momentary glance at the man, and that he had probably been looking at her anyhow. Nevertheless, she was horrified, and it is to be doubted whether Jimmy Long enjoyed her company enough to compensate him for the cut-price, twentieth-row tickets he had obtained at Black's Drug Store.

But if Jimmy as a decoy had proved a lamentable failure, an occurrence of Thursday offered her considerable satisfaction and paid tribute to her quickness of mind. She had invented an engagement for luncheon, and Scott was going to meet her at two o'clock to take her to the Hippodrome. She lunched alone somewhat imprudently in the Ritz dining room and sauntered out almost side by side with a good-looking young man who had been at the table next to her. She expected to meet Scott in the outer lobby, but as she reached the entrance to the restaurant she saw him standing not far away.

On a lightning impulse she turned to the good-looking man abreast of her, bowed sweetly and said in an audible, friendly voice, " Well, I'll see you later." Then before he could even register astonishment she faced about quickly and joined Scott.

"Who was that?" he asked, frowning.

"Isn't he darling looking?"

"If you like that sort of looks."

Scott's tone implied that the gentleman referred to was effete and overdressed. Yanci laughed, impersonally admiring the skillfulness of her ruse. It was in preparation for that all-important Saturday night that on Thursday she went into a shop on Forty-second Street to buy some long gloves. She made her purchase and handed the clerk a fifty-dollar bill so that her lightened pocketbook would feel heavier with the change she could put in. To her surprise the clerk tendered her the package and a twenty-five-cent piece.

"Is there anything else?"

"The rest of my change."

"You've got it. You gave me five dollars. Four-seventy-five for the gloves leaves twenty-five cents."

"I gave you fifty dollars."

"You must be mistaken."

Yanci searched her purse.

"I gave you fifty!" she repeated frantically.

"No, ma'am, I saw it myself."

They glared at each other in hot irritation. A cash girl was called to testify, then the floor manager; a small crowd gathered.

"Why, I'm perfectly sure !" cried Yanci, two angry tears trembling in her eyes. "I'm positive!"

The floor manager was sorry, but the lady really must have

left it at home. There was no fifty-dollar bill in the cash drawer. The bottom was creaking out of Yanci's rickety world.

"If you'll leave your address," said the floor manager, "I'll let you know if anything turns up."

"Oh, you damn fools!" cried Yanci, losing control. "I'll get the police!"

And weeping like a child she left the shop. Outside, helplessness overpowered her. How could she prove anything? It was after six and the store was closing even as she left it. Whichever employee had the fifty-dollar bill would be on her way home now before the police could arrive, and why should the New York police believe her, or even give her fair play?

In despair she returned to the Ritz, where she searched through her trunk for the bill with hopeless and mechanical gestures.

The Floor Manager Was Sorry, But the Lady Really Must Have Left it at Home. There Was No Fifty-Dollar Bill in the Cash Drawer

It was not there. She had known it would not be there. She gathered every penny together and found that she had fifty-one dollars and thirty cents. Telephoning the office, she asked that her bill be made out up to the following noon—she was too dispirited to think of leaving before then.

She waited in her room, not daring even to send for ice water. Then the phone rang and she heard the room clerk's voice, cheerful and metallic.

"Miss Bowman?"

"Yes."

"Your bill, including tonight, is exactly fifty-one twenty."

"Fifty-one twenty?" Her voice was trembling.

"Yes, ma'am."

"Thank you very much."

Breathless, she sat there beside the telephone, too frightened now to cry. She had ten cents left in the world!

Friday. She had scarcely slept. There were dark rings under her eyes, and even a hot bath followed by a cold one failed to arouse her from a despairing lethargy. She had never fully realized what it would mean to be without money in New York; her determination and vitality seemed to have vanished at last with her fifty-dollar bill. There was no help for it now—she must attain her desire today or never.

She was to meet Scott at the Plaza for tea. She wondered— was it her imagination, or had his manner been consciously cool the afternoon before? For the first time in several days she had needed to make no effort to keep the conversation from growing sentimental. Suppose he had decided that it must come to nothing—that she was too extravagant, too frivolous. A hundred eventualities presented themselves to her during the morning—a dreary morning, broken only by her purchase of a ten-cent bun at a grocery store.

It was her first food in twenty hours, but she self-consciously pretended to the grocer to be having an amusing and facetious time in buying one bun. She even asked to see his grapes, but told him, after looking at them appraisingly—and hungrily—that she didn't think she'd buy any. They didn't look ripe to her, she said. The store was full of prosperous women who, with thumb and first finger joined and held high in front of them, were inspecting food. Yanci would have liked to ask one of them for a bunch of grapes. Instead she went up to her room in the hotel and ate her bun.

When four o'clock came she found that she was thinking more about the sandwiches she would have for tea than of what else must occur there, and as she walked slowly up Fifth Avenue toward the Plaza she felt a sudden faintness which she took several deep

She Went Up to Her Room in the Most Fashionable Hotel in New York and Ate Her Bun

breaths of air to overcome. She wondered vaguely where the bread line was. That was where people in her condition should go—but where was it? How did one find out? She imagined fantastically that it was in the phone book under B, or perhaps under N, for New York Bread Line.

She reached the Plaza. Scott's figure, as he stood waiting for her in the crowded lobby, was a personification of solidity and hope.

"Let's hurry!" she cried with a tortured smile. "I feel rather punk and I want some tea."

She ate a club sandwich, some chocolate ice cream and six tea biscuits. She could have eaten much more, but she dared not. The eventuality of her hunger having been disposed of, she must turn at bay now and face this business of life, represented by the handsome young man who sat opposite watching her with some emotion whose import she could not determine just behind his level eyes.

But the words, the glance, subtle, pervasive and sweet, that she had planned, failed somehow to come.

"Oh, Scott," she said in a low voice, "I'm so tired."

"Tired of what?" he asked coolly.

" Of—everything."

There was a silence.

"I'm afraid," she said uncertainly—"I'm afraid I won't be able to keep that date with you tomorrow."

There was no pretense in her voice now. The emotion was apparent in the waiver of each word, without intention or control.

"I'm going away."

"Are you? Where?"

His tone showed a strong interest, but she winced as she saw that that was all.

"My aunt's come back. She wants me to join her in Florida right away."

"Isn't this rather unexpected?"

"Yes."

"You'll be coming back soon?" he said after a moment.

"I don't think so. I think we'll go to Europe from—from New Orleans."

"Oh!"

Again there was a pause. It lengthened. In the shadow of a moment it would become awkward, she knew. She had lost—well? Yet, she would go on to the end.

"Will you miss me?"

"Yes."

One word. She caught his eyes, wondered for a moment if she saw more there than kindly interest; then she dropped her own again.

"I like it—here at the Plaza," she heard herself saying. They spoke of things like that.

Afterwards she could never remember what they said. They spoke—even of the tea, of the thaw that was ended and the cold coming down outside. She was sick at heart and she seemed to herself very old. She rose at last.

"I've got to tear," she said. "I'm going out to dinner."

To the last she would keep on—the illusion, that was the important thing. To hold her proud lies inviolate—there was only a moment now. They walked toward the door.

"Put me in a taxi," she said quietly. "I don't feel equal to walking."

He helped her in. They shook hands.

"Good-by, Scott," she said.

"Good-by, Yanci," he answered slowly.

"You've been awfully nice to me. I'll always remember what a good time you helped to give me this two weeks."

"The pleasure was mine. Shall I tell the driver the Ritz?"

"No. Just tell him to drive out Fifth. I'll tap on the glass when I want him to stop."

Out Fifth! He would think, perhaps, that she was dining on Fifth. What an appropriate finish that would be! She wondered if he were impressed. She could not see his face clearly, because the air was dark with the snow and her own eyes were blurred by tears.

"Good-by," he said simply.

He seemed to realize that any pretense of sorrow on his part would be transparent.

She knew that he did not want her.

The door slammed, the car started, skidding in the snowy street. Yanci leaned back dismally in the corner.

Try as she might, she could not see where she had failed or what it was that had changed his attitude toward her. For the first time in her life she had ostensibly offered herself to a man—and he had not wanted her. The precariousness of her position paled beside the tragedy of her defeat.

She let the car go on—the cold air was what she needed, of course. Ten minutes had slipped away drearily before she realized that she had not a penny with which to pay the driver.

"It doesn't matter," she thought. "They'll just send me to jail, and that's a place to sleep."

She began thinking of the taxi driver.

"He'll be mad when he finds out, poor man. Maybe he's very poor, and he'll have to pay the fare himself." With a vague sentimentality she began to cry.

"Poor taxi man," she was saying half aloud. "Oh, people have such a hard time—such a hard time!"

She rapped on the window and when the car drew up at a curb she got out. She was at the end of Fifth Avenue and it was dark and cold.

"Send for the police!" she cried in a quick low voice. "I haven't any money!"

The taxi man scowled down at her. "Then what'd you get in for?"

She had not noticed that another car had stopped about twenty-five feet behind them. She heard running footsteps in the snow and then a voice at her elbow.

"It's all right," someone was saying to the taxi man. "I've got it right here.'

A bill was passed up. Yanci slumped sideways against Scott's overcoat.

Scott knew—he knew because he had gone to Princeton to surprise her, because the stranger she had spoken to in the Ritz had been his best friend, because the check of her father's for three hundred dollars had been returned to him marked "No funds." Scott knew—he had known for days.

But he said nothing; only stood there holding her with one arm as her taxi drove away.

"Oh, it's you," said Yanci faintly. "Lucky you came along. I left my purse back at the Ritz, like an awful fool. I do such ridiculous things —"

Scott laughed with some enjoyment. There was a light snow falling, and lest she should slip in the damp he picked her up and carried her back toward his waiting taxi.

"Such ridiculous things," she repeated.

"Go to the Ritz first," he said to the driver. "I want to get a trunk."

Appendix One
PAGES OF THE SATURDAY EVENING POST

16   THE SATURDAY EVENING POST   February 21, 192

HEAD AND SHOULDERS

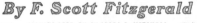

By F. Scott Fitzgerald

ILLUSTRATED BY CHARLES D. MITCHELL

IN 1915 Horace Tarbox was thirteen years old. In that year he took the examinations for entrance to Princeton University and received the Grade A—excellent—in Cæsar, Cicero, Vergil, Xenophon, Homer, Algebra, Plane Geometry, Solid Geometry and Chemistry.

Two years later, while George M. Cohan was composing Over There, Horace was leading the sophomore class by several lengths and digging out theses on The Syllogism as an Obsolete Scholastic Form, and during the Battle of Château-Thierry he was sitting at his desk deciding whether or not to wait until his seventeenth birthday before beginning his series of essays on The Pragmatic Bias of the New Realists.

After a while some newsboy told him that the war was over, and he was glad, because it meant that Peat Brothers, publishers, would get out their new edition of Spinoza's Improvement of the Understanding. Wars were all very well in their way, made young men self-reliant or something, but Horace felt that he could never forgive the President for allowing a brass band to play under his window on the night of the false Armistice, causing him to leave three important sentences out of his thesis on German Idealism.

The next year he went up to Yale to take his degree as Master of Arts.

He was seventeen then, tall and slender, with near-sighted gray eyes and an air of keeping himself utterly detached from the mere words he let drop.

"I never feel as though I'm talking to him," expostulated Professor Dillinger to a sympathetic colleague. "He makes me feel as though I were talking to his representative. I always expect him to say, 'Well, I'll ask myself and find out.'"

And then, just as nonchalantly as though Horace Tarbox had been Mr. Beef the butcher or Mr. Hat the haberdasher, life reached in, seized him, handled him, stretched him and unrolled him like a piece of Irish lace on a Saturday-afternoon bargain counter.

To move in the literary fashion I should say that this was all because when way back in colonial days the hardy pioneers had come to a bald place in Connecticut and asked of each other, "Now what shall we build here?" the hardiest one among 'em had answered, "Let's build a town where theatrical managers can try out musical comedies!" How afterward they founded Yale College there, to try the musical comedies on, is a story everyone knows. At any rate one December, Home James opened at the Shubert and all the students encored Marcia Meadow, who sang a song about the Blundering Blimp in the first act and did a shaky, shivery, celebrated dance in the last.

Marcia was nineteen. She didn't have wings, but audiences agreed generally that she didn't need them. She was a blonde by natural pigment and she wore no paint on the streets at high noon. Outside of that she was no better than most women.

It was Charlie Moon who promised her five thousand cigarettes if she would pay a call on Horace Tarbox, prodigy extraordinary. Charlie was a senior in Sheffield and he and Horace were first cousins. They liked and pitied each other.

Horace had been particularly busy that night. The failure of the Frenchman, Laurier, to synchronize the sources of the new realists was preying on his mind. In fact, his only reaction to a low, clear-cut rap at his study was to make him speculate as to whether any rap would have actual existence without an ear there to hear it. He fancied he was verging more and more toward pragmatism. But at that moment, though he did not know it, he was verging with astounding rapidity toward something quite different.

The rap sounded—three seconds leaked by—the rap sounded.

"Come in," muttered Horace automatically.

He heard the door open and then close, but, bent over his book in the big armchair before the fire, he did not look up.

"Leave it on the bed in the other room," he said absently.

"Leave what on the bed in the other room?"

Marcia Meadow had to talk her songs, but her speaking voice was like byplay on a harp.

"The laundry."

"I can't."

Horace stirred impatiently in his chair.

"Why can't you?"

"Why, because I haven't got it."

"H'm!" he replied testily. "Suppose you go back and get it."

Across the fire from Horace was another easy chair. He was accustomed to change to it in the course of an evening by way of exercise and variety. One chair he called

Berkeley, the other he called Hume. He su ̣ denly heard a sound as of a rustling, diaphano ̣ form sinking into Hume. He glanced up.

"Well," said Marcia with the sweet smile she used Act Two—"Oh, so the Duke liked my dancing!"

"Well, Omar Khayyám, here I am beside you singi ̣ in the wilderness."

Horace stared at her dazedly. The momentary suspici ̣ came to him that she existed there only as a phantom of ̣ imagination. Women didn't come into men's rooms a ̣ sink into men's Humes. Women brought laundry and to ̣ your seat in the street car and married you later on whe ̣ you were old enough to know fetters.

This woman had clearly materialized out of Hur ̣ Why, the very froth of her brown gauzy dress was ̣ emanation from Hume's leather arm there! If he look ̣ long enough he would see Hume right through her a ̣ then he would be alone again in the room. He passed h ̣ fist across his eyes. He really must take up those trape ̣ exercises again.

"For Pete's sake don't look so critical!" objected t ̣ emanation pleasantly. "I feel as if you were going to w ̣ me away with that patent dome of yours. And then the ̣ wouldn't be anything left of me except my shadow in yo ̣ eyes."

Horace coughed. Coughing was one of his two gestur ̣ When he talked then he forgot he had a body at all. It w ̣ like hearing a phonograph record by a singer who had be ̣ dead a long time.

"What do you want?" he asked.

"I want them letters," whined Marcia melodrama ̣ cally—"them letters of mine you bought from my gra ̣ sire in 1881."

Horace considered.

"I haven't got your letters," he said evenly. "I ̣ only seventeen years old. My father was not born un ̣ March 3, 1879. You evidently have me confused w ̣ someone else."

"You're only seventeen?" repeated Marcia suspiciou ̣

"Only seventeen."

"I knew a girl," said Marcia reminiscently, "who we ̣ on the ten-twenty-thirty when she was sixteen. She wa ̣ stuck on herself that she could never say 'sixteen' witho ̣ putting the 'only' before it. We got to calling her 'O ̣ Jessie.' And she's just where she was when she starte ̣ only worse. 'Only' is a bad habit, Omar—it sounds like ̣ alibi."

"My name is not Omar."

"I know," agreed Marcia, nodding—"your nam ̣ Horace. I just call you Omar because you remind ̣ of a smoked cigarette."

"And I haven't your letters. I doubt if I've ever ̣ your grandfather. In fact, I think it very improbable t ̣ you yourself were alive in 1881."

Marcia stared at him in wonder.

"Me—1881? Why sure! I was second-line stuff w ̣ the Florodora Sextette was still in the convent. I was ̣ original nurse to Mrs. Sol Smith's Juliette. Why, Oma ̣ was a canteen singer during the War of 1812."

Horace's mind made a sudden successful leap and smiled.

"Did Charlie Moon put you up to this?"

Marcia regarded him inscrutably.

"Who's Charlie Moon?"

"Small—wide nostrils—big ears."

She grew several inches and sniffed.

"I'm not in the habit of noticing my friends' nostrils."

"Then it was Charlie?"

Marcia bit her lip—and then yawned.

"Oh, let's change the subject, Omar. I'll pull a sno ̣ in this chair in a minute."

"Yes," replied Horace gravely, "Hume has often be ̣ considered soporific."

"Who's your friend—and will he die?"

Then of a sudden Horace Tarbox rose slenderly and ̣ gan to pace the room with his hands in his pockets. ̣ was his other gesture.

"I don't care for this," he said as if he were talking ̣ himself—"at all. Not that I mind your being here ̣ don't. You're quite a pretty little thing, but I don't ̣ Charlie Moon's sending you up here. Am I a laborat ̣ experiment on which the janitors as well as the chem ̣ can make experiments? Is my intellectual developm ̣ humorous in any way? Do I look like the pictures of ̣ little Boston boy in the comic magazines? Has that caf ̣ ass, Moon, with his eternal tales about his week in Pa ̣ any right to——"

"No!" interrupted Marcia emphatically. "And you ̣ sweet boy. Come here and kiss me."

Horace stopped quickly in front of her.

"Why do you want me to kiss you?" he asked inten ̣ "Do you just go round kissing people?"

"I Hope I Haven't Given You the Impression That I Consider Kissing Intrinsically Irrational"

"Why, yes," said Marcia, unruffled. "'At's all life is. Just going round kissing people."

"Well," replied Horace emphatically, "I must say your ideas are horribly garbled! In the first place life isn't just that, and in the second place I won't kiss you. It might get to be a habit and I can't get rid of habits. This year I've got in the habit of lolling in bed until even-thirty."

Marcia nodded understandingly.

"Do you ever have any fun?" she asked.

"What do you mean by fun?"

"See here," said Marcia sternly, "I like you, Omar, but I wish you'd talk as if you had a line on what you were saying. You sound as if you were gargling a lot of words in your mouth and lost a bet every time you spilled a few. I asked you if you ever had any fun."

Horace shook his head.

"Later perhaps," he answered. "You see I'm a plan. I'm an experiment. I don't say that I don't get tired of it sometimes—I do. Yet—oh, I can't explain! But what you and Charlie Moon call fun wouldn't be fun to me."

"Please explain."

Horace stared at her, started to speak and then changing his mind resumed his walk. After an unsuccessful attempt to determine whether or not he was looking at her Marcia smiled at him.

"Please explain."

Horace turned.

"If I do, will you promise to tell Charlie Moon that I wasn't in?"

"Uh-uh."

"Very well then. Here's my history: I was a 'why' child. I wanted to see the wheels go round. My father was a young economics professor at Princeton. He brought me up on the system of answering every question I asked him to the best of his ability. My response to that gave him the idea of making an experiment in precocity. To aid in the massacre I had ear trouble—seven operations between the ages of nine and twelve. Of course this kept me apart from other boys and made me ripe for forcing. Anyway, while my generation was boring through Uncle Remus I was honestly enjoying Catullus in the original.

"I passed off my college examinations when I was thirteen because I couldn't help it. My chief associates were professors and I took a tremendous pride in knowing that I had a fine intelligence, for though I was unusually precocious I was not abnormal in other ways. When I was sixteen I got tired of being a freak; I decided that some one had made a bad mistake. Still as I gone that far I concluded to finish up by taking my degree of Master of Arts. My chief interest in life is the study of modern philosophy. I am a realist of the School of Anton Laurier—with Bergsonian trimmings—and I'll be eighteen years old in two months. That's all."

"Whew!" exclaimed Marcia. "That's enough! You do neat job with the parts of speech."

"Satisfied?"

"No, you haven't kissed me."

"It's not in my program," demurred Horace. "Understand that I don't pretend to be above physical things, they have their place, but——"

"Oh, don't be so darned reasonable!"

"I can't help it."

"I hate these slot-machine people."

"I assure you I——" began Horace.

"Oh, shut up!"

"My own rationality——"

"I didn't say anything about your nationality. You're Amuricun, ar'n't you?"

"Yes."

"Well, that's O. K. with me. I got a notion I want to you do something that isn't in your highbrow program. want to see if a what-ch-call-em with Brazilian trimmings—that thing you said you were—can be a little human."

Horace shook his head again.

"I won't kiss you."

"My life is blighted," muttered Marcia tragically. "I'm a beaten woman. I'll go through life without ever having been kissed with Brazilian trimmings." She sighed. "Anyways, Omar, will you come and see my show?"

"What show?"

"I'm a wicked actress from Home James!"

"Light opera?"

"Yes—at a stretch. One of the characters is a Brazilian rice planter. That might interest you."

"I saw The Bohemian Girl once," reflected Horace aloud. "I enjoyed it—to some extent."

"Then you'll come?"

"Well, I'm—I'm ——"

"Oh, I know—you've got to run down to Brazil for the week-end."

"Not at all. I'd be delighted to come."

Marcia clapped her hands.

"Goody for you! I'll mail you a ticket—Thursday night?"

"Why, I ——"

"Good! Thursday night it is."

She stood up and walking close to him laid both hands on his shoulders.

"I like you, Omar. I'm sorry I tried to kid you. I thought you'd be sort of frozen, but you're a nice boy."

He eyed her sardonically.

"I'm several thousand generations older than you are."

"You carry your age well."

They shook hands gravely.

"My name's Marcia Meadow," she said emphatically. "Member it—Marcia Meadow. And I won't tell Charlie Moon you were in."

An instant later as she was skimming down the last flight of stairs three at a time she heard a voice call over the upper banister, "Oh, say ——"

She stopped and looked up—made out a vague form leaning over.

"Oh, say!" called the prodigy again. "Can you hear me?"

"Here's your connection, Omar."

"I hope I haven't given you the impression that I consider kissing intrinsically irrational."

"Impression? Why, you didn't even give me the kiss! Never fret—so long."

Two doors near her opened curiously at the sound of a feminine voice. A tentative cough sounded from above. Gathering her skirts, Marcia dived wildly down the last flight and was swallowed up in the murky Connecticut air outside.

Upstairs Horace paced the floor of his study. From time to time he glanced toward Berkeley waiting there in suave dark-red respectability, an open book lying suggestively on his cushions. And then he found that his circuit of the floor was bringing him each time nearer to Hume. There was something about Hume that was strangely and inexplicably different. The diaphanous form still seemed hovering near and had Horace sat there he would have felt as if he were sitting on a lady's lap. And though Horace couldn't have named the quality of difference, there was such a quality—quite intangible to the speculative mind, but real nevertheless. Hume was radiating something that in all the two hundred years of his influence he had never radiated before.

Hume was radiating attar of roses.

II

ON THURSDAY night Horace Tarbox sat in an aisle seat in the fifth row and witnessed Home James. Oddly enough he found that he was enjoying himself. The cynical students near him were annoyed at his audible appreciation of time-honored jokes in the Hammerstein tradition. But Horace was waiting with anxiety for Marcia Meadow singing her song about a Jazz-bound Blundering Blimp. When she did appear, radiant under a floppity flower-faced hat, a warm glow settled over him, and when the song was over he did not join in the storm of applause. He felt somewhat numb.

In the intermission after the second act an usher materialized beside him, demanded to know if he were Mr. Tarbox and then handed him a note written in a round adolescent hand. Horace read it in some confusion, while the usher lingered with withering patience in the aisle.

Dear Omar: After the show I always grow an awful hunger. If you want to satisfy it for me in the Taft Grill just communicate your answer to the big-timber guide that brought this and oblige.   Your friend,
MARCIA MEADOW.

"Tell her"—he coughed—"tell her that it will be quite all right. I'll meet her in front of the theater."

The big-timber guide smiled arrogantly.

"I giss she meant for you to come roun' t' the stage door."

"Where—where is it?"

"Ou'side. Tunayulef. Down ee alley."

"What?"

"Ou'side. Turn to y'left! Down ee alley!"

The arrogant person withdrew. A freshman behind Horace snickered.

Then half an hour later, sitting in the Taft Grill opposite the hair that was yellow by natural pigment, the prodigy was saying an odd thing.

"Do you have to do that dance in the last act?" he was asking earnestly—"I mean, would they dismiss you if you refused to do it?"

Marcia grinned.

"It's fun to do it. I like to do it."

And then Horace came out with a faux pas.

"I should think you'd detest it," he remarked succinctly.

"The people behind me were making remarks about your bosom."

Marcia blushed fiery red.

(Continued on Page 81)

"What Do They Expect for a Hundred a Week—Perpetual Motion?" She Grumbled to Herself in the Wings

THE SATURDAY EVENING POST

HEAD AND SHOULDERS

(Continued from Page 17)

"I can't help that," she said quickly. "The dance to me is only a sort of acrobatic stunt. Lord, it's hard enough to do! I rub liniment into my shoulders for an hour every night."

"Do you have—fun while you're on the stage?"

"Uh-huh—sure! I got in the habit of having people look at me, Omar, and I like it."

"H'm!" Horace sank into a brownish study.

"How's the Brazilian trimmings?"

"H'm!" repeated Horace, and then after a pause—"Where does the play go from here?"

"New York."

"For how long?"

"All depends. Winter—maybe."

"Oh!"

"Coming up to lay eyes on me, Omar, or aren't you int'rested? Not as nice here, is it, as it was up in your room? I wish we was there now."

"I feel idiotic in this place," confessed Horace, looking round him nervously.

"Too bad! We got along pretty well."

At this he looked suddenly so melancholy that she changed her tone and reaching over patted his hand.

"Ever take an actress out to supper before?"

"No," said Horace miserably, "and I never will again. I don't know why I came to-night. Here under all these lights and with all these people laughing and chattering I feel completely out of my sphere. I don't know what to talk to you about."

"We'll talk about me. We talked about you last time."

"Very well."

"Well, my name really is Meadow, but my first name isn't Marcia—it's Veronica. I'm nineteen. Question—how did the girl make her leap to the footlights? Answer—she was born in Passaic, New Jersey, and up to a year ago she got the right to breathe by pushing biscuits in Marcel's tea room in Trenton. She started going with a guy named Robbins, a singer in the Trent House cabaret, and he got her to try a song and dance with him one evening. In a month we were filling the supper room every night. Then we went to New York with meet-my-friend letters thick as a pile of napkins.

"In two days we'd landed a job at Divinerries' and I learned to shimmy from a kid at the Palais Royal. We stayed at Divinerries' six months until one night Peter Boyce Wendell, the columnist, ate his milk toast there. Next morning a poem about Marvelous Marcia came out in his newspaper and within two days I had three vaudeville offers and a chance at the Midnight Frolic. I wrote Wendell a thank-you letter and he printed it in his column—said that the style was like Carlyle's, only more rugged, and that I ought to quit dancing

and do North American literature. This got me a coupla more vaudeville offers and a chance as an ingénue in a regular show. I took it—and here I am, Omar."

When she finished they sat for a moment in silence, she draping the last skeins of a Welsh rabbit on her fork and waiting for him to speak.

"Let's get out of here," he said suddenly. Marcia's eyes hardened.

"What's the idea? Am I making you sick?"

"No, but I don't like it here. I don't like to be sitting here with you."

Without another word Marcia signaled for the waiter.

"What's the check?" she demanded briskly. "My part—the rabbit and the ginger ale."

Horace watched blankly as the waiter figured it.

"See here," he began, "I intended to pay for yours too. You're my guest."

With a half sigh Marcia rose from the table and walked from the room. Horace, his face a document in bewilderment, laid a bill down and followed her out, up the stairs and into the lobby. He overtook her in front of the elevator and they faced each other.

"See here," he repeated, "you're my guest. Have I said something to offend you?"

After an instant of wonder Marcia's eyes softened.

"You're a rude fella," she said slowly. "Don't you know you're rude?"

"I can't help it," said Horace with a directness she found quite disarming. "You know I like you."

"You said you didn't like being with me."

"I didn't like it."

"Why not?"

Fire blazed suddenly from the gray forests of his eyes.

"Because I didn't. I've formed the habit of liking you. I've been thinking of nothing much else for two days."

"Well, if you——"

"Wait a minute," he interrupted. "I've got something to say. It's this: in six weeks I'll be eighteen years old. When I'm eighteen years old I'm coming up to New York to see you. Is there some place in New York where we can go and not have a lot of people in the room?"

"Sure!" smiled Marcia. "You can come up to my 'partment. Sleep on the couch if you want to."

"I can't sleep on couches," he said shortly. "But I want to talk to you."

"Why sure," repeated Marcia—"in my 'partment."

In his excitement Horace put his hands in his pockets.

"All right—just so I can see you alone. I want to talk to you as we talked up in my room."

"Honey boy," cried Marcia laughing, "is it that you want to kiss me?"

"Yes," Horace almost shouted, "I'll kiss you if you want me to."

The elevator man was looking at them reproachfully. Marcia edged toward the grated door.

"I'll drop you a post card," she said.

Horace's eyes were quite wild.

"Send me a post card! I'll come up any time after January first. I'll be eighteen then."

And as she stepped into the elevator he coughed enigmatically, yet with a vague challenge, at the ceiling, and walked quickly away.

III

HE WAS there again. She saw him when she took her first glance at the restless Manhattan audience—down in the front row with his head bent a bit forward and his gray eyes fixed on her. And she knew that to him they were alone together in a world where the high-rouged row of ballet faces and the massed whines of the violins were as imperceivable as powder on a marble Venus. An instinctive defiance rose within her.

"Silly boy!" she said to herself hurriedly and she didn't take her encore.

"What do they expect for a hundred a week—perpetual motion?" she grumbled to herself in the wings.

"What's the trouble, Marcia?"

"Guy I don't like down in front."

During the last act as she waited for her specialty she had an odd attack of stage fright. She had never sent Horace the promised post card. Last night she had pretended not to see him—had hurried from the theater immediately after her dance to pass a sleepless night in her apartment, thinking—as she had so often in the last month—of his pale, rather intent face, his slim, boyish figure, the merciless, unworldly abstraction that made him charming to her.

And now that he had come she felt vaguely sorry—as though an unwonted responsibility was being forced on her.

"Infant prodigy!" she said aloud.

"What?" demanded the negro comedian standing beside her.

"Nothing—just talking about myself."

On the stage she felt better. This was her dance—and she always felt that the way she did it wasn't suggestive any more than to some men every pretty girl is suggestive. She made it a stunt.

Uptown, downtown, jelly on a spoon,
After sundown shiver by the moon.

He was not watching her now. She saw that clearly. He was looking very deliberately at a castle on the back drop, wearing that expression he had worn in the Taft Grill. A wave of exasperation swept over her—he was criticizing her.

That's the vibration that thr-ills me,
Funny how affection fi-ills me,
Uptown, downtown ——

Unconquerable revulsion seized her. She was suddenly and horribly conscious of herself. For a moment she had never been since her first appearance. Was that a leer on a pallid face in the front row, a droop of disgust on one young girl's mouth? These shoulders of hers—these shoulders shaking—were they hers? Were they real? Surely shoulders weren't made for this!

Then—you'll—see at a glance
I'll need some funeral ushers with St. Vitus dance
At the end of the world I'll ——

The bassoon and two cellos crashed into a final chord. She paused and poised a moment on her toes with every muscle tense, her young face looking out dully at the audience in what one young girl afterward called "such a curious, puzzled look" and then without bowing rushed from the stage. Into the dressing room she sped, kicked out of one dress and into another and caught a taxi outside.

Her apartment was very warm—small, it was, with a row of professional pictures and sets of Kipling and O. Henry which she had bought once from a blue-eyed agent and read occasionally. And there were several chairs which matched, but were none of them comfortable, and a pink-shaded lamp with blackbirds painted on it and an atmosphere of rather-stifled pink throughout. There were nice things in it—nice unrelentingly hostile to each other, springs of a vicarious, impatient taste acquired in stray moments.

The worst was typified by a great picture framed in oak bark of Passaic as seen from the Erie Railroad—altogether a frantic, oddly extravagant, oddly penurious attempt to make a cheerful room. Marcia knew it was a failure.

Into this room came the prodigy; he took her two hands awkwardly.

"I followed you this time," he said.

"Oh!"

"I want you to marry me," he said.

Her arms went out to him. She kissed his mouth with a sort of passionate whole someness.

"There!"

"I love you," he said.

She kissed him again and then with a little sigh flung herself into an armchair and lay there, shaken with absurd laughter.

"Why, you infant prodigy!" she cried.

"Very well, call me that if you want. I once told you that I was ten thousand years older than you—I am."

She laughed again.

"I don't like to be disapproved of."

"No one's ever going to approve of you again."

"Omar," she asked, "wh you want to marry me?"

"I Know," Agreed Marcia, Nodding—"Your Name's Horace. I Just Call You Omar Because You Remind Me of a Smoked Cigarette"

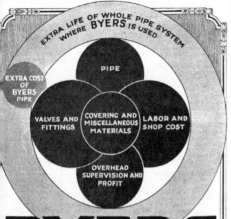
The prodigy rose and put his hands in his pockets.

"Because I love you, Marcia Meadow."

And then she stopped calling him Omar.

"Dear boy," she said, "you know I sort of love you. There's something about you—I can't tell what—that just puts my heart through the wringer every time I'm round you. But, honey ——" she paused.

"But what?"

"But lots of things. But you're only just eighteen and I'm nearly twenty."

"Nonsense!" he interrupted. "Put it this way—that I'm in my nineteenth year and you're nineteen. That makes us pretty close—without counting that other ten thousand years I mentioned."

Marcia laughed.

"But there are some more 'buts.' Your people ——"

"My people!" exclaimed the prodigy ferociously. "My people tried to make a monstrosity out of me." His face grew quite crimson at the enormity of what he was going to say. "My people can go way back and sit down!"

"My heavens!" cried Marcia in alarm. "All that? On tacks, I suppose."

"Tacks—yes," he agreed wildly—"on anything. The more I think of how they allowed me to become a little dried-up mummy ——"

"What makes you think you're that?" asked Marcia quietly—"me?"

"Yes, every person I've met on the streets since I met you has made me jealous because they knew what love was before I did. I used to call it the 'sex impulse.' Heavens!"

"There's more 'buts,'" said Marcia.

"What are they?"

"How could we live?"

"I'll make a living."

"You're in college."

"Do you think I care anything about taking a Master of Arts degree?"

"You want to be Master of Me, hey?"

"Yes! What? I mean, no!"

Marcia laughed, and crossing swiftly over sat in his lap. He put his arm round her wildly and implanted the vestige of a kiss somewhere near her neck.

"There's something white about you," mused Marcia, "but it doesn't sound very logical."

"Oh, don't be so darned reasonable!"

"I can't help it," said Marcia.

"I hate these slot-machine people!"

"But we ——"

"Oh, shut up!"

And as Marcia couldn't talk through her ears she had to.

IV

HORACE and Marcia were married early in February. The sensation in academic circles both at Yale and Princeton was tremendous. Horace Tarbox, who at fourteen had been played up in the Sunday magazine sections of metropolitan newspapers, was throwing over his career, his chance of being a world authority on American philosophy, by marrying a chorus girl—they made Marcia a chorus girl. But like all modern stories it was a four-and-a-half-day wonder.

They took a flat in Harlem. After two weeks' search, during which his idea of the value of academic knowledge faded unmercifully, Horace took a position as clerk with a South American export company—someone had told him that exporting was the coming thing. Marcia was to stay in her show for a few months—anyway until he got on his feet. He was getting a hundred and twenty-five to start with, and though of course they told him it was only a question of months until he would be earning double that, Marcia refused even to consider giving up the hundred and fifty a week that she was getting at the time.

"We'll call ourselves Head and Shoulders, dear," she said softly, "and the shoulders 'll have to keep shaking a little longer until the old head gets started."

"I hate it," he objected gloomily.

"Well," she replied emphatically, "your salary wouldn't keep us in a tenement. Don't think I want to be public—I don't. I want to be yours. But I'd be a half-wit to sit in one room and count the sunflowers on the wall pap.. while I waited for you. When you pull down three hundred a month I'll quit."

And much as it hurt his pride, Horace had to admit that hers was the wiser course.

March mellowed into April. May read a gorgeous riot act to the parks and waters of Manhattan and they were very happy. Horace, who had no habits whatsoever—he had never had time to form any—proved

the most adaptable of husbands, and as Marcia entirely lacked opinions on the subjects that engrossed him there were very few joltings and bumpings. Their minds moved in different spheres. Marcia acted as practical factotum and Horace lived either in his old world of abstract ideas or in a sort of triumphantly earthy worship and adoration of his wife. She was a continual source of astonishment to him—the freshness and originality of her mind, her dynamic, clear-headed energy and her unfailing good humor.

And Marcia's coworkers in the nine-o'clock show, whither she had transferred her talents, were impressed with her tremendous pride in her husband's mental powers. Horace they knew only as a very slim, tight-lipped and immature-looking young man who waited every night to take her home.

"Horace," said Marcia one evening when she met him as usual at eleven, "you looked like a ghost standing there against the street lights. You losing weight?"

He shook his head vaguely.

"I don't know. They raised me to a hundred and thirty-five to-day and ——"

"I don't care," said Marcia severely. "You're killing yourself working at night. You read those big books on economy ——"

"Economics," corrected Horace.

"Well, you read 'em every night long after I'm asleep. And you're getting all stooped over like you were before we married."

"But, Marcia, I've got to ——"

"No, you haven't, dear. I guess I'm running this shop for the present and I won't let my fella ruin his health and eyes. You got to get some exercise."

"I do. Every morning I ——"

"Oh, I know! But those dumb-bells of yours wouldn't give a consumptive two degrees of fever. I mean real exercise. You've got to join a gymnasium. 'Member you told me you were such a trick gymnast once that they tried to get you out for the team in college and they couldn't because you had a standing date with Herb Spencer?"

"I used to enjoy it," mused Horace, "but it would take up too much time now."

"All right," said Marcia. "I'll make a bargain with you. You join a gym and I'll read one of those books from the brown row of 'em."

"Pepys' Diary? Why, that ought to be enjoyable. He's very light."

"Not for me—he isn't. It'll be like digesting plate glass. But you've been telling me how much it'd broaden my lookout. Well, you go to a gym three nights a week and I'll take one big dose of Sammy."

Horace hesitated.

"Well ——"

"Come on now! You do some giant swings for me and I'll chase some culture for you."

So Horace finally consented and all through a baking summer he spent three and sometimes four evenings a week experimenting on the trapeze in Skipper's Gymnasium. And in August he admitted to Marcia that it made him capable of more mental work during the day.

"*Mens sana in corpore sano*," he said.

"Don't believe in it," replied Marcia. "I tried one of those patent medicines once and they're all bunk. You stick to gymnastics."

One night in early September while he was going through one of his contortions on the rings in the nearly deserted room he was addressed by a meditative fat man whom he had noticed watching him for several nights.

"Say, lad, do that stunt you were doin' last night."

Horace grinned at him from his perch.

"I invented it," he said. "I got the idea from the fourth proposition of Euclid."

"What circus he with?"

"He's dead."

"Well, he must of broke his neck doin' that stunt. I set here last night thinkin' sure you was goin' to break yours."

"Like this!" said Horace, and swinging onto the trapeze he did his stunt.

"Don't it kill your neck an' shoulder muscles?"

"It did at first, but inside of a week I wrote the *quod erat demonstrandum* on it."

"H'm!"

Horace swung idly on the trapeze.

"Ever think of takin' it up professionally?" asked the fat man.

"Not I."

(Continued on Page 85)

THE SATURDAY EVENING POST

(Continued from Page 82)

"Good money in it if you're willin' to do stunts like 'at an' can get away with it."

"Here's another," chirped Horace eagerly, and the fat man's mouth dropped suddenly agape as he watched this pink-jerseyed Prometheus again defy the gods and Isaac Newton.

The night following this encounter Horace got home from work to find a rather pale Marcia stretched out on the sofa waiting for him.

"I fainted twice to-day," she began without preliminaries.

"What?"

"Yep. You see baby's due in three months now. Doctor says I ought to have quit dancing two weeks ago."

Horace sat down and thought it over.

"I'm glad of course," he said pensively—"I mean glad that we're going to have a baby. But this means a lot of expense."

"I've got two hundred and fifty in the bank," said Marcia hopefully, "and two weeks' pay coming."

Horace computed quickly.

"Including my salary, that'll give us nearly fourteen hundred for the next six months."

Marcia looked blue.

"That all? Course I can get a job singing somewhere this month. And I can go to work again in March."

"Of course, nothing!" said Horace gruffly. "You'll stay right here. Let's see now—there'll be doctor's bills and a nurse, besides the maid. We've got to have some more money."

"Well," said Marcia wearily, "I don't know where it's coming from. It's up to the old head now. Shoulders is out of business."

Horace rose and pulled on his coat.

"Where are you going?"

"I've got an idea," he answered. "I'll be right back."

Ten minutes later as he headed down the street toward Skipper's Gymnasium he felt a placid wonder quite unmixed with humor at what he was going to do. How he would have gaped at himself a year before! How everyone would have gaped! But when you opened your door at the rap of life you let in many things.

The gymnasium was brightly lit and when his eyes became accustomed to the glare he found the meditative fat man seated on a pile of canvas mats smoking a big cigar.

"Say," began Horace directly, "were you in earnest last night when you said I could make money on my trapeze stunts?"

"Why, yes," said the fat man in surprise.

"Well, I've been thinking it over and I believe I'd like to try it. I could work at night and on Saturday afternoons—and regularly if the pay is high enough."

The fat man looked at his watch.

"Well," he said, "Charlie Paulson's the man to see. He'll book you inside of four days, once he sees you work out. He won't be in now, but I'll get hold of him for to-morrow night."

The fat man was as good as his word. Charlie Paulson arrived next night and put in a wondrous hour watching the prodigy swoop through the air in amazing parabolas and on the night following he brought two large men with him who looked as though they had been born smoking black cigars and talking about money in low passionate voices. Then on the succeeding Saturday Horace Tarbox's torso made its first professional appearance in a gymnastic exhibition at the Coleman Street Gardens. But though the audience numbered nearly five thousand people, Horace felt no nervousness.

From his childhood he had read papers to audiences—learned that trick of detaching himself.

"Marcia," he said cheerfully later that same night, "I think we're out of the woods. Paulson thinks he can get me an opening at the Hippodrome and that means an all-winter engagement. The Hippodrome, you know, is a big ——"

"Yes, I believe I've heard of it," interrupted Marcia, "but I want to know about this stunt you're doing. It isn't any spectacular suicide, is it?"

"It's nothing," said Horace quietly. "But if you can think of any nicer way of a man killing himself than taking a risk for you, why that's the way I want to die."

Marcia reached up and wound both arms tightly round his neck.

"Kiss me," she whispered, "and call me 'dear heart.' I love to hear you say 'dear heart.' And bring me the book to read to-morrow. No more Sam Pepys, but something trick and trashy. I've been wild for something to do all day. I felt like writing letters, but I didn't have anybody to write to."

"Write to me," said Horace. "I'll read them."

"I wish I could," breathed Marcia. "If I knew words enough I could write you the longest love letter in the world—and never get tired."

But after two more months Marcia grew very tired indeed and for a row of nights it was a very anxious, weary-looking young athlete who walked out before the Hippodrome crowd. Then there were two days when his place was taken by a young man who wore pale blue instead of white and got very little applause. But after the two days Horace appeared again, and those who sat close to the stage remarked an expression of beatific happiness on that young acrobat's face, even when he was twisting breathlessly in the air in the middle of his amazing and original shoulder swing. After that performance he laughed at the elevator man and dashed up the stairs to the flat five steps at a time—and then tiptoed very carefully into a quiet room.

"Marcia," he whispered.

"Hello!" She smiled up at him wanly. "Horace, there's something I want you to do. Look in my top bureau drawer and you'll find a big stack of paper. It's a book—sort of—Horace. I wrote it down in these last three months while I've been laid up. I wish you'd take it to that Peter Boyce Wendell, who put my letter in his paper. He could tell you whether it'd be a good book. I wrote it just the way I talk, just the way I wrote that letter to him. It's just a story about a lot of things that happened to me. Will you take it to him, Horace?"

"Yes, darling."

He leaned over the bed until his head was beside her on the pillow and began stroking back her yellow hair.

"Dearest Marcia," he said softly.

"No," she murmured, "call me what I told you to call me."

"Dear heart," he whispered passionately—"dearest, dearest heart."

"What'll we call her?"

They rested a minute in happy drowsy content, while Horace considered.

"We'll call her Marcia Hume Tarbox," he said at length.

"Why the Hume?"

"Because he's the fellow who first introduced us."

"That so?" she murmured, sleepily surprised. "I thought his name was Moon."

Her eyes closed and after a moment the slow, lengthening surge of the bedclothes over her breast showed that she was asleep.

Horace tiptoed over to the bureau and opening the top drawer found a heap of closely scrawled, lead-smeared pages. He looked at the first sheet:

SANDRA PEPYS, SYNCOPATED
By Marcia Tarbox

He smiled. So Samuel Pepys had made an impression on her after all. He turned a page and began to read. His smile deepened—he read on. Half an hour passed and he became aware that Marcia had waked and was watching him from the bed.

"Honey," came in a whisper.

"What, Marcia?"

"Do you like it?"

Horace coughed.

"I seem to be reading on. It's bright."

"Take it to Peter Boyce Wendell. Tell 'him you got the highest marks in Princeton once and that you ought to know when a book's good. Tell him this one's a world beater."

"All right, Marcia," said Horace gently.

Her eyes closed again and Horace crossing over kissed her forehead—stood there for a moment with a look of tender pity. Then he left the room.

All that night the sprawly writing on the pages, the constant mistakes in spelling and grammar and the weird punctuation danced before his eyes. He woke several times in the night, each time full of a welling chaotic sympathy for this desire of Marcia's soul to express itself in words. To him there was something infinitely pathetic about it, and for the first time in months he began to turn over in his mind some half-forgotten dreams.

He had meant to write a series of books, to popularize the new realism as Schopenhauer had popularized pessimism and William James pragmatism.

But life hadn't come that way. Life took hold of people and forced them into flying rings. He laughed to think of that rap at his door, the diaphanous shadow in Hume, Marcia's threatened kiss.

"And it's still me," he said aloud in wonder as he lay awake in the darkness. "I'm the man who sat in Berkeley with temerity to wonder if that rap would have had actual existence had my ear not been there to hear it. I'm still that man. I could be electrocuted for the crimes he committed.

"Poor gauzy souls trying to express ourselves in something tangible. Marcia with her written book; I with my unwritten ones. Trying to choose our mediums and then taking what we get—and being glad."

v

SANDRA PEPYS, SYNCOPATED, with an introduction by Peter Boyce Wendell, the columnist, appeared serially in Jordan's Magazine and came out in book form in March. From its first published installment it attracted attention far and wide. A trite enough subject—a girl from a small New Jersey town coming to New York to go on the stage—treated simply, with a peculiar vividness of phrasing and a haunting undertone of sadness in the very inadequacy of its vocabulary, it made an irresistible appeal.

Peter Boyce Wendell, who happened at that time to be advocating the enrichment of the American language by the immediate adoption of expressive vernacular words, stood as its sponsor and thundered his indorsement over the placid bromides of the conventional reviewers.

Marcia received three hundred dollars an installment for the serial publication, which came at an opportune time, for though Horace's monthly salary at the Hippodrome was now more than Marcia's had ever been, young Marcia was emitting shrill cries which interpreted as a demand for country air. So early April found them installed in a bungalow in Westchester County with a place for a lawn, a place for a garage and a place for everything, including a sound-proof impregnable study in which Marcia faithfully promised Mr. Jordan she would shut herself up when her daughter's demands began to be abated and compose immortally illiterate literature.

"It's not half bad," thought Horace one night as he was on his way from the station to his house. He was considering several prospects that had opened up, a four months' vaudeville offer in five figures, a chance to go back to Princeton in charge of all gymnasium work. Odd! He had once intended to go back there in charge of all philosophic work, and now he had not even been stirred by the arrival in New York of Anton Laurier, his old idol.

The gravel crunched raucously under his heel. He saw the lights of his sitting room gleaming and noticed a big car standing in the drive. Probably Mr. Jordan again, come to persuade Marcia to settle down to work.

She had heard the sound of his approach and her form was silhouetted against the lighted door as she came out to meet him.

"There's some Frenchman here," she whispered nervously. "I can't pronounce his name, but he sounds awful deep. You'll have to jaw with him."

"What Frenchman?"

"You can't prove it by me. He drove up an hour ago with Mr. Jordan and said he wanted to meet Sandra Pepys, and all that sort of thing."

Two men rose from chairs as they went inside.

"Hello, Tarbox," said Jordan. "I've just been bringing together two celebrities. M'sieur Laurier, let me present Mr. Tarbox, Mrs. Tarbox's husband."

"Not Anton Laurier!"

"But, yes. I must come. I have to come. I have read the book of madame and I have been charmed"—he fumbled in his pocket—"ah, I have read of you too. In this newspaper which I read to-day it has your name."

He finally produced a clipping from a magazine.

"Read it!" he said eagerly. "It has about you too."

Horace's eye skipped down the page.

"A distinct contribution to American dialect literature," it said. "No attempt at literary tone; the book derives its very quality from this fact, as did Huckleberry Finn."

Horace's eyes caught a passage lower down; he became suddenly aghast—read on hurriedly.

"Marcia Tarbox's connection with the stage is not only as a spectator but as the wife of a performer. She was married last year to Horace Tarbox, who every evening delights the children at the Hippodrome with his wondrous flying-ring performance. It is said that the young couple have dubbed themselves Head and Shoulders, referring doubtless to the fact that Mrs. Tarbox supplies the literary and mental qualities while the supple and agile shoulders of her husband contribute their share to the family fortunes.

"Mrs. Tarbox seems to merit that much-abused title—'prodigy.' Only twenty——"

Horace stopped reading and with a very odd expression in his eyes gazed intently at Anton Laurier.

"I want to advise you——" he began hoarsely.

"What?"

"About raps. Don't answer them! Let them alone—have a padded door."

MYRA MEETS HIS FAMILY

By F. Scott Fitzgerald

ILLUSTRATED BY MAY WILSON PRESTON

"Dearest, Dearest!" He Cried. "I Shouldn't Have Told You! I Shouldn't Have Told You!"

PROBABLY every boy who has attended an Eastern college in the last ten years has met Myra half a dozen times, for the Myras live on the Eastern colleges, as kittens live on warm milk. When Myra is young, seventeen or so, they call her a "wonderful kid"; in her prime—say, at nineteen—she is tendered the subtle compliment of being referred to by her name alone; and after that she is a "prom trotter" or "the famous coast-to-coast Myra."

You can see her practically any winter afternoon if you stroll through the Biltmore lobby. She will be standing in a group of sophomores just in from Princeton or New Haven, trying to decide whether to dance away the mellow hours at the Club de Vingt or the Plaza Red Room. Afterward one of the sophomores will take her to the theater and ask her down to the February prom—and then dive for a taxi to catch the last train back to college.

Invariably she has a somnolent mother sharing a suite with her on one of the floors above.

When Myra is about twenty-four she thinks over all the nice boys she might have married at one time or other, sighs a little and does the best she can. But no remarks, please! She has given her youth to you; she has blown fragrantly through many ballrooms to the tender tribute of many eyes; she has roused strange surges of romance in a hundred pagan young breasts; and who shall say she hasn't counted?

The particular Myra whom this story concerns will have to have a paragraph of history. I will get it over with as swiftly as possible.

When she was sixteen she lived in a big house in Cleveland and attended Derby School in Connecticut, and it was while she was still there that she started going to prep-school dances and college proms. She decided to spend the war at Smith College, but in January of her freshman year falling violently in love with a young infantry officer she failed all her midyear examinations and retired to Cleveland in disgrace. The young infantry officer arrived about a week later.

Just as she had about decided that she didn't love him after all he was ordered abroad, and in a great revival of sentiment she rushed down to the port of embarkation with her mother to bid him good-by. She wrote him daily for two months, and then weekly for two months, and then once more. This last letter he never got, for a machine-gun bullet ripped through his head one rainy July morning. Perhaps this was just as well, for the letter informed him that it had all been a mistake, and that something told her they would never be happy together, and so on.

The "something" wore boots and silver wings and was tall and dark. Myra was quite sure that it was the real thing at last, but as an engine went through his chest at Kelly Field in mid-August she never had a chance to find out.

Instead she came East again, a little slimmer, with a becoming pallor and new shadows under her eyes, and throughout armistice year she left the ends of cigarettes all over New York on little china trays marked "Midnight Frolic" and "Coconut Grove" and "Palais Royal." She was twenty-one now, and Cleveland people said that her mother ought to take her back home—that New York was spoiling her.

You will have to do your best with that. The story should have started long ago.

It was an afternoon in September when she broke a theater date in order to have tea with young Mrs. Arthur Elkins, once her roommate at school.

"I wish," began Myra as they sat down exquisitely, "that I'd been a señorita or a mademoiselle or something. Good grief! What is there to do over here once you're out, except marry and retire!"

Lilah Elkins had seen this form of ennui before.

"Nothing," she replied coolly; "do it."

"I can't seem to get interested, Lilah," said Myra, bending forward earnestly. "I've played round so much that even while I'm kissing the man I just wonder how soon I'll get tired of him. I never get carried away like I used to."

"How old are you, Myra?"

"Twenty-one last spring."

"Well," said Lilah complacently, "take it from me don't get married unless you're absolutely through playing round. It means giving up an awful lot, you know."

"Through! I'm sick and tired of my whole pointless existence. Funny, Lilah, but I do feel ancient. Up at New Haven last spring men danced with me that seemed like little boys—and once I overheard a girl say in the dressing room 'There's Myra Harper! She's been coming up here for eight years.' Of course she was about three years off, but it did give me the calendar blues."

"You and I went to our first prom when we were sixteen—five years ago."

"Heavens!" sighed Myra. "And now some men are afraid of me. Isn't that odd? Some of the nicest boys. One man dropped me like a hotcake after coming down from Morristown for three straight week-ends. Some kind friend told him I was husband hunting this year and he was afraid of getting in too deep."

"Well, you *are* husband hunting, aren't you?"

"I suppose so—after a fashion." Myra paused and looked about rather cautiously. "Have you ever met Knowleton Whitney? You know what a wiz he is on looks, and his father's worth a fortune, they say. Well, I noticed that the first time he met me he started when he heard my name and fought shy—and, Lilah darling, not so ancient and homely as all that, am I?"

"You certainly are not!" laughed Lilah. "And here's my advice: Pick out the best thing in sight—the man who has all the mental, physical, social and financial qualities you want, and then go after him hammer and tongs—way we used to. After you've got him don't say to yourself 'Well, he can't sing like Billy,' or 'I wish he played better golf.' You can't have everything. Shut your eyes and turn off your sense of humor, and then after you're married it'll be very different and you'll be mighty glad."

"Yes," said Myra absently; "I've had that advice before."

"Drifting into romance is easy when you're eighteen," continued Lilah emphatically; "but after five years of it your capacity for it simply burns out."

"I've had such nice times," sighed Myra, "and such sweet men. To tell you the truth I have decided to go after someone."

"Who?" *(Continued on Page 42)*

294

(Continued from Page 40)

"Knowleton Whitney. Believe me, I may be a bit blasé, but I can still get any man I want."

"You really want him?"

"Yes — as much as I'll ever want anyone. He's smart as a whip, and shy—rather sweetly shy—and they say his family have the best-looking place in Westchester County."

Lilah sipped the last of her tea and glanced at her wrist watch.

"I've got to tear, dear."

They rose together and, sauntering out on Park Avenue, hailed taxicabs.

"I'm awfully glad, Myra; and I know you'll be glad too."

Myra skipped a little pool of water and, reaching her taxi, balanced on the running board like a ballet dancer.

"By, Lilah. See you soon."

"Good-by, Myra. Good luck!"

And knowing Myra as she did, Lilah felt that her last remark was distinctly superfluous.

II

THAT was essentially the reason that one Friday night six weeks later Knowleton Whitney paid a taxi bill of seven dollars and ten cents and with a mixture of emotions paused beside Myra on the Biltmore steps.

The outer surface of his mind was deliriously happy, but just below that was a slowly hardening fright at what he had done. He, protected since his freshman year at Harvard from the snares of fascinating fortune hunters, had dragged away from several sweet young things by the acquiescent nape of his neck, had taken advantage of his family's absence in the West to become so enmeshed in the toils that it was hard to say which was toils and which was he.

The afternoon had been like a dream: November twilight along Fifth Avenue after the matinée, and he and Myra looking out at the swarming crowds from the romantic privacy of a hansom cab—quaint device—then tea at the Ritz and her white hand gleaming on the arm of a chair beside him; and suddenly quick broken words. After that had come the trip to the jeweler's and a mad dinner in some little Italian restaurant where he had written "Do you?" on the back of the bill of fare and pushed it over to her to add the ever-miraculous "You know I do!" And now at the day's end they paused on the Biltmore steps.

"Say it," breathed Myra close to his ear.

He said it. Ah, Myra, how many ghosts must have flitted across your memory then!

"You've made me so happy, dear," she said softly.

"No—you've made me happy. Don't you know—Myra——"

"I know."

"For good?"

"For good. I've got this, you see." And she raised the diamond solitaire to her lips. She knew how to do things, did Myra.

"Good night."

"Good night. Good night."

Like a gossamer fairy in shimmering rose she ran up the wide stairs and her cheeks were glowing wildly as she rang the elevator bell.

At the end of a fortnight she got a telegram from him saying that his family had returned from the West and expected her up in Westchester County for a week's visit. Myra wired her train time, bought three new evening dresses and packed her trunk.

It was a cool November evening when she arrived, and stepping from the train in the late twilight she shivered slightly and looked eagerly round for Knowleton. The station platform warmed for a moment with men returning from the city; there was a shouting medley of wives and

chauffeurs, and a great snorting of automobiles as they backed and turned and slid away. Then before she realized it the platform was quite deserted and not a single one of the luxurious cars remained. Knowleton must have expected her on another train.

With an almost inaudible "Damn!" she started toward the Elizabethan station to telephone, when suddenly she was accosted by a very dirty, dilapidated man who touched his ancient cap to her and addressed her in a cracked, querulous voice.

"You Miss Harper?"

"Yes," she confessed, rather startled. Was this unmentionable person by any wild chance the chauffeur?

"The chauffeur's sick," he continued in a high whine. "I'm his son."

Myra gasped.

"You mean Mr. Whitney's chauffeur?"

"Yes; he only keeps just one since the war. Great on economizin'—regelar Hoover." He stamped his feet nervously and smacked enormous gauntlets together. "Well, no use waitin' here gabbin' in the cold. Le's have your grip."

Too amazed for words and not a little dismayed, Myra followed her guide to the edge of the platform, where she looked in vain for a car. But she was not left to wonder long, for the person led her steps to a battered old flivver, wherein was deposited her grip.

"Big car's broke," he explained. "Have to use this or walk."

He opened the front door for her and nodded.

"Step in."

"I b'lieve I'll sit in back if you don't mind."

"Surest thing you know," he cackled, opening the back door. "I thought the trunk bumpin' round back there might make you nervous."

"What trunk?"

"Yourn?"

"Oh, didn't Mr. Whitney—can't you make two trips?"

He shook his head obstinately.

"Wouldn't allow it. Not since the war. Up to rich people to set 'n example; that's what Mr. Whitney says. Le's have your check, please."

As he disappeared Myra tried in vain to conjure up a picture of the chauffeur if this was his son. After a mysterious argument with the station agent he returned, gasping violently, with the trunk on his back. He deposited it in the rear seat and climbed up in front beside her.

It was quite dark when they swerved out of the road and up a long dusky driveway to the Whitney place, whence lighted windows flung great blots of cheerful

"As for You, My Exquisite Young Lady, You'd Better Understand That the Best Thing You Can Do is to Decide to Settle Down Right Here. This is My Home, and I Mean to Keep It So!"

yellow light over the gravel and grass and trees. Even now she could see that it was very beautiful, that its blurred outline was Georgian Colonial and that great shadowy garden parks were flung out at both sides. The car plumped to a full stop before a square stone doorway and the chauffeur's son climbed out after her and pushed open the outer door.

"Just go right in," he cackled; and as she passed the threshold she heard him softly shut the door, closing out himself and the dark.

Myra looked round her. She was in a large somber hall paneled in old English oak and lit by dim shaded lights clinging like luminous yellow turtles at intervals along the wall. Ahead of her was a broad staircase and on both sides there were several doors, but there was no sight or sound of life, and an intense stillness seemed to rise ceaselessly from the deep crimson carpet.

She must have waited there a full minute before she began to have the unmistakable sense of someone looking at her. She forced herself to turn casually round.

A sallow little man, bald and clean shaven, trimly dressed in a frock coat and white spats, was standing a few yards away regarding her quizzically. He must have been fifty at the least, but even before he moved she had noticed a curious alertness about him—something in his pose which promised that it had been instantaneously assumed and would be instantaneously changed in a moment. His tiny hands and feet and the odd twist to his eyebrows gave him a faintly elfish expression, and she had one of those vague transient convictions that she had seen him before, many years ago.

For a minute they stared at each other in silence and then she flushed slightly and discovered a desire to swallow.

"I suppose you're Mr. Whitney." She smiled faintly and advanced a step toward him. "I'm Myra Harper."

For an instant longer he remained silent and motionless, and it flashed across Myra that he might be deaf; then suddenly he jerked into spirited life exactly like a mechanical toy started by the pressure of a button.

"Why, of course—why, naturally, I know—ah!" he exclaimed excitedly in a high-pitched elfin voice. Then raising himself on his toes in a sort of attenuated ecstasy of enthusiasm and smiling a wizened smile, he minced toward her across the dark carpet.

She blushed appropriately.

"That's awfully nice of ——"

"Ah!" he went on. "You must be tired; a rickety, cindery, ghastly trip, I know. Tired and hungry and thirsty, no doubt, no doubt!" He looked round him indignantly. "The servants are frightfully inefficient in this house!"

Myra did not know what to say to this, so she made no answer. After an instant's abstraction Mr. Whitney crossed over with his furious energy and pressed a button; then almost as if he were dancing he was by her side again, making thin, disparaging gestures with his hands.

"A little minute," he assured her, "sixty seconds, scarcely more. Here!"

He rushed suddenly to the wall and with some effort lifted a great carved Louis Fourteenth chair and set it down carefully in the geometrical center of the carpet.

"Sit down—won't you? Sit down! I'll go get you something. Sixty seconds at the outside."

She demurred faintly, but he kept on repeating "Sit down!" in such an aggrieved yet hopeful tone that Myra sat down. Instantly her host disappeared.

She sat there for five minutes and a feeling of oppression fell over her. Of all the receptions she had ever received this was decidedly the oddest—for though she had read somewhere that Ludlow Whitney was considered one of the most eccentric figures in the financial world, to find a sallow, elfin little man who, when he walked, danced was rather a blow to her sense of form. He had gone to get Knowleton! She revolved her thumbs in interminable concentric circles.

Then she started nervously at a quick cough at her elbow. It was Mr. Whitney again. In one hand he held a glass of milk and in the other a blue kitchen bowl full of those hard cubical crackers used in soup.

(Continued on Page 44)

(Continued from Page 42)

"Hungry from your trip!" he exclaimed compassionately. "Poor girl, poor little girl, starving!" He brought out this last word with such emphasis that some of the milk plopped gently over the side of the glass.

Myra took the refreshments submissively. She was not hungry, but it had taken him ten minutes to get them so it seemed ungracious to refuse. She sipped gingerly at the milk and ate a cracker, wondering vaguely what to say. Mr. Whitney, however, solved the problem for her by disappearing again—this time by way of the wide stairs—four steps at a hop—the back of his bald head gleaming oddly for a moment in the half dark.

Minutes passed. Myra was torn between resentment and bewilderment that she should be sitting on a high comfortless chair in the middle of this big hall munching crackers. By what code was a visiting fiancée ever thus received!

Her heart gave a jump of relief as she heard a familiar whistle on the stairs. It was Knowleton at last, and when he came in sight he gasped with astonishment.

"Myra!"

She carefully placed the bowl and glass on the carpet and rose, smiling.

"Why," he exclaimed, "they didn't tell me you were here!"

"Your father—welcomed me."

"Lordy! He must have gone upstairs and forgotten all about it. Did he insist on your eating this stuff? Why didn't you just tell him you didn't want any?"

"Why—I don't know."

"You mustn't mind father, dear. He's forgetful and a little unconventional in some ways, but you'll get used to him."

He pressed a button and a butler appeared.

"Show Miss Harper to her room and have her bag carried up—and her trunk if it isn't there already." He turned to Myra. "Dear, I'm awfully sorry I didn't know you were here. How long have you been waiting?"

"Oh, only a few minutes."

It had been twenty at the least, but she saw no advantage in stressing it. Nevertheless it had given her an oddly uncomfortable feeling.

Half an hour later as she was hooking the last eye on her dinner dress there was a knock on the door.

"It's Knowleton, Myra; if you're about ready we'll go in and see mother for a minute before dinner."

She threw a final approving glance at her reflection in the mirror and turning out the light joined him in the hall. He led her down a central passage which crossed to the other wing of the house, and stopping before a closed door he pushed it open and ushered Myra into the weirdest room upon which her young eyes had ever rested.

It was a large luxurious boudoir, paneled, like the lower hall, in dark English oak and bathed by several lamps in a mellow orange glow that blurred its every outline into misty amber. In a great armchair piled high with cushions and draped with a curiously figured cloth of silk reclined a very sturdy old lady with bright white hair, heavy features, and an air about her of having been there for many years. She lay somnolently against the cushions, her eyes half closed, her great bust rising and falling under her black negligee.

But it was something else that made the room remarkable, and Myra's eyes scarcely rested on the woman, so engrossed was she in another feature of her surroundings. On the carpet, on the chairs and sofas, on the great canopied bed and on the soft Angora rug in front of the fire sat and sprawled and slept a great army of white poodle dogs. There must have been almost two dozen of them, with curly hair twisting in front of their wistful eyes and wide yellow bows flaunting from their necks. As Myra and Knowleton entered a stir went over the dogs; they raised one-and-twenty cold black noses in the air and from one-and-twenty little throats went up a great clatter of staccato barks until the room was filled

(Continued on Page 46)

"Myra, I've Done a Ghastly Thing—to You, to Me, to Us. I Haven't a Word to Say in Favor of Myself"

46   THE SATURDAY EVENING POST   March 20, 1920

Macey Filing Equipment

—designed according to business requirements, embodies only the highest standard of quality. The Macey trade mark, known the world over, assures the purchaser of the utmost in utility, convenience and long service.

Protect Yourself With The

(Continued from Page 44)

with such an uproar that Myra stepped back in alarm.

But at the din the somnolent fat lady's eyes trembled open and in a low husky voice that was in itself oddly like a bark she snapped out: "Hush that racket!" and the clatter instantly ceased. The two or three poodles round the fire turned their silky eyes on each other reproachfully, and lying down with little sighs faded out on the white Angora rug; the tousled ball on the lady's lap dug his nose into the crook of an elbow and went back to sleep, and except for the patches of white wool scattered about the room Myra would have thought it all a dream.

"Mother," said Knowleton after an instant's pause, "this is Myra."

From the lady's lips flooded one low husky word: "Myra?"

"She's visiting us, I told you."

Mrs. Whitney raised a large arm and passed her hand across her forehead wearily.

"Child!" she said—and Myra started, for again the voice was like a low sort of growl—"you want to marry my son Knowleton?"

Myra felt that this was putting the tonneau before the radiator, but she nodded. "Yes, Mrs. Whitney."

"How old are you?" This very suddenly.

"I'm twenty-one, Mrs. Whitney."

"Ah—and you're from Cleveland?" This was in what was surely a series of articulate barks.

"Yes, Mrs. Whitney."

"Ah——"

Myra was not certain whether this last ejaculation was conversation or merely a groan, so she did not answer.

"You'll excuse me if I don't appear downstairs," continued Mrs. Whitney; "but when we're in the East I seldom leave this room and my dear little doggies."

Myra nodded and a conventional health question was trembling on her lips when she caught Knowleton's warning glance and checked it.

"Well," said Mrs. Whitney with an air of finality, "you seem like a very nice girl. Come in again."

"Good night, mother," said Knowleton.

"Night!" barked Mrs. Whitney drowsily, and her eyes sealed gradually up as her head receded back again into the cushions.

Knowleton held open the door and Myra feeling a bit blank left the room. As they walked down the corridor she heard a burst of furious sound behind them; the noise of the closing door had again roused the poodle dogs.

When they went downstairs they found Mr. Whitney already seated at the dinner table.

"Utterly charming, completely delightful!" he exclaimed, beaming nervously. "One big family, and you the jewel of it, my dear."

Myra smiled, Knowleton frowned and Mr. Whitney tittered.

"It's been lonely here," he continued; "desolate, with only us three. We expect you to bring sunlight and warmth, the peculiar radiance and efflorescence of youth. It will be quite delightful. Do you sing?"

"Why—I have. I mean, I do, some."

He clapped his hands enthusiastically.

"Splendid! Magnificent! What do you sing? Opera? Ballads? Popular music?"

"Well, mostly popular music."

"Good; personally I prefer popular music. By the way, there's a dance tonight."

"Father," demanded Knowleton sulkily, "did you go and invite a crowd here?"

"I had Monroe call up a few people—just some of the neighbors," he explained to Myra. "We're all very friendly hereabouts; give informal things continually. Oh, it's quite delightful!"

Myra caught Knowleton's eye and gave him a sympathetic glance. It was obvious that he had wanted to be alone with her this first evening and was quite put out.

"I want them to meet Myra," continued his father. "I want them to know this delightful jewel we've added to our little household."

"Father," said Knowleton suddenly, "eventually of course Myra and I will want to live here with you and mother, but for the first two or three years I think an apartment in New York would be more the thing for us."

Crash! Mr. Whitney had raked across the tablecloth with his fingers and swept his silver to a jangling heap on the floor.

"Nonsense!" he cried furiously, pointing a tiny finger at his son. "Don't talk that utter nonsense! You'll live here, do you understand me? Here! What's a home without children?"

"But, father——"

In his excitement Mr. Whitney rose and a faint unnatural color crept into his sallow face.

"Silence!" he shrieked. "If you expect one bit of help from me you can have it under my roof—nowhere else! Is that clear? As for you, my exquisite young lady," he continued, turning his wavering finger on Myra, "you'd better understand that the best thing you can do is to decide to settle down right here. This is my home, and I mean to keep it so!"

He stood then for a moment on his tiptoes, bending furiously indignant glances first on one, then on the other, and then suddenly he turned and skipped from the room.

"Well," gasped Myra, turning to Knowleton in amazement, "what do you know about that!"

III

SOME hours later she crept into bed in a great state of restless discontent. One thing she knew—she was not going to live in this house. Knowleton would have to make his father see reason to the extent of giving them an apartment in the city. The sallow little man made her nervous; she was sure Mrs. Whitney's dogs would haunt her dreams; and there was a general casualness in the chauffeur, the butler, the maids and even the guests she had met that night, that did not in the least coincide with her ideas on the conduct of a big estate.

She had lain there an hour perhaps when she was startled from a slow reverie by a sharp cry which seemed to proceed from the adjoining room. She sat up in bed and listened, and in a minute it was repeated. It sounded exactly like the plaint of a weary child stopped summarily by the placing of a hand over its mouth. In the dark silence her bewilderment shaded gradually off into uneasiness. She waited for the cry to recur, but straining her ears she heard only the intense crowded stillness of three o'clock. She wondered where Knowleton slept, remembered that his bedroom was over in the other wing just beyond his mother's. She was alone over here—or was she?

With a little gasp she slid down into bed again and lay listening. Not since childhood had she been afraid of the dark, but the unforeseen presence of someone next door startled her and sent her imagination racing through a host of mystery stories that at one time or another had whisked away a long afternoon.

She heard the clock strike four and found she was very tired. A curtain drifted slowly down in front of her imagination, and changing her position she fell suddenly to sleep.

Next morning, walking with Knowleton under starry frosted bushes in one of the bare gardens, she grew quite light-hearted and wondered at her depression of the night before. Probably all families seemed odd when one visited them for the first time in such an intimate capacity. Yet her determination that she and Knowleton were going to live elsewhere than with the white dogs and the jumpy little man was not abated. And if the near-by Westchester County society was typified by the chilly crowd she had met at the dance——

"The family," said Knowleton, "must seem rather unusual. I've been brought up in an odd atmosphere, I suppose, but mother is really quite normal outside of her penchant for poodles in great quantities, and father in spite of his eccentricities seems to hold a secure position in Wall Street."

"Knowleton," she demanded suddenly, "who lives in the room next door to me?"

Did he start and flush slightly—or was that her imagination?

"Because," she went on deliberately, "I'm almost sure I heard someone crying in there during the night. It sounded like a child, Knowleton."

"There's no one in there," he said decidedly. "It was either your imagination or something you ate. Or possibly one of the maids was sick."

Seeming to dismiss the matter without effort he changed the subject.

The day passed quickly. At lunch Mr. Whitney seemed to have forgotten his temper of the previous night; he was as nervously enthusiastic as ever; and watching him Myra again had that impression

(Continued on Page 49)

297

APPENDIX ONE

(Continued from Page 46)

that she had seen him somewhere before. She and Knowleton paid another visit to Mrs. Whitney—and again the poodles stirred uneasily and set up a barking, to be summarily silenced by the harsh throaty voice. The conversation was short and of inquisitional flavor. It was terminated as before by the lady's drowsy eyelids and a pæan of farewell from the dogs.

In the evening she found that Mr. Whitney had insisted on organizing an informal neighborhood vaudeville. A stage had been erected in the ballroom and Myra sat beside Knowleton in the front row and watched proceedings curiously. Two slim and haughty ladies sang, a man performed some ancient card tricks, a girl gave impersonations, and then to Myra's astonishment Mr. Whitney appeared and did a rather effective buck-and-wing dance. There was something inexpressibly weird in the motion of the well-known financier flitting solemnly back and forth across the stage on his tiny feet. Yet he danced well, with an effortless grace and an unexpected suppleness, and he was rewarded with a storm of applause.

In the half dark the lady on her left suddenly spoke to her.

"Mr. Whitney is passing the word along that he wants to see you behind the scenes."

Puzzled, Myra rose and ascended the side flight of stairs that led to the raised platform. Her host was waiting for her anxiously.

"Ah," he chuckled, "splendid!"

He held out his hand, and wonderingly she took it. Before she realized his intention he had half led, half drawn her out on to the stage. The spotlight's glare bathed them, and the ripple of conversation washing the audience ceased. The faces before her were pallid splotches on the gloom and she felt her ears burning as she waited for Mr. Whitney to speak.

"Ladies and gentlemen," he began, "most of you know Miss Myra Harper. You had the honor of meeting her last night. She is a delicious girl, I assure you. I am in a position to know. She intends to become the wife of my son."

He paused and nodded and began clapping his hands. The audience immediately took up the clapping and Myra stood there in motionless horror, overcome by the most violent confusion of her life.

The piping voice went on: "Miss Harper is not only beautiful but talented. Last night she confided to me that she sang. I asked whether she preferred the opera, the ballad or the popular song, and she confessed that her taste ran to the latter. Miss Harper will now favor us with a popular song."

And then Myra was standing alone on the stage, rigid with embarrassment. She fancied that on the faces in front of her she saw critical expectation, boredom, ironic disapproval. Surely this was the height of bad form—to drop a guest unprepared into such a situation.

In the first hush she considered a word or two explaining that Mr. Whitney had been under a misapprehension—then anger came to her assistance, then anger and those in front saw her lips close together sharply.

Advancing to the platform's edge she said succinctly to the orchestra leader: "Have you got Wave That Wishbone?"

"Lemme see. Yes, we got it."

"All right. Let's go!"

She hurriedly reviewed the words, which she had learned quite by accident at a dull house party the previous summer. It was perhaps not the song she would have chosen for her first public appearance, but it would have to do. She smiled radiantly, nodded at the orchestra leader and began the verse in a light clear alto.

As she sang a spirit of ironic humor slowly took possession of her—a desire to give them all a run for their money. And she did. She injected an East Side snarl into every word of slang; she ragged; she shimmied; she did a tickle-toe step she had learned once in an amateur musical comedy; and in a burst of inspiration finished up in an Al Jolson position, on her knees with her arms stretched out to her audience in syncopated appeal.

Then she rose, bowed and left the stage.

For an instant there was silence, the silence of a cold tomb; then perhaps half a dozen hands joined in a faint, perfunctory applause that in a moment had died completely away.

"Heavens!" thought Myra. "Was it as bad as all that? Or did I shock 'em?"

Mr. Whitney, however, seemed delighted. He was waiting for her in the wings and seizing her hand shook it enthusiastically.

"Quite wonderful!" he chuckled. "You are a delightful little actress—and you'll be a valuable addition to our little plays. Would you like to give an encore?"

"No!" said Myra shortly, and turned away.

In a shadowy corner she waited until the crowd had filed out, with an angry unwillingness to face them immediately after their rejection of her effort.

When the ballroom was quite empty she walked slowly up the stairs, and there she came upon Knowleton and Mr. Whitney alone in the dark hall, evidently engaged in a heated argument.

They ceased when she appeared and looked toward her eagerly.

"Father," said Mr. Whitney, "Knowleton wants to talk to you."

"Father," said Knowleton intensely, "I ask you——"

"Silence!" cried his father, his voice ascending testily. "You'll do your duty—now."

Knowleton cast one more appealing glance at him, but Mr. Whitney only shook his head excitedly and, turning, disappeared phantomlike up the stairs.

Knowleton stood silent a moment and finally with a look of dogged determination took her hand and led her toward a room that opened off the hall at the back. The yellow light fell through the door after them and she found herself in a dark wide chamber where she could just distinguish on the walls great square shapes which she took to be frames. Knowleton pressed a button, and immediately forty portraits sprang into life—old gallants from colonial days, ladies with floppity Gainsborough hats, fat women with ruffs and placid clasped hands.

She turned to Knowleton inquiringly, but he led her forward to a row of pictures on the side.

"Myra," he said slowly and painfully, "there's something I have to tell you. These"—he indicated the pictures with his hand—"are family portraits."

There were seven of them, three men and three women, all of them of the period just before the Civil War. The one in the middle, however, was hidden by crimson-velvet curtains.

"Ironic as it may seem," continued Knowleton steadily, "that frame contains a picture of my great-grandmother."

Reaching out, he pulled a little silken cord and the curtains parted, to expose a portrait of a lady dressed as a European but with the unmistakable features of a Chinese.

"My great-grandfather, you see, was an Australian tea importer. He met his future wife in Hong-Kong."

Myra's brain was whirling. She had a sudden vision of Mr. Whitney's yellowish face, peculiar eyebrows and tiny hands and feet—she remembered ghastly tales she had heard of reversions to type—of Chinese babies—and then with a final surge of horror she thought of that sudden hushed cry in the night. She gasped, her knees seemed to crumple up and she sank slowly to the floor.

In a second Knowleton's arms were round her.

"Dearest, dearest!" he cried. "I shouldn't have told you! I shouldn't have told you!"

As he said this Myra knew definitely and unmistakably that she could never marry him, and when she realized it she cast at him a wild pitiful look, and for the first time in her life fainted dead away.

IV

When she next recovered full consciousness she was in bed. She imagined a maid had undressed her, for on turning up the reading lamp she saw that her clothes had been neatly put away. For a minute she lay there, listening idly while the hall clock struck two, and then her overwrought nerves jumped in terror as she heard again that child's icy cry from the room next door. The morning seemed suddenly infinitely far away. There was some shadowy secret near her—her feverish imagination pictured a Chinese child brought up there in the half dark.

In a quick panic she crept into a negligee and, throwing open the door, slipped down the corridor toward Knowleton's room. It was very dark in the other wing, but when she pushed open his door she could see by the faint hall light that his bed was empty

March Rain Hints

ON rainy days wear sturdy out-door shoes. Wear rubbers. And when you get home don't dry your shoes by artificial heat. Let them dry naturally on shoe trees. Then will you get the most wear.

Wear in a shoe is hidden. Hence the necessity of a brand that means something to you when selecting a shoe. The name CROSSETT on your shoes is a definite guarantee of full value and longer wear.

and had not been slept in. Her terror increased. What could take him out at this hour of the night? She started for Mrs. Whitney's room, but at the thought of the dogs and her bare ankles she gave a little discouraged cry and passed by the door.

Then she suddenly heard the sound of Knowleton's voice issuing from a faint crack of light far down the corridor, and with a glow of joy she fled toward it. When she was within a foot of the door she found she could see through the crack—and after one glance all thought of entering left her.

Before an open fire, his head bowed in an attitude of great dejection, stood Knowleton, and in the corner, feet perched on the table, sat Mr. Whitney in his shirt sleeves, very quiet and calm, and pulling contentedly on a huge black pipe. Seated on the table was a part of Mrs. Whitney—that is, Mrs. Whitney without any hair. Out of the familiar great bust projected Mrs. Whitney's head, but she was bald; on her cheeks was the faint stubble of a beard, and in her mouth was a large black cigar, which she was puffing with obvious enjoyment.

"A thousand," groaned Knowleton as if in answer to a question. "Say twenty-five hundred and you'll be nearer the truth. I got a bill from the Graham Kennels to-day for those poodle dogs. They're soaking me two hundred and saying that they've got to have 'em back to-morrow."

"Well," said Mrs. Whitney in a low barytone voice, "send 'em back. We're through with 'em."

"That's a mere item," continued Knowleton glumly. "Including your salary, and Appleton's here, and that fellow who did the chauffeur, and seventy supes for two nights, and an orchestra—that's nearly twelve hundred, and then there's the rent on the costumes and that darn Chinese portrait and the bribes to the servants. Lord! There'll probably be bills for one thing or another coming in for the next month."

"Well, then," said Appleton, "for pity's sake pull yourself together and carry it through to the end. Take my word for it, that girl will be out of the house by twelve noon."

Knowleton sank into a chair and covered his face with his hands.

"Oh——"

"Brace up! It's all over. I thought for a minute there in the hall that you were going to balk at that Chinese business."

"It was the vaudeville that knocked the spots out of me," groaned Knowleton. "it was about the meanest trick ever pulled on any girl, and when she was so darned game about it!"

"She had to be," said Mrs. Whitney cynically.

"Oh, Kelly, if you could have seen the girl look at me to-night just before she fainted in front of that picture. Lord, I believe she loves me! If, oh, if you could have seen her!"

Outside Myra flushed crimson. She leaned closer to the door, biting her lip until she could taste the faintly bitter savor of blood.

"If there was anything I could do now," continued Knowleton—"anything in the world that would smooth it over I believe I'd do it."

Kelly crossed ponderously over, his bald shiny head ludicrous above his feminine negligee, and put his hand on Knowleton's shoulder.

"See here, my boy—your trouble is just nerves. Look at it this way: You undertook somep'n to get yourself out of an awful mess. It's a cinch the girl was after your money—now you've beat her at her own game an' saved yourself an unhappy marriage and your family a lot of suffering. Ain't that so, Appleton?"

"Absolutely!" said Appleton emphatically. "Go through with it."

"Well," said Knowleton with a dismal attempt to be righteous, "if she really loved me she wouldn't have let it all affect her this much. She's not marrying my family."

Appleton laughed.

"I thought we'd tried to make it pretty obvious that she is."

"Oh, shut up!" cried Knowleton miserably.

Myra saw Appleton wink at Kelly.

"At's right," he said; "she's shown she was after your money. Well, now then, there's no reason for not going through with it. See here. On one side you've proved she didn't love you and you're rid of her and free as air. She'll creep away and never say a word about it—and your family never the wiser. On the other side

twenty-five hundred thrown to the howwows, miserable marriage, girl sure to hate you as soon as she finds out, and your family all broken up and probably disownin' you for marryin' her. One big mess, I'll tell the world."

"You're right," admitted Knowleton gloomily. "You're right, I suppose—but oh, the look in that girl's face! She's probably in there now lying awake, listening to the Chinese baby——"

Appleton rose and yawned.

"Well ——" he began.

But Myra waited to hear no more. Pulling her silk kimono close about her she sped like lightning down the soft corridor, to dive headlong and breathless into her room.

"My heavens!" she cried, clenching her hands in the darkness. "My heavens!"

v

JUST before dawn Myra drowsed into a jumbled dream that seemed to act on through interminable hours. She awoke about seven and lay listlessly with one blue-veined arm hanging over the side of the bed. She who had danced in the dawn at many proms was very tired.

A clock outside her door struck the hour, and with her nervous start something seemed to collapse within her—she turned over and began to weep furiously into her pillow, her tangled hair spreading like a dark aura round her head. To her, Myra Harper, had been done this cheap vulgar trick by a man she had thought shy and kind.

Lacking the courage to come to her and tell her the truth he had gone into the highways and hired men to frighten her.

Between her fevered broken sobs she tried in vain to comprehend the workings of a mind which could have conceived this in all its subtlety. Her pride refused to let her think of it as a deliberate plan of Knowleton's. It was probably an idea fostered by this little actor Appleton or by the fat Kelly with his horrible poodles. But it was all unspeakable—unthinkable. It gave her an intense sense of shame.

But when she emerged from her room at eight o'clock and, disdaining breakfast, walked into the garden she was a very self-possessed young beauty, with dry cool eyes only faintly shadowed. The ground was firm and frosty with the promise of winter, and she found gray sky and dull air vaguely comforting and one with her mood. It was a day for thinking and she needed to think.

And then turning a corner suddenly she saw Knowleton seated on a stone bench, his head in his hands, in an attitude of profound dejection. He wore his clothes of the night before and it was quite evident that he had not been to bed.

He did not hear her until she was quite close to him, and then as a dry twig snapped under her heel he looked up wearily. She saw that the night had played havoc with him—his face was deathly pale and his eyes were pink and puffed and tired. He jumped up with a look that was very like dread.

"Good morning," said Myra quietly.

"Sit down," he began nervously. "Sit down; I want to talk to you! I've got to talk to you."

Myra nodded and taking a seat beside him on the bench clasped her knees with her hands and half closed her eyes.

"Myra, for heaven's sake have pity on me!"

She turned wondering eyes on him.

"What do you mean?"

He groaned.

"Myra, I've done a ghastly thing—to you, to me, to us. I—I haven't a word to say in favor of myself—I've been just rotten. I think it was a sort of madness that came over me."

"You'll have to give me a clew to what you're talking about."

"Myra—Myra"—like all large bodies his confession seemed difficult to imbue with momentum—"Myra—Mr. Whitney is not my father."

"You mean you were adopted?"

"No; I mean—Ludlow Whitney is my father, but this man you've met isn't Ludlow Whitney."

"I know," said Myra coolly. "He's Warren Appleton, the actor."

Knowleton leaped to his feet.

"How on earth ——"

"Oh," lied Myra easily, "I recognized him the first night. I saw him five years ago in The Swiss Grapefruit."

(Concluded on Page 53)

(Concluded from Page 50)

At this Knowleton seemed to collapse utterly. He sank down limply on to the bench.

"You knew?"

"Of course! How could I help it? It simply made me wonder what it was all about."

With a great effort he tried to pull himself together.

"I'm going to tell you the whole story, Myra."

"I'm all ears."

"Well, it starts with my mother—my real one, not the woman with those idiotic dogs; she's an invalid and I'm her only child. Her one idea in life has always been for me to make a fitting match, and her idea of a fitting match centers round social position in England. Her greatest disappointment was that I wasn't a girl so I could marry a title; instead she wanted to drag me to England—marry me off to the sister of an earl or the daughter of a duke. Why, before she'd let me stay up here alone this fall she made me promise I wouldn't go to see any girl more than twice. And then I met you."

"I was," murmured Myra.

"Well, that first intoxication lasted a week, and then one day a letter came from mother saying she was bringing home some wonderful English girl, Lady Helena Something-or-Other. And the same day a man told me that he'd heard I'd been caught by the most famous husband hunter in New York. Well, between these two things I went half crazy. I came into town to see you and call it off—got as far as the Biltmore entrance and didn't dare. I started wandering down Fifth Avenue like a wild man, and then I met Kelly. I told him the whole story—and within an hour we'd hatched up this ghastly plan. It was his plan—all the details. His histrionic instinct got the better of him and he had me thinking it was the kindest way out."

"Finish," commanded Myra crisply.

"Well, it went splendidly, we thought. Everything—the station meeting, the dinner scene, the scream in the night, the vaudeville—though I thought that was a little too much—until—until —— Oh, Myra, when you fainted under that picture and I held you there in my arms, helpless as a baby, I knew I loved you. I was sorry then, Myra."

There was a long pause while she sat motionless, her hands still clasping her knees—then he burst out with a wild plea of passionate sincerity.

"Myra!" he cried. "If by any possible chance you can bring yourself to forgive and forget I'll marry you when you say, let my family go to the devil, and love you all my life."

For a long while she considered, and Knowleton rose and began pacing nervously up and down the aisle of bare bushes, his hands in his pockets, his tired eyes pathetic now, and full of dull appeal. And then she came to a decision.

"You're perfectly sure?" she asked calmly.

"Yes."

"Very well, I'll marry you to-day."

With her words the atmosphere cleared and his troubles seemed to fall from him like a ragged cloak. An Indian summer sun drifted out from behind the gray clouds and the dry bushes rustled gently in the breeze.

"It was a bad mistake," she continued, "but if you're sure you love me now, that's the main thing. We'll go to town this morning, get a license, and I'll call up my cousin, who's a minister in the First Presbyterian Church. We can go West to-night."

"Myra!" he cried jubilantly. "You're a marvel and I'm not fit to tie your shoe strings. I'm going to make up to you for this, darling girl."

And taking her supple body in his arms he covered her face with kisses.

The next two hours passed in a whirl. Myra went to the telephone and called her cousin, and then rushed upstairs to pack. When she came down a shining roadster was waiting miraculously in the drive and by ten o'clock they were bowling happily toward the city.

They stopped for a few minutes at the City Hall and again at the jeweler's, and then they were in the house of the Reverend Walter Gregory on Sixty-ninth Street, where a sanctimonious gentleman with twinkling eyes and a slight stutter received them cordially and urged them to a breakfast of bacon and eggs before the ceremony.

On the way to the station they stopped only long enough to wire Knowleton's father, and then they were sitting in their compartment on the Broadway Limited.

"Darn!" exclaimed Myra. "I forgot my bag. Left it at Cousin Walter's in the excitement."

"Never mind. We can get a whole new outfit in Chicago."

She glanced at her wrist watch.

"I've got time to telephone him to send it on."

She rose.

"Don't be long, dear."

She leaned down and kissed his forehead.

"You know I couldn't. Two minutes, honey."

Outside Myra ran swiftly along the platform and up the steel stairs to the great waiting room, where a man met her—a twinkly-eyed man with a slight stutter.

"How d-did it go, M-myra?"

"Fine! Oh, Walter, you were splendid! I almost wish you'd join the ministry so you could officiate when I do get married."

"Well—I r-rehearsed for half an hour after I g-got your telephone call."

"Wish we'd had more time. I'd have had him lease an apartment and buy furniture."

"H'm," chuckled Walter. "Wonder how far he'll go on his honeymoon."

"Oh, he'll think I'm on the train till he gets to Elizabeth." She shook her little fist at the great contour of the marble dome. "Oh, he's getting off too easy—far too easy!"

"I haven't f-figured out what the f-fellow did to you, M-myra."

"You never will, I hope."

They had reached the side drive and he hailed her a taxicab.

"You're an angel!" beamed Myra. "And I can't thank you enough."

"Well, any time I can be of use t-to you —— By the way, what are you going to do with all the rings?"

Myra looked laughingly at her hand.

"That's the question," she said. "I may send them to Lady Helena Something-or-Other—and—well, I've always had a strong penchant for souvenirs. Tell the driver 'Biltmore,' Walter."

SAVING MILLIONS
for
American Industry

HERE is a message for every man in America,—a business message.

During the war a great corporation built an industrial plant and manned it with ten thousand workmen. Here they toiled grinding out munitions. Maximum production was imperative, but it dropped—dropped far below what had been expected.

Experts were engaged to conduct an exhaustive survey which developed these facts:

It was found that 68% of the workers on the non-effective list each day were listed because of the venereal diseases.

Measurements of output showed that a man so infected was 33% below normal in production.

Scientific treatment facilities were introduced at small cost by the corporation and 2,000 employees were treated during the year.

Every man's output returned to normal after treatment was concluded and the men were returned to health!

The company estimates that the work was worth at least $150,000 net for the year in increased production.

The corporation was urged to these measures by the national agencies at work on the American Plan to combat venereal diseases. Today more than two thousand other corporations have found that it pays. They are conducting educational campaigns and are providing treatment facilities.

Today the United States is rapidly organizing against the most dangerous of all plagues. These diseases can be conquered as completely as were smallpox, yellow fever and typhoid. It will pay the nation as completely as it pays industry.

Every man and woman must help. The Government has declared it a duty of citizenship for everyone to know about the American Plan of action. Send today for Will Irwin's absorbing booklet, "Conquering an Old Enemy," a stirring book that should be read by the millions. It explains social and economic reasons that obligate you as a citizen to back up the campaign. First learn the facts. A copy will be mailed on receipt of ten cents to cover printing and mailing. Get it today.

The AMERICAN SOCIAL HYGIENE ASSOCIATION, Inc.
105 West Fortieth Street, New York City

The national agencies coöperating in the American Plan and backing up the state and local boards of health are:

**The United States Public Health Service,
The Interdepartmental Social Hygiene Board,
The American Social Hygiene Association,
The Army and the Navy.**

This advertisement paid for by public spirited men and women who realize that the greatest menace to public health can be stamped out!

THE CAMEL'S BACK

By F. Scott Fitzgerald

ILLUSTRATED BY ARTHUR WILLIAM BROWN

THE restless, wearied eye of the tired magazine reader resting for a critical second on the above title will judge it to be merely metaphorical. Stories about the cup and the lip nd the bad penny and the new broom rarely ave anything to do with cups and lips and pennies nd brooms. This story is the great exception. It as to do with an actual, material, visible and large-life camel's back.

Starting from the neck we shall work tailward. Meet Mr. Perry Parkhurst, twenty-eight, lawyer, ative of Toledo. Perry has nice teeth, a Harvard ducation, and parts his hair in the middle. You ave met him before—in Cleveland, Portland, St. aul, Indianapolis, Kansas City and elsewhere. aker Brothers, New York, pause on their semi-nnual trip through the West to clothe him; Mont-orency & Co. dispatch a young man posthaste every ree months to see that he has the correct number f little punctures on his shoes. He has a domestic adster now, will have a French roadster if he lives ng enough, and doubtless a Chinese one if it comes o fashion. He looks like the advertisement of the oung man rubbing his sunset-colored chest with iniment, goes East every year to the Harvard re-nion—does everything—smokes a little o much —— Oh, you've seen him.

Meet his girl. Her name is Betty Medill. And d she would take well in the movies. Her ther gives her her two hundred a month dress on and she has tawny eyes and ir, and feather fans of three colors. eet her father, Cyrus Medill. Though is to all appearances flesh and blood is, strange to say, commonly known Toledo as the Aluminum Man. But en he sits in his club window with o or three Iron Men and the White e Man and the Brass Man they look y much as you and I do, only more if you know what I mean. Meet the camel's back—or —don't meet the camel's back . Meet the story.

During the Christmas holidays 1919, the first real Christmas days since the war, there took ce in Toledo, counting only people with the italicized forty-one dinner parties, six-n dances, six luncheons male d female, eleven luncheons ale, twelve teas, four stag ners, two weddings and thir-n bridge parties. It was the ulative effect of all this that ved Perry Parkhurst on the nty-ninth day of December a desperate decision.

Betty Medill would marry him and wouldn't marry him. She was hav-such a good time that she hated ake such a definite step. Mean-le, their secret engagement had so long that it seemed as if any it might draw off of its own ght. A little man named Warbur- , who knew it all, persuaded Perry to superman her, et a marriage license and go up to the Medill house tell her she'd have to marry him at once or call it off ver. This is some stunt—but Perry tried it on Decemb-the twenty-ninth. He presented self, heart, license and matum, and within five minutes they were in the midst violent quarrel, a burst of sporadic open fighting such ccurs near the end of all long wars and engagements. It ught about one of those ghastly lapses in which two ble who are in love pull up sharp, look at each other ly and think it's all been a mistake. Afterward they aily kiss wholesomely and assure the other person it all their fault. Say it all was my fault! Say it was! I t to hear you say it!

at while reconciliation was trembling in the air, while was, in a measure, stalling it off, so that they might more voluptuously and sentimentally enjoy it when it e, they were permanently interrupted by a twenty-ate phone call for Betty from a garrulous aunt who d in the country. At the end of eighteen minutes Perry hurst, torn by pride and suspicion and urged on by red dignity, put on his long fur coat, picked up his brown soft hat and stalked out the door.

t's all over," he muttered brokenly as he tried to jam ar into first. "It's all over—if I have to choke you

A Little Man Who Knew It All Persuaded Perry to Superman Her, to Tell Her She'd Have to Marry Him at Once or Call it Off Forever. This is Some Stunt

for an hour, darn you!" This last to the car, which had been standing some time and was quite cold.

He drove downtown—that is, he got into a snow rut that led him downtown.

He sat slouched down very low in his seat, much too dispirited to care where he went. He was living over the next twenty years without Betty.

In front of the Clarendon Hotel he was hailed from the sidewalk by a bad man named Baily, who had big huge teeth and lived at the hotel and had never been in love.

"Perry," said the bad man softly when the roadster drew up beside him at the curb, "I've got six quarts of the dog-goodest champagne you ever tasted. A third of it's yours, Perry, if you'll come upstairs and help Martin Macy and me drink it."

"Baily," said Perry tensely, "I'll drink your champagne. I'll drink every drop of it. I don't care if it kills me. I don't care if it's fifty-proof wood alcohol."

"Shut up, you nut!" said the bad man gently. "They don't put wood alcohol in champagne. This is the stuff that proves the world is more than six thousand years old. It's so ancient that the cork is petrified. You have to pull it with a stone drill."

"Take me upstairs," said Perry moodily. "If that cork sees my heart it'll fall out from pure mortification."

The room upstairs was full of those innocent hotel pictures of little girls eating apples and sitting in swings and talking to dogs. The other decorations were neckties and a pink man reading a pink paper devoted to ladies in pink tights.

"When you have to go into the highways and byways ——" said the pink man, looking reproachfully at Baily and Perry.

"Hello, Martin Macy," said Perry shortly, "where's this stone-age champagne?"

"What's the rush? This isn't an operation, understand. This is a party."

Perry sat down dully and looked disapprovingly at all the neckties.

Baily leisurely opened the door of a wardrobe and brought out six wicked-looking bottles and three glasses.

"Take off that darn fur coat!" said Martin Macy to Perry. "Or maybe you'd like to have us open all the windows."

"Give me champagne," said Perry.

"Going to the Town-sends' circus ball to-night?"

"Am not!"

"'Vited?"

"Uh-huh."

"Why not go?"

"Oh, I'm sick of parties," exclaimed Perry. "I'm sick of 'em. I've been to so many that I'm sick of 'em."

"Maybe you're going to the Howard Tates' party?"

"No, I tell you; I'm sick of 'em."

"Well," said Macy consolingly, "the Tates' is just for college kids anyways."

"I tell you ——"

"I thought you'd be going to one of 'em anyways. I see by the papers you haven't missed a one this Christmas."

"Hm," grunted Perry morosely.

He would never go to any more parties. Classical phrases played in his mind—that side of his life was closed, closed. Now when a man says "closed, closed" like that, you can be pretty sure that some woman has double-closed him, so to speak. Perry was also thinking that other classical thought, about how cowardly suicide is. A noble thought that one—warm and uplifting. Think of all the fine men we should lose if suicide were not so cowardly!

An hour later was six o'clock, and Perry had lost all resemblance to the young man in the liniment advertisement. He looked like a rough draft for a riotous cartoon. They were singing—an impromptu song of Baily's improvisation:

One Lump Perry, the parlor snake,
  Famous through the city for the way he drinks his tea;
  Plays with it, toys with it,
Makes no noise with it,
  Balanced on a napkin on his well-trained knee.

"Trouble is," said Perry, who had just banged his hair with Baily's comb and was tying an orange tie round it to get the effect of Julius Cæsar, "that you fellas can't sing worth a damn. Soon's I leave th' air an' start singin' tenor you start singin' tenor too."

"'M a natural tenor," said Macy gravely. "Voice lacks cultivation, tha's all. Gotta natural voice, m'aunt used say. Naturally good singer."

"Singers, singers, all good singers," remarked Baily, who was at the telephone. "No, not the cabaret; I want night clerk. I mean refreshment clerk or some dog-gone clerk 'at's got food—food! I want ——"

"Julius Cæsar," announced Perry, turning round from the mirror. "Man of iron will and stern 'termination."

"Shut up!" yelled Baily. "Say, iss Mr. Baily. Sen' up enormous supper. Use y'own judgment. Right away."

He connected the receiver and the hook with some difficulty, and then with his lips closed and an air of solemn intensity in his eyes went to the lower drawer of his dresser and pulled it open.

"Lookit!" he commanded. In his hands he held a truncated garment of pink gingham.

"Pants," he explained gravely. "Lookit!" This was a pink blouse, a red tie and a Buster Brown collar.

"Lookit!" he repeated. "Costume for the Townsends' circus ball. This is what li'l' boy carries water for the elephants."

Perry was impressed in spite of himself.

"I'm going to be Julius Cæsar," he announced after a moment of concentration.

"Thought you weren't going!" said Macy.

"Me? Sure, I'm goin'. Never miss a party. Good for the nerves—like celery."

"Cæsar!" scoffed Baily. "Can't be Cæsar! He's not about a circus. Cæsar's Shakspere. Go as a clown."

Perry shook his head.

"Nope, Cæsar."

"Cæsar?"

"Sure. Chariot."

Light dawned on Baily.

"That's right. Good idea."

Perry looked round the room searchingly.

"You lend me a bathrobe and this tie," he said finally.

Baily considered.

"No good."

"Sure, tha's all I need. Cæsar was a savage. They can't kick if I come as Cæsar if he was a savage."

"No," said Baily, shaking his head slowly. "Get a costume over at a costumer's. Over at Nolak's."

"Closed up."

"Find out."

After a puzzling five minutes at the phone a small, weary voice managed to convince Perry that it was Mr. Nolak speaking, and that they would remain open until eight because of the Townsends' ball. Thus assured, Perry ate a great amount of filet mignon and drank his third of the last bottle of champagne. At eight-fifteen the man in the tall hat who stands in front of the Clarendon found him trying to start his roadster.

"Froze up," said Perry wisely. "The cold froze it. The cold air."

"Froze, eh?"

"Yes. Cold air froze it."

"Can't start it?"

"Nope. Let it stand here till summer. One those hot ole August days'll thaw it out awright."

"Goin' let it stand?"

"Sure. Let 'er stand. Take a hot thief to steal it. Gemme taxi."

The man in the tall hat summoned a taxi.

"Where to, mister?"

"Go to Nolak's—costume fella."

II

MRS. NOLAK was short and ineffectual looking, and on the cessation of the world war had belonged for a while to one of the new nationalities. Owing to the unsettled European conditions she had never since been quite sure what she was. The shop in which she and her husband performed their daily stint was dim and ghostly and peopled with suits of armor and Chinese mandarins and enormous papier-mâché birds suspended from the ceiling. In a vague background many rows of masks glared eyelessly at the visitor, and there were glass cases full of crowns and scepters and jewels and enormous stomachers and paints and powders and crape hair and face creams and wigs of all colors.

When Perry ambled into the shop Mrs. Nolak was folding up the last troubles of a strenuous day, so she thought, in a drawer full of pink silk stockings.

"Something for you?" she queried pessimistically.

"Want costume of Julius Hur, the charioteer."

Mrs. Nolak was sorry, but every stitch of charioteer had been rented long ago. Was it for the Townsends' circus ball? It was.

"Sorry," she said, "but I don't think there's anything left that's really circus."

This was an obstacle.

"Hm," said Perry. An idea struck him suddenly. "If you've got a piece of canvas I could go's a tent."

"Sorry, but we haven't anything like that. A hardware store is where you'd have to go to. We have some very nice Confederate soldiers."

"No, no soldiers."

"And I have a very handsome king."

He shook his head.

"Several of the gentlemen," she continued hopefully, "are wearing stovepipe hats and swallow-tail coats and going as ringmasters—but we're all out of tall hats. I can let you have some crape hair for a mustache."

"Want somep'm 'stinctive."

"Something—let's see. Well, we have a lion's head, and a goose, and a camel ——"

"Camel?" The idea seized Perry's imagination, gripped it fiercely.

"Yes, but it needs two people."

"Camel. That's an idea. Lemme see it."

The camel was produced from his resting place on a top shelf. At first glance he appeared to consist entirely of a very gaunt, cadaverous head and a sizable hump, but on being spread out he was found to possess a dark brown, unwholesome-looking body made of thick, cottony cloth.

"You see it takes two people," explained Mrs. Nolak, holding the camel up in frank admiration. "If you have a friend he could be part of it. You see there's sorta pants for two people. One pair is for the fella in front and the other pair for the fella in back. The fella in front does the lookin' out through these here eyes an' the fella in back he's just gotta stoop over an' folla the front fella round."

"Put it on," commanded Perry.

Obediently Mrs. Nolak put her tabby-cat face inside the camel's head and turned it from side to side ferociously.

Perry was fascinated.

"What noise does a camel make?"

"What?" asked Mrs. Nolak as her face emerged, somewhat smudgy. "Oh, what noise? Why, he sorta brays."

"Lemme see it in a mirror."

Before a wide mirror Perry tried on the head and turned from side to side appraisingly. In the dim light the effect was distinctly pleasing. The camel's face was a study in pessimism, decorated with numerous abrasions, and it must be admitted that his coat was in that state of general negligence peculiar to camels—in fact, he needed to be cleaned and pressed—but distinctive he certainly was. He was majestic. He would have attracted attention in any gathering if only by his melancholy cast of feature and the look of pensive hunger lurking round his shadowy eyes.

"You see you have to have two people," said Mrs. Nolak again.

Perry tentatively gathered up the body and legs and wrapped them about him, tying the hind legs as a girdle round his waist. The effect on the whole was bad. It was even irreverent—like one of those medieval pictures of a monk changed into a beast by the ministrations of Satan. At the very best the ensemble resembled a humpbacked cow sitting on her haunches among blankets.

"Don't look like anything at all," objected Perry gloomily.

"No," said Mrs. Nolak; "you see you got to have two people." *(Continued on Page 157)*

"You 'Fraid of Me?" Said Betty. "Don't Be. You See I'm a Snake Charmer, But I'm Pretty Good at Camels Too"

THE CAMEL'S BACK

(Continued from Page 17)

A solution flashed upon Perry.

"You got a date to-night?"

"Oh, I couldn't possibly ——"

"Oh, come on," said Perry encouragingly. "Sure you can! Here! Be a good sport and climb into these hind legs."

With difficulty he located them and extended their yawning depths ingratiatingly. But Mrs. Nolak seemed loath. She backed perversely away.

"Oh, no ——"

"C'm on! Why, you can be the front if you want to. Or we'll flip a coin."

"Oh, no ——"

"Make it worth your while."

Mrs. Nolak set her lips firmly together.

"Now you just stop!" she said with no coyness implied. "None of the gentlemen ever acted up this way before. My husband ——"

"You got a husband?" demanded Perry. "Where is he?"

"He's home."

"Wha's telephone number?"

After considerable parley he obtained the telephone number pertaining to the Nolak penates and got into communication with that small, weary voice he had heard once before that day. But Mr. Nolak, though taken off his guard and somewhat confused by Perry's brilliant flow of logic, stuck staunchly to his point. He refused firmly but with dignity to help out Mr. Parkhurst in the capacity of back part of a camel.

Having rung off, or rather having been rung off on, Perry sat down on a three-legged stool to think it over. He named over to himself those friends on whom he might call, and then his mind paused as betty Medill's name hazily and sorrowfully occurred to him. He had a sentimental thought. He would ask her. Their love affair was over, but she could not refuse this last request. Surely it was not much to ask—to help him keep up his end of social obligation for one short night. And if she insisted she could be the front part of the camel and he would go as the back. His magnanimity pleased him. His mind even turned to rosy-colored dreams of a tender reconciliation inside the camel—there hidden away from all the world.

"Now you'd better decide right off."

The bourgeois voice of Mrs. Nolak broke upon his mellow fancies and roused him to action. He went to the phone and called up the Medill house. Miss Betty was out; had gone out to dinner.

Then, when all seemed lost, the camel's back wandered curiously into the store. He was a dilapidated individual with a cold in his head and a general trend about him of downwardness. His cap was pulled down low on his head, and his chin was pulled down low on his chest, his coat hung down to his shoes, he looked run-down, down at the heels, and—Salvation Army the contrary—down and out. He said that he was the taxicab driver that the gentleman had hired at the Clarendon Hotel. He had been instructed to wait outside, but he had waited some time and had grown a suspicion that the gentleman had gone out the back way with purpose to defraud him—gentlemen sometimes did—so he had come in. He sank down onto the three-legged stool.

"Wanta go to a party?" demanded Perry sternly.

"I gotta work," answered the taxi driver lugubriously. "I gotta keep my job."

"It's a very good party."

"'S a very good job."

"Come on!" urged Perry. "Be a good fella. See—it's pretty!" He held the camel up and the taxi driver looked at it cynically.

"Huh!"

Perry searched feverishly among the folds of the cloth.

"See!" he cried enthusiastically, holding up a selection of folds. "This is your part. You don't even have to talk. All you have to do is to walk—and sit down occasionally. You do all the sitting down. Think of it—you're on my feet all the time and you can sit down some of the time. The only time I can sit down is when we're lying down, and you can sit down when—oh, any time. See?"

"What's 'at thing?" demanded the individual dubiously. "A shroud?"

"Not at all," said Perry hurriedly. "It's a camel."

"Huh?"

Then Perry mentioned a sum of money, and the conversation left the land of grunts and assumed a practical tinge. Perry and the taxi driver tried on the camel in front of the mirror.

"You can't see it," explained Perry, peering anxiously out through the eyeholes, "but honestly, ole man, you look sim'ly great! Honestly!"

A grunt from the hump acknowledged this somewhat dubious compliment.

"Honestly, you look great!" repeated Perry enthusiastically. "Move round a little."

The hind legs moved forward, giving the effect of a huge cat-camel hunching his back preparatory to a spring.

"No; move sideways."

The camel's hips went neatly out of joint; a hula dancer would have writhed in envy.

"Good, isn't it?" demanded Perry, turning to Mrs. Nolak for approval.

"It looks lovely," agreed Mrs. Nolak.

"We'll take it," said Perry.

The bundle was safely stowed under Perry's arm and they left the shop.

"Go to the party!" he commanded as he took his seat in the back.

"What party?"

"Fanzy-dress party."

"Where'bouts is it?"

This presented a new problem. Perry tried to remember, but the names of all those who had given parties during the holidays danced confusedly before his eyes. He could ask Mrs. Nolak, but on looking out the window he saw that the shop was dark. Mrs. Nolak had already faded out, a little black smudge far down the snowy street.

"Drive uptown," directed Perry with fine confidence. "If you see a party, stop. Otherwise I'll tell you when we get there."

He fell into a hazy daydream and his thoughts wandered again to Betty—he imagined vaguely that they had had a disagreement because she refused to go to the party as the back part of the camel. He was just slipping off into a chilly doze when he was wakened by the taxi driver opening the door and shaking him by the arm.

"Here we are, maybe."

Perry looked out sleepily. A striped awning led from the curb up to a spreading gray stone house, from inside which issued the low drummy whine of expensive jazz. He recognized the Howard Tate house.

"Sure," he said emphatically; "at's it! Tate's party to-night. Sure, everybody's goin'."

"Say," said the individual anxiously after another look at the awning, "you sure these people ain't gonna romp on me for comin' here?"

Perry drew himself up with dignity.

"'F anybody says anything to you, just tell 'em you're part of my costume."

The visualization of himself as a thing rather than a person seemed to reassure the individual.

"All right," he said reluctantly.

Perry stepped out under the shelter of the awning and began unrolling the camel.

"Let's go," he commanded.

Several minutes later a melancholy, hungry-looking camel, emitting clouds of smoke from his mouth and from the tip of his noble hump, might have been seen crossing the threshold of the Howard Tate residence, passing a startled footman without so much as a snort, and heading directly for the main stairs that led up to the ballroom. The beast walked with a peculiar gait which varied between an uncertain lockstep and a stampede—but can best be described by the word "halting." The camel had a halting gait—and as he walked he alternately elongated and contracted like a gigantic concertina.

III

THE Howard Tates are, as everyone who lives in Toledo knows, the most formidable people in town. Mrs. Howard Tate was a Chicago Todd before she became a Toledo Tate, and the family generally affect that conscious simplicity which has begun to be the earmark of American aristocracy. The Tates have reached the stage where they talk about pigs and farms and look at you icy-eyed if you are not amused. They have begun to prefer retainers rather than friends as dinner guests, spend a lot of money in a quiet way and, having lost all sense of competition, are in process of growing quite dull.

The dance this evening was for little Millicent Tate, and though there was a scattering of people of all ages present the dancers were mostly from school and college—the younger married crowd was at the Townsends' circus ball up at the Tallyho Club. Mrs. Tate was standing just inside the ballroom, following Millicent round with her eyes and beaming whenever she caught her eye. Beside her were two middle-aged sycophants who were saying what a perfectly exquisite child Millicent was. It was at this moment that Mrs. Tate was grasped firmly by the skirt and her youngest daughter, Emily, aged eleven, hurled herself with an "Oof!" into her mother's arms.

"Why, Emily, what's the trouble?"

"Mamma," said Emily, wild-eyed but voluble, "there's something out on the stairs."

"What?"

"There's a thing out on the stairs, mamma. I think it's a big dog, mamma, but it doesn't look like a dog."

"What do you mean, Emily?"

The sycophants waved their heads and hemmed sympathetically.

"Mamma, it looks like a—like a camel."

Mrs. Tate laughed.

"You saw a mean old shadow, dear, that's all."

"No, I didn't. No, it was some kind of thing, mamma—big. I was going downstairs to see if there were any more people and this dog or something, he was coming upstairs. Kinda funny, mamma, like he was lame. And then he saw me and gave a sort of growl and then he slipped at the top of the landing and I ran."

Mrs. Tate's laugh faded.

"The child must have seen something," she said.

The sycophants agreed that the child must have seen something—and suddenly all three women took an instinctive step away from the door as the sounds of muffled footsteps were audible just outside.

And then three startled gasps rang out as a dark brown form rounded the corner and they saw what was apparently a huge beast looking down at them hungrily.

"Oof!" cried Mrs. Tate.

(Continued on Page 161)

"Julius Cæsar," Announced Perry, Turning Round From the Mirror.
"Man of Iron Will and Stern Termination"

Appendix One

(Continued from Page 157)

"O-o-oh!" cried the ladies in a chorus.

The camel suddenly humped his back, and the gasps turned to shrieks.

"Oh—look!"

"What is it?"

The dancing stopped, but the dancers hurrying over got quite a different impression of the invader from that of the ladies by the door; in fact, the young people immediately suspected that it was a stunt, a hired entertainer come to amuse the party. The boys in long trousers looked at it rather disdainfully and sauntered over with their hands in their pockets, feeling that their intelligence was being insulted. But the girls ran over with much handclapping and many little shouts of glee.

"It's a camel!"

"Well, if he isn't the funniest!"

The camel stood there uncertainly, swaying slightly from side to side and seeming to take in the room in a careful, appraising glance; then as if he had come to an abrupt decision he turned and ambled swiftly out the door.

Mr. Howard Tate had just come out of his den on the lower floor and was standing chatting with a good-looking young man in the hall. Suddenly they heard the noise of shouting upstairs and almost immediately a succession of bumping sounds, followed by the precipitous appearance at the foot of the stairway of a large brown beast who seemed to be going somewhere in a great hurry.

"Now what the devil!" said Mr. Tate, starting.

The beast picked itself up with some dignity and affecting an air of extreme nonchalance, as if he had just remembered an important engagement, started at a mixed gait toward the front door. In fact, his front legs began casually to run.

"See here now," said Mr. Tate sternly. "Here! Grab it, Butterfield! Grab it!"

The young man enveloped the rear of the camel in a pair of brawny arms, and evidently realizing that further locomotion was quite impossible the front end submitted to capture and stood resignedly in a state of some agitation. By this time a flood of young people was pouring downstairs, and Mr. Tate, suspecting everything from an ingenious burglar to an escaped lunatic, gave crisp directions to the good-looking young man:

"Hold him! Lead him in here; we'll soon see."

The camel consented to be led into the den, and Mr. Tate, after locking the door, took a revolver from a table drawer and instructed the young man to take the thing's head off. Then he gasped and returned the revolver to its hiding place.

"Well, Perry Parkhurst!" he exclaimed in amazement.

"'M in the wrong pew," said Perry sheepishly. "Got the wrong party, Mr. Tate. Hope I didn't scare you."

"Well—you gave us a thrill, Perry." Realization dawned on him. "Why, of course; you're bound for the Townsends' circus ball."

"That's the general idea."

"Let me introduce Mr. Butterfield, Mr. Parkhurst. Parkhurst is our most famous young bachelor here." Then turning to Perry: "Butterfield is staying with us for a few days."

"I got a little mixed up," mumbled Perry. "I'm very sorry."

"Heavens, it's perfectly all right; most natural mistake in the world. I've got a clown costume and I'm going down there myself after a while. Silly idea for a man of my age." He turned to Butterfield. "Better change your mind and come down with us."

The good-looking young man demurred. He was going to bed.

"Have a drink, Perry?" suggested Mr. Tate.

"Thanks, I will."

"And, say," continued Tate quickly, "I'd forgotten all about your—friend here." He indicated the rear part of the camel. "I didn't mean to seem discourteous. Is it anyone I know? Bring him out."

"It's not a friend," explained Perry hurriedly. "I just rented him."

"Does he drink?"

"Do you?" demanded Perry, twisting himself tortuously round.

There was a faint sound of assent.

"Sure he does!" said Mr. Tate heartily. "A really efficient camel ought to be able to drink enough so it'd last him three days."

"Tell you, sir," said Perry anxiously, "he isn't exactly dressed up enough to come out. If you give me the bottle I can hand it back to him and he can take his inside."

From under the cloth was audible the enthusiastic smacking sound inspired by this suggestion. When a butler had appeared with bottles, glasses and siphon one of the bottles was handed back, and thereafter the silent partner could be heard imbibing long potations at frequent intervals.

Thus passed a peaceful hour. At ten o'clock Mr. Tate decided that they'd better be starting. He donned his clown's costume; Perry replaced the camel's head with a sigh; and side by side they progressed on foot the single block between the Tate house and the Tallyho Club.

The circus ball was in full swing. A great tent fly had been put up inside the ballroom and round the walls had been built rows of booths representing the various attractions of a circus side show, but these were now vacated and on the floor swarmed a shouting, laughing medley of youth and color—clowns, bearded ladies, acrobats, bareback riders, ringmasters, tattooed men and charioteers. The Townsends had determined to assure their party of success, so a great quantity of liquor had been surreptitiously brought over from their house in automobiles and it was flowing freely. A green ribbon ran along the wall completely round the ballroom, with pointing arrows alongside of it and signs which instructed the uninitiated to "Follow the green line!" The green line led down to the bar, where waited pure punch and wicked punch and plain dark-green bottles.

On the wall above the bar was another arrow, red and very wavy, and under it the slogan: "Now follow this!"

But even amid the luxury of costume and high spirits represented there the entrance of the camel created something of a stir, and Perry was immediately surrounded by a curious, laughing crowd who were anxious to penetrate the identity of this beast who stood by the wide doorway eying the dancers with his hungry, melancholy gaze.

And then Perry saw Betty. She was standing in front of a booth talking to a group of clowns, comic policemen and ringmasters. She was dressed in the costume of an Egyptian snake charmer, a costume carried out to the smallest detail. Her tawny hair was braided and drawn through brass rings, the effect crowned with a glittering Oriental tiara. Her fair face was stained to a warm olive glow and on her bare arms and the half moon of her back writhed painted serpents with single eyes of venomous green. Her feet were in sandals and her skirt was slit to the knees, so that when she walked one caught a glimpse of other slim serpents painted just above her bare ankles. Wound about her neck was a huge, glittering, cotton-stuffed cobra, and her bracelets were in the form of tiny garter snakes. Altogether a very charming and beautiful costume—one that made the more nervous among the older women shrink away from her when she passed, and the more troublesome ones to make great talk about "shouldn't be allowed" and "perfectly disgraceful."

But Perry, peering through the uncertain eyes of the camel, saw only her face, radiant, animated and glowing with excitement, and her arms and shoulders, whose mobile, expressive gestures made her always the outstanding figure in any gathering. He was fascinated and his fascination exercised a strangely sobering effect on him. With a growing clarity the events of the day came back—he had lost forever this shimmering princess in emerald green and black. Rage rose within him, and with a half-formed intention of taking her away from the crowd he started toward her—or rather he elongated slightly, for he had neglected to issue the preparatory command necessary to locomotion.

But at this point fickle Kismet, who for a day had played with him bitterly and sardonically, decided to reward him in full for the amusement he had afforded her. Kismet turned the tawny eyes of the snake charmer to the camel. Kismet led her to lean toward the man beside her and say, "Who's that? That camel?"

They all gazed.

"Darned if I know."

But a little man named Warburton, who knew it all, found it necessary to hazard an opinion:

"It came in with Mr. Tate. I think it's probably Warren Butterfield, the architect, who's visiting the Tates."

Something stirred in Betty Medill—that age-old interest of the provincial girl in the visiting man.

"Oh," she said casually after a slight pause.

At the end of the next dance Betty and her partner finished up within a few feet of the camel. With the informal audacity that was the keynote of the evening she reached out and gently rubbed the camel's nose.

"Hello, old camel."

The camel stirred uneasily.

"You 'fraid of me?" said Betty, lifting her eyebrows in mock reproof. "Don't be. You see I'm a snake charmer, but I'm pretty good at camels too."

The camel bowed very low and the groups round laughed and made the obvious remark about the beauty and the beast.

Mrs. Townsend came bustling up.

"Well, Mr. Butterfield," she beamed, "I wouldn't have recognized you."

Perry bowed again and smiled gleefully behind his mask.

"And who is this with you?" she inquired.

"Oh," said Perry in a disguised voice, muffled by the thick cloth and quite unrecognizable, "he isn't a fellow, Mrs. Townsend. He's just part of my costume."

This seemed to get by, for Mrs. Townsend laughed and bustled away. Perry turned again to Betty.

"So," he thought, "this is how much she cares! On the very day of our final rupture she starts a flirtation with another man—an absolute stranger."

On an impulse he gave her a soft nudge with his shoulder and waved his head suggestively toward the hall, making it clear that he desired her to leave her partner and accompany him. Betty seemed quite willing.

"By-by, Bobby," she called laughingly to her partner. "This old camel's got me. Where are we going, Prince of Beasts?"

The noble animal made no rejoinder, but stalked gravely along in the direction of a secluded nook on the side stairs.

There Betty seated herself, and the camel, after some seconds of confusion which included gruff orders and sounds of a heated dispute going on in his interior, placed himself beside her—his hind legs stretching out uncomfortably across two steps.

"Well, camel," said Betty cheerfully, "how do you like our happy party?"

The camel indicated that he liked it by rolling his head ecstatically and executing a gleeful kick with his hoofs.

"This is the first time that I ever had a tête-à-tête with a man's valet round"—she pointed to the hind legs—"or whatever that is."

"Oh," said Perry, "he's deaf and blind. Forget about him."

"That sure is some costume! But I should think you'd feel rather handicapped—you can't very well shimmy, even if you want to."

The camel hung his head lugubriously.

"I wish you'd say something," continued Betty sweetly. "Say you like me, camel. Say you think I'm pretty. Say you'd like to belong to a pretty snake charmer."

The camel would.

"Will you dance with me, camel?"

The camel would try.

Betty devoted half an hour to the camel. She devoted at least half an hour to all visiting men. It was usually sufficient. When she approached a new man the current débutantes were accustomed to scatter right and left like a close column deploying before a machine gun. And so to Perry Parkhurst was awarded the unique privilege of seeing his love as others saw her. He was flirted with violently!

IV

THIS paradise of frail foundation was broken into by the sound of a general ingress to the ballroom; the cotillion was beginning. Betty and the camel joined the crowd, her brown hand resting lightly on his shoulder, defiantly symbolizing her complete adoption of him.

When they entered, the couples were already seating themselves at tables round the walls, and Mrs. Townsend, resplendent as a super bareback rider with rather too rotund calves, was standing in the center with the ringmaster who was in charge of arrangements. At a signal to the band everyone rose and began to dance.

"Isn't it just slick!" breathed Betty.

"You bet!" said the camel.

"Do you think you can possibly dance?"

Perry nodded enthusiastically. He felt suddenly exuberant. After all, he was here incognito talking to his girl—he felt lik winking patronizingly at the world.

"I think it's the best idea," cried Betty "to give a party like this! I don't see ho they ever thought of it. Come on, let dance!"

So Perry danced the cotillion. I sa danced, but that is stretching the word f beyond the wildest dreams of the jazzie terpsichorean. He suffered his partner put her hands on his helpless shoulders ar pull him here and there gently over th floor while he hung his huge head docile over her shoulder and made futile dumn motions with his feet. His hind legs dance in a manner all their own, chiefly by ho ping first on one foot and then on the othe Never being sure whether dancing w going on or not, the hind legs played sa by going through a series of steps whe ever the music started playing. So t spectacle was frequently presented of t front part of the camel standing at ease an the rear keeping up a constant energet motion calculated to rouse a sympathet perspiration in any soft-hearted observe

He was frequently favored. He danc first with a tall lady covered with straw w announced jovially that she was a bale hay and coyly begged him not to eat her.

"I'd like to; you're so sweet," said t camel gallantly.

Each time the ringmaster shouted call of "Men up!" he lumbered ferociou for Betty with the cardboard wienerwu or the photograph of the bearded lady whatever the favor chanced to be. Som times he reached her first, but usually rushes were unsuccessful and resulted intense interior arguments.

"For heaven's sake," Perry would sn fiercely between his clenched teeth, "ge little pep! I could have gotten her th time if you'd picked your feet up."

"Well, gimme a little warnin'!"

"I did, darn you."

"I can't see a dog-gone thing in here."

"All you have to do is follow me. I just like dragging a load of sand round walk with you."

"Maybe you wanta try back here."

"You shut up! If these people fou you in this room they'd give you the wo beating you ever had. They'd take yo taxi license away from you!"

Perry surprised himself by the ease w which he made this monstrous threat, it seemed to have a soporific influence his companion, for he muttered an " gwan" and subsided into abashed siler

The ringmaster mounted to the top the piano and waved his hand for silence

"Prizes!" he cried. "Gather round!"

"Yea! Prizes!"

Self-consciously the circle swayed ward. The rather pretty girl who had m tered the nerve to come as a bearded la trembled with excitement, hoping to be warded for an evening's hideousness. man who had spent the afternoon hav tattoo marks painted on him by a s painter skulked on the edge of the cro blushing furiously when anyone told him was sure to get it.

"Lady and gent performers of the cus," announced the ringmaster jovia "I am sure we will all agree that a g time has been had by all. We will now stow honor where honor is due by best ing the prizes. Mrs. Townsend has as me to bestow the prizes. Now, fel performers, the first prize is for that la who has displayed this evening the m striking, becoming"—at this point bearded lady sighed resignedly—"and o inal costume." Here the bale of pricked up her ears. "Now I am sure t the decision which has been decided u will be unanimous with all here pres The first prize goes to Miss Betty Me the charming Egyptian snake charmer.

There was a great burst of applau chiefly masculine, and Miss Betty Me blushing beautifully through her o paint, was passed up to receive her awa With a tender glance the ringmaster han down to her a huge bouquet of orchids.

"And now," he continued, looking ro him, "the other prize is for that man has the most amusing and original tume. This prize goes without dispute guest in our midst, a gentleman wh visiting here but whose stay we all h will be long and merry—in short to noble camel who has entertained us al his hungry look and his brilliant dan throughout the evening."

He ceased and there was a hearty b of applause, for it was a popular ch

(Concluded on Page 165)

(Concluded from Page 161)

'he prize, a huge box of cigars, was put side for the camel, as he was anatomically nable to accept it in person.

"And now," continued the ringmaster, we will wind up the cotillon with the arriage of Mirth to Folly!

"Form for the grand wedding march, the eautiful snake charmer and the noble amel in front!"

Betty skipped forward cheerily and ound an olive arm round the camel's eck. Behind them formed the procession little boys, little girls, country jakes, olicemen, fat ladies, thin men, sword vallowers, wild men of Borneo, armless onders and charioteers, some of them well their cups, all of them excited and happy d dazzled by the flow of light and color und them and by the familiar faces rangely unfamiliar under bizarre wigs d barbaric paint. The voluminous chords the wedding march done in mad synco-tion issued in a delirious blend from the xophones and trombones—and the march gan.

"Aren't you glad, camel?" demanded etty sweetly as they stepped off. "Aren't u glad we're going to be married and u're going to belong to the nice snake armer ever afterward?"

The camel's front legs pranced, express-g exceeding joy.

"Minister, minister! Where's the minis-?" cried voices out of the revel. "Who's ng to be the cler-gy-man?"

The head of Jumbo, rotund negro waiter the Tallyho Club for many years, ap-ared rashly through a half-opened pantry or.

'Oh, Jumbo!"

'Get old Jumbo. He's the fella!"

'Come on, Jumbo. How 'bout marrying a couple?"

'Yea!"

Jumbo despite his protestations was zed by four brawny clowns, stripped of apron and escorted to a raised dais at head of the ball. There his collar was noved and replaced back side forward give him a sanctimonious effect. He od there grinning from ear to ear, evi-tly not a little pleased, while the parade arated into two lines leaving an aisle for bride and groom.

Lawdy, man," chuckled Jumbo, "Ah ole Bible 'n' ev'ythin', sho nuff."

He produced a battered Bible from a sterious interior pocket.

Yea! Old Jumbo's got a Bible!"

Razor, too, I'll bet!"

Marry 'em off, Jumbo!"

ogether the snake charmer and the el ascended the cheering aisle and oped in front of Jumbo, who adopted a ve pontifical air.

Where's your license, camel?"

Make it legal, camel."

man near by prodded Perry.

Give him a piece of paper, camel. thing'll do."

erry fumbled confusedly in his pocket, ad a folded paper and pushed it out ugh the camel's mouth. Holding it de down Jumbo pretended to scan it estly.

Dis yeah's a special camel's license," aid. "Get you ring ready, camel."

side the camel Perry turned round and ressed his worse half.

Gimme a ring, for Pete's sake!"

I ain't got none," protested a weary e.

You have. I saw it."

I ain't goin' to take it offen my hand."

If you don't I'll kill you."

here was a gasp and Perry felt a huge r of rhinestone and brass inserted into hand.

gain he was nudged from the outside.

Speak up!"

do!" cried Perry quickly.

e heard Betty's responses given in a ning debonair tone, and the sound of even in this burlesque thrilled him.

it was only real! he thought. If it was!

hen he had pushed the rhinestone ugh a tear in the camel's coat and was ing it on her finger, muttering ancient historic words after Jumbo. He didn't anyone to know about this ever. His idea was to slip away without having sclose his identity, for Mr. Tate had r kept his secret well. A dignified g man, Perry—and this might injure fant law practice.

Kiss her, camel!"

Embrace the bride!"

Unmask, camel, and kiss her!"

Instinctively his heart beat high as Betty turned to him laughingly and began play-fully to stroke the cardboard muzzle. He felt his self-control giving away, he longed to seize her in his arms and declare his identity and kiss those scarlet lips that smiled teasingly at him from only a foot away—when suddenly the laughter and applause round them died away and a curi-ous hush fell over the hall. Perry and Betty looked up in surprise. Jumbo had given vent to a huge "Hello!" in such a startled and amazed voice that all eyes were bent on him.

"Hello!" he said again. He had turned round the camel's marriage license, which he had been holding upside down, pro-duced spectacles and was studying it in-tently.

"Why," he exclaimed, and in the per-vading silence his words were heard plainly by everyone in the room, "this yeah's a sho-nuff marriage permit."

"What?"

"Huh?"

"Say it again, Jumbo!"

"Sure you can read?"

Jumbo waved them to silence and Perry's blood burned to fire in his veins as he realized the break he had made.

"Yassuh!" repeated Jumbo. "This yeah's a sho-nuff license, and the pa'ties concerned one of 'em is dis yeah young lady, Miz Betty Medill, and th' other's Mistah Perry Pa'khurst."

There was a general gasp, and a low rumble broke out as all eyes fell on the camel. Betty shrank away from him quickly, her tawny eyes giving out sparks of fury.

"Is you Mistah Pa'khurst, you camel?"

Perry made no answer. The crowd pressed up closer and stared at him as he stood frozen rigid with embarrassment, his cardboard face still hungry and sardonic, regarding the ominous Jumbo.

"You-all bettah speak up!" said Jumbo slowly, "this yeah's a mighty serous mat-tah. Outside mah duties at this club ah happens to be a sho-nuff minister in the Firs' Cullud Baptis' Church. It done look to me as though you-all is gone an' got married."

V

THE scene that followed will go down forever in the annals of the Tallyho Club. Stout matrons fainted, strong men swore, wild-eyed débutantes babbled in lightning groups instantly formed and in-stantly dissolved, and a great buzz of chat-ter, virulent yet oddly subdued, hummed through the chaotic ballroom. Feverish youths swore they would kill Perry or Jumbo or themselves or someone and the Baptis' preacheh was besieged by a tem-pestuous covey of clamorous amateur lawyers, asking questions, making threats, demanding precedents, ordering the bonds annulled, and especially trying to ferret out any hint or suspicion of prearrangement in what had occurred.

In the corner Mrs. Townsend was crying softly on the shoulder of Mr. Howard Tate, who was trying vainly to comfort her; they were exchanging "all my fault's" volubly and voluminously. Outside on a snow cov-ered walk Mr. Cyrus Medill, the Aluminum Man, was being paced slowly up and down between two brawny charioteers, giving vent now to a grunt, now to a string of unrepeatables, now to wild pleadings that they'd just let him get at Jumbo. He was facetiously attired for the evening as a wild man of Borneo, and the most exacting stage manager after one look at his face would have acknowledged that any improvement in casting the part would have been quite impossible.

Meanwhile the two principals held the real center of the stage. Betty Medill—or was it Betty Parkhurst?—weeping furi-ously, was surrounded by the plainer girls—the prettier ones were too busy talking about her to pay much attention to her—and over on the other side of the hall stood the camel, still intact except for his head-piece, which dangled pathetically on his chest. Perry was earnestly engaged in making protestations of his innocence to a ring of angry, puzzled men. Every few min-utes just as he had apparently proved his case someone would mention the marriage certificate, and the inquisition would begin again.

A girl named Marion Cloud, considered the second best belle of Toledo, changed the gist of the situation by a remark she made to Betty.

"Well," she said maliciously, "it'll all blow over, dear. The courts will annul it without question."

Betty's tears dried miraculously in her eyes, her lips shut tightly together, and she flashed a withering glance at Marion. Then she rose and scattering her sympathizers right and left walked directly across the room to Perry, who also rose and stood looking at her in terror. Again silence crept down upon the room.

"Will you have the decency," she said, "to grant me five minutes' conversation—or wasn't that included in your plans?"

He nodded, his mouth unable to form words.

Indicating coldly that he was to follow her she walked out into the hall with her chin uptilted and headed for the privacy of one of the little card rooms.

Perry started after her, but was brought to a jerky halt by the failure of his hind legs to function.

"You stay here!" he commanded sav-agely.

"I can't," whined a voice from the hump, "unless you get out first and let me get out."

Perry hesitated, but the curious crowd was unbearable, and unable any longer to tolerate eyes he muttered a command and with as much dignity as possible the camel moved carefully out on its four legs.

Betty was waiting for him.

"Well," she began furiously, "you see what you've done! You and that crazy license! I told you you shouldn't have got-ten it! I told you!"

"My dear girl, I ——"

"Don't dear-girl me! Save that for your real wife if you ever get one after this dis-graceful performance."

"I ——"

"And don't try to pretend it wasn't all arranged. You know you gave that col-ored waiter money! You know you did! Do you mean to say you didn't try to marry me?"

"No—I mean, yes—of course ——"

"Yes, you'd better admit it! You tried it, and now what are you going to do? Do you know my father's nearly crazy? It'll serve you right if he tries to kill you. He'll take his gun and put some cold steel in you. O-o-oh! Even if this marr—this thing can be annulled it'll hang over me all the rest of my life!"

Perry could not resist quoting softly: "'Oh, camel, wouldn't you like to belong to the pretty snake charmer for all your ——'"

"Shut up!" cried Betty.

There was a pause.

"Betty," said Perry finally with a very faint hopefulness, "there's only one thing to do that will really get us out clear. That's for you to marry me."

"Marry you!"

"Yes. Really it's the only ——"

"You shut up! I wouldn't marry you if—if ——"

"I know. If I were the last man on earth. But if you care anything about your reputation ——"

"Reputation!" she cried. "You're a nice one to think about my reputation *now*. Why didn't you think about my reputa-tion before you hired that horrible Jumbo to—to ——"

Perry tossed up his hands hopelessly.

"Very well. I'll do anything you want. Lord knows I renounce all claims!"

"But," said a new voice, "I don't."

Perry and Betty started, and she put her hand to her heart.

"For heaven's sake, what was that?"

"It's me," said the camel's back.

In a minute Perry had whipped off the camel's skin, and a lax, limp object, his clothes hanging on him damply, his hand clenched tightly on an almost empty bot-tle, stood defiantly before them.

"Oh," cried Betty, tears starting again to her eyes, "you brought that object in here to frighten me! You told me he was deaf—that awful person!"

The ex-camel's back sat down on a chair with a sigh of satisfaction.

"Don't talk 'at way about me, lady. I ain't no person. I'm your husband."

"Husband!"

The cry was wrung simultaneously from Betty and Perry.

"Why, sure. I'm as much your husband as that gink is. The smoke didn't marry you to the camel's front. He married you to the whole camel. Why, that's my ring you got on your finger!"

With a little cry she snatched the ring from her finger and flung it passionately at the floor.

"What's all this?" demanded Perry dazedly.

"Jes' that you better fix me an' fix me right. If you don't I'm a-gonna have the same claim you got to bein' married to her!"

"That's bigamy," said Perry, turning gravely to Betty.

Then came the supreme moment of Perry's early life, the ultimate chance on which he risked his fortunes. He rose and looked first at Betty, where she sat weakly, her face aghast at this new complication, and then at the individual who swayed from side to side on his chair, uncertainly yet menacingly.

"Very well," said Perry slowly to the in-dividual, "you can have her. Betty, I'm going to prove to you that as far as I'm concerned our marriage was entirely acci-dental. I'm going to renounce utterly my rights to have you as my wife, and give you to—to the man whose ring you wear—your lawful husband."

There was a pause and four horror-stricken eyes were turned on him.

"Good-by, Betty," he said brokenly. "Don't forget me in your new-found happi-ness. I'm going to leave for the Far West on the morning train. Think of me kindly, Betty."

With a last glance at them he turned on his heel and his head bowed on his chest as his hand touched the door knob.

"Good-by," he repeated. He turned the door knob.

But at these words a flying bundle of snakes and silk and tawny hair hurled itself at him.

"Oh, Perry, don't leave me! I can't face it alone! Perry, Perry, take me with you!"

Her tears rained down in a torrent and flowed damply on his neck. Calmly he folded his arms about her.

"I don't care," she cried tearfully. "I love you and if you can wake up a minister at this hour and have it done over again I'll go West with you."

Over her shoulder the front part of the camel looked at the back part of the camel—and they exchanged a particularly subtle, esoteric sort of wink that only true camels can understand.

BERNICE BOBS HER HAI

By F. Scott Fitzgerald

ILLUSTRATED BY MAY WILSON PRESTON

A FTER dark on Saturday night one could stand on the first tee of the golf course and see the country club windows as a yellow expanse over a very black and wavy ocean. The waves of this ocean, so to speak, were the heads of many curious caddies, a few of the more ingenious chauffeurs, the golf professional's deaf sister—and there were usually several stray, diffident waves who might have rolled inside had they so desired. This was the gallery.

The balcony was inside. It consisted of the circle of wicker chairs that lined the wall of the combination clubroom and ballroom. At these Saturday-night dances it was largely feminine; a great babel of middle-aged ladies with sharp eyes and icy hearts behind lorgnettes and large bosoms. The main function of the balcony was critical. It occasionally showed grudging admiration, but never approval, for it is well known among ladies over thirty-five that when the younger set dance in the summer time it is with the very worst intentions in the world, and if they are not bombarded with stony eyes stray couples will dance weird barbaric interludes in the corners, and the more popular, more dangerous girls will sometimes be kissed in the parked limousines of unsuspecting dowagers.

But after all, this critical circle is not close enough to the stage to see the actors' faces and catch the subtler byplay. It can only frown and lean, ask questions and make satisfactory deductions from its set of postulates, such as the one which states that every young man with a large income leads the life of a hunted partridge. It never really appreciates the drama of the shifting, semicruel world of adolescence. No; boxes, orchestra circle, principals and chorus are represented by the medley of faces and voices that sway to the plaintive African rhythm of Dyer's dance orchestra.

From sixteen-year-old Otis Ormonde, who has two more years at Hill School, to G. Reece Stoddard, over whose bureau at home hangs a Harvard law diploma; from little Madeleine Hogue, whose hair still feels strange and uncomfortable on top of her head, to Bessie MacRae, who has been the life of the party a little too long—more than ten years—the medley is not only the center of the stage but contains the only people capable of getting an unobstructed view of it.

With a flourish and a bang the music stops. The couples exchange artificial, effortless smiles, facetiously repeat "*la-de-da-dadum-dum*," and then the clatter of young feminine voices soars over the burst of clapping.

A few disappointed stags caught in midfloor as they had been about to cut in subsided listlessly back to the walls, because this was not the riotous Christmas dances. These summer hops were considered just pleasantly warm and exciting, where even the younger marrieds rose and performed ancient waltzes and terrifying fox trots to the tolerant amusement of their younger brothers and sisters.

Warren McIntyre, who casually attended Yale, being one of the unfortunate stags, felt in his dinner-coat pocket for a cigarette and strolled out onto the wide, semidark veranda, where couples were scattered at tables, filling the lantern-hung night with vague words and hazy laughter. He nodded here and there at the less absorbed and as he passed each couple some half-forgotten fragment of a story played in his mind, for it was not a large city and everyone was Who's Who to everyone else's past. There, for example, were Jim Strain and Ethel Demorest, who had been privately engaged for three years. Everyone knew that as soon as Jim managed to hold a job for more than two months she would marry him. Yet how bored

they both looked and how wearily Ethel regarded Jim sometimes, as if she wondered why she had trained the vines of her affection on such a wind-shaken poplar.

Warren was nineteen and rather pitying with those of his friends who hadn't gone East to college. But like most boys he bragged tremendously about the girls of his city when he was away from it. There was Genevieve Ormonde, who regularly made the rounds of dances, house parties and football games at Princeton, Yale, Williams and Cornell; there was black-eyed Roberta Dillon, who was quite as famous to her own generation as Hiram Johnson or Ty Cobb; and, of course, there was Marjorie Harvey, who besides having a fairylike face and a dazzling, bewildering tongue was already justly celebrated for having turned five cart wheels in succession during the last pump-and-slipper dance at New Haven.

Warren, who had grown up across the street from Marjorie, had long been wildly in love with her. Sometimes she seemed to reciprocate his feelings with a faint gratitude, but she had tried him by her infallible test and informed him gravely that she did not love him. Her test was that when she was away from him she forgot him and had affairs with other boys. Warren found this discouraging, especially as Marjorie had been making little trips all summer, and for the first two or three days after each arrival home he saw great heaps of mail on the Harveys' hall table addressed to her in various masculine handwritings. To make matters worse, all during the month of August she had been visited by her Cousin Bernice from Eau Claire, and it seemed impossible to see her alone. It was always necessary to hunt round and find someone to take care of Bernice. As August waned this was becoming more and more difficult.

Much as Warren loved Marjorie, he had to admit that Cousin Bernice was sorta hopeless. She was pretty, with dark hair and high color, but she was no fun on a party.

Every Saturday night he danced a long an duty dance with her to please Marjorie, but never been anything but bored in her com "Warren"—a soft voice at his elbow broke in up thoughts, and he turned to see Marjorie, flushe radiant as usual. She laid a hand on his shoulder glow settled almost imperceptibly over him.

"Warren," she whispered, "do something for dance with Bernice. She's been stuck with littl Ormonde for almost an hour."

Warren's glow faded.

"Why—sure," he answered half-heartedly.

"You don't mind, do you? I'll see that you do stuck."

"'Sall right."

Marjorie smiled—that smile that was thanks enou "You're an angel, and I'm obliged harshly."

With a sigh the angel glanced round the verand Bernice and Otis were not in sight. He wandered inside, and there in front of the women's dressing re found Otis in the center of a group of young men wh convulsed with laughter. Otis was brandishing a p timber he had picked up, and discoursing volubly.

"She's gone in to fix her hair," he announced v "I'm waiting to dance another hour with her."

Their laughter was renewed.

"Why don't some of you cut cried Otis resentfully. "She likes variety."

"Why, Otis," suggested a f "you've just barely got used to be "Why the two-by-four, Otis? quired Warren, smiling.

"The two-by-four? Oh, this? T club. When she comes out I'll b on the head and knock her in aga

Warren collapsed on a settee and howle glee.

"Never mind, Otis," he articulated f "I'm relieving you this time."

Otis simulated a sudden fainting attac handed the stick to Warren.

"If you need it, old man," he said hoarse

No matter how beautiful or brilliant a gi be, the reputation of not being frequently on makes her position at a dance unfort Perhaps boys prefer her company to stag butterflies with whom they dance a dozen an evening, but youth in this jazz-nourishe eration is temperamentally restless, and th of fox trotting more than one full fox tro the same girl is distasteful, not to say When it comes to several dances and the missions between she can be quite sure young man, once relieved, will never tre her wayward feet again.

Warren danced the next full dance with Bernic finally, thankful for the intermission, he led her to on the veranda. There was a moment's silence wh did unimpressive things with her fan.

"It's hotter here than in Eau Claire," she said.

Warren stifled a sigh and nodded. It might be fo knew or cared. He wondered idly whether she was conversationalist because she got no attention or attention because she was a poor conversationalist.

"You going to be here much longer?" he aske then turned rather red. She might suspect his reas asking.

"Another week," she answered, and stared at hi to lunge at his next remark when it left his lips.

Warren fidgeted. Then with a sudden charitabl pulse he decided to try part of his line on her. He and looked at her eyes.

"You've got an awfully kissable mouth," he quietly.

This was a remark that he sometimes made to college proms when they were talking in just su dark as this. Bernice distinctly jumped. She tur ungraceful red and became clumsy with her fan. had ever made such a remark to her before.

"Fresh!"—the word had slipped out before she w it, and she bit her lip. Too late she decided to be w and offered him a flustered smile.

Warren was annoyed. Though not accustomed that remark taken seriously, still it usually prov laugh or a paragraph of sentimental banter. And h to be called fresh, except in a joking way. His cla impulse died and he switched the topic.

"Jim Strain and Ethel Demorest sitting out as he commented.

This was more in Bernice's line, but a faint regr gled with her relief as the subject changed. Men

He Wondered Idly Whether She Was a Poor Conversationalist Because She Got No Attention or Got No Attention Because She Was a Poor Conversationalist

alk to her about kissable mouths, but she knew that they alked in some such way to other girls.

"Oh, yes," she said, and laughed. "I hear they've been nooning round for years without a red penny. Isn't it lly?"

Warren's disgust increased. Jim Strain was a close iend of his brother's, and anyway he considered it bad erm to sneer at people for not having money. But Bernice had had no intention of sneering. She was merely ervous.

II

WHEN Marjorie and Bernice reached home at half after midnight they said good night at the top of the airs. Though cousins, they were not intimates. As a atter of fact Marjorie had no female intimates—she considered girls stupid. Bernice on the contrary all through his parent-arranged visit had rather longed to exchange iose confidences flavored with giggles and tears that she nsidered an indispensable factor in all feminine interurse. But in this respect she found Marjorie rather cold; lt somehow the same difficulty in talking to her that she ad in talking to men. Marjorie never giggled, was never ightened, seldom embarrassed, and in fact had very few the qualities which Bernice considered appropriately d blessedly feminine.

As Bernice busied herself with toothbrush and paste is night she wondered for the hundredth time why she ver had any attention when she was away from home. hat her family were the wealthiest in Eau Claire; that r mother entertained tremendously, gave little dinners r her daughter before all dances and bought her a car of r own to drive round in never occurred to her as factors her home-town social success. Like most girls she had en brought up on the warm milk prepared by Annie llows Johnston and on novels in which the female was loved because of certain mysterious womanly qualities, ways mentioned but never displayed.

Bernice felt a vague pain that she was not at present gaged in being popular. She did not know that had it t been for Marjorie's campaigning she would have nced the entire evening with one man; but she knew that en in Eau Claire other girls with less position and less lchritude were given a much bigger rush. She attribd this to something subtly unscrupulous in those girls. had never worried her, and if it had her mother would

have assured her that the other girls cheapened themselves and that men really respected girls like Bernice.

She turned out the light in her bathroom, and on an impulse decided to go in and chat for a moment with her Aunt Josephine, whose light was still on. Her soft slippers bore her noiselessly down the carpeted hall, but hearing voices inside she stopped near the partly opened door. Then she caught her own name, and without any definite intention of eavesdropping lingered—and the thread of the conversation going on inside pierced her consciousness sharply as if it had been drawn through with a needle.

"She's absolutely hopeless!" It was Marjorie's voice. "Oh, I know what you're going to say! So many people have told you how pretty and sweet she is, and how she can cook! What of it? She has a bum time. Men don't like her."

"What's a little cheap popularity?"

Mrs. Harvey sounded annoyed.

"It's everything when you're eighteen," said Marjorie emphatically. "I've done my best. I've been polite and I've made men dance with her, but they just won't stand being bored. When I think of that gorgeous coloring wasted on such a ninny, and think what Martha Carey could do with it—oh!"

"There's no courtesy these days."

Mrs. Harvey's voice implied that modern situations were too much for her. When she was a girl all young ladies who belonged to nice families had glorious times.

"Well," said Marjorie, "no girl can permanently bolster up a lame-duck visitor, because these days it's every girl for herself. I've even tried to drop her hints about clothes and things, and she's been furious—given me the funniest looks. She's sensitive enough to know she's not getting away with much, but I'll bet she consoles herself by thinking that she's very virtuous and that I'm too gay and fickle and will come to a bad end. All unpopular girls think that way. Sour grapes! Sarah Hopkins refers to Genevieve and Roberta and me as gardenia girls! I'll bet she'd give ten years of her life and her European education to be a gardenia girl and have three or four men in love with her and be cut in on every few feet at dances."

"It seems to me," interrupted Mrs. Harvey rather wearily, "that you ought to be able to do something for Bernice. I know she's not very vivacious."

Marjorie groaned.

"Vivacious! Good grief! I've never heard her say anything to a boy except that it's hot or the floor's crowded or that she's going to school in New York next year. Sometimes she asks them what kind of car they have and tells them the kind she has. Thrilling!"

There was a short silence, and then Mrs. Harvey took up her refrain:

"All I know is that other girls not half so sweet and attractive get partners. Martha Carey, for instance, is stout and loud, and her mother is distinctly common. Roberta Dillon is so thin this year that she looks as though Arizona were the place for her. She's dancing herself to death."

"But, mother," objected Marjorie impatiently, "Martha is cheerful and awfully witty and an awfully slick girl, and Roberta's a marvelous dancer. She's been popular for ages!"

Mrs. Harvey yawned.

"I think it's that crazy Indian blood in Bernice," continued Marjorie. "Maybe she's a reversion to type. Indian women all just sat round and never said anything."

"Go to bed, you silly child," laughed Mrs. Harvey. "I wouldn't have told you that if I'd thought you were going to remember it. And I think most of your ideas are perfectly idiotic," she finished sleepily.

There was another silence, while Marjorie considered whether or not convincing her mother was worth the trouble. People over forty can seldom be permanently convinced of anything. At eighteen our convictions are hills from which we look; at forty-five they are caves in which we hide.

Having decided this, Marjorie said good night. When she came out into the hall it was quite empty.

III

WHILE Marjorie was breakfasting late next day Bernice came into the room with a rather formal good morning, sat down opposite, stared intently over and slightly moistened her lips.

(Continued on Page 159)

Bob Set

BERNICE BOBS HER HAIR

(Continued from Page 15)

"What's on your mind?" inquired Marjorie, rather puzzled.

Bernice paused before she threw her hand grenade.

"I heard what you said about me to your mother last night."

Marjorie was startled, but she showed only a faintly heightened color and her voice was quite even when she spoke.

"Where were you?"

"In the hall. I didn't mean to listen—at first."

After an involuntary look of contempt Marjorie dropped her eyes and became very interested in balancing a stray corn flake on her finger.

"I guess I'd better go back to Eau Claire—if I'm such a nuisance." Bernice's lower lip was trembling violently and she continued on a wavering note: "I've tried to be nice, and—and I've been first neglected and then insulted. No one ever visited me and got such treatment."

Marjorie was silent.

"But I'm in the way, I see. I'm a drag on you. Your friends don't like me." She paused, and then remembered another one of her grievances. "Of course I was furious last week when you tried to hint to me that that dress was unbecoming. Don't you think I know how to dress myself?"

"No," murmured Marjorie less than half aloud.

"What?"

"I didn't hint anything," said Marjorie succinctly. "I said, as I remember, that it was better to wear a becoming dress three times straight than to alternate it with two frights."

"Do you think that was a very nice thing to say?"

"I wasn't trying to be nice." Then after a pause: "When do you want to go?"

Bernice drew in her breath sharply.

"Oh!" It was a little half cry.

Marjorie looked up in surprise.

"Didn't you say you were going?"

"Yes, but——"

"Oh, you were only bluffing!"

They stared at each other across the breakfast table for a moment. Misty waves were passing before Bernice's eyes, while Marjorie's face wore that rather hard expression that she used when slightly intoxicated undergraduates were making love to her.

"So you were bluffing," she repeated as if it were what she might have expected.

Bernice admitted it by bursting into tears. Marjorie's eyes showed boredom.

"You're my cousin," sobbed Bernice. "I'm v-v-visiting you. I was to stay a month, and if I go home my mother will know and she'll wah-wonder——"

Marjorie waited until the shower of broken words collapsed into little sniffles.

"I'll give you my month's allowance," she said coldly, "and you can spend this last week anywhere you want. There's a very nice hotel——"

Bernice's sobs rose to a flute note, and rising of a sudden she fled from the room.

An hour later, while Marjorie was in the library absorbed in composing one of those noncommittal, marvelously elusive letters that only a young girl can write, Bernice reappeared, very red-eyed and consciously calm. She cast no glance at Marjorie but took a book at random from the shelf and sat down as if to read. Marjorie seemed absorbed in her letter and continued writing. When the clock showed noon Bernice closed her book with a snap.

"I suppose I'd better get my ticket."

This was not the beginning of the speech she had rehearsed upstairs, but as Marjorie was not getting her cues—wasn't urging her to be reasonable; it's all a mistake—it was the best opening she could muster.

"Just wait till I finish this letter," said Marjorie without looking round. "I want to get it off in the next mail."

After another minute, during which her pen scratched busily, she turned round and relaxed with an air of "at your service."

"Do you want me to go home?"

"Well," said Marjorie, considering, "I suppose if you're not having a good time you'd better go. No use being miserable."

"Don't you think common kindness——"

"Oh, please don't quote Little Women!" cried Marjorie impatiently. "That's out of style."

"You think so?"

"Heavens, yes! What modern girl could live like those inane females?"

"They were the models for our mothers."

Marjorie laughed.

"Yes, they were—not! Besides our mothers were all very well in their way, but they know very little about their daughters' problems."

Bernice drew herself up.

"Please don't talk about my mother."

Marjorie laughed.

"I don't think I mentioned her."

Bernice felt that she was being led away from her subject.

"Do you think you've treated me very well?"

"I've done my best. You're rather hard haven't a feminine quality in you."

The lids of Bernice's eyes reddened.

"I think you're hard and selfish, and you haven't a feminine quality in you."

"Oh, my Lord!" cried Marjorie in desperation. "You little nut! Girls like you are responsible for all the tiresome colorless marriages; all those ghastly inefficiencies that pass as feminine qualities. What a blow it must be when a man with imagination marries the beautiful bundle of clothes that he's been building ideals round, and finds that she's just a weak, whining, cowardly mass of affectations!"

Bernice's mouth had slipped half open.

"The womanly woman!" continued Marjorie. "Her whole early life is occupied in whining criticisms of girls like me who really do have a good time."

Bernice's jaw descended further as Marjorie's voice rose.

(Continued on Page 163)

"Well," said Marjorie, "No Girl Can Permanently Bolster Up a Lame-Duck Visitor, Because These Days it's Every Girl for Herself"

(Continued from Page 159)

"There's some excuse for an ugly girl hining. If I'd been irretrievably ugly I'd ever have forgiven my parents for bring- g me into the world. But you're starting 'e without any handicap——" Marjorie's tle fist clenched. "If you expect me to eep with you you'll be disappointed. Go stay, just as you like." And picking up er letters she left the room.

Bernice claimed a headache and failed to pear at luncheon. They had a matinée te for the afternoon, but the headache rsisting Marjorie made explanation to a t very downcast boy. But when she re- rned late in the afternoon she found ernice with a strangely set face waiting r her in her bedroom.

"I've decided," began Bernice without eliminaries, "that maybe you're right out things—possibly not. But if you'll l me why your friends aren't—aren't in- ested in me I'll see if I can do what you nt me to."

Marjorie was at the mirror shaking down r hair.

"Do you mean it?"

"Yes."

"Without reservations? Will you do ex- tly what I say?"

"Well, I —— "

"Well nothing! Will you do exactly as ay?"

"If they're sensible things."

"They're not! You're no case for sen- le things."

"Are you going to make—to recom- nd —— "

"Yes, everything. If I tell you to take cing lessons you'll have to do it. Write ne and tell your mother you're going to y another two weeks."

'If you'll tell me —— "

'All right—I'll just give you a few ex- ples now. First, you have no ease of nner. Why? Because you're never sure out your personal appearance. When a feels that she's perfectly groomed and ssed she can forget that part of her. at's charm. The more parts of yourself can afford to forget the more charm have."

'Don't I look all right?"

"No; for instance, you never take care of r eyebrows. They're black and lus- us, but by leaving them straggly they're lemish. They'd be beautiful if you'd e care of them in one-tenth the time you e doing nothing. You're going to brush m so that they'll grow straight."

'ernice raised the brows in question.

Do you mean to say that men notice brows?"

Yes—subconsciously. And when you home you ought to have your teeth ightened a little. It's almost imper- tible, still —— "

But I thought," interrupted Bernice in wilderment, "that you despised little nty feminine things like that."

I hate dainty minds," answered Mar- e. "But a girl has to be dainty in person. he looks like a million dollars she can about Russia, ping-pong or the League Nations and get away with it."

What else?"

Oh, I'm just beginning! There's your cing."

Don't I dance all right?"

No, you don't—you lean on a man; yes, do—ever so slightly. I noticed it when were dancing together yesterday. And dance standing up straight instead of ding over a little. Probably some old on the side line once told you that you ked so dignified that way. But except a very small girl it's much harder on man, and he's the one that counts."

Go on." Bernice's brain was reeling.

Well, you've got to learn to be nice to who are sad birds. You look as if 'd been insulted whenever you're own with any except the most popular s. Why, Bernice, I'm cut in on every feet—and who does most of it? Why, e very sad birds. No girl can afford to ect them. They're the big part of any vd. Young boys too shy to talk are the best conversational practice. Clumsy s are the best dancing practice. If you follow them and yet look graceful you follow a baby tank across a barb-wire craper."

ernice sighed profoundly, but Marjorie not through.

If you go to a dance and really amuse, three sad birds that dance with you; u talk so well to them that they forget 're stuck with you you've done some- g. They'll come back next time, and gradually so many sad birds will dance with you that the attractive boys will see there's no danger of being stuck—then they'll dance with you."

"Yes," agreed Bernice faintly. "I think I begin to see."

"And finally," concluded Marjorie, "poise and charm will just come. You'll wake up some morning knowing you've attained it, and men will know it too."

Bernice rose.

"It's been awfully kind of you—but nobody's ever talked to me like this before, and I feel sort of startled."

Marjorie made no answer but gazed pensively at her own image in the mirror.

"You're a peach to help me," continued Bernice.

Still Marjorie did not answer, and Bernice thought she had seemed too grateful.

"I know you don't like sentiment," she said timidly.

Marjorie turned to her quickly.

"Oh, I wasn't thinking about that. I was considering whether we hadn't better bob your hair."

Bernice collapsed backward upon the bed.

IV

ON THE following Wednesday evening there was a dinner dance at the country club. When the guests strolled in Bernice found her place card with a light feeling of irritation. Though at her right sat G. Reece Stoddard, a most desirable and distinguished young bachelor, the all-important left held only Charley Paulson. Charley lacked height, beauty and social shrewdness, and in her new enlightenment Bernice decided that his only qualification to be her partner was that he had never been stuck with her. But this feeling of irritation left with the last of the soup plates, and Marjorie's specific instruction came to her. Swallowing her pride she turned to Charley Paulson and plunged.

"Do you think I ought to bob my hair, Mr. Charley Paulson?"

Charley looked up in surprise.

"Why?"

"Because I'm considering it. It's such a sure and easy way of attracting attention."

Charley smiled pleasantly. He could not know this had been rehearsed. He replied that he didn't know much about bobbed hair. But Bernice was there to tell him.

"I want to be a society vampire, you see," she announced coolly, and went on to inform him that bobbed hair was the necessary prelude. She added that she wanted to ask his advice, because she had heard he was so critical about girls.

Charley, who knew as much about the psychology of women as he did of the mental states of Buddhist contemplatives, felt vaguely flattered.

"So I've decided," she continued, her voice rising slightly, "that early next week I'm going down to the Sevier Hotel barber shop, sit in the first chair and get my hair bobbed." She faltered, noticing that the people near her had paused in their conversation and were listening; but after a confused second Marjorie's coaching told, and she finished her paragraph to the vicinity at large. "Of course I'm charging admission, but if you'll all come down and encourage me I'll issue passes for the inside seats."

There was a ripple of appreciative laughter, and under cover of it G. Reece Stoddard leaned over quickly and said close to her ear: "I'll take a box right now."

She met his eyes and smiled as if he had said something surpassingly brilliant.

"Do you believe in bobbed hair?" asked G. Reece in the same undertone.

"I think it's unmoral," affirmed Bernice gravely. "But, of course, you've either got to amuse people or feed 'em or shock 'em." Marjorie had culled this from Oscar Wilde. It was greeted with a ripple of laughter from the men and a series of quick, intent looks from the girls. And then as though she had said nothing of wit or moment Bernice turned again to Charley and spoke confidentially in his ear.

"I want to ask you your opinion of several people. I imagine you're a wonderful judge of character."

Charley thrilled faintly—paid her a subtle compliment by overturning her water.

Two hours later, while Warren McIntyre was standing passively in the stag line abstractedly watching the dancers and wondering whither and with whom Marjorie had disappeared, an unrelated perception began to creep slowly upon him—a perception that Bernice, cousin to Marjorie, had been cut in on several times in the past five minutes. He closed his eyes, opened them and looked again. Several minutes back she had been dancing with a visiting boy, a matter easily accounted for; a visiting boy would know no better. But now she was dancing with someone else, and there was Charley Paulson headed for her with enthusiastic determination in his eye. Funny—Charley seldom danced with more than three girls an evening.

Warren was distinctly surprised when—the exchange having been effected—the man relieved proved to be none other than G. Reece Stoddard himself. And G. Reece seemed not at all jubilant at being relieved. Next time Bernice danced near, Warren regarded her intently. Yes, she was pretty, distinctly pretty; and to-night her face seemed really vivacious. She had that look that no woman, however histrionically proficient, can successfully counterfeit—she looked as if she were having a good time. He liked the way she had her hair arranged, wondered if it was brilliantine that made it glisten so. And that dress was becoming—a dark red that set off her shadowy eyes and high coloring. He remembered that he had thought her pretty when she first came to town, before he had realized that she was dull. Too bad she was dull—dull girls unbearable—certainly pretty though.

His thoughts zigzagged back to Marjorie. This disappearance would be like other disappearances. When she reappeared he would demand where she had been—would be told emphatically that it was none of his business. What a pity she was so sure of him! She basked in the knowledge that no other girl in town interested him; she defied him to fall in love with Genevieve or Roberta.

Warren sighed. The way to Marjorie's affections was a labyrinth indeed. He looked up. Bernice was again dancing with the visiting boy. Half unconsciously he took a step out from the stag line in her direction, and hesitated. Then he said to himself that it was charity. He walked toward her—collided suddenly with G. Reece Stoddard.

"Pardon me," said Warren.

But G. Reece had not stopped to apologize. He had again cut in on Bernice.

That night at one o'clock Marjorie, with one hand on the electric-light switch in the hall, turned to take a last look at Bernice's sparkling eyes.

"So it worked?"

"Oh, Marjorie, yes!" cried Bernice.

"I saw you were having a gay time."

"I did! The only trouble was that about midnight I ran short of talk. I had to repeat myself—with different men of course. I hope they won't compare notes."

"Men don't," said Marjorie, yawning, "and it wouldn't matter if they did—they'd think you were even trickier."

She snapped out the light, and as they started up the stairs Bernice grasped the banister thankfully. For the first time in her life she had been danced tired.

"You see," said Marjorie at the top of the stairs, "one man sees another man cut in and he thinks there must be something there. Well, we'll fix up some new stuff to-morrow. Good night."

"Good night."

As Bernice took down her hair she passed the evening before her in review. She had followed instructions exactly. Even when Charley Paulson cut in for the eighth time she had simulated delight and had apparently been both interested and flattered. She had not talked about the weather or Eau Claire or automobiles or her school, but had confined her conversation to me, you and us.

But a few minutes before she fell asleep a rebellious thought was churning drowsily in her brain—after all, it was she who had done it. Marjorie, to be sure, had given her her conversation, but then Marjorie got much of her conversation out of things she read. Bernice had bought the red dress, though she had never valued it highly before—and her own voice had said the words, her own lips had smiled, her own feet had danced. Marjorie nice girl—vain, though—nice evening—nice boys—like Warren—Warren—Warren—what's-his-name—Warren ——

She fell asleep.

V

TO BERNICE the next week was a revelation. With the feeling that people really enjoyed looking at her and listening to her came the foundation of self-confidence. Of course there were numerous mistakes at first. She did not know, for instance, that Draycott Deyo was studying for the ministry; she was unaware that he had cut in on her because he thought she was a quiet, reserved girl. Had she known these things she would not have treated him to the line which began "Hello, Shell Shock!" and continued with the bathtub story—"It takes a frightful lot of energy to fix my hair in the summer—there's so much of it—so I always fix it first and powder my face and put on my hat; then I get into the bathtub, and dress afterward. Don't you think that's the best plan?"

Though Draycott Deyo was in the throes of difficulties concerning baptism by immersion and might possibly have seen a connection, it must be admitted that he did not. He considered feminine bathing an immoral subject, and gave her some of his ideas on the depravity of modern society.

But to offset that unfortunate occurrence Bernice had several signal successes to her credit. Little Otis Ormonde pleaded off from a trip East and elected instead to follow her with a puppylike devotion, to the amusement of his crowd and to the irritation of G. Reece Stoddard, several of whose afternoon calls Otis completely ruined by the disgusting tenderness of the glances he bent on Bernice. He even told her the story of the two-by-four and the dressing room to show her how frightfully mistaken he and everyone else had been in their first judgment of her. Bernice laughed off that incident with a slight sinking sensation.

Of all Bernice's conversation perhaps the best known and most universally approved was the line about the bobbing of her hair.

"Oh, Bernice, when you goin' to get the hair bobbed?"

"Day after to-morrow maybe," she would reply, laughing. "Will you come and see me? Because I'm counting on you, you know."

"Will we? You know! But you better hurry up."

Bernice, whose tonsorial intentions were strictly dishonorable, would laugh again.

"Pretty soon now. You'd be surprised."

But perhaps the most significant symbol of her success was the gray car of the hypercritical Warren McIntyre, parked daily in front of the Harvey house. At first the parlor maid was distinctly startled when he asked for Bernice instead of Marjorie; after a week of it she told the cook that Miss Bernice had gotta holda Miss Marjorie's best fella.

And Miss Bernice had. Perhaps it began with Warren's desire to rouse jealousy in Marjorie; perhaps it was the familiar though unrecognized strain of Marjorie in Bernice's conversation; perhaps it was both of these and something of sincere attraction besides. But somehow the collective mind of the younger set knew within a week that Marjorie's most reliable beau had made an amazing face-about and was giving an indisputable rush to Marjorie's guest. The question of the moment was how Marjorie would take it. Warren called Bernice on the phone twice a day, sent her notes, and they were frequently seen together in his roadster, obviously engrossed in one of those tense, significant conversations as to whether or not he was sincere.

Marjorie on being twitted only laughed. She said she was mighty glad that Warren had at last found someone who appreciated him. So the younger set laughed, too, and guessed that Marjorie didn't care and let it go at that.

One afternoon when there were only three days left of her visit Bernice was waiting in the hall for Warren, with whom she was going to a bridge party. She was in rather a blissful mood, and when Marjorie—also bound for the party—appeared beside her and began casually to adjust her hat in the mirror Bernice was utterly unprepared for anything in the nature of a clash. Marjorie did her work very coldly and succinctly in three sentences.

"You may as well get Warren out of your head," she said coldly.

"What?" Bernice was utterly astounded.

"You may as well stop making a fool of yourself over Warren McIntyre. He doesn't care a snap of his fingers about you."

For a tense moment they regarded each other—Marjorie scornfu' aloof; Bernice astounded, half angry, half afraid. Then two cars drove up in front ot the house and there was a riotous honking. Both of them gasped faintly, turned, and side by side hurried out.

(Concluded on Page 167)

Appendix One

(Concluded from Page 163)

All through the bridge party Bernice strove in vain to master a rising uneasiness. She had offended Marjorie, the sphinx of sphinxes. With the most wholesome and innocent intentions in the world she had stolen Marjorie's property. She felt suddenly and horribly guilty. After the bridge game, when they sat in an informal circle and the conversation became general, the storm gradually broke. Little Otis Ormonde inadvertently precipitated it.

"When you going back to kindergarten, Otis?" someone had asked.

"Me? Day Bernice gets her hair bobbed."

"Then your education's over," said Marjorie quickly. "That's only a bluff of hers. I should think you'd have realized."

"That a fact?" demanded Otis, giving Bernice a reproachful glance.

Bernice's ears burned as she tried to think up an effectual come-back. In the face of this direct attack her imagination was paralyzed.

"There's a lot of bluffs in the world," continued Marjorie quite pleasantly. "I should think you'd be young enough to know that, Otis."

"Well," said Otis, "maybe so. But gee! With a line like Bernice's —— "

"Really?" yawned Marjorie. "What's her latest bon mot?"

No one seemed to know. In fact, Bernice, having trifled with her muse's beau, had said nothing memorable of late.

"Was that really all a line?" asked Roberta curiously.

Bernice hesitated. She felt that wit in some form was demanded of her, but under her cousin's suddenly frigid eyes she was completely incapacitated.

"I don't know," she stalled.

"Splush!" said Marjorie. "Admit it!"

Bernice saw that Warren's eyes had left a ukulele he had been tinkering with and were fixed on her questioningly.

"Oh, I don't know!" she repeated steadily. Her cheeks were glowing.

"Splush!" remarked Marjorie again.

"Come through, Bernice," urged Otis. "Tell her where to get off."

Bernice looked round again—she seemed unable to get away from Warren's eyes.

"I like bobbed hair," she said hurriedly, as if he had asked her a question, "and I intend to bob mine."

"When?" demanded Marjorie.

"Any time."

"No time like the present," suggested Roberta.

Otis jumped to his feet.

"Swell stuff!" he cried. "We'll have a summer bobbing party. Sevier Hotel barber shop, I think you said."

In an instant all were on their feet. Bernice's heart throbbed violently.

"What?" she gasped.

Out of the group came Marjorie's voice, very clear and contemptuous.

"Don't worry—she'll back out!"

"Come on, Bernice!" cried Otis, starting toward the door.

Four eyes—Warren's and Marjorie's—stared at her, challenged her, defied her. For another second she wavered wildly.

"All right," she said swiftly, "I don't care if I do."

An eternity of minutes later, riding down town through the late afternoon beside Warren, the others following in Roberta's car close behind, Bernice had all the sensations of Marie Antoinette bound for the guillotine in a tumbrel. Vaguely she wondered why she did not cry out that it was all a mistake. It was all she could do to keep from clutching her hair with both hands to protect it from the suddenly hostile world. Yet she did neither. Even the thought of her mother was no deterrent now. This was the test supreme of her sportsmanship; her right to walk unchallenged in the starry heaven of popular girls.

Warren was moodily silent, and when they came to the hotel he drew up at the curb and nodded to Bernice to precede him out. Roberta's car emptied a laughing crowd into the shop, which presented two bold plate-glass windows to the street.

Bernice stood on the curb and looked at the sign, Sevier Barber Shop. It was a guillotine indeed, and the hangman was the first barber, who, attired in a white coat and smoking a cigarette, leaned nonchalantly against the first chair. He must have heard of her; he must have been waiting all week, smoking eternal cigarettes beside that portentous, too-often-mentioned first chair. Would they blindfold her? No, but they would tie a white cloth round her neck lest any of her blood—nonsense—hair—should get on her clothes.

"All right, Bernice," said Warren quickly.

With her chin in the air she crossed the sidewalk, pushed open the swinging screen door, and giving not a glance to the uproarious, riotous row that occupied the waiting bench went up to the first barber.

"I want you to bob my hair."

The first barber's mouth slid somewhat open. His cigarette dropped to the floor.

"Huh?"

"My hair—bob it!"

Refusing further preliminaries, Bernice took her seat on high. A man in the chair next to her turned on his side and gave her a glance, half lather, half amazement. One barber started and spoiled little Willy Schuneman's monthly haircut. Mr. O'Reilly in the last chair grunted and swore musically in ancient Gaelic as a razor bit into his cheek. Two bootblacks became wide-eyed and rushed for her feet. No, Bernice didn't care for a shine.

Outside a passer-by stopped and stared; a couple joined him; half a dozen small boys' noses sprang into life, flattened against the glass; and snatches of conversation borne on the summer breeze drifted in through the screen door.

"Lookada long hair on a kid!"

"Where'd yuh get 'at stuff? 'At's a bearded lady he just finished shavin'."

But Bernice saw nothing, heard nothing. Her only living sense told her that this man in the white coat had removed one tortoise-shell comb and then another; that his fingers were fumbling clumsily with unfamiliar hairpins; that this hair, this wonderful hair of hers, was going—she would never again feel its long voluptuous pull as it hung in a dark-brown glory down her back. For a second she was near breaking down, and then the picture before her swam mechanically into her vision—Marjorie's mouth curling in a faint ironic smile as if to say:

"Give up and get down! You tried to buck me and I called your bluff. You see you haven't got a prayer."

And some last energy rose up in Bernice, for she clenched her hands under the white cloth, and there was a curious narrowing of her eyes that Marjorie remarked on to someone long afterward.

Twenty minutes later the barber swung her round to face the mirror, and she flinched at the full extent of the damage that had been wrought. Her hair was not curly, and now it lay in lank lifeless blocks on both sides of her suddenly pale face. It was ugly as sin—she had known it would be ugly as sin. Her face's chief charm had been a Madonna-like simplicity. Now that was gone and she was—well, frightfully mediocre—not stagy; only ridiculous, like a Greenwich Villager who had left her spectacles at home.

As she climbed down from the chair she tried to smile—failed miserably. She saw two of the girls exchange glances; noticed Marjorie's mouth curved in attenuated mockery—and that Warren's eyes were suddenly very cold.

"You see"—her words fell into an awkward pause—"I've done it."

"Yes, you've—done it," admitted Warren.

"Do you like it?"

There was a half-hearted "Sure" from two or three voices, another awkward pause, and then Marjorie turned swiftly and with serpentlike intensity to Warren.

"Would you mind running me down to Derry's shop?" she asked. "I've simply got to get a hat there before supper. Roberta's driving right home and she can take the others."

Warren stared abstractedly at some infinite speck out the window. Then for an instant his eyes rested coldly on Bernice before they turned to Marjorie.

"Be glad to," he said slowly.

VI

BERNICE did not fully realize the outrageous trap that had been set for her until she met her aunt's amazed glance just before dinner.

"Why, Bernice!"

"I've bobbed it, Aunt Josephine."

"Why, child!"

"Do you like it?"

"Why, Ber-nice!"

"I suppose I've shocked you."

"No, but what'll Mrs. Deyo think to-morrow night? Bernice, you should have waited until after the Deyos' dance—you should have waited if you wanted to do that."

"It was sudden, Aunt Josephine. Anyway, why does it matter to Mrs. Deyo particularly?"

"Why, child," cried Mrs. Harvey, "in her paper on The Foibles of the Younger Generation that she read at the last meeting of the Thursday Club she devoted fifteen minutes to bobbed hair. It's her pet abomination. And the dance is for you and Marjorie!"

"I'm sorry."

"Oh, Bernice, what'll your mother say? She'll think I let you do it."

"I'm sorry."

Dinner was an agony. She had made a hasty attempt with a curling iron, and burned her finger and much hair. She could see that her aunt was both worried and grieved, and her uncle kept saying, "Well, I'll be darned!" over and over in a hurt and faintly hostile tone. And Marjorie sat very quietly, intrenched behind a faint smile, a faintly mocking smile.

Somehow she got through the evening. Three boys called; Marjorie disappeared with one of them, and Bernice made a listless mechanical attempt to entertain the two others—sighed thankfully as she climbed the stairs to her room at half past ten. What a day!

When she had undressed for the night the door opened and Marjorie came in.

"Bernice," she said, "I'm awfully sorry about the Deyo dance. I'll give you my word of honor I'd forgotten all about it."

"'Sall right," said Bernice shortly. Standing before the mirror she passed her comb slowly through her short hair.

"I'll take you downtown to-morrow," continued Marjorie, "and the hairdresser'll fix it so you'll look slick. I didn't imagine you'd go through with it. I'm really mighty sorry."

"Oh, 'sall right!"

"Still it's your last night, so I suppose it won't matter much."

Then Bernice winced as Marjorie tossed her own hair over her shoulders and began to twist it slowly into two long blond braids until in her cream-colored negligee she looked like a delicate painting of some Saxon princess. Fascinated, Bernice watched the braids grow. Heavy and luxurious they were, moving under the supple fingers like restive snakes—and to Bernice remained this relic and the curling iron and a to-morrow full of eyes. She could see G. Reece Stoddard, who liked her, assuming his Harvard manner and telling his din partner that Bernice shouldn't have be allowed to go to the movies so mu she could see Draycott Deyo exchang glances with his mother and then being c scientiously charitable to her. But t perhaps by to-morrow Mrs. Deyo wo have heard the news; would send round icy little note requesting that she fai appear—and behind her back they wo all laugh and know that Marjorie had m a fool of her; that her chance at beauty been sacrificed to the jealous whim of a s ish girl. She sat down suddenly before mirror, biting the inside of her cheek.

"I like it," she said with an effort. think it'll be becoming."

Marjorie smiled.

"It looks all right. For heaven's sa don't let it worry you!"

"I won't."

"Good night, Bernice."

But as the door closed someth snapped within Bernice. She sprang namically to her feet, clenching her ha then swiftly and noiselessly crossed ove her bed and from underneath it drag out her suitcase. Into it she tossed t articles and a change of clothing. Then turned to her trunk and quickly dumpe two drawerfuls of lingerie and sum dresses. She moved quietly, but with de efficiency, and in three-quarters of an h her trunk was locked and strapped and was fully dressed in a becoming new tra ing suit that Marjorie had helped her out.

Sitting down at her desk she wro short note to Mrs. Harvey, in which briefly outlined her reasons for going. sealed it, addressed it and laid it on pillow. She glanced at her watch. train left at one, and she knew that i walked down to the Marborough Hotel blocks away she could easily get a tax

Suddenly she drew in her breath sh and an expression flashed into her eyes a practiced character reader might connected vaguely with the set look had worn in the barber's chair—someh development of it. It was quite a new for Bernice—and it carried conseque

She went stealthily to the bureau, pi up an article that lay there, and turnin all the lights stood quietly until her became accustomed to the darkness. S she pushed open the door to Marj room. She heard the quiet even brea of an untroubled conscience asleep.

She was by the bedside now, very erate and calm. She acted swiftly. Ber over she found one of the braids of jorie's hair, followed it up with her ha the point nearest the head, and then ing it a little slack so that the sleeper w feel no pull she reached down with shears and severed it. With the pigt her hand she held her breath. Marjori muttered something in her sleep. B deftly amputated the other braid, pa for an instant, and then flitted swiftly silently back to her own room.

Downstairs she opened the big front sed it carefully behind her, and f idly happy and exuberant stepped porch into the moonlight, swingin heavy grip like a shopping bag. A minute's brisk walk she discovered th left hand still held the two blond b She laughed unexpectedly—had to sh mouth hard to keep from emitting an lute peal. She was passing Warren's now, and on the impulse she set dow baggage, and swinging the braids pieces of rope flung them at the w porch, where they landed with a thud. She laughed again, no longe straining herself.

"Huh!" she giggled wildly. "Sca selfish thing!"

Then picking up her suitcase she s at a half run down the moonlit street.

THE SATURDAY EVENING POST   May 22, 1920

THE ICE PALACE

By F. Scott Fitzgerald

ILLUSTRATED BY JAMES H. CRANK

THE sunlight dripped over the house like golden paint over an art jar and the freckling shadows here and there only intensified rigor of the bath of light. The Butterworth great stodgy trees; only the Happer house took the sun and all day long faced the dusty road-street with errant kindly patience. This was the city of Tarleton southernmost Georgia—September afternoon.

o in her bedroom window Sally Carrol Happer rested nineteen-year-old chin on a fifty-two-year-old sill watched Clark Darrow's ancient flivver turn the er. The car was hot—being partly metallic it retained he heat it absorbed or evolved—and Clark Darrow g bolt upright at the wheel wore a pained, strained ssion as though he considered himself a spare part rather likely to break. He laboriously crossed two ruts, the wheels squeaking indignantly at the encounand then with a terrifying expression he gave the ng gear a final wrench and deposited self and car oximately in front of the Happer steps. There was a tive heaving sound, a death rattle, followed by a silence; and then the air was rent by a startling le.

ly Carrol gazed down sleepily. She started to yawn, nding this quite impossible unless she raised her chin the window sill changed her mind and continued ly to regard the car, whose owner sat brilliantly if nctorily at attention as he waited for an answer to his air. After a moment the whistle once more split the air.

ood mawnin'."

ch difficulty Clark twisted his tall body round and a distorted glance on the window.

'ain't mawnin', Sally Carrol."

n't it, sure enough?"

'hat you doin'?"

atin' 'n apple."

ome on go swimmin'—want to?"

eckon so."

ow 'bout hurryin' up?"

are enough?"

y Carrol sighed voluminously and raised herself with and inertia from the floor, where she had been oc in alternately destroying parts of a green apple ainting paper dolls for her younger sister. She ached a mirror, regarded her expression with a d and pleasant languor, dabbed two spots of rouge lips and a grain of powder on her nose and cov er bobbed corn-colored hair with a rose-littered nnet. Then she kicked over the painting water, "Oh, damn!"—but let it lie—and left the room.

w you, Clark?" she inquired a min er as she slipped nimbly over the the car.

ighty fine, Sally Carrol."

here we go swimmin'?"

t to Walley's Pool. Told Marylyn all by an' get her an' Joe Ewing." k was dark and lean and when on s rather inclined to

His eyes were omi nd his expression petulant except startlingly illumi ny one of his fre miles. Clark had was locally called me"—just enough himself in ease and n gasoline—and he ent the two years e graduated from Tech in dozing the lazy streets of e town discussing could best invest tal for an immedi une.

Swathed in Furs Sally Carrol Put in a Morning Tobogganing on the Country-Club Hill

Hanging round he found not at all difficult; a crowd of little girls had grown up beautifully, the amazing Sally Carrol foremost among them; and they enjoyed being swum with and danced with and made love to in the flower-filled summery evenings—and they all liked Clark immensely. When feminine company palled there were half a dozen other youths who were always just about to do something and meanwhile were quite willing to join him in a few holes of golf or a game of billiards or the consumption of a quart of "hard yella licker." Every once in a while one of these contemporaries made a farewell round of calls before going up to New York or Philadelphia or Pittsburgh to go into business, but mostly they just stayed round in this languid paradise of dreamy skies and firefly evenings and noisy street

fairs—and especially of gracious soft-voiced girls who were brought up on memories instead of money.

The flivver having been excited into a sort of restless resentful life Clark and Sally Carrol rolled and rattled down Valley Avenue into Jefferson Street, where the dust road became a pavement; along opiate Millicent Place, where there were half a dozen prosperous substantial mansions; and on into the downtown section.

Driving was perilous here, for it was shopping time; the population idled casually across the streets and a drove of low-moaning oxen were being urged along in front of a placid street car; even the shops seemed only yawning their doors and blinking their windows in the sunshine before retiring into a state of utter and finite coma.

"Sally Carrol," said Clark suddenly, "it a fact that you're engaged?"

She looked at him quickly.

"Where'd you hear that?"

"Sure enough, you engaged?"

"'At's a nice question to ask a girl!"

"Girl told me you were engaged to a Yankee you met up in Asheville last summah."

Sally Carrol sighed.

"Never saw such an old town faw rumors."

"Don't marry a Yankee, Sally Carrol. We need you round here."

Sally Carrol was silent a moment.

"Clark," she demanded suddenly, "who on earth shall I marry?"

"I offah my services."

"Honey, you couldn't suppawt a wife," she answered cheerfully. "Anyway, I know you too well to fall in love with you."

"'At doesn't mean you ought to marry a Yankee."

"S'pose I love him?"

He shook his head.

"You couldn't. He'd be a lot different from us, every way."

He broke off as he halted the car in front of a rambling dilapidated house. Marylyn Wade and Joe Ewing appeared in the doorway.

"'Lo, Sally Carrol."

"Hi!"

"How you-all?"

"Sally Carrol," demanded Marylyn as they started off again, "you engaged?"

"Lawdy, where'd all this start? Can't I look at a man 'thout everybody in town engagin' me to him?"

Clark stared straight in front of him at a bolt on the clattering wind shield.

"Sally Carrol," he said with a curious intensity, "don't you like us?"

"What?"

"Us down here?"

"Why, Clark, you know I do. I adore all you boys."

"Then why you gettin' engaged to a Yankee?"

"Clark, I don't know. I'm not sure what I'll do, but—well, I want to go places and see people. I want my mind to grow. I want to live where things happen on a big scale."

"What you mean?"

"Oh, Clark, I love you, and I love Joe here, and Ben Arrot, and you all, but you'll—you'll ——"

"We'll all be failures?"

"Yes. I don't mean only money failures but just sort of—of ineffectual and sad and—oh, how can I tell you?"

"You mean because we stay here in Tarleton?"

"Yes, Clark; and because you like it and never want to change things or think or go ahead."

He nodded and she reached over and pressed his hand.

"Clark," she said softly, "I wouldn't change you for the world. You're sweet the way you are. The things that'll make you fail I'll love always—the living in the past, the lazy days and nights you have, and all your carelessness and generosity."

"But you're goin' away?"

"Yes—because I couldn't ever marry you. You've a place in my heart no one else ever could have, but tied down here I'd get restless. I'd feel I was—wastin' myself. There's two sides to me, you see. There's the sleepy old side you love; an' there's a sawt of energy—the feelin' that makes me do wild things. That's the part of me that may be useful somewhere, that'll last when I'm not beautiful any more."

She broke off with characteristic suddenness and sighed, "Oh, sweet cooky!" as her mood changed.

Half closing her eyes and tipping back her head till it rested on the seat back she let the savory breeze fan her eyes and ripple the fluffy curls of her bobbed hair. They were in the country now, hurrying between tangled growths of bright-green coppice and grass and tall trees that sent sprays of foliage to hang a cool welcome over the road. Here and there they passed a battered negro cabin, its oldest white-haired inhabitant smoking a corncob pipe beside the door and half a dozen scantily clothed

They Passed Through the Gateway and Followed a Path That Led Through a Wavy Valley of Graves

...monies parading tattered dolls on the wild grown grass in front. Further out were lazy cotton fields, where even the workers seemed intangible shadows lent by the sun to the earth not for toil but to while away some age-old tradition in the golden September fields. And round the drowsy picturesqueness, over the trees and shacks and muddy rivers, flowed the heat, never hostile, only comforting like a great warm nourishing bosom for the infant earth.

"Sally Carrol, we're here!"

"Poor chile's soun' asleep."

"Honey, you dead at last outa sheer laziness?"

"Water, Sally Carrol! Cool water waitin' faw you!"

Her eyes opened sleepily.

"Hi!" she murmured, smiling.

II

IN NOVEMBER Harry Bellamy, tall, broad and brisk, came down from his Northern city to spend four days. His intention was to settle a matter that had been hanging fire since he and Sally Carrol had met in Asheville, North Carolina, in midsummer. The settlement took only a quiet afternoon and an evening in front of a glowing open fire, for Harry Bellamy had everything Sally Carrol wanted; and, besides, she loved him—loved him with that side of her she kept especially for loving. Sally Carrol had several rather clearly defined sides.

On his last afternoon they walked, and she found their steps tending half-unconsciously toward one of her favorite haunts, the cemetery. When it came in sight, gray-white and golden-green under the cheerful late sun, she paused irresolute by the iron gate.

"Are you mournful by nature, Harry?" she asked with a faint smile.

"Mournful? Not I."

"Then let's go in here. It depresses some folks, but I like it."

They passed through the gateway and followed a path that led through a wavy valley of graves—dusty-gray and moldy for the fifties; quaintly carved with flowers and jars for the seventies; ornate and hideous for the nineties, with fat marble cherubs lying in sodden sleep on stone pillows, and great impossible growths of nameless granite flowers. Occasionally they saw a kneeling figure with

tributary flowers, but over most of the graves lay silence and withered leaves with only the fragrance that their own shadowy memories could waken in living minds.

They reached the top of a hill where they were fronted by a tall round headstone, freckled with dark spots of damp and half grown over with vines.

"'Margery Lee,'" she read; "'1844–1873.' Wasn't she nice? She died when she was twenty-nine. Dear Margery Lee," she added softly. "Can't you see her, Harry?"

"Yes, Sally Carrol."

He felt a little hand insert itself into his.

"She was dark, I think; and she always wore her hair with a ribbon in it, and gorgeous hoopskirts of bright blue and old rose."

"Yes."

"Oh, she was sweet, Harry! And she was the sort of girl born to stand on a wide pillared porch and welcome folks in. I think perhaps a lot of men went away to war meanin' to come back to her; but maybe none of 'em ever did."

He stooped down close to the stone, hunting for any record of marriage.

"There's nothing here to show."

"Of course not. How could there be anything there better than just 'Margery Lee,' and that eloquent date?"

She drew close to him and an unexpected lump came into his throat as her yellow hair brushed his cheek.

"You see how she was, don't you, Harry?"

"I see," he agreed gently. "I see through your precious eyes. You're beautiful now, so I know she must have been."

Silent and close they stood, and he could feel her shoulders trembling a little. An ambling breeze swept up the hill and stirred the brim of her floppidy hat.

"Let's go down there!"

She was pointing to a flat stretch on the other side of the hill where along the green turf were a thousand grayish-white crosses stretching in endless ordered rows like the stacked arms of a battalion.

"Those are the Confederate dead," said Sally Carrol simply.

They walked along and read the inscriptions, always only a name and a date, sometimes quite indecipherable.

"The last row is the saddest—see, 'way over there. Every cross has just a date on it and the word 'Unknown.'"

She looked at him and her eyes brimmed with tears.

"I can't tell you how real it is to me, darling—if you don't know."

"How you feel about it is beautiful to me."

"No, no, it's not me, it's them—that old time that I tried to have live in me. These were just men, unimportant, evidently, or they wouldn't have been 'unknown'; but they died for the most beautiful thing in the world—the dead South. You see," she continued, her voice husky, her eyes glistening with tears, "people have dreams they fasten on to things, and I've always grown up with that dream. It was so easy because it was all dead and there weren't any disillusions comin' to me, tried in a way to live up to those past standards of nobless oblige—there's just the last remnants of it, you know, the roses of an old garden dying all round us—stray stories I used to hear from a Confederate soldier who lived next door, and a few old darkies. Oh, Harry, there was something, there was something! I couldn't ever make you understand, but it was there."

"I understand," he assured her again quietly.

Sally Carrol smiled and dried her eyes on the tip of a handkerchief protruding from his breast pocket.

"You don't feel depressed, do you, lover? Even when I cry I'm happy here, and I get a sawt of strength from it."

Hand in hand they turned and walked slowly away. Finding soft grass she drew him down to a seat beside her with their backs against the remnants of a low broken wall.

"Wish those three old women would clear out," she complained. "I want to kiss you, Sally Carrol."

"Me, too."

They waited impatiently for the three bent figures to move off, and then she kissed him until the sky seemed to fade out and all her smiles and tears to vanish in an ecstasy of eternal seconds.

Afterward they walked slowly back together, while the corners twilight played at somnolent black-and-white checkers with the end of day.

"You'll be up about mid-January," he said, "and you got to stay a month at least. It'll be slick. There's a winter carnival on, and if you've never really seen snow it'll be like fairyland to you. There'll be skating and skiing

(Continued on Page 163)

THE ICE PALACE

(Continued from Page 19)

tobogganing and sleigh riding and all sorts of torchlight parades on snowshoes. They haven't had one for years, so they're going to make it a knock-out."

"Will it be cold, Harry?" she asked suddenly.

"You certainly won't. You may freeze your nose, but you won't be shivery cold. It's hard and dry, you know."

"I guess I'm a summer child. I don't like any cold I've ever seen."

She broke off and they were both silent for a minute.

"Sally Carrol," he said very slowly, "what do you say to—March?"

"I say I love you."

"March?"

"March, Harry."

III

ALL night in the Pullman it was very cold. She rang for the porter to ask for another blanket, and when he couldn't give her one she tried vainly, by squeezing down into the bottom of her berth and doubling back the bedclothes, to snatch a few hours' sleep.

Sally Carrol wanted to look her best in the morning.

She rose at six and sliding uncomfortably into her clothes stumbled up to the diner for a cup of coffee. The snow had filtered into the vestibules and covered the floor with a slippery coating. It was intriguing, this cold, it crept in everywhere. Her breath was quite visible and she blew into the air with a naïve enjoyment. Seated in the diner she stared out the window at white hills and valleys and scattered pines with each branch a green platter for a cold feast of snow.

Sometimes a solitary farmhouse would fly by, ugly and bleak and lone on the white waste; and with each one she had an instant of chill compassion for the souls shut in there waiting for spring.

As she left the diner and swayed back into the Pullman she experienced a surging rush of energy and wondered if she was feeling the bracing air of which Harry had spoken. This was the North, the North— her land now!

Then blow, ye winds, heigho!
A-roving I will go,

she chanted exultantly to herself.

"What's 'at?" inquired the porter politely.

"I said, 'Brush me off.'"

The long wires of the telegraph poles doubled; two tracks ran up beside the train—three—four; came a succession of white-roofed houses, a glimpse of a trolley car with frosted windows, streets—more streets—the city.

She stood for a dazed moment in the frosty station before she saw three fur-bundled figures descending upon her.

"There she is!"

"Oh, Sally Carrol!"

Sally Carrol dropped her bag.

"Hi!"

A faintly familiar icy-cold face kissed her, and then she was in a group of faces all apparently emitting great clouds of heavy smoke; she was shaking hands. There was Gordon, a short, eager man of thirty who looked like an amateur knocked-about model for Harry; and his wife Myra, a listless lady with flaxen hair under a fur automobile cap. Almost immediately Sally Carrol thought of her as vaguely Scandinavian. A cheerful chauffeur adopted her bag and amid ricochets of half phrases, exclamations and perfunctory, listless "my dear's" from Myra they swept each other from the station.

Then they were in a sedan bound through a crooked succession of snowy streets where dozens of little boys were hitching sleds behind grocery wagons and automobiles.

"Oh," cried Sally Carrol, "I want to do that! Can we, Harry?"

"That's for kids. But we might ——"

"It looks like such a circus!" she said regretfully.

Home was a rambling frame house set on a white lap of snow, and there she met a big, gray-haired man of whom she approved, and a lady who was like an egg and who kissed her—these were Harry's parents. There was a breathless, indescribable hour crammed full of half sentences, hot water, bacon and eggs and confusion; and after that she was alone with Harry in the library asking him if she dared smoke.

It was a large room with a Madonna over the fireplace and rows upon rows of books in covers of light gold and dark gold and shiny red. All the chairs had little lace squares where one's head should rest, the couch was just comfortable, the books looked as if they had been read—some— and Sally Carrol had an instantaneous vision of the battered old library at home with her father's huge medical books and the oil paintings of her three great-uncles and the old couch that had been mended up for forty-five years and was still luxurious to dream in. This room struck her as being neither attractive nor particularly otherwise. It was simply a room with a lot of fairly expensive things in it that all looked about fifteen years old.

"What do you think of it up here?" demanded Harry eagerly. "Does it surprise you? Is it what you expected, I mean?"

"You are, Harry," she said quietly, and reached out her arms to him.

But after a brief kiss he seemed anxious to extort enthusiasm from her.

"The town, I mean. Do you like it? Can you feel the pep in the air?"

"Oh, Harry," she laughed, "you'll have to give me time. You can't just fling questions at me."

She puffed at her cigarette with a sigh of contentment.

"One thing I want to ask you," he began rather apologetically; "you Southerners put quite an emphasis on family and all that—not that it isn't quite all right, but you'll find it a little different here. I mean—you'll notice a lot of things that'll seem to you sort of vulgar display at first, Sally Carrol; but just remember that this is a three-generation town. Everybody has a father and about half of us have grandfathers. Back of that we don't go."

"Of course," she murmured.

"Our grandfathers, you see, founded the place, and a lot of them had to take some pretty queer jobs while they were doing the founding.

"For instance, there's one woman who at present is about the social model for the town; well, her father was the first public ash man—things like that."

"Why," said Sally Carrol, puzzled, "did you s'pose I was goin' to make remarks about people?"

"Not at all," interrupted Harry; "and I'm not apologizing for anyone either. It's just that—well, a Southern girl came up here last summer and said some unfortunate things, and—oh, I just thought I'd tell you."

Sally Carrol felt suddenly indignant—as though she had been unjustly spanked— but Harry evidently considered the subject closed, for he went on with a great surge of enthusiasm.

"It's carnival time, you know. First in ten years. And there's an ice palace they're building now that's the first they've had since Eighty-five. Built out of blocks of the clearest ice they could find—on a tremendous scale."

She rose and walking to the window pushed aside the heavy Turkish portières and looked out.

"Oh!" she cried suddenly. "There's two little boys makin' a snow man! Harry, do you reckon I can go out an' help 'em?"

"You dream! Come here and kiss me."

She left the window rather reluctantly.

"I don't guess this is a very kissable climate, is it? I mean, it makes you so you don't want to sit round, doesn't it?"

"We're not going to. I've got a vacation for the first week you're here, and there's a dinner dance to-night."

"Oh, Harry," she confessed, subsiding in a heap, half in his lap, half in the pillows, "I sure do feel confused. I haven't got an idea whether I'll like it or not, an' I don't know what people expect or anythin'. You'll have to tell me, honey."

(Continued on Page 167)

"I Told You I Wouldn't Want to Tie My Life to Any of the Boys That are Round Tarleton Now, But I Never Made Any Sweepin' Generalities"

Appendix One

(Continued from Page 163)

"I'll tell you," he said softly, "if you'll just tell me you're glad to be here."

"Glad—just awful glad!" she whispered, insinuating herself into his arms in her own peculiar way. "Where you are is home for me, Harry."

And as she said this she had the feeling for almost the first time in her life that she was acting a part.

That night, amid the gleaming candles of a dinner party where the men seemed to do most of the talking while the girls sat in a haughty and expensive aloofness, even Harry's presence on her left failed to make her feel at home.

"They're a good-looking crowd, don't you think?" he demanded. "Just look round. There's Spud Hubbard, tackle at Princeton last year, and Junie Morton—he and the red-haired fellow next to him were both Yale hockey captains; Junie was in my class. Why, the best athletes in the world come from these states round here. This is a man's country, I tell you. Look at John J. Fishburn!"

"Who's he?" asked Sally Carrol innocently.

"Don't you know?"

"I've heard the name."

"Greatest wheat man in the Northwest, and one of the greatest financiers in the country."

She turned suddenly to a voice on her right.

"I guess they forgot to introduce us. My name's Roger Patton."

"My name is Sally Carrol Happer," she said graciously.

"Yes, I know. Harry told me you were coming."

"You a relative?"

"No, I'm a professor."

"Oh," she laughed.

"At the university. You're from the South, aren't you?"

"Yes; Tarleton, Georgia."

She liked him immediately—a reddish-brown mustache under watery blue eyes that had something in them that these other eyes lacked, some quality of appreciation. They exchanged stray sentences through dinner and she made up her mind to see him again.

After coffee she was introduced to numerous good-looking young men who danced with conscious precision and seemed to take it for granted that she wanted to talk about nothing except Harry.

"Heavens," she thought, "they talk as if my being engaged made me older than they are—as if I'd tell their mothers on them!"

In the South an engaged girl, even a young married woman, expected the same amount of half-affectionate badinage and flattery that would be accorded a débutante, but here all that seemed banned. One young man, after getting well started on the subject of Sally Carrol's eyes and how they had allured him ever since she entered the room, went into a violent confusion when he found she was visiting the Bellamys—was Harry's fiancée. He seemed to feel as though he had made some risqué and inexcusable blunder, became immediately formal and left her at the first opportunity.

She was rather glad when Roger Patton cut in on her, and suggested that they sit out a while.

"Well," he inquired, blinking cheerily, "how's Carmen from the South?"

"Mighty fine. How's—how's Dangerous Dan McGrew? Sorry, but he's the only Northerner I know much about."

He seemed to enjoy that.

"Of course," he confessed, "as a professor of literature I'm not supposed to have read Dangerous Dan McGrew."

"Are you a native?"

"No, I'm a Philadelphian. Imported from Harvard to teach seventeenth-century French. But I've been here ten years."

"Nine years, three hundred an' sixty-four days longer than me."

"Like it here?"

"Uh-huh. Sure do!"

"Really?"

"Well, why not? Don't I look as if I were havin' a good time?"

"I saw you look out the window a minute ago—and shiver."

"Just my imagination," laughed Sally Carrol. "I'm used to havin' everythin' quiet outside, an' sometimes I look out an' see a flurry of snow, an' it's just as if somethin' dead was movin'."

He nodded appreciatively.

"Ever been North before?"

"Spent two Julys in Asheville, North Carolina."

"Nice-looking crowd, aren't they?" suggested Patton, indicating the swirling floor.

Sally Carrol started. This had been Harry's remark.

"Sure are! They're—canine."

"What?"

She flushed.

"I'm sorry; that sounded worse than I meant it. You see I always think of people as feline or canine, irrespective of sex."

"Which are you?"

"I'm feline. So are you. So are most Southern men an' most of these girls here."

"What's Harry?"

"Harry's canine, distinctly. All the men I've met to-night seem to be canine."

"What does 'canine' imply? A certain conscious masculinity as opposed to subtlety?"

"Reckon so. I never analyzed it—only I just look at people an' say 'canine' or 'feline' right off. It's right absurd, I guess."

"Not at all. I'm interested. I used to have a theory about these people. I think they're freezing up."

"What?"

"I think they're growing like Swedes—Ibsenesque, you know. Very gradually getting gloomy and melancholy. It's these long winters. Ever read any Ibsen?"

She shook her head.

"Well, you find in his characters a certain brooding rigidity. They're righteous, narrow and cheerless, without infinite possibilities for great sorrow or joy."

"Without smiles or tears?"

"Exactly. That's my theory. You see there are thousands of Swedes up here. They come, I imagine, because the climate is very much like their own, and there's been a gradual mingling. They're probably not half a dozen here to-night, but—we've had four Swedish governors. Am I boring you?"

"I'm mighty interested."

"Your future sister-in-law is half Swedish. Personally I like her, but my theory is that Swedes react rather badly on us as a whole. Scandinavians, you know, have the largest suicide rate in the world."

"Why do you live here if it's so depressing?"

"Oh, it doesn't get me. I'm pretty well cloistered, and I suppose books mean more than people to me anyway."

"But writers all speak about the South being tragic. You know—Spanish señoritas, black hair and daggers an' hauntin' music."

He shook his head.

"No, the Northern races are the tragic races—they don't indulge in the cheering luxury of tears."

Sally Carrol thought of her graveyard. She supposed that that was vaguely what she had meant when she said it didn't depress her.

"The Italians are about the gayest people in the world—but it's a dull subject," he broke off. "Anyway, I want to tell you you're marrying a pretty fine man."

Sally Carrol was moved by an impulse of confidence.

"I know. I'm the sort of person who wants to be taken care of after a certain point, and I feel sure I will be."

"Shall we dance? You know," he continued as they rose, "it's encouraging to find a girl who knows what she's marrying for. Nine-tenths of them think of it as a sort of walking into a moving-picture sunset."

She laughed, and liked him immensely.

Two hours later on the way home she nestled near Harry in the back seat.

"Oh, Harry," she whispered, "it's so co-old!"

"But it's warm in here, darling girl."

"But outside it's cold; and oh, that howling wind!"

She buried her face deep in his fur coat and trembled involuntarily as his cold lips kissed the tip of her ear.

IV

THE first week of her visit passed in a whirl. She had her promised toboggan ride at the back of an automobile through a chill January twilight. Swathed in furs she put in a morning tobogganing on the country-club hill; even tried skiing, to sail through the air for a glorious moment and then land in a tangled, laughing bundle on a soft snowdrift. She liked all the winter sports, except an afternoon spent snow-shoeing over a glaring plain under pale yellow sunshine; but she soon realized that these things were for children—that she was being humored and that the enjoyment round her was only a reflection of her own.

At first the Bellamy family puzzled her. The men were reliable and she liked them; to Mr. Bellamy especially, with his iron-gray hair and energetic dignity, she took an immediate fancy once she found that he was born in Kentucky; this made of him a link between the old life and the new. But toward the women she felt a definite hostility. Myra, her future sister-in-law, seemed the essence of spiritless conventionality. Her conversation was so utterly devoid of personality that Sally Carrol, who came from a country where a certain amount of charm and assurance could be taken for granted in the women, was inclined to despise her.

"If those women aren't beautiful," she thought, "they're nothing. They just fade out when you look at them. They're glorified domestics. Men are the center of every mixed group."

Lastly there was Mrs. Bellamy, whom Sally Carrol detested. The first day's impression of an egg had been confirmed—an egg with a cracked, veiny voice and such an ungracious dumpiness of carriage that Sally Carrol felt that if she once fell she would surely scramble. In addition, Mrs. Bellamy seemed to typify the town in being innately hostile to strangers. She called Sally Carrol "Sally," and could not be persuaded that the double name was anything more than a tedious, ridiculous nickname. To Sally Carrol this shortening of her name was like presenting her to the public half clothed. She loved "Sally Carrol"; she loathed "Sally." She knew also that Harry's mother disapproved of her bobbed hair; and she had never dared smoke downstairs after that first day when Mrs. Bellamy had come into the library sniffing violently.

Of all the men she met she preferred Roger Patton, who was a frequent visitor at the house. He never again alluded to the Ibsenesque tendency of the populace, but when he came in one day and found her curled up on the sofa bent over Peer Gynt he laughed and told her to forget what he'd said—that it was all rot.

And then one afternoon in her second week she and Harry hovered on the edge of a dangerously steep quarrel. She considered that he precipitated it entirely, though the Serbia in the case was an unknown man who had not had his trousers pressed.

They had been walking homeward between mounds of high-piled snow and under a sun which Sally Carrol scarcely recognized. They passed a little girl done up in gray wool until she resembled a small Teddy bear, and Sally Carrol could not resist a gasp of maternal appreciation.

"Look! Harry!"

"What?"

"That little girl—did you see her face?"

"Yes, why?"

"It was red as a little strawberry. Oh, she was cute!"

"Why, your own face is almost as red as that already! Everybody's healthy here. We're out in the cold as soon as we're old enough to walk. Wonderful climate!"

She looked at him and had to agree. He was mighty healthy looking; so was his brother.

And she had noticed the new red in her own cheeks that very morning.

Suddenly their glances were caught and held and they stared for a moment at the street corner ahead of them. A man was standing there, his knees bent, his eyes gazing upward with a tense expression as though he were about to make a leap toward the chilly sky. And then they both exploded into a shout of laughter, for coming closer they discovered it had been a ludicrous momentary illusion produced by the extreme bagginess of the man's trousers.

"Reckon that's one on us," she laughed.

"He must be a Southerner, judging by those trousers," suggested Harry mischievously.

"Why, Harry!"

Her surprised look must have irritated him.

"Those damn Southerners!"

Sally Carrol's eyes flashed.

"Don't call 'em that!"

"I'm sorry, dear," said Harry, malignantly apologetic, "but you know what I think of them. They're sort of—sort of degenerates—not at all like the old Southerners. They've lived so long down there with all the colored people that they've gotten lazy and shiftless."

"Hush your mouth, Harry!" she cried angrily. "They're not! They may be lazy—anybody would be in that climate—but they're my best friends, an' I don't want to hear 'em criticized in any such sweepin' way. Some of 'em are the finest men in the world."

"Oh, I know. They're all right when they come North to college, but of all the hangdog, ill-dressed, slovenly lot I ever saw a bunch of small-town Southerners are the worst!"

Sally Carrol was clenching her gloved hands and biting her lip furiously.

"Why," continued Harry, "there was one in my class at New Haven and we all thought that at last we'd found the true type of Southern aristocrat, but it turned out that he wasn't an aristocrat at all—just the son of a Northern carpetbagge who owned about all the cotton round Birmingham."

"A Southerner wouldn't talk the way you're talking now," she said evenly.

"They haven't the energy!"

"Or the somethin' else."

"I'm sorry, Sally Carrol, but I'v heard you say yourself that you'd neve marry ——"

"That's quite different. I told you I wouldn't want to tie my life to any of th boys that are round Tarleton now, but never made any sweepin' generalities."

They walked along in silence.

"I probably spread it on a bit thick Sally Carrol. I'm sorry."

She nodded, but made no answer. Fiv minutes later as they stood in the hallwa she suddenly threw her arms round him.

"Oh, Harry," she cried, her eyes full tears, "let's get married next week. I'r afraid of having fusses like that. I'm afraic Harry. It wouldn't be that way if we we married."

But Harry being in the wrong was sti irritated.

"That'd be idiotic. We decided March."

The tears in Sally Carrol's eyes fade her expression hardened slightly.

"Very well—I suppose I shouldn't hav said that."

Harry melted.

"Dear little nut!" he cried. "Come ar kiss me and let's forget."

That very night at the end of a vaud ville performance the orchestra play Dixie, and Sally Carrol felt somethi stronger and more enduring than her tea and smiles of the day brim up inside he She leaned forward, gripping the arms of h chair until her face grew crimson.

"Sort of get you, dear?" whisper Harry.

But she did not hear him. To the spirit throb of the violins and the inspiring be of the kettledrums her own old ghosts we marching by and on into the darkness, ar as fifes whistled and sighed in the l encore they seemed so nearly out of sig that she could have waved good-by.

Away, away, away down South in Dixie
Away, away, away down South in Dixie.

V

IT WAS a particularly cold night. sudden thaw had nearly cleared t streets the day before, but now they we traversed again with a powdery wraith loose snow that traveled in wavy lines fore the feet of the wind and filled t lower air with a fine-particled mist. Th was no sky—only a dark, ominous tent th draped in the tops of the streets and was reality a vast approaching army of sno flakes—while over it all, chilling away comfort from the brown-and-green glow lighted windows and muffling the stea trot of the horse pulling their sleigh, int minably washed the north wind. It wa dismal town after all, she thought—dism

Sometimes at night it had seemed to as though no one lived here—they had gone long ago, leaving lighted houses to covered in time by tombing heaps of sl Oh, if there should be snow on her gra To be beneath great piles of it all win long, where even her headstone would b light shadow against light shadows. grave—a grave that should be flow strewn and washed with sun and rain.

She thought again of those isola country houses that her train had pass and of the life there the long wir through—the ceaseless glare through windows, the crust forming on the drifts of snow, finally the slow, cheer melting and the harsh spring of wh Roger Patton had told her. Her spring to lose it forever—with its lilacs and

(Concluded on Page 170)

Vulcanize Your Tube Punctures

with the simple

SHALER

5-Minute Vulcanizer

Easier than patching or changing tubes. Makes the tube as good as new. The Shaler operates automatically, and without fail. Just touch a match to the chemical fuel. In five minutes the puncture is repaired—a permanent *heat vulcanized* repair that will not come off—stronger than the tube itself. No gasoline; cement or flame. Carry it in your car—use it anywhere—in any weather. Cannot burn or injure your tubes.

Over a Million Motorists Use It

Complete Outfit $1.50

The outfit includes the Vulcanizer—12 Patch-&-Heat Units (6 round for punctures and 6 oblong for cuts)—price complete $1.50. Extra Patch-&-Heat Units, 75 cents a dozen. Prices are slightly higher west of the Rockies and in Canada.

All Accessory Dealers Sell It

C. A. SHALER COMPANY

1402 Fourth St. Waupun, Wisconsin

"Old Town Canoes"

YOU can lazy-paddle an "Old Town" all day long. "Old Towns" are light, buoyant canoes that answer the slightest pressure of the blade. They are strong, sturdy canoes built for years of service. The "Sponson Model" is safer than a row boat. Write for catalog—3000 canoes in stock.

OLD TOWN CANOE CO.

956 Middle Street

Old Town, Maine, U. S. A.

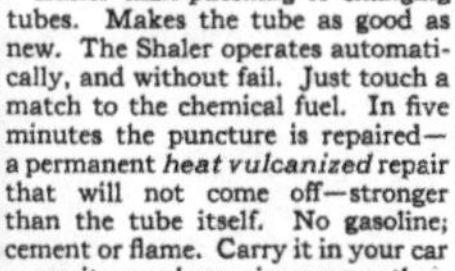

PATENTS. WRITE for free illustrated guide book and "EVIDENCE OF CONCEPTION BLANK." Send model or sketch and description of invention for our free opinion of its patentable nature.

Highest References. Prompt Service. Reasonable Terms.

Victor J. Evans & Co., 727 Ninth, Washington, D.C.

PATENT-SENSE

"The Book for Inventors & Mfrs."

By Return Mail FREE. Write

LACEY & LACEY, Dept. W Washington, D.C.

Worthington Quality

Chairs and Tricycles

The Colson Co.

968 Cedar St., Elyria, O.

(Concluded from Page 167)

lazy sweetness it stirred in her heart. She was laying away that spring—afterward she would lay away that sweetness.

With a gradual insistence the storm broke. Sally Carrol felt a film of flakes melt quickly on her eyelashes and Harry reached over a furry arm and drew down her complicated flannel cap. Then the small flakes came in skirmish line and the horse bent his neck patiently as a transparency of white appeared momentarily on his coat.

"Oh, he's cold, Harry," she said quickly.

"Who? The horse? Oh, no, he isn't. He likes it!"

After another ten minutes they turned a corner and came in sight of their destination. On a tall hill outlined in vivid glaring green against the wintry sky stood the ice palace. It was three stories in the air, with battlements and embrasures and narrow icicled windows, and the innumerable electric lights inside made a gorgeous transparency of the great central hall. Sally Carrol clutched Harry's hand under the fur robe.

"It's beautiful!" he cried excitedly. "My golly, it's beautiful, isn't it? They haven't had one here since eighty-five!"

Somehow the notion of there not having been one since eighty-five oppressed her. Ice was a ghost, and this mansion of it was surely peopled by those shades of the eighties, with pale faces and blurred snow-filled hair.

"Come on, dear," said Harry.

She followed him out of the sleigh and waited while he hitched the horse. A party of four—Gordon, Myra, Roger Patton and another girl—drew up beside them with a mighty jingle of bells. There was quite a crowd already, bundled in fur or sheepskin, shouting and calling to each other as they moved through the snow, which was now so thick that people could scarcely be distinguished a few yards away.

"It's a hundred and seventy feet tall," Harry was saying to a muffled figure beside him as they trudged toward the entrance; "covers six thousand square yards."

She caught snatches of conversation: "One main hall"—"walls twenty to forty inches thick"—"and the ice cave has almost a mile of"—"This Canuck who built it ——"

They found their way inside, and dazed by the magic of the great crystal walls Sally Carrol found herself repeating over and over two lines from Kubla Khan:

It was a miracle of rare device,
A sunny pleasure-dome with caves of ice!

In the great glittering cavern with the dark shut out she took a seat on a wooden bench, and the evening's oppression lifted. Harry was right—it was beautiful; and her gaze traveled the smooth surface of the walls, the blocks for which had been selected for their purity and clearness to obtain this opalescent, translucent effect.

"Look! Here we go—oh, boy!" cried Harry.

A band in a far corner struck up Hail, Hail, the Gang's All Here! which echoed over to them in wild muddled acoustics, and then the lights suddenly went out; silence seemed to flow down the icy sides and sweep over them. Sally Carrol could still see her white breath in the darkness, and a dim row of pale faces over on the other side.

The music eased to a sighing complaint, and from outside drifted in the full-throated resonant chant of the marching clubs. It grew louder like some pæan of a viking tribe traversing an ancient wild; it swelled—they were coming nearer; then a row of torches appeared, and another and another, and keeping time with their moccasined feet a long column of gray-mackinawed figures swept in, snowshoes slung at their shoulders, torches soaring and flickering as their voices rose along the great walls.

The gray column ended and another followed, the light streaming luridly this time over red toboggan caps and flaming crimson mackinaws, and as it entered it took up the refrain; then came a long platoon of blue and white, of green, of white, of brown and yellow.

"Those white ones are the Wacouta Club," whispered Harry eagerly. "Those are the men you've met round at dances."

The volume of the voices grew; the great cavern was a phantasmagoria of torches waving in great banks of fire, of colors and the rhythm of soft leather steps. The leading column turned and halted, platoon deployed in front of platoon until the whole procession made a solid flag of flame, and then from thousands of voices burst a mighty shout that filled the air like a crash of thunder and sent the torches wavering. It was magnificent, it was tremendous! To Sally Carrol it was the North offering sacrifice on some mighty altar to the gray pagan God of Snow.

As the shout died the band struck up again and there came more singing, and then long reverberating cheers by each club. She sat very quiet listening while the staccato cries rent the stillness; and then she started, for there was a volley of explosion, and great clouds of smoke went up here and there through the cavern—the flashlight photographers at work—and the council was over. With the band at their head the clubs formed in column once more, took up their chant and began to march out.

"Come on!" shouted Harry. "We want to see the labyrinths downstairs before they turn the lights off!"

They all rose and started toward the chute—Harry and Sally Carrol in the lead, her little glove buried in his big fur gauntlet. At the bottom of the chute was a long empty room of ice with the ceiling so low that they had to stoop—and their hands were parted. Before she realized what he intended Harry had darted down one of the half dozen glittering passages that opened into the room, and was only a vague receding blot against the green shimmer.

"Harry!" she called.

"Come on!" he cried back.

She looked round the empty chamber; the rest of the party had evidently decided to go home, were already outside somewhere in the blundering snow. She hesitated and then darted in after Harry.

"Harry!" she shouted.

She had reached a turning point thirty feet down; she heard a faint muffled answer far to the left, and with a touch of panic fled toward it. She passed another turning, two more yawning alleys.

"Harry!"

No answer. She started to run straight forward, and then turned like lightning and sped back the way she had come, enveloped in a sudden ice terror.

She reached a turn—was it here?—took the left and came to what should have been the outlet into the long low room, but it was only another glittering passage with darkness at the end. She called again, but the walls gave back a flat lifeless echo with no reverberations. Retracing her steps she turned another corner, this time following a wide passage. It was like the green lane between the parted waters of the red sea, like a damp vault connecting empty tombs.

She slipped a little now as she walked, for ice had formed on the bottom of her overshoes; she had to run her gloves along the half-slippery, half-sticky walls to keep her balance.

"Harry!"

Still no answer. The sound she made bounced mockingly down to the end of the passage.

Then on an instant the lights went out and she was in complete darkness. She gave a small frightened cry and sank down into a cold little heap on the ice. She felt her left knee do something as she fell, but she scarcely noticed it as some deep terror far greater than any fear of being lost settled upon her. She was alone with this presence that came out of the North, the dreary loneliness that rose from ice-bound whalers in the Arctic seas, from smokeless trackless wastes where were strewn the whitened bones of adventure. It was an icy breath of death; it was rolling down low across the land to clutch at her.

With a furious despairing energy she rose again and started blindly down the darkness. She must get out. She might be lost in here for days, freeze to death and lie embedded in the ice like corpses she had read of, kept perfectly preserved until the melting of a glacier. Harry probably thought she had left with the others—he had gone by now; no one would know until late next day. She reached pitifully for the wall. Forty inches thick they had said—forty inches thick!

"Oh!"

On both sides of her along the walls she felt things creeping, damp souls that haunted this palace, this town, this North.

"Oh, send somebody—send somebody!" she cried aloud.

Clark Darrow—he would understand; or Joe Ewing; she couldn't be left here to wander forever—to be frozen, heart, body and soul. This her—this Sally Carrol! Why, she was a happy thing. She was a happy little girl. She liked warmth and summer and Dixie. These things were foreign—foreign.

"You're not crying," something said aloud. "You'll never cry any more. Your tears would just freeze; all tears freeze up here!"

She sprawled full length on the ice.

"O God!" she faltered.

A long single file of minutes went by, and with a great weariness she felt her eyes closing. Then someone seemed to sit down near her and take her face in warm soft hands. She looked up gratefully.

"Why, it's Margery Lee," she crooned softly to herself. "I knew you'd come." It really was Margery Lee, and she was just as Sally Carrol had known she would be, with a young white brow and wide welcoming eyes and a hoop skirt of some soft material that was quite comforting to rest on.

"Margery Lee."

It was getting darker now and darker—all those tombstones ought to be repainted, sure enough, only that would spoil 'em of course. Still, you ought to be able to see 'em.

Then after a succession of moments that went fast and then slow, but seemed to be ultimately resolving themselves into a multitude of blurred rays converging toward a pale yellow sun, she heard a great cracking noise break her new-found stillness.

It was the sun, it was a light; a torch, and a torch beyond that, and another one, and voices; a face took flesh below the torch, heavy arms raised her and she felt something on her cheek, it felt wet. Someone had seized her and was rubbing her face with snow. How ridiculous—with snow!

"Sally Carrol! Sally Carrol!"

It was Dangerous Dan McGrew; and two other faces she didn't know.

"Child, child! We've been looking for you two hours. Harry's half crazy!"

Things came rushing back into place—the singing, the torches, the great shout of the marching clubs. She squirmed in Patton's arms and gave a long low cry.

"Oh, I want to get out of here! I'm going back home. Take me home"—her voice rose to a scream that sent a chill to Harry's heart as he came racing down the next passage—"to-morrow!" she cried with delirious, unrestrained passion—"To-morrow! To-morrow! To-morrow!"

VI

THE wealth of golden sunlight poured a quite enervating yet oddly comforting heat over the house where day long it faced the dusty stretch of road. Two birds were making a great to-do in a cool spot found among the branches of a tree next door, and down the street a colored woman was announcing herself melodiously as a purveyor of strawberries. It was April afternoon.

Sally Carrol Happer, resting her chin on her arm and her arm on an old window seat, gazed sleepily down over the spangled dust whence the heat waves were rising for the first time this spring. She was watching a very ancient flivver turn a perilous corner and rattle and groan to a jolting stop at the end of the walk. She made no sound, and in a minute a strident familiar whistle rent the air. Sally Carrol smiled and blinked.

"Good mawnin'."

A head appeared tortuously from under the car top below.

"'Taint mawnin', Sally Carrol."

"Sure enough," she said in affected surprise. "I guess maybe not."

"What you doin'?"

"Eatin' green peach. 'Spect to die any minute."

Clark twisted himself a last impossible notch to get a view of her face.

"Water's warm as a kettla steam, Sally Carrol. Wanta go swimmin'?"

"Hate to move," sighed Sally Carrol lazily, "but I reckon so."

THE OFFSHORE PIRATE

By F. Scott Fitzgerald

ILLUSTRATED BY LESLIE L. BENSON

T HIS un-
likely story
begins on
a sea that was a
blue dream, as
colorful as blue silk stockings, and beneath a sky as blue
as the irises of children's eyes. From the western half of
the sky the sun was shying little golden disks at the
sea—if you gazed intently enough you could see them
skip from wave tip to wave tip until they joined a broad
collar of golden coin that was collecting half a mile out
and would eventually be a dazzling sunset. About halfway
between the Florida shore and the golden collar a white
steam yacht, very young and graceful, was riding at anchor
and under a blue-and-white awning aft a yellow-haired
girl reclined in a wicker settee reading The Revolt of the
Angels, by Anatole France.

She was about nineteen, slender and supple, with a
spoiled, alluring mouth and quick gray eyes full of a radiant
curiosity. Her feet, stockingless, and adorned rather than
clad in blue satin slippers which swung nonchalantly from
her toes, were perched on the arm of a settee adjoining the
one she occupied. And as she read she intermittently regaled herself by a faint application to her tongue of a half
lemon that she held in her hand. The other half, sucked
dry, lay on the deck at her feet and rocked very gently to
and fro at the almost imperceptible motion of the tide.

The second half lemon was well-nigh pulpless and the
golden collar had grown astonishing in width when suddenly the drowsy silence which enveloped the yacht was
broken by the sound of heavy footsteps and an elderly man
topped with orderly gray hair and clad in a white flannel
suit appeared at the head of the companionway. There he
paused for a moment until his eyes became accustomed to
the sun, and then seeing the girl under the awning he
uttered a long, even grunt of disapproval.

If he had intended thereby to obtain a rise of any sort he
was doomed to disappointment. The girl calmly turned
over two pages, turned back one, raised the lemon mechanically and then faintly but quite unmistakably yawned.

"Ardita!" said the gray-haired man sternly.

Ardita uttered a small sound indicating nothing.

"Ardita!" he repeated. "Ardita!"

Ardita raised the lemon languidly, allowing three words
to slip out before it reached her tongue.

"Oh, shut up."

"Ardita!"

"What?"

"Will you listen to me—or will I have to get a servant
to hold you while I talk to you?"

The lemon de-
scended slowly and
scornfully.

"Put it in writing."

"Will you have the
decency to close that
abominable book and
discard that damn
lemon for two min-
utes?"

"Oh, can't you lemme alone for a second?"

"Ardita, I have just received a telephone message from the shore——"

"Telephone?" She showed for the first time
a faint interest.

"Yes, it was——"

"Do you mean to say," she interrupted wonderingly, "'at they let you run a wire out here?"

"Yes, and just now——"

"Won't other boats bump into it?"

"No. It's too
low. It's run
along the bot-
tom. Five
min——"

"Well, I'll be darned! Gosh! Science is golden
or something—isn't it?"

"Will you let me say what I started to?"

"Shoot!"

"Well, it seems—well, I am up here——" He
paused and swallowed several times distractedly.
"Oh, yes. Young woman, Colonel Moreland has
called up again to ask me to be sure to
bring you in to dinner. His son Toby has
come all the way from New York to meet
you and he's invited several other young
people. For the last time, will you——"

"No," said
Ardita shortly,
"I won't. I
came along on
this darn cruise
with the one
idea of going to
Palm Beach,
and you knew it, and
I absolutely refuse to
meet any darn old
colonel or any darn
young Toby or any
darn old young people
or to set foot in any
other darn old town
in this crazy state. So you either take
me to Palm Beach or else shut up and
go away."

"Very well. This is the last straw. In your infatuation
for this man—a man who is notorious for his excesses, a
man your father would not have allowed so much as to
mention your name—you have reflected the demi-monde
rather than the circles in which you have presumably
grown up. From now on——"

"I know," interrupted Ardita ironically, "from now on
you go your way and I go mine. I've heard that story
before. You know I'd like nothing better."

"From now on," he announced grandiloquently, "you
are no niece of mine. I——"

"O-o-o-oh!" The cry was wrung from Ardita with the
agony of a lost soul. "Will you stop boring me! Will you
go way! Will you jump overboard and drown! Do you
want me to throw this book at you!"

"If you dare do any——"

Smack!

The Revolt of the Angels sailed through the air, missed
its target by the length of a short nose and bumped cheerfully down the companionway.

The gray-haired man made an instinctive step backward and then two
cautious steps forward. Ardita jumped

*Her Feet, in Blue Satin Slippers Which Swung Nonchalant[ly]
From Her Toes, Were Perched on the Arm of a Settee*

to her five feet four and stared at him defiantly, her g[ray]
eyes blazing.

"Keep off!"

"How dare you!" he cried.

"Because I darn please!"

"You've grown unbearable! Your disposition ——"

"You've made me that way! No child ever has a [bad]
disposition unless it's her family's fault! Whatever I [am]
you did it."

Muttering something under his breath her uncle tur[ned]
and, walking forward, called in a loud voice for the laur[nch.]
Then he returned to the awning, where Ardita had ag[ain]
seated herself and resumed her attention to the lemon.

"I am going ashore," he said slowly. "I will be
again at nine o'clock to-night. When I return we
start back to New York, where I shall turn you ove[r to]
your aunt for the rest of your natural, or rather unnatu[ral]
life."

He paused and looked at her, and then all at once so[me-]
thing in the utter childishness of her beauty seemed [to]
puncture his anger like an inflated tire and render [him]
helpless, uncertain, utterly fatuous.

"Ardita," he said not unkindly, "I'm no fool. I've b[een]
round. I know men. And, child, confirmed liberti[nes]
don't reform until they're tired—and then they're [no use to]
themselves—they're husks of themselves." He looke[d at]
her as if expecting agreement, but receiving no sigh[t or]
sound of it he continued. "Perhaps the man loves yo[u—]
that's possible. He's loved many women and he'll l[ove]
many more. Less than a month ago,
month, Ardita, he was involved in a ne[fa-]
rious affair with that red-haired M[rs.]
Merril; promised to give her the diam[ond]
bracelet that the Czar of Russia gave [his]
mother. You know—you read the pape[rs.]"

"Thrilling scandals by an anxious unc[le,]"
yawned Ardita. "Have it filmed. Wic[ked]
clubman making eyes at virtuous flap[per.]
Virtuous flapper conclusively vamped [by]
his lurid past. Plans to meet him at P[alm]
Beach. Foiled by anxious uncle."

"Will you tell me why the devil you w[ant]
to marry him?"

"I'm sure I couldn't say," said Ardita sho[rtly.]
"Maybe because he's the only man I k[now]
good or bad, who has an imagination and
courage of his convictions. Maybe it's to [get]
away from the young fools that spend [their]
vacuous hours pursuing me round the country. [But]
as for the famous Russian bracelet, you can set y[our]
mind at rest on that score. He's going to give [it to]
me at Palm Beach—if you'll have a little sen[se.]"

"How about the—red-haired woman?"

"He hasn't seen her for six months," she said ang[rily.]
"I have enough pride to see to that. Don't you know [that]
I can do any darn thing with any darn man I want t[o?]"

*"Go on," She Urged. "Lie to Me by
the Moonlight. Do a Fabulous Story"*

She put her chin in the air like the statue of France
Aroused, and then spoiled the pose somewhat by raising
the lemon for action.

"Is it the Russian bracelet that fascinates you?"

"No, I'm merely trying to give you the sort of argument
that would appeal to your intelligence. And I wish you'd
go way," she said, her temper rising again. "You know I
never change my mind. You've been boring me for three
days until I'm about to go crazy. I won't go ashore!
Won't! Do you hear? Won't!"

"Very well," he said, "and you won't go to Palm Beach
either. Of all the selfish, spoiled, uncontrolled, disagreeable, impossible girls I have ——"

Splash! The half lemon caught him in the neck. Simultaneously came a hail from over the side.

"The launch is ready, Mr. Farnam."

Too full of words and rage to speak, Mr. Farnam cast
one utterly condemning glance at his niece and, turning,
ran swiftly down the ladder.

II

FIVE o'clock rolled down from the sun and plumped
soundlessly into the sea. The golden collar widened
into a glittering island; and a faint breeze that had been
playing with the edges of the awning and swaying one of
the dangling blue slippers became suddenly freighted with
song. It was a chorus of men in close harmony and in
perfect rhythm to an accompanying sound of oars cleaving
the blue waters. Ardita lifted her head and listened:

    Carrots and peas,
    Beans on their knees,
    Pigs in the seas,
        Lucky fellows!
    Blow us a breeze,
    Blow us a breeze,
    Blow us a breeze,
        With your bellows.

Ardita's brow wrinkled in astonishment. Sitting very
still she listened eagerly as the chorus took up a second
verse:

    Onions and beans,
    Marshalls and Deans,
    Goldbergs and Greens
        And Costellos.
    Blow us a breeze,
    Blow us a breeze,
    Blow us a breeze,
        With your bellows.

With an exclamation she tossed her book to the deck,
where it sprawled at a straddle, and hurried to the rail.
Fifty feet away a large rowboat was approaching containing seven men, six of them rowing and one standing up in
the stern keeping time to their song with an orchestra
leader's baton:

    Oysters and rocks,
    Sawdust and socks,
    Who could make clocks
        Out of cellos?

The leader's eyes suddenly rested on Ardita, who was
leaning over the rail spellbound with curiosity. He made
a quick movement with his baton and the singing instantly
ceased. She saw that he was the only white man in the
boat—the six rowers were negroes.

"Narcissus ahoy!" he called politely.

"What's the idea of all the discord?" demanded Ardita
cheerfully. "Is this the varsity crew from the county nut
farm?"

By this time the boat was scraping the side of the yacht
and a great hulking negro in the bow turned round and
grasped the ladder. Thereupon the leader left his position
in the stern and before Ardita had realized his intention he
ran up the ladder and stood breathless before her on the
deck.

"The women and children will be spared!" he said
briskly. "All crying babies will be immediately drowned
and all males put in double irons!"

Digging her hands excitedly down into the pockets of
her dress Ardita stared at him, speechless with astonishment.

He was a young man with a scornful mouth and the
bright blue eyes of a healthy baby set in a dark, sensitive
face. His hair was pitch black, damp and curly—the hair
of a Grecian statue gone brunet. He was trimly built,
trimly dressed and graceful as an agile quarterback.

"Well, I'll be a son of a gun!" she said dazedly.

They eyed each other coolly.

"Do you surrender the ship?"

"Is this an outburst of wit?" demanded Ardita. "Are
you an idiot—or just being initiated to some fraternity?"

"I asked you if you surrendered the ship."

"I thought the country was dry," said Ardita disdainfully. "Have you been drinking finger-nail enamel? You
better get off this yacht!"

"What?" The young man's voice expressed incredulity.

"Get off the yacht! You heard me!"

He looked at her for a moment as if considering what she
had said.

"No," said his scornful mouth slowly; "no, I won't get
off the yacht. You can get off if you wish."

Going to the rail he gave a curt command and immediately the crew of the rowboat scrambled up the ladder and
ranged themselves in line before him, a coal black and
burly darky at one end and a miniature mulatto of four
feet nine at the other. They seemed to be uniformly
dressed in some sort of blue costume ornamented with
dust, mud and tatters; over the shoulder of each was
slung a small, heavy-looking white sack, and under their
arms they carried large black cases apparently containing
musical instruments.

"Ten-shun!" commanded the young man, snapping his
own heels together crisply. "Right driss! Front! Step
out here, Babe!"

The smallest negro took a quick step forward and
saluted.

"Yas-suh!"

"Take command; go down below, catch the crew and
tie 'em up—all except the engineer. Bring him up to me.
Oh, and pile those bags by the rail there."

"Yas-suh!"

He saluted again and, wheeling about, motioned for the
five others to gather about him. Then after a short whispered consultation they all filed noiselessly down the
companionway.

"Now," said the young man cheerfully to Ardita, who
had witnessed this last scene in withering silence, "if you
will swear on your honor as a flapper—which probably
isn't worth much—that you'll keep that spoiled little
mouth of yours tight shut for forty-eight hours you can
row yourself ashore in our rowboat."

"Otherwise what?"

"Otherwise you're going to sea in a ship."

With a little sigh as for a crisis well passed the young
man sank into the settee Ardita had lately vacated, and
stretched his arms lazily. The corners of his mouth relaxed
appreciatively as he looked round at the rich striped awning, the polished brass and the luxurious fittings of the
deck. His eye fell on the book and then on the exhausted
lemon.

"Hm," he said, "Stonewall Jackson claimed that lemon
juice cleared his head. Your head feel pretty clear?"

Ardita disdained to answer.

(Continued on Page 99)

"Is it a Proposal of Marriage? Extra! Ardita Farnam Becomes Pirate's Bride. Society Girl Kidnaped by Ragtime Bank Robber"

Appendix One

THE OFFSHORE PIRATE

(Continued from Page 11)

"Because inside of five minutes you'll have to make a clear decision whether it's go or stay."

He picked up the book and opened it curiously.

"The Revolt of the Angels. Sounds pretty good. French, eh?" He stared at her with new interest. "You French?"

"No."

"What's your name?"

"Farnam."

"Farnam what?"

"Ardita Farnam."

"Well, Ardita, no use standing up there and chewing out the insides of your mouth. You ought to break those nervous habits while you're young. Come over here and sit down."

Ardita took a carved jade case from her pocket, extracted a cigarette and lit it with a conscious coolness, though she knew her hand was trembling a little; then she crossed over with her supple, swinging walk and sitting down in the other settee blew a mouthful of smoke at the awning.

"You can't get me off this yacht," she said steadily; "and you haven't got very much sense if you think you'll get far with it. My uncle'll have wirelesses zigzagging all over this ocean by half past six."

"Hm."

She looked quickly at his face, caught anxiety stamped there plainly in the faintest depression of the mouth's corners.

"It's all the same to me," she said, shrugging her shoulders. "'Tisn't my yacht. I don't mind going for a coupla hours' cruise. I'll even lend you that book so you'll have something to read on the revenue boat that takes you up to Sing Sing."

He laughed scornfully.

"If that's advice you needn't bother. This is part of a plan arranged before I ever knew this yacht existed. If it hadn't been this one it'd have been the next one we passed anchored along the coast."

"Who are you?" demanded Ardita suddenly. "And what are you?"

"You've decided not to go ashore?"

"I never even faintly considered it."

"We're generally known," he said, "all seven of us, as Curtis Carlyle and his Six Black Buddies, late of the Winter Garden and the Midnight Frolic."

"You're singers?"

"We were until to-day. At present, due to those white bags you see there, we're fugitives from justice, and if the reward offered for our capture hasn't by this time reached twenty thousand dollars I miss my guess."

"What's in the bags?" asked Ardita curiously.

"Well," he said, "for the present we'll call it—mud—Florida mud."

III

WITHIN ten minutes after Curtis Carlyle's interview with a very frightened engineer the yacht Narcissus was under way, steaming south through a balmy tropical twilight. The little mulatto, Babe, who seemed to have Carlyle's implicit confidence, took full command of the situation. Mr. Farnam's valet and the chef, the only members of the crew on board except the engineer, having shown fight, were now reconsidering, strapped securely to their bunks below. Trombone Mose, the biggest negro, was set busy with a can of paint obliterating the name Narcissus from the bow and substituting the name Hula Hula, and the others congregated aft and became intently involved in a game of craps.

Having given orders for a meal to be prepared and served on deck at seven-thirty Carlyle rejoined Ardita and, sinking back into his settee, half closed his eyes and fell into a state of profound abstraction.

Ardita scrutinized him carefully—and classed him immediately as a romantic figure. He gave the effect of towering self-confidence erected on a slight foundation; just under the surface of each of his decisions she discerned a hesitancy that was in decided contrast to the arrogant curl of his lips.

"He's not like me," she thought. "There's a difference somewhere."

Being a supreme egotist Ardita frequently thought about herself; never having had her egotism disputed she did it entirely naturally and with no distraction from her unquestioned charm. Though she was nineteen she gave the effect of a high-spirited precocious child, and in the present glow of her youth and beauty all the men and women she had known were but driftwood on the ripples of her temperament. She had met other egotists; in fact, she found that selfish people bored her rather less than unselfish people—but as yet there had not been one she had not eventually defeated and brought to her feet.

But though she recognized an egotist in the settee next to her she felt none of that usual shutting of doors in her mind which meant clearing ship for action; on the contrary her instinct told her that this man was somehow completely pregnable and quite defenseless. When Ardita defied convention—and of late it had been her chief amusement—it was from an intense desire to be herself, and she felt that this man on the contrary was preoccupied with his own defiance.

She was much more interested in him than she was in her own situation, which affected her as the prospect of a matinée might affect a ten-year-old child. She had implicit confidence in her ability to take care of herself under any and all circumstances.

The night deepened. A pale new moon smiled misty-eyed upon the sea, and as the shore faded dimly out and dark clouds were blown like leaves along the far horizon a great haze of moonshine suddenly bathed the yacht and spread an avenue of glittering mail in her swift path. From time to time there was the bright flare of a match as one of them lighted a cigarette, but except for the low undertone of the throbbing engines and the even wash of the waves about the stern the yacht was quiet as a dream boat star-bound through the heavens. Round them flowed the smell of the night sea, bringing with it an infinite languor.

Carlyle broke the silence at last.

"Lucky girl," he sighed, "I've always wanted to be rich—and buy all this beauty."

Ardita yawned.

"I'd rather be you," she said frankly.

"You would—for about a day. But you do seem to possess a lot of nerve for a flapper."

"I wish you wouldn't call me that."

"Beg your pardon."

"As to nerve," she continued slowly, "it's my one redeeming feature. I'm not afraid of anything in heaven or earth."

"Hm, I am."

"To be afraid," said Ardita, "a person has either to be very great and strong—or else a coward. I'm neither." She paused for a moment, and eagerness crept into her tone. "But I want to talk about you. What on earth have you done—and how did you do it?"

"Why?" he demanded cynically. "Going to write a movie about me?"

"Go on," she urged. "Lie to me by the moonlight. Do a fabulous story."

A negro appeared, switched on a string of small lights under the awning and began setting the wicker table for supper. And while they ate cold sliced chicken, salad, artichokes and strawberry jam from the plentiful larder below, Carlyle began to talk, hesitatingly at first, but eagerly as he saw she was interested. Ardita scarcely touched her food as she watched his dark young face—handsome, ironic, faintly ineffectual.

He began life as a poor kid in a Tennessee town, he said, so poor that his people were the only white family in their street. He never remembered any white children—but there were always a dozen pickaninnies streaming in his trail, passionate admirers whom he kept in tow by the vividness of his imagination and the amount of trouble he was always getting them in and out of. And it seemed that this association diverted a rather unusual musical gift into a strange channel.

There had been a colored woman named Belle Pope Calhoun who played the piano at parties given for white children—nice white children that would have passed Curtis Carlyle with a sniff. But the ragged little "po' white" used to sit beside her piano by the hour and try to get in an alto with one of those kazoos that boys hum through. Before he was thirteen he was picking up a living teasing ragtime out of a battered violin in little cafés round Nashville. Eight years later the ragtime craze hit the country and he took six darkies on the Orpheum circuit. Five of them were boys he had grown up with; the other was the little mulatto, Babe Dívine, who was a wharf nigger round New York and long before that a plantation hand in Bermuda, until he stuck an eight-inch stiletto in his master's back. Almost before Carlyle realized his good fortune he was on Broadway, with offers of engagements on all sides, and more money than he had ever dreamed of.

It was about then that a change began in his whole attitude, a rather curious, embittering change. It was when he realized that he was spending the golden years of his life gibbering round a stage with a lot of black men. His act was good of its kind—three trombones, three saxophones and Carlyle's flute—and it was his own peculiar sense of rhythm that made all the difference; but he began to grow strangely sensitive about it, began to hate the thought of appearing, dreaded it from day to day.

They were making money—each contract he signed called for more—but when he went to managers and told them that he wanted to separate from his sextet and go on as a regular pianist they laughed at him and told him he was crazy—it would be an artistic suicide. He used to laugh afterward at the phrase "artistic suicide." They all used it.

Half a dozen times they played at private dances at three thousand dollars a night, and it seemed as if these crystallized all his distaste for his mode of livelihood. They took place in clubs and houses that he couldn't have gone into in the daytime. After all, he was merely playing the rôle of the eternal monkey, a sort of sublimated chorus man. He was sick of the very smell of the theater, of powder and rouge and the chatter of the green room and the patronizing approval of the boxes. He couldn't put his heart into it any more. The idea of a slow approach to the luxury of leisure drove him wild. He was, of course, progressing toward it but, like a child, eating his ice cream so slowly that he couldn't taste it at all.

He wanted to have a lot of money, and time and opportunity to read and play, and the sort of men and women round him that he could never have—the kind who, if they thought of him at all, would have considered him rather contemptible; in short he wanted all those things which he was beginning to lump under the general head of aristocracy, an aristocracy which it seemed almost any money could buy except money made as he was making it. He was twenty-five then, without family or education or any promise that he would succeed in a business career. He began speculating wildly, and within three weeks he had lost every cent he had saved.

Then the war came. He went to Plattsburg, and even there his profession followed him. A brigadier general called him up to headquarters and told him he could serve the country better as a band leader—so he spent the war entertaining celebrities behind the line with a headquarters band. It was not so bad—except that when the infantry came limping back from the trenches he wanted to be one of them. The sweat and mud they wore seemed only one of those ineffable symbols of aristocracy that were forever eluding him.

"It was the private dances that did it. After I came back from the war the old routine started. We had an offer from a syndicate of Florida hotels. It was only a question of time then."

He broke off and Ardita looked at him expectantly, but he shook his head.

"No," he said, "I'm not going to tell you about it. I'm enjoying it too much, and I'm afraid I'd lose a little of that enjoyment if I shared it with anyone else. I want to hang on to those few breathless, heroic moments when I stood out before them all and let them know I was more than a damn bobbing, squawking clown."

From up forward came suddenly the low sound of singing. The negroes had gathered together on the deck and their voices rose together in a haunting melody that soared in poignant harmonies toward the moon. And Ardita listened in enchantment:

Oh down—
Oh down,
Mammy wanna take me downa milky way,
Oh down—
Oh down,
Pappy say to-morra-a-a-ah!
But mammy say to-day,
Yes—mammy say to-day!

Carlyle sighed and was silent for a mo
ment, looking up at the gathered host
stars blinking like arc lights in the war
sky. The negroes' song had died away
a plaintive humming and it seemed as
minute by minute the brightness and th
great silence were increasing until he coul
almost hear the midnight toilet of the me
maids as they combed their silver-drippir
curls under the moon and gossiped to eac
other of the fine wrecks they lived in on th
green opalescent avenues below.

"You see," said Carlyle softly, "this
the beauty I want. Beauty has got to
astonishing, astounding—it's got to bur
in on you like a dream, like the exquisi
eyes of a girl."

He turned to her, but she was silent.

"You see, don't you, Anita—I mea
Ardita?"

Again she made no answer. She ha
been sound asleep for some time.

IV

IN THE dense sun-flooded noon of ne
day a spot in the sea before them r
solved casually into a green-and-gray isle
apparently composed of a great grani
cliff at its northern end which slanted sou
through a mile of vivid coppice and gra
to a sandy beach melting lazily into th
surf. When Ardita, reading in her favori
seat, came to the last page of The Revolt
the Angels and slamming the book sh
looked up and saw it, she gave a little c
of delight and called to Carlyle, who w
standing moodily by the rail.

"Is this it? Is this where you're going
Carlyle shrugged his shoulders careless

"You've got me." He raised his vo
and called up to the acting skipper. "
Babe, is this your island?"

The mulatto's miniature head appear
from round the corner of the deckhouse.

"Yas-suh! This yeah's it."

Carlyle joined Ardita.

"Looks sort of sporting, doesn't it?"

"Yes," she agreed; "but it doesn't lo
big enough to be much of a hiding plac

"You still putting your faith in th
wirelesses your uncle was going to ha
zigzagging round?"

"No," said Ardita frankly. "I'm all
you. I'd really like to see you make
get-away."

He laughed.

"You're our Lady Luck. Guess we'll ha
to keep you with us as a mascot—
the present anyway."

"You couldn't very well ask me to sw
back," she said coolly. "If you do I
going to start writing dime novels found
on that interminable history of your
you gave me last night."

He flushed and stiffened slightly.

"I'm very sorry I bored you."

"Oh, you didn't—until just at the
with some story about how furious y
were because you couldn't dance with
ladies you played music for."

He rose angrily.

"You have got a darn mean little tongu

"Excuse me," she said, melting i
laughter, "but I'm not used to having m
regale me with the story of their life am
tions—especially if they've lived su
deathly platonic lives."

"Why? What do men usually regale y
with?"

"Oh, they talk about me," she yawn
"They tell me I'm the spirit of youth a
beauty."

"What do you tell them?"

"Oh, I agree quietly."

"Does every man you meet tell you
loves you?"

Ardita nodded.

"Why shouldn't he? All life is jus
progression toward and then a recess
from one phrase—'I love you.'"

Carlyle laughed and sat down.

"That's very true. That's—that's
bad. Did you make that up?"

"Yes—or rather I found it out.
doesn't mean anything especially. It's j
clever."

"It's the sort of remark," he said grave
"that's typical of your class."

"Oh," she interrupted impatien
"don't start that lecture on aristocr
again! I distrust people who can be inte
at this hour in the morning. It's a r
form of insanity—a sort of breakfast-f
jag. Morning's the time to sleep, swim
be careless."

(Continued on Page 101)

(Continued from Page 99)

Ten minutes later they had swung round a wide circle as if to approach the island rom the north.

"There's a trick somewhere," commented Ardita thoughtfully. "He can't can just to anchor up against this cliff."

They were heading straight in now toward he solid rock, which must have been well rer a hundred feet tall, and not until they were within fifty yards of it did Ardita see eir objective. Then she clapped her ands in delight.

There was a break in the cliff entirely idden by a curious overlapping of rock id through this break the yacht entered id very slowly traversed a narrow channel crystal-clear water between high gray alls. Then they were riding at anchor ded bay smooth as glass and set round ith tiny palms, the whole resembling the irror lakes and twig trees that children it up in sand piles.

"Not so darned bad!" cried Carlyle exedly. "I guess that little coon knows his iy round this corner of the Atlantic."

His exuberance was contagious and Arta became quite jubilant.

"It's an absolutely sure-fire hiding ace!"

"Lordy, yes! It's the sort of island you id about."

The rowboat was lowered into the golden ce and they pulled ashore.

"Come on," said Carlyle as they landed the slushy sand; "we'll go exploring."

The fringe of palms was in turn ringed in a round mile of flat sandy country. They lowed it south and, brushing through a ther rim of tropical vegetation, came out a pearl-gray virgin beach where Ardita ked off her brown gold shoes—she seemed iave permanently abandoned stockings— it went wading. Then they sauntered ck to the yacht, where the indefatigable be had luncheon ready for them. He I posted a lookout on the high cliff to the th to watch the sea on both sides, ugh he doubted if the entrance to the was generally known—he had never n a map on which the island was even rked.

"What's its name," asked Ardita—"the nd, I mean?"

"No name 'tall," chuckled Babe. eckin she jus' Island, 'at's all." Ardita thought for a moment.

"I'll name it," she said. "It'll be the of Illusion."

"Or of Disillusion," murmured Carlyle. "Disillusion, if more people know about han Babe seems to think."

n the late afternoon they sat with their ks against great boulders on the highest t of the cliff and Carlyle sketched for her vague plans. He was sure they were hot er him by this time. The total proceeds he coup he had pulled off, and concern— which he still refused to enlighten her, estimated as just under a million dollars.

counted on lying up here several weeks then setting off southward, keeping l outside the usual channels of travel, eckin the Horn and heading for Callao, Peru. The details of coaling and proioning he was leaving entirely to Babe, i, it seemed, had sailed these seas in iy capacity from cabin boy aboard a ee trader to virtual first mate on a zilian pirate craft, whose skipper had since been hung.

If he'd been white he'd have been king iouth America long ago," said Carlyle ihatically. "When it comes to intelnce he makes Booker T. Washington : like a moron. He's got the guile of ry race and nationality whose blood is is veins, and that's half a dozen or I'm ar. He worships me because I'm the y man in the world who can play better ime than he can. We used to sit to- er on the wharves down on the New k water front, he with a bassoon and ith an oboe, and we'd blend minor is African harmonics a thousand years until the rats would crawl up the posts sit round groaning and squeaking like s will in front of a phonograph."

rdita roared.

How you can tell 'em!"

arlyle grinned.

I swear that's the gos——"

What you going to do when you get to ao?" she interrupted.

Take ship for India. I want to be iah. I mean it. My idea is to go up into anistan somewhere, buy up a palace rdita roared.

a reputation, and then after about five s appear in England with a foreign accent and a mysterious past. But India first. Do you know, they say that all the gold in the world drifts very gradually back to India? Something fascinating about that to me. And I want leisure to read— an immense amount."

"How about after that?"

"Then," he answered defiantly, "comes aristocracy. Laugh if you want to—but at least you'll have to admit that I know what I want—which I imagine is more than you do."

"On the contrary," contradicted Ardita, reaching in her pocket for her cigarette case, "when I met you I was in the midst of a great uproar of all my friends and relatives because I did know what I wanted."

"What was it?"

"A man."

He started.

"You mean you were engaged?"

"After a fashion. If you hadn't come aboard I had every intention of slipping ashore yesterday evening—how long ago it seems—and meeting him in Palm Beach. He's waiting there for me with a bracelet that once belonged to Catharine of Russia. Now don't mutter anything about aristocracy," she put in quickly. "I liked him simply because he had an imagination and the utter courage of his convictions."

"But your family disapproved, eh?"

"What there is of it—only a silly uncle and a sillier aunt. It seems he got into some scandal with a red-haired woman named Mimi something—it was frightfully exaggerated, he said, and men don't lie to me—and anyway I didn't care what he'd done; it was the future that counted. And I'd see to that. When a man's in love with me he doesn't care for other amusements. I told him to drop her like a hot cake, and he did."

"I feel rather jealous," said Carlyle, frowning—and then he laughed. "I guess I'll just keep you along with us until we get to Callao. Then I'll lend you enough money to get back to the States. By that time you'll have had a chance to think that gentleman over a little more."

"Don't talk to me like that!" fired up Ardita. "I won't tolerate the parental attitude from anybody! Do you understand me?"

He chuckled and then stopped, rather abashed, as her cold anger seemed to fold him about and chill him.

"I'm sorry," he offered uncertainly.

"Oh, don't apologize! I can't stand men who say 'I'm sorry' in that manly, reserved tone. Just shut up!"

A pause ensued, a pause which Carlyle found rather awkward, but which Ardita seemed not to notice at all as she sat contentedly enjoying her cigarette and gazing out at the shining sea. After a minute she crawled out on the rock and lay with her face over the edge, looking down. Carlyle, watching her, reflected how it seemed impossible for her to assume an ungraceful attitude.

"Oh, look!" she cried. "There's a lot of sort of ledges down there. Wide ones of all different heights."

He joined her and together they gazed down the dizzy height.

"We'll go swimming to-night!" she said excitedly. "By moonlight."

"Wouldn't you rather go in at the beach on the other end?"

"Not a chance. I like to dive. You can use my uncle's bathing suit, only it'll fit you like a gunny sack, because he's a very flabby man. I've got a one-piece affair that's shocked the natives all along the Atlantic coast from Biddeford Pool to St. Augustine."

"I suppose you're a shark."

"Yes, I'm pretty good. And I look cute too. A sculptor last summer told me my calves were worth five hundred dollars."

There didn't seem to be any answer to this, so Carlyle was silent, permitting himself only a discreet interior smile.

WHEN the night crept down in shadowy blue and silver they threaded the shimmering channel in the rowboat and tying it to a jutting rock began climbing the cliff together. The first shelf was ten feet up, wide and furnishing a natural diving platform. There they sat down in the bright moonlight and watched the faint incessant surge of the waters, almost stilled now as the tide set seaward.

"Are you happy?" he asked suddenly.

She nodded.

"Always happy near the sea. You know," she went on, "I've been thinking all day

that you and I are somewhat alike. We're both rebels—only for different reasons. One year ago, when I was just eighteen, and you were ——"

"Twenty-five."

"—— well, we were both conventional successes. I was an utterly devastating débutante and you were a prosperous musician just commissioned in the army ——"

"Gentleman by act of Congress," he put in ironically.

"Well, at any rate, we both fitted. If our corners were not rubbed off they were at least pulled in. But deep in us both was something that made us require more for happiness. I didn't know what I wanted. I went from man to man, restless, impatient, month by month getting less acquiescent and more dissatisfied. I used to sit sometimes chewing at the insides of my mouth and thinking I was going crazy—I had a frightful sense of transiency. I wanted things now—now—now! Here I was—beautiful —— I am, aren't I?"

"Yes," agreed Carlyle tentatively.

Ardita rose suddenly.

"Wait a second. I want to try this delightful-looking sea."

She walked to the end of the ledge and shot out over the water, doubling up in midair and then straightening out and entering the water straight as a blade in a perfect jackknife dive.

In a minute her voice floated up to him.

"You see, I used to read all day and most of the night. I began to resent society ——"

"Come on up here," he interrupted. "What on earth are you doing?"

"Just floating round on my back. I'll be up in a minute. Let me tell you. The only thing I enjoyed was shocking people; wearing something quite impossible and quite charming to fancy-dress parties, going round with the fastest men in New York and getting into some of the most hellish scrapes imaginable."

The sounds of splashing mingled with her words, and then he heard her hurried breathing as she began climbing up the side to the ledge.

"Go on in!" she called.

Obediently he rose and dived. When he emerged, dripping, and made the climb he found that she was no longer on the ledge, but after a frightened second he heard her light laughter from another shelf ten feet up. There he joined her and they both sat quietly for a moment, their arms clasped round their knees, panting a little from the climb.

"The family were wild," she said suddenly. "They tried to marry me off. And then when I'd begun to feel that after all life was scarcely worth living I found something"—her eyes went skyward exultantly—"I found something!"

Carlyle waited and her words came with a rush.

"Courage—just that; courage as a rule of life and something to cling to always. I began to build up this enormous faith in myself. I began to see that in all my idols in the past some manifestation of courage had unconsciously been the thing that attracted me. I began separating courage from the other things of life. All sorts of courage—the beaten, bloody prize fighter coming up for more—I used to make men take me to prize fights; the *déclassée* woman sailing through a nest of cats and looking at them as if they were mud under her feet; the liking what you like always; the utter disregard for other people's opinions—just to live as I liked always and to die in my own way. Did you bring up the cigarettes?"

He handed one over and held a match for her silently.

"Still," Ardita continued, "the men kept gathering—old men and young men, my mental and physical inferiors, most of them, but all intensely desiring to have me—to own this rather magnificent proud tradition I'd built up round me. Do you see?"

"Sort of. You never were beaten and you never apologized."

"Never!"

She sprang to the edge, poised for a moment like a crucified figure against the sky; then describing a dark parabola plunked without a splash between two silver ripples twenty feet below.

Her voice floated up to him again.

"And courage to me meant plowing through that dull gray mist that comes down on life—not only overriding people and circumstances but overriding the bleakness of living. A sort of insistence on the value of life and the worth of transient things."

She was climbing up now, and at her last words her head, with the damp yellow hair slicked symmetrically back, appeared on his level.

"All very well," objected Carlyle. "You can call it courage, but your courage is really built, after all, on a pride of birth. You were bred to that defiant attitude. On my gray days even courage is one of the things that's gray and lifeless."

She was sitting near the edge, hugging her knees and gazing abstractedly at the white moon; he was farther back, crammed like a grotesque god into a niche in the rock.

"I don't want to sound like Pollyanna," she began, "but you haven't grasped me yet. My courage is faith—faith in the eternal resilience of me—that joy'll come back, and hope and spontaneity. And I feel that till it does I've got to keep my lips shut and my chin high and my eyes wide—not necessarily any silly smiling. Oh, I've been through hell without a whine quite often—and the female hell is deadlier than the male."

"But supposing," suggested Carlyle, "that before joy and hope and all that came back the curtain was drawn on you for good?"

Ardita rose, and going to the wall climbed with some difficulty to the next ledge, another ten or fifteen feet above.

"Why," she called back, "then I'd have won!"

He edged out till he could see her.

"Better not dive from there! You'll break your back," he said quickly.

She laughed.

"Not I!"

Slowly she spread her arms and stood there swanlike, radiating a pride in the young life within her that lit a warm glow in Carlyle's heart.

"We're going through the black air with our arms wide," she called, "and our feet straight out behind like a dolphin's tail, and we're going to think we'll never hit the silver down there till suddenly it'll be all warm round us and full of little kissing, caressing waves."

Then she was in the air and Carlyle involuntarily held his breath. He had not realized that the dive was nearly forty feet. It seemed an eternity before he heard the swift compact sound as she reached the sea.

And it was with his glad sigh of relief when her light watery laughter curled up the side of the cliff and into his anxious ears that he knew he loved her.

VI

TIME, having no ax to grind, showered down upon them three days of afternoons. When the sun cleared the porthole of Ardita's cabin an hour after dawn she rose cheerily, donned her bathing suit and went up on deck. The negroes would leave their work when they saw her, and crowd, chuckling and chattering, to the rail as she floated, an agile minnow, on and under the surface of the clear water. Again in the cool of the afternoon she would swim—and loll and smoke with Carlyle upon the cliff; or else they would lie on their sides in the sands of the southern beach, talking little, but watching the day fade colorfully and tragically into the infinite languor of a tropical evening.

And with the long sunny hours Ardita's idea of the episode as incidental, madcap, a sprig of romance in a desert of reality, gradually left her. She dreaded the time when he would strike off southward; she dreaded all the eventualities that presented themselves to her; thoughts were suddenly troublesome and decisions odious. Had prayers found place in the pagan rituals of her soul she would have asked of life only to be unmolested for a while, lazily acquiescent to the ready, untutored flow of Carlyle's ideas, his vivid boyish imagination and the vein of monomania that seemed to run crosswise through his temperament and colored his every action.

But this is not a story of two on an island nor concerned primarily with love bred of isolation. It is merely the presentation of two personalities, and its idyllic setting among the palms of the Gulf Stream is quite incidental. Most of us are content to exist and breed, and fight for the right to do both, and the dominant idea, the foredoomed attempt to control one's destiny, is reserved for the fortunate or unfortunate few. To me the interesting thing about Ardita is the courage that will tarnish with her beauty and youth.

"Take me with you," said Ardita late one night as they sat lazily in the grass under the shadowy spreading palms. The negroes had brought ashore their instruments and the sound of weird ragtime was drifting over softly on the warm breath of the night. "I'd love to reappear in ten years as a fabulously wealthy high-caste Indian lady," she continued.

Carlyle looked at her quickly.

"You can, you know."

She laughed.

"Is it a proposal of marriage? Extra! Ardita Farnam becomes pirate's bride. Society girl kidnaped by ragtime bank robber."

"It wasn't a bank."

"What was it? Why won't you tell me?"

"I don't want to break down your illusions."

"My dear man, I have no illusions about you."

"I mean your illusions about yourself."

She looked up in surprise.

"About myself! What on earth have I got to do with whatever stray felonies you've committed?"

"That remains to be seen."

She reached over and patted his hand.

"Dear Mr. Curtis Carlyle," she said softly, "are you in love with me?"

"As if it mattered."

"But it does—because I think I'm in love with you."

He looked at her ironically.

"Thus swelling your January total to half a dozen," he suggested. "Suppose I call your bluff and ask you to come to India with me?"

"Shall I?"

He shrugged his shoulders.

"We can get married in Callao."

"What sort of life can you offer me? I don't mean that unkindly, but seriously; what would become of me if the people who want that twenty-thousand-dollar reward ever catch up with you?"

"I thought you weren't afraid."

"I never am—but I won't throw my life away just to show one man I'm not."

"I wish you'd been poor. Just a little poor girl dreaming over a fence in a warm cow country."

"Wouldn't it have been nice?"

"I'd have enjoyed astonishing you—watching your eyes open on things. If you only wanted things! Don't you see?"

"I know—like girls who stare into the windows of jewelry stores."

"Yes—and want the big oblong watch that's platinum and has diamonds all round the edge. Only you'd decide it was too expensive and choose one of white gold for a hundred dollars. Then I'd say, 'Expensive? I should say not!' And we'd go into the store and pretty soon the platinum one would be gleaming on your wrist."

"That sounds so nice and vulgar—and fun, doesn't it?" murmured Ardita.

"Doesn't it? Can't you see us traveling round and spending money right and left and being worshiped by bell boys and waiters? Oh, blessed are the simple rich, for they inherit the earth!"

"I honestly wish we were that way."

"I love you, Ardita," he said gently.

Her face lost its childish look for a moment and became oddly grave.

"I love to be with you," she said, "more than with any man I've ever met. And I like your looks and your dark old hair and the way you go over the side of the rail when we come ashore. In fact, Curtis Carlyle, I like all the things you do when you're perfectly natural. I think you've got nerve, and you know how I feel about that. Sometimes when you're round I've been tempted to kiss you suddenly and tell you that you were just an idealistic boy with a lot of caste nonsense in his head. Perhaps if I were just a little bit older and a little more bored I'd go with you. As it is, I think I'll go back and marry—that other man."

Over across the silver lake the figures of the negroes writhed and squirmed in the moonlight, like acrobats who, having been too long inactive, must go through their tricks from sheer surplus energy. In single file they marched, weaving in concentric circles, now with their heads thrown back, now bent over their instruments like piping fauns. And from trombone and saxophone ceaselessly whined a blended melody, sometimes riotous and jubilant, sometimes haunting and plaintive as a death dance from the Congo's heart.

"Let's dance!" cried Ardita. "I can't sit still with that perfect jazz going on."

Taking her hand, he led her out into a broad stretch of hard sandy soil that the

(Continued on Page 106)

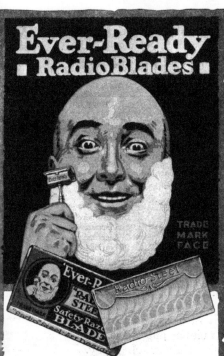

Ever-Ready
▪ Radio Blades ▪

More and Better Shaves!

Talk about exact science and fine art! Talk about diamond cutting! In what other factory must such precision prevail as in the Ever-Ready Radio Blade factory?

If there's one little defect in your blade, your shave isn't right. But there ISN'T one little defect in Radio Blades.

At the Ever-Ready factory, they say that is their business—making those little thin edges of beard-slicing steel. All thoughts are focused on that edge. It must be perfect, more than perfect.

The tougher your beard and the tenderer your skin, the more you'll appreciate the Ever-Ready Radio Blade.

6 for 40c — Sold the World Over

AMERICAN SAFETY RAZOR CORPORATION
Brooklyn, N. Y.

Makers of the famous Ever-Ready Safety Razors and Ever-Ready Shaving Brushes

Factories:
New York
Brooklyn
Toronto
London
Paris

(Continued from Page 102)

moon flooded with grand splendor. They floated out like drifting moths under the rich hazy light, and as the fantastic symphony wept and exulted and wavered and despaired Ardita's last sense of reality dropped away and she abandoned her imagination to the dreamy summer scents of tropical flowers and the infinite starry spaces overhead, feeling that if she opened her eyes it would be to find herself dancing with a ghost in a land created by her own fancy.

"This is what I should call an exclusive private dance," he whispered.

"I feel quite mad — but delightfully mad!"

"We're enchanted. The shades of unnumbered generations of cannibals are watching us from high up on the side of the cliff there."

"And I'll bet the cannibal women are saying that we dance too close and that it was immodest of me to come without my nose ring."

They both laughed softly — and then their laughter died as over across the lake they heard the trombones stop in the middle of a bar and the saxophones give a startled moan and fade out.

"What's the matter?" called Carlyle.

After a moment's silence they made out the dark figure of a man rounding the silver lake at a run. As he came closer they saw it was Babe in a state of unusual excitement. He drew up before them and gasped out his news in a breath.

"Ship stan'in' off sho' 'bout half a mile, suh. Mose, he uz on watch, he say look's if she's done anchor'd."

"A ship — what kind of a ship?" demanded Carlyle anxiously.

Dismay was in his voice and Ardita's heart gave a sudden wrench as she saw his whole face suddenly droop.

"He say he don't know, suh."

"Are they landing a boat?"

"No, suh."

"We'll go up," said Carlyle.

They ascended the hill in silence, Ardita's hand still resting in Carlyle's as it had when they finished dancing. She felt it clench nervously from time to time as though he were unaware of the contact, but though he hurt her she made no attempt to remove it. It seemed an hour's climb before they reached the top and crept cautiously across the silhouetted plateau to the edge of the cliff. After one short look Carlyle involuntarily gave a little cry. It was a revenue boat with six-inch guns mounted fore and aft.

"They know!" he said with a short intake of breath. "They know! They picked up the trail somewhere."

"Are you sure they know about the channel? They may be only standing by to take a look at the island in the morning. From where they are they couldn't see the opening in the cliff."

"They could with field glasses," he said hopelessly. He looked at his wrist watch.

"It's nearly two now. They won't do anything until dawn, that's certain. Of course there's always the faint possibility that they're waiting for some other ship to join; or for a coaler."

"I suppose we may as well stay right here."

The hours passed and they lay there side by side, very silently, their chins in their hands like dreaming children. In back of them squatted the negroes, patient, resigned, acquiescent, announcing now and then with sonorous snores that not even the presence of danger could subdue their unconquerable African craving for sleep.

Just before five o'clock Babe approached Carlyle.

There were half a dozen rifles aboard the Narcissus, he said. Had it been decided to offer no resistance? A pretty good fight might be made, he thought, if they worked out some plan.

Carlyle laughed and shook his head.

"That isn't a Spic army out there, Babe. That's a revenue boat. It'd be like a bow and arrow trying to fight a machine gun. If you want to bury those bags somewhere and take a chance on recovering them later, go on do it. But it won't work — they'd dig this island over from one end to another. It's a lost battle all round, Babe."

Babe inclined his head silently and turned away, and Carlyle's voice was husky as he turned to Ardita.

"There's the best friend I ever had. He'd die for me, and be proud to, if I'd let him."

"You've given up?"

"I've no choice. Of course there's always one way out — the sure way — but that can wait. I wouldn't miss my trial for anything — it'll be an interesting experiment in notoriety. 'Miss Farnam testifies that the pirate's attitude to her was at all times that of a gentleman.'"

"Don't!" she said. "I'm awfully sorry."

When the color faded from the sky and lusterless blue changed to leaden gray a commotion was visible on the ship's deck and they made out a group of officers clad in white duck, gathered near the rail. They had field glasses in their hands and were attentively examining the islet.

"It's all up," said Carlyle grimly.

"Damn!" whispered Ardita. She felt tears gathering in her eyes.

"We'll go back to the yacht," he said. "I prefer that to being hunted out up here like a 'possum."

Leaving the plateau they descended the hill, and reaching the lake were rowed out to the yacht by the silent negroes. Then, pale and weary, they sank into the settees and waited.

Half an hour later in the dim gray light the nose of the revenue boat appeared in the channel and stopped, evidently fearing that the bay might be too shallow. From the peaceful look of the yacht, the man and the girl in the settees and the negroes lounging curiously against the rail, they evidently judged that there would be no resistance.

Two boats were lowered casually over the side, one containing an officer and six bluejackets, and the other, four rowers and in the stern two gray-haired men in yachting flannels. Ardita and Carlyle stood up and half unconsciously started toward each other. Then he paused and putting his hand suddenly into his pocket he pulled out a round glittering object and held it out to her.

"What is it?" she asked wonderingly.

"I'm not positive, but I think from the Russian inscription inside that it's your promised bracelet."

"Where — where on earth ——"

"It came out of one of those bags. You see, Curtis Carlyle and his Six Black Buddies, in the middle of their performance in the tea room of the hotel at Palm Beach, suddenly changed their instruments for automatics and held up the crowd. I took this bracelet from a pretty overrouged woman with red hair."

Ardita frowned and then smiled.

"So that's what you did! You have got nerve!"

He bowed.

"A well-known bourgeois quality," he said.

And then dawn slanted dynamically across the deck and flung the shadows reeling into gray corners. The dew rose and turned to golden mist, thin as a dream, enveloping them until they seemed gossamer relics of the late night, infinitely transient and already fading. For a moment sea and sky were breathless and dawn held a pink hand over the young mouth of life — then from out in the lake came the complaint of a rowboat and the swish of oars.

Suddenly against the golden furnace low in the east their two graceful figures melted into one and he was kissing her spoiled young mouth.

"It's a sort of glory," he murmured after a second.

She smiled up at him.

"Happy, are you?"

Her sigh was a benediction — an ecstatic surety that she was youth and beauty now as much as she would ever know. For another instant life was radiant and time a phantom and their strength eternal — then there was a bumping, scraping sound as the rowboat scraped alongside.

Up the ladder scrambled the two gray-haired men, the officer and two of the sailors with their hands on their revolvers. Mr. Farnam folded his arms and stood looking at his niece.

"So," he said, nodding his head slowly.

With a sigh her arms unwound from Carlyle's neck, and her eyes, transfigured and far away, fell upon the boarding party. Her uncle saw her upper lip slowly unveil into that arrogant pout he knew so well.

"So," he repeated savagely. "So this is your idea of romance. A runaway affair, with a — a high-seas pirate."

Ardita considered him carelessly.

"What an old fool you are!" she said quietly.

"Is that the best you can say for yourself?" *(Concluded on Page 109)*

(Concluded from Page 106)

"No," she said as if considering. "No, there's something else. There's that well-known phrase with which I have ended most of our conversations for the past few years—'Shut up!'"

And with that she turned, included the two old men, the officer and the two sailors in a curt glance of contempt, and walked proudly down the companionway.

But had she waited an instant longer she would have heard a sound from her uncle quite unfamiliar in most of their interviews. Her uncle gave vent to a wholehearted amused chuckle, in which the second old man joined.

The latter turned briskly to Carlyle, who had been regarding this scene with an air of cryptic amusement.

"Well, Toby," he said genially, "you incurable, harebrained, romantic chaser of rainbows, did you find that she was the person you wanted?"

Carlyle smiled confidently.

"Why—naturally," he said. "I've been perfectly sure ever since I first heard tell of her wild career. That's why I had Babe send up the rocket last night."

"I'm glad you did," said Colonel Moreland gravely. "We've been keeping pretty close to you in case you should have trouble with those six strange nigers. And we hoped we'd find you two in some such compromising position," he sighed. "Well, set a crank to catch a crank!"

"Your father and I sat up all night hoping for the best—or perhaps it's the worst. Lord knows you're welcome to her, my boy. She's run me crazy. Did you give her the Russian bracelet my detective got from that Mimi woman?"

Carlyle nodded.

"Sh!" he said. "She's coming on deck."

Ardita appeared at the head of the companionway and gave a quick involuntary glance at Carlyle's wrists. A puzzled look came over her face. Back aft the negroes

had begun to sing, and the cool lake, fresh with dawn, echoed serenely to their low voices.

"Ardita," said Carlyle unsteadily.

She swayed a step toward him.

"Ardita," he repeated breathlessly, "I've got to tell you the—the truth. It was all a plant, Ardita. My name isn't Carlyle. It's Moreland, Toby Moreland. The story was invented, Ardita, invented out of thin Florida air."

She stared at him, bewildered amazement, disbelief and anger flowing in quick waves across her face. The three men held their breaths. Moreland, Senior, took a step toward her; Mr. Farnam's mouth dropped a little open as he waited, panic-stricken, for the expected crash.

But it did not come. Ardita's face became suddenly radiant, and with a little laugh she went swiftly to young Moreland and looked up at him without a trace of wrath in her gray eyes.

"Will you swear," she said quietly, "that it was entirely a product of your own brain?"

"I swear," said young Moreland eagerly. She drew his head down and kissed him gently.

"What an imagination!" she said softly and almost enviously. "I want you to lie to me just as sweetly as you know how for the rest of my life."

The negroes' voices floated drowsily back, mingled in an air that she had heard them sing before:

Time is a thief;
Gladness and grief
Cling to the leaf
As it yellows ——

"What was in the bags?" she asked softly.

"Florida mud," he answered. "That was one of the two true things I told you."

And Ardita placed a girl of some perspicacity had no difficulty in guessing the other.

SCHOOL-TEACHERS

WHEN men wore whiskers and girls wore red-flannel petticoats and boys wore copper-toed shoes, the business of teaching a rural school was listed as one of the hazardous occupations, and one who applied for a position was not questioned closely concerning his intellectual attainments if his breadth of shoulder gave promise of ability to maintain order in the schoolroom. The teacher earned a little more than the plow hand, and his board was part of his pay.

In later years, when schoolboys had grown tamer, girl pedagogues appeared. For the most part the girls became teachers because their earnings were needed at home. If there were several girls in the family and the head of the house decreed that one should become a teacher the lot usually fell to the one least beautiful, the assumption being that she had less reasonable hope of catching a husband. If homely girls develop more brains than pretty girls it is because they have need of more.

Girl pedagogues were considered desirable because they lived at home and were thus enabled to work for a smaller salary than men demanded. Then, as now, citizens made fine talk concerning the benefits of education and whined about the taxes levied for educational purposes.

Teaching was not a profession. Men without capital taught school until something better should offer, and girls taught while waiting for a man. Their social standing was near that of the preacher. Like the preacher they were respected for their knowledge and despised for their poverty, and those who furnished their support purchased the right to hold them in mild contempt. It is not surprising that pedagogy progressed but slowly to the dignity of a profession.

A profession it is to-day. Reputable schools teach the art of teaching as others teach medicine and the law. One who would teach must know his trade. And as we demand more of our teachers so do we respect them more. Indeed, in most communities the pedagogue is a superior person, deferred to and consulted in many matters not rightly pertaining to his craft.

He holds the respect he deserves, but he does not receive the pay he deserves. Business men gauge the value of an employee by his ability to make a profit for his employer. The profit made by the pedagogue for his employers is an indefinite one, not readily comprehended, and since it cannot be counted in dollars and cents must be accepted on faith. As an incentive to continued investment, faith is less effective than the sight of immediate profits in cash.

The pedagogue has devoted years to the task of learning his trade, but he will not always pay the price of poverty for the privilege of doing his work. The ever-widening gulf between his earnings and the earnings of those whose sole stock in trade is brawn will in time persuade him to venture into a new field and the schools will come upon an evil day.

We prate of our civilization, and mouth pretty phrases concerning the blessings of education; but we do not show our faith by our works. If we valued education as we profess to value it, brains would have a reasonable cash value in the schoolroom as they have in commerce and industry, and college-bred experts would not be held down to a wage that is demanded and received by apprentices in other trades.

It will always be possible to hire teachers at the price now paid; it will not long be possible to hold competent teachers at that price.

Published Weekly
The Curtis Publishing Company
Cyrus H. K. Curtis, President
C. H. Ludington, Vice-President and Treasurer
F. S. Collins, General Business Manager
Walter D. Fuller, Secretary
William Boyd, Advertising Director

Independence Square, Philadelphia

London: 6 Henrietta Street
Covent Garden, W. C.

THE SATURDAY EVENING POST
Founded A°D¹ 1728 by Benj. Franklin
Copyright, 1922, by The Curtis Publishing Company in the United States and Great Britain
Title Registered in U. S. Patent Office and in Foreign Countries

George Horace Lorimer
EDITOR
Churchill Williams, F. S. Bigelow,
A. W. Neall, Arthur McKeogh,
T. D. Costain, Associate Editors

Entered as Second-Class Matter, November 16,
1879, at the Post Office at Philadelphia,
Under the Act of March 3, 1879
Additional Entry as Second-Class Matter
at Columbus, Ohio, at Decatur, Illinois, and
at Indianapolis, Ind.

Entered as Second-Class Matter at the
Post-Office Department, Ottawa, Canada

Volume 194   5c. THE COPY   PHILADELPHIA, PA., FEBRUARY 11, 1922 $2.00 THE YEAR   Number 33

THE POPULAR GIRL

"Who Was the Gentleman With the Invisible Tie?" Scott Asked. "Is His Personality as Diverting as His Haberdashery?"

By F. Scott Fitzgerald
ILLUSTRATED BY CHARLES D. MITCHELL

LONG about half past ten every Saturday night Yanci Bowman eluded her partner by some graceful subterfuge and from the dancing floor went to point of vantage overlooking the country-club bar. When she saw her father she would either beckon to him, if he chanced to be looking in her direction, or else she would dispatch a waiter to call attention to her impendent presence. If it were no later than half past ten—that is, if he had had no more than an hour of synthetic gin rickeys—he would get up from his chair and suffer himself to be persuaded into the ballroom.

"Ballroom," for want of a better word. It was that room, filled by day with wicker furniture, which was always connoted in the phrase "Let's go in and dance." It was referred to as "Inside" or "downstairs." It was that nameless chamber wherein occur the principal transactions of all the country clubs in America.

Yanci knew that if she could keep her father there for an hour, talking, watching her dance, or even on rare occasions dancing himself, she could safely release him at the end of that time. In the period that would elapse before midnight ended the dance he could scarcely become sufficiently stimulated to annoy anyone.

All this entailed considerable exertion on Yanci's part, and it was less for her father's sake than for her own that she went through with it. Several rather unpleasant experiences were scattered through this past summer. One night when she had been detained by the impassioned and impossible-to-interrupt speech of a young man from Chicago her father had appeared swaying gently in the ballroom doorway; in his hand a glass, and on his handsome face two faded blue eyes were squinted half shut as he tried to focus on the dancers, and he was obviously preparing to offer himself to the first dowager who caught his eye. He was ludicrously injured when Yanci insisted upon an immediate withdrawal.

After that night Yanci went through her Fabian maneuver to the minute.

Yanci and her father were the handsomest two people in the Middle Western city where they lived. Tom Bowman's complexion was hearty from twenty years spent in the service of good whisky and bad golf. He kept an office downtown, where he was thought to transact some vague real-estate business; but in point of fact his chief concern in life was the exhibition of a handsome profile and an easy well-bred manner at the country club, where he had spent the greater part of the ten years that had elapsed since his wife's death.

Yanci was twenty, with a vague die-away manner which was partly the setting for her languid disposition and partly the effect of a visit she had paid to some Eastern relatives at an impressionable age. She was intelligent, in a flitting way, romantic under the moon and unable to decide whether to marry for sentiment or for comfort, the latter of these two abstractions being well enough personified by one of the most ardent among her admirers. Meanwhile she kept house, not without efficiency, for her father, and tried in a placid unruffled tempo to regulate his constant tippling to the sober side of inebriety.

She admired her father. She admired him for his fine appearance and for his charming manner. He had never quite lost the air of having been a popular Bones man at Yale. This charm of his was a standard by which her susceptible temperament unconsciously judged the men she knew. Nevertheless, father and daughter were far from that sentimental family relationship which is a stock plant in fiction, but in life

3

323

usually exists in the mind of only the older party to it. Yanci Bowman had decided to leave her home by marriage within the year. She was heartily bored.

Scott Kimberly, who saw her for the first time this November evening at the country club, agreed with the lady whose house guest he was that Yanci was an exquisite little beauty. With a sort of conscious sensuality surprising in such a young man—Scott was only twenty-five—he avoided an introduction that he might watch her undisturbed for a fanciful hour, and sip the pleasure or the disillusion of her conversation at the drowsy end of the evening.

"She never got over the disappointment of not meeting the Prince of Wales when he was in this country," remarked Mrs. Orrin Rogers, following his gaze. "She said so, anyhow; whether she was serious or not I don't know. I hear that she has her walls simply plastered with pictures of him."

"Who?" asked Scott suddenly.

"Why, the Prince of Wales."

"Who has plaster pictures of him?"

"Why, Yanci Bowman, the girl you said you thought was so pretty."

"After a certain degree of prettiness, one pretty girl is as pretty as another," said Scott argumentatively.

"Yes, I suppose so."

Mrs. Rogers' voice drifted off on an indefinite note. She had never in her life compassed a generality until it had fallen familiarly on her ear from constant repetition.

"Let's talk her over," Scott suggested.

With a mock reproachful smile Mrs. Rogers lent herself agreeably to slander. An encore was just beginning. The orchestra trickled a light overflow of music into the pleasant green-latticed room and the two score couples who for the evening comprised the local younger set moved placidly into time with its beat. Only a few apathetic stags gathered one by one in the doorways, and to a close observer it was apparent that the scene did not attain the gayety which was its aspiration. These girls and men had known each other from childhood; and though there were marriages incipient upon the floor to-night, they were marriages of environment, of resignation, or even of boredom.

Their trappings lacked the sparkle of the seventeen-year-old affairs that took place through the short and radiant holidays. On such occasions as this, thought Scott as his eyes still sought casually for Yanci, occurred the matings of the left-overs, the plainer, the duller, the poorer of the social world; matings actuated by the same urge toward perhaps a more glamorous destiny, yet, for all that, less beautiful and less young. Scott himself was feeling very old.

But there was one face in the crowd to which his generalization did not apply. When his eyes found Yanci Bowman among the dancers he felt much younger. She was the incarnation of all in which the dance failed—graceful youth, arrogant, languid freshness and beauty that was sad and perishable as a memory in a dream. Her partner, a young man with one of those fresh red complexions ribbed with white streaks, as though he had been slapped on a cold day, did not appear to be holding her interest, and her glance fell here and there upon a group, a face, a garment, with a far-away and oblivious melancholy.

"Dark-blue eyes," said Scott to Mrs. Rogers. "I don't know that they mean anything except that they're beautiful, but that nose and upper lip and chin are certainly aristocratic—if there is any such thing," he added apologetically.

"Oh, she's very aristocratic," agreed Mrs. Rogers. "Her grandfather was a senator or governor or something in one of the Southern States. Her father's very aristocratic looking too. Oh, yes, they're very aristocratic; they're aristocratic people."

"She looks lazy."

Scott was watching the yellow gown drift and submerge among the dancers.

"She doesn't like to move. It's a wonder she dances so well. Is she engaged? Who is the man who keeps cutting in on her, the one who tucks his tie under his collar so rakishly and affects the remarkable slanting pockets?"

He was annoyed at the young man's persistence, and his sarcasm lacked the ring of detachment.

"Oh, that's"—Mrs. Rogers bent forward, the tip of her tongue just visible between her lips—"that's the O'Rourke boy. He's quite devoted, I believe."

"I believe," Scott said suddenly, "that I'll get you to introduce me if she's near when the music stops."

They arose and stood looking for Yanci—Mrs. Rogers, small, stoutening, nervous, and Scott Kimberly, her husband's cousin, dark and just below medium height. Scott was an orphan with half a million of his own, and he was in this city for no more reason than that he had missed a train. They looked for several minutes, and in vain. Yanci, in her yellow dress, no longer moved with slow loveliness among the dancers.

The clock stood at half past ten.

II

"GOOD evening," her father was saying to her at that moment in syllables faintly slurred. "This seems to be getting to be a habit."

They were standing near a side stairs, and over his

She Was Overstrained With Grief and Loneliness; Almost Any Shoulder Would Have Done as Well

shoulder through a glass door Yanci could see a party of half a dozen men sitting in familiar joviality about a round table.

"Don't you want to come out and watch for a while?" she suggested, smiling and affecting a casualness she did not feel.

"Not to-night, thanks."

Her father's dignity was a bit too emphasized to be convincing.

"Just come out and take a look," she urged him. "Everybody's here, and I want to ask you what you think of somebody."

This was not so good, but it was the best that occurred to her.

"I doubt very strongly if I'd find anything to interest me out there," said Tom Bowman emphatically. "I observe that f'some insane reason I'm always taken out and aged on the wood for half an hour as though I was irresponsible."

"I only ask you to stay a little while."

"Very considerate, I'm sure. But to-night I happ'n be interested in a discussion that's taking place in here."

"Come on, father."

Yanci put her arm through his ingratiatingly; but he released it by the simple expedient of raising his own arm and letting hers drop.

"I'm afraid not."

"I'll tell you," she suggested lightly, concealing her annoyance at this unusually protracted argument, "you

come in and look, just once, and then if it bores you y can go right back."

He shook his head.

"No, thanks."

Then without another word he turned suddenly an reëntered the bar. Yanci went back to the ballroom. S glanced easily at the stag line as she passed, and maki a quick selection murmured to a man near her, "Danc with me, will you, Carty? I've lost my partner."

"Glad to," answered Carty truthfully.

"Awfully sweet of you."

"Sweet of me? Of you, you mean."

She looked up at him absently. She w furiously annoyed at her father. Next mor ing at breakfast she would radiate a consum ing chill, but for to-night she could only wa hoping that if the worst happened he would least remain in the bar until the dance w over.

Mrs. Rogers, who lived next door to t Bowmans, appeared suddenly at her elb with a strange young man.

"Yanci," Mrs. Rogers was saying with social smile. "I want to introduce Mr. Ki berly. Mr. Kimberly's spending the wee end with us, and I particularly wanted him meet you."

"How perfectly slick!" drawled Yanci wi lazy formality.

Mr. Kimberly suggested to Miss Bowm that they dance, to which proposal Miss Bo man dispassionately acquiesced. They min their arms in the gesture prevalent and stepp into time with the beat of the drum. Sim taneously it seemed to Scott that the roc and the couples who danced up and down up it converted themselves into a backgrou behind her. The commonplace lamps, rhythm of the music playing some paraphra of a paraphrase, the faces of many girls, pret undistinguished or absurd, assumed a cert solidity as though they had grouped themsel in a retinue for Yanci's languid eyes a dancing feet.

"I've been watching you," said Scott si ply. "You look rather bored this evenin

"Do I?" Her dark-blue eyes expose borderland of fragile iris as they opened a delicate burlesque of interest. "How p feetly kill-ing!" she added.

Scott laughed. She had used the exagg ated phrase without smiling, indeed with any attempt to give it verisimilitude. He heard the adjectives of the year—"heck "marvelous" and "slick"—delivered casua but never before without the faintest me ing. In this lackadaisical young beauty it inexpressibly charming.

The dance ended. Yanci and Scott strolled towar lounge set against the wall, but before they could t possession there was a shriek of laughter and a bra damsel dragging an embarrassed boy in her wake skid by them and plumped down upon it.

"How rude!" observed Yanci.

"I suppose it's her privilege."

"A girl with ankles like that has no privileges."

They seated themselves uncomfortably on two chairs.

"Where do you come from?" she asked of Scott v polite disinterest.

"New York."

This having transpired, Yanci deigned to fix her eye him for the best part of ten seconds.

"Who was the gentleman with the invisible tie," S asked rudely, in order to make her look at him ag "who was giving you such a rush? I found it impos to keep my eyes off him. Is his personality as diver as his haberdashery?"

"I don't know," she drawled; "I've only been enga to him for a week."

"My Lord!" exclaimed Scott, perspiring suddenly der his eyes.

"I beg your pardon. I didn't ——"

"I was only joking," she interrupted with a sig laugh. "I thought I'd see what you'd say to that."

Then they both laughed, and Yanci continued, not engaged to anyone. I'm too horribly unpopul Still the same key, her languorous voice humorously tradicting the content of her remark. "No one'll marry me."

"How pathetic!"

"Really," she murmured; "because I have to compliments all the time, in order to live, and no thinks I'm attractive any more, so no one ever gives t to me."

Seldom had Scott been so amused.

"Why, you beautiful child," he cried, "I'll ne never hear anything else from morning till night!"

"Oh, yes I do," she responded, obviously pleased. "I never get compliments unless I fish for them."

"Everything's the same," she was thinking as she gazed around her in a peculiar mood of pessimism. Same boys sober and same boys tight; same old women sitting by the walls—and one or two girls sitting with them who were dancing this time last year.

Yanci had reached the stage where these country-club dances seemed little more than a display of sheer idiocy. An enchanted carnival where jeweled and immaculate maidens rouged to the pinkest propriety displayed themselves to strange and fascinating men, the picture had faded to a medium-sized hall where was an almost indecent display of unclothed motives and obvious failures. So much for several years! And the dance had changed scarcely by a ruffle in the fashions or a new flip in a figure of speech.

Yanci was ready to be married.

Meanwhile the dozen remarks rushing to Scott Kimberly's lips were interrupted by the apologetic appearance of Mrs. Rogers.

"Yanci," the older woman was saying, "the chauffeur's just telephoned to say that the car's broken down. I wonder if you and your father have room for us going home. If it's the slightest inconvenience don't hesitate to tell—"

"I know he'll be terribly glad to. He's got loads of room, because I came out with someone else."

She was wondering if her father would be presentable at twelve.

He could always drive at any rate—and, besides, people who asked for a lift could take what they got.

"That'll be lovely. Thank you so much," said Mrs. Rogers.

Then, as she had just passed the kittenish late thirties when women still think they are *persona grata* with the young and entered upon the early forties when their children convoy to them tactfully that they no longer are, Mrs. Rogers obliterated herself from the scene. At that moment the music started and the unfortunate young man with white streaks in his red complexion appeared in front of Yanci.

Just before the end of the end of the next dance Scott Kimberly cut in on her again.

"I've come back," he began, "to tell you how beautiful you are."

"I'm not, really," she answered. "And, besides, you tell everyone that."

The music gathered gusto for its finale, and they sat down upon the comfortable lounge.

"I've told no one that for three years," said Scott.

There was no reason why he should have made it three years, yet somehow it sounded convincing to both of them. Her curiosity was stirred. She began finding out about him. She put him to a lazy questionnaire which began with his relationship to the Rogerses and ended, he knew not by what steps, with a detailed description of his apartment in New York.

"I want to live in New York," she told him; "on Park Avenue, in one of those beautiful white buildings that have twelve big rooms in each apartment and cost a fortune to rent."

"That's what I'd want, too, if I were married. Park Avenue—it's one of the most beautiful streets in the world, I think, perhaps chiefly because it hasn't any leprous park trying to give it an artificial suburbanity."

"Whatever that is," agreed Yanci. "Anyway, father and I go to New York about three times a year. We always go to the Ritz."

This was not precisely true. Once a year she generally pried her father from his placid and not unbeneficent existence that she might spend a week lolling the Fifth Avenue shop windows, lunching or having tea with some former school friend from Farmover, and occasionally going to dinner and the theater with boys who came up from Yale or Princeton for the occasion. These had been pleasant adventures—not one but was filled to the brim with colorful hours—dancing at Mont Martre, dining at the Ritz, with some movie star or supereminent society woman at the next table, or else dreaming of what she might buy at Hempel's or Waxe's or Thrumble's if her father's income had but one additional naught on the happy side of the decimal. She adored New York with a great impersonal affection—adored it as only a Middle Western or Southern girl can. In its gaudy bazaars she felt her soul transported with turbulent delight, for to her eyes it held nothing ugly, nothing sordid, nothing plain.

She had stayed once at the Ritz—once only. The Manhattan, where they usually registered, had been torn down. She knew that she could never induce her father to afford the Ritz again.

After a moment she borrowed a pencil and paper and scribbled a notification "To Mr. Bowman in the grill" that he was expected to drive Mrs. Rogers and her guest home, "by request"—this last underlined. She hoped that he would be able to do so with dignity. This note she sent by a waiter to her father. Before the next dance began it was returned to her with a scrawled O. K. and her father's initials.

The remainder of the evening passed quickly. Scott Kimberly cut in on her as often as time permitted, giving her those comforting assurances of her enduring beauty which not without a whimsical pathos she craved. He laughed at her also, and she was not so sure that she liked that. In common with all vague people, she was unaware

that she was vague. She did not entirely comprehend when Scott Kimberly told her that her personality would endure long after she was too old to care whether it endured or not.

She liked best to talk about New York, and each of their interrupted conversations gave her a picture or a memory of the metropolis on which she speculated as she looked over the shoulder of Jerry O'Rourke or Carty Braden or some other beau, to whom, as to all of them, she was comfortably anæsthetic. At midnight she sent another note to her father, saying that Mrs. Rogers and Mrs. Rogers' guest would meet him immediately on the porch by the main driveway. Then, hoping for the best, she walked out into the starry night and was assisted by Jerry O'Rourke into his roadster.

III

"GOOD night, Yanci." With her late escort she was standing on the curbstone in front of the rented stucco house where she lived. Mr. O'Rourke was attempting to put significance into his lingering rendition of her name. For weeks he had been straining to boost their relations almost forcibly onto a sentimental plane; but Yanci, with her vague impassivity, which was a defense against almost anything, had brought to naught his efforts. Jerry O'Rourke was an old story. His family had money; but he—he worked in a brokerage house along with most of the rest of his young generation. He sold bonds—bonds were now the thing; real estate was once the thing—in the days of the boom; then automobiles were the thing. Bonds were the thing now. Young men sold them who had nothing else to go into.

"Don't bother to come up, please." Then as he put his car into gear, "Call me up soon!"

A minute later he turned the corner of the moonlit street and disappeared, his cut-out resounding voluminously through the night as it declared that the rest of two dozen weary inhabitants was of no concern to his gay meanderings.

Yanci sat down thoughtfully upon the porch steps. She had no key and must wait for her father's arrival. Five minutes later a roadster turned into the street, and approaching with an exaggerated caution stopped in front of the Rogers' large house next door. Relieved, Yanci arose and strolled slowly down the walk. The door of the car had swung open and Mrs. Rogers, assisted by Scott Kimberly, had alighted safely upon the sidewalk; but to Yanci's surprise Scott Kimberly, after escorting Mrs. Rogers to her steps, returned to the car. Yanci was close enough to notice that he took the driver's seat. As he drew up at the Bowmans' curbstone Yanci saw that her father was occupying the far corner, fighting with ludicrous dignity against a sleep that had come upon him. She groaned. The fatal last hour had done its work—Tom Bowman was once more *hors de combat*.

The Maid Found Her Next Morning, Asleep, Sprawled Across the Toilet Things on the Dresser in a Room That Was Heavy and Sweet With the Scent of Spilled Perfume

"Hello," cried Yanci as she reached the curb.

"Yanci," muttered her parent, simulating, unsuccessfully, a brisk welcome. His lips were curved in an ingratiating grin.

"Your father wasn't feeling quite fit, so he let me drive home," explained Scott cheerfully as he got himself out and came up to her.

"Nice little car. Had it long?"

Yanci laughed, but without humor.

"Is he paralyzed?"

"Is who paralyze'?" demanded the figure in the car with an offended sigh.

Scott was standing by the car.

"Can I help you out, sir?"

"I c'n get out. I c'n get out," insisted Mr. Bowman. "Just step a li'l' out my way. Someone must have given me some stremely bad wisk'."

"You mean a lot of people must have given you some," retorted Yanci in cold unsympathy.

Mr. Bowman reached the curb with astonishing ease; but this was a deceitful success, for almost immediately he clutched at a handle of air perceptible only to himself, and was saved by Scott's quickly proffered arm. Followed by the two men, Yanci walked toward the house in a furor of

(Continued on Page 82)

82   *THE SATURDAY EVENING POST*   *February 11, 1922*

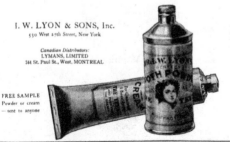
THE POPULAR GIRL
(Continued from Page 5)

embarrassment. Would the young man think that such scenes went on every night? It was chiefly her own presence that made it humiliating for Yanci. Had her father been carried to bed by two butlers each evening she might even have been proud of the fact that he could afford such dissipation; but to have it thought that she assisted, that she was burdened with the worry and the care! And finally she was annoyed with Scott Kimberly for being there, and for his officiousness in helping to bring her father into the house.

Reaching the low porch of tapestry brick, Yanci searched in Tom Bowman's vest for the key and unlocked the front door. A minute later the master of the house was deposited in an easy-chair.

"Thanks very much," he said, recovering for a moment. "Sit down. Like a drink? Yanci, get some crackers and cheese, if there's any, won't you, dear?"

At the unconscious coolness of this Scott and Yanci laughed.

"It's your bedtime, father," she said, her anger struggling with diplomacy.

"Give me my guitar," he suggested, "and I'll play you tune."

Except on such occasions as this, he had not touched his guitar for twenty years. Yanci turned to Scott.

"He'll be fine now. Thanks a lot. He'll fall asleep in a minute and when I wake him he'll go to bed like a lamb."

"Well ——"

They strolled together out the door.

"Sleepy?" he asked.

"No, not a bit."

"Then perhaps you'd better let me stay here with you a few minutes until you see if he's all right. Mrs. Rogers gave me a key so I can get in without disturbing her."

"It's quite all right," protested Yanci. "I don't mind a bit, and he won't be any trouble. He must have taken a glass too much, and this whisky we have out here—you know! This has happened once before—last year," she added.

Her words satisfied her; as an explanation it seemed to have a convincing ring.

"Can I sit down for a moment, anyway?" They sat side by side upon a wicker porch settee.

"I'm thinking of staying over a few days," Scott said.

"How lovely!" Her voice had resumed its die-away note.

"Cousin Pete Rogers wasn't well today, but tomorrow he's going duck shooting, and he wants me to go with him."

"Oh, how thrill-ing! I've always been mad to go, and father's always promised to take me, but he never has."

"We're going to be gone about three days, and then I thought I'd come back here and stay over the next week-end——"

He broke off suddenly and bent forward in a listening attitude.

"Now what on earth is that?"

The sounds of music were proceeding brokenly from the room they had lately left—a ragged chord on a guitar and half a dozen feeble starts.

"It's father!" cried Yanci.

And now a voice drifted out to them, drunken and murmurous, taking the long notes with attempted melancholy:

> Sing a song of cities,
> Ridin' on a rail,
> A nigga's ne'er so happy
> As when he's out-a jail.

"How terrible!" exclaimed Yanci. "He'll wake up everybody in the block."

The chorus ended, the guitar jangled again, then gave out a last harsh spang! and was still. A moment later these disturbances were followed by a low but quite definite snore. Mr. Bowman, having indulged his musical proclivity, had dropped off to sleep.

"Let's go to ride," suggested Yanci impatiently. "This is too hectic for me."

Scott arose with alacrity and they walked down to the car.

"Where'll we go?" she wondered.

"I don't care."

"We might go up half a block to Crest Avenue—that's our show street—and then ride out to the river boulevard."

IV

AS THEY turned into Crest Avenue the new cathedral, immense and unfinished, in imitation of a cathedral left unfinished by accident in some little Flemish

town, squatted just across the way like a plump white bulldog on its haunches. The ghosts of four moonlit apostles looked down at them wanly from wall niches still littered with the white, dusty trash of the builders. The cathedral inaugurated Crest Avenue. After it came the great brown stone mass built by R. R. Comerford, the flour king, followed by a half mile of pretentious stone houses put up in the gloomy 90's. These were adorned with monstrous driveways and porte-cochères which had once echoed to the hoofs of good horses and with huge circular windows that corseted the second stories.

The continuity of these mausoleums was broken by a small park, a triangle of grass where Nathan Hale stood ten feet tall with his hands bound behind his back by stone cord and stared over a great bluff at the slow Mississippi. Crest Avenue ran along the bluff, but neither faced it nor seemed aware of it, for all the houses fronted inward toward the street. Beyond the first half mile it became newer, essayed ventures in terraced lawns, in concoctions of stucco or in granite mansions which imitated through a variety of gradual refinements the marble contours of the Petit Trianon. The houses of this phase rushed by the roadster for a succession of minutes, then the way turned and the car was headed directly into the moonlight which swept toward it like the lamp of some gigantic motorcycle far up the avenue.

Past the low Corinthian lines of the Christian Science Temple, past a block of dark frame horrors, a deserted row of grim red brick—an unfortunate experiment of the late 90's—then new houses again, bright-red brick now, with trimmings of white, black iron fences and hedges binding flowery lawns. These swept by, faded, passed, enjoying their moment of grandeur; then waiting there in the moonlight to be outmoded as had the frame, cupolaed mansions of lower town and the brownstone piles of older Crest Avenue in their turn.

The roofs lowered suddenly, the lots narrowed, the houses shrank up in size and shaded off into bungalows. These held the street for the last mile, to the bend in the river which terminated the prideful avenue at the statue of Chelsea Arbuthnot. Arbuthnot was the first governor—and, some said, the last real aristocrat—and most the last of Anglo-Saxon blood.

All the way thus far Yanci had not spoken, absorbed still in the annoyance of the evening, yet soothed somehow by the fresh air of Northern November that rushed by them. She must take her fur coat out of storage next day, she thought.

"Where are we now?" he asked.

As they slowed down Scott looked curiously at the pompous stone figures clear in the crisp moonlight, with one hand on a book and the forefinger of the other pointing, as though with reproachful symbolism, directly at some construction work going on in the street.

"This is the end of Crest Avenue," said Yanci, turning to him. "This is our show street."

"A museum of American architectural failures."

"What?"

"Nothing," he murmured.

"I should have explained it to you. I forgot. We can go along the river boulevard if you'd like—or are you tired?"

Scott assured her that he was not tired—not in the least.

Entering the boulevard, the cement road twisted under darkling trees.

"The Mississippi—how little it means to you now!" said Scott suddenly.

"What?" Yanci looked around. "Oh, the river."

"I guess it was once pretty important to your ancestors up here."

"My ancestors weren't up here then," said Yanci with some dignity. "My ancestors were from Maryland. My father came out here when he left Yale."

"Oh!" Scott was politely impressed.

"My mother was from here. My father came out here from Baltimore because of his health."

"Oh!"

"Of course we belong here now, I suppose"—this with faint condescension—"much as anywhere else."

"Of course."

"Except that I want to live in the East and I can't persuade father to," she finished. *(Continued on Page 84)*

"D. O." Means Four Years' Intensive Training

LETTERS attached to a person's name, signifying certain degrees, are a fraud unless the person has earned them and unless they stand for special and specific training.

A professional man is one who professes knowledge. And knowledge worthy of a profession can not be gained in a brief period. No man can become a "D. O." (Doctor of Osteopathy) until by virtue of extended and standard study he becomes a true professional.

No school of healing or medicine is more exacting in its curriculum or trains its students longer than Osteopathic Colleges—for a system based on the manifold truths of Anatomy and Physiology must be thorough.

Qualified men and women who are considering the study of Osteopathy should obtain information from one of the following recognized institutions:

American School of Osteopathy
Kirksville, Mo.
Founded in 1892

Des Moines Still College of Osteopathy
Des Moines, Iowa
Founded in 1898

Chicago College of Osteopathy
Chicago, Ill.
Founded in 1900

College of Osteopathic Physicians and Surgeons
Los Angeles, Cal.
Founded in 1907

Philadelphia College of Osteopathy
Philadelphia, Pa.
Founded in 1899

Massachusetts College of Osteopathy
Boston, Mass.
Founded in 1897

Kansas City College of Osteopathy and Surgery
Kansas City, Mo.
Founded in 1915

All of these schools conform to the same rigid entrance and graduation requirements. The young man or woman who enters an Osteopathic College studies long and hard, but graduates trained to creditably live up to letters standing for a Doctorship well earned.

Osteopathy is the science of healing by adjustment of the body, more specifically of the spinal column.

The Osteopathic Physician is trained through four separate school years of nine months each, in all branches necessary for correct diagnosis and processes fundamental to healing.

State laws universally recognize Osteopathy as a thoroughly responsible and capable system of healing.

Bureau of Osteopathic Education

*An interesting booklet will be forwarded to those who care to know more about Osteopathy.
Address the Bureau at 1103 F. & M. Bank Bldg.
Fort Worth, Texas*

(Continued from Page 82)

It was after one o'clock and the boulevard was almost deserted. Occasionally two yellow disks would top a rise ahead of them and take shape as a late-returning automobile. Except for that they were alone in a continual rushing dark. The moon had gone down.

"Next time the road goes near the river let's stop and watch it," he suggested.

Yanci smiled inwardly. This remark was obviously what one boy of her acquaintance had named an international petting cue, by which was meant a suggestion that aimed to create naturally a situation for a kiss. She considered the matter. As yet the man had made no particular impression on her. He was good-looking, apparently well-to-do and from New York. She had begun to like him during the dance, increasingly as the evening had drawn to a close; then the incident of her father's appalling arrival had thrown cold water upon this tentative warmth; and now—it was November, and the night was cold. Still—

"All right," she agreed suddenly.

The road divided; she swerved around and brought the car to a stop in an open place high above the river.

"Well?" she demanded in the deep quiet that followed the shutting off of the engine.

"Thanks."

"Are you satisfied here?"

"Almost. Not quite."

"Why not?"

"I'll tell you in a minute," he answered. "Why is your name Yanci?"

"It's a family name."

"It's very pretty." He repeated it several times caressingly. "Yanci—it has all the grace of Nancy, and it isn't prim."

"What's your name?" she inquired.

"Scott."

"Scott what?"

"Kimberly. Didn't you know?"

"I wasn't sure. Mrs. Rogers introduced you in such a mumble."

There was a slight pause.

"Yanci," he repeated; "beautiful Yanci, with her dark-blue eyes and her lazy soul. Do you know why I'm not quite satisfied, Yanci?"

"Why?"

Imperceptibly she had moved her face nearer until as she waited for an answer with her lips faintly apart he knew that in asking she had granted.

Without haste he bent his head forward and touched her lips.

He sighed, and both of them felt a sort of relief—relief from the embarrassment of playing up to what conventions of this sort of thing remained.

"Thanks," he said as he had when she first stopped the car.

"Now are you satisfied?"

Her blue eyes regarded him unsmilingly in the darkness.

"After a fashion; of course, you can never say—definitely."

Again he bent toward her, but she stooped and started the motor. It was late and Yanci was beginning to be tired. What purpose there was in the experiment was accomplished. He had had what he asked. If he liked it he would want more, and that put her one move ahead in the game which she felt she was beginning.

"I'm hungry," she complained. "Let's go down and eat."

"Very well," he acquiesced sadly. "Just when I was so enjoying—the Mississippi."

"Do you think I'm beautiful?" she inquired almost plaintively as they backed out.

"What an absurd question!"

"But I like to hear people say so."

"I was just about to—when you started the engine."

Downtown in a deserted all-night lunch room they ate bacon and eggs. She was pale as ivory now. The night had drawn the lazy vitality and languid color out of her face. She encouraged him to talk to her of New York until he was beginning every sentence with, "Well, now, let's see——"

The repast over, they drove home. Scott helped her put the car in the little garage, and just outside the front door she let him her lips again for the faint brush of a kiss. Then she went in.

The long living room where Yanci left was red-denend by a dying fire which had been high when Yanci left and now was faded to a steady undancing glow. She took a log from the fire box and threw it on the embers, then started as a voice came out of

the half darkness at the other end of the room.

"Back so soon?"

It was her father's voice, not yet quite sober, but alert and intelligent.

"Yes. Went riding," she answered shortly, sitting down in a wicker chair before the fire.

"Then went down and had something to eat."

"Oh!"

Her father left his place and moved to a chair nearer the fire, where he stretched himself out with a sigh. Glancing at him from the corner of her eye, for she was going to show an appropriate coldness, Yanci was fascinated by his complete recovery of dignity in the space of two hours. His graying hair was scarcely rumpled; his handsome face was ruddy as ever. Only his eyes, crisscrossed with tiny red lines, were evidence of his late dissipation.

"Have a good time?"

"Why should you care?" she answered rudely.

"Why shouldn't I?"

"You didn't seem to care earlier in the evening. I asked you to take two people home for me, and you weren't able to drive your own car."

"The deuce I wasn't!" he protested. "I could have driven in—in a race in an arana, arcaena. That Mrs. Rogers insisted that her young admirer should drive, so what could I do?"

"That isn't her young admirer," retorted Yanci crisply. There was no drawl in her voice now. "She's as old as you are. That's her niece—I mean her nephew."

"Excuse me!"

"I think you owe me an apology." She found suddenly that she bore him no resentment. She was rather sorry for him, and it occurred to her that in asking him to take Mrs. Rogers home she had somehow imposed on his liberty. Nevertheless, discipline was necessary—there would be other Saturday nights. "Don't you?" she concluded.

"I apologize, Yanci."

"Very well, I accept your apology," she answered stiffly.

"What's more, I'll make it up to you."

Her blue eyes contracted. She hoped—she hardly dared to hope that he might take her to New York.

"Let's see," he said. "November, isn't it? What date?"

"The twenty-third."

"Well, I'll tell you what I'll do." He knocked the tips of his fingers together tentatively. "I'll give you a present. I've been meaning to let you have a trip all fall, but business has been bad." She almost smiled—as though business was of any consequence in his life. "But then you need a trip. I'll make you a present of it."

He rose again, and crossing over to his desk sat down.

"I've got a little money in a New York bank that's been lying there quite a while," he said as he fumbled in a drawer for a check book. "I've been intending to close out the account. Let—me—see. There's just——" His pen scratched. "Where the devil's the blotter? Uh!"

He came back to the fire and a pink oblong paper fluttered into her lap.

"Why, father!"

It was a check for three hundred dollars.

"But can you afford this?" she demanded.

"It's all right," he reassured her, nodding. "That can be a Christmas present, too, and you'll probably need a dress or a hat or something before you go."

"Why," she began uncertainly, "I hardly know whether I ought to take this much or not! I've got two hundred of my own downtown, you know. Are you sure——"

"Oh, yes!" He waved his hand with magnificent carelessness. "You need a holiday. You've been talking about New York, and I want you to go down there. Tell some of your friends at Yale and the other colleges and they'll ask you to the prom or something. That'll be nice. You'll have a good time."

He sat down abruptly in his chair and gave vent to a long sigh. Yanci folded up the check and tucked it into the low bosom of her dress.

"Well," she drawled softly with a return to her usual manner, "you're a perfect lamb to be so sweet about it, but I don't want to be horribly extravagant."

Her father did not answer. He gave another little sigh and relaxed sleepily into his chair.

(Continued on Page 86)

(Continued from Page 84)

"Of course I do want to go," went on
Yanci.

Still her father was silent. She wondered
if he were asleep.

"Are you asleep?" she demanded, cheerfully now. She bent toward him; then she
stood up and looked at him.

"Father," she said uncertainly.

Her father remained motionless; the
ruddy color had melted suddenly out of his
face.

"Father!"

It occurred to her—and at the thought
she grew cold, and a brassière of iron
clutched at her breast—that she was alone
in the room. After a frantic instant she
said to herself that her father was dead.

▼

YANCI judged herself with inevitable
gentleness—judged herself very much
as a mother might judge a wild, spoiled
child. She was not hard-minded, nor did
she live by any ordered and considered
philosophy of her own. To such a catastrophe as the death of her father her immediate reaction was a hysterical self-pity.
The first three days were something of a
nightmare; but sentimental civilization,
being as infallible as Nature in healing the
wounds of its more fortunate children, had
inspired a certain Mrs. Oral, whom Yanci
had always loathed, with a passionate interest in all such crises. To all intents and
purposes Mrs. Oral buried Tom Bowman.
The morning after his death Yanci had
wired her maternal aunt in Chicago, but
as yet that undemonstrative and well-to-do
lady had sent no answer.

All day long, for four days, Yanci sat in
her room upstairs, hearing steps come and
go on the porch, and it merely increased
her nervousness that the doorbell had been
disconnected. This by order of Mrs. Oral!
Doorbells were always disconnected! After
the burial of the dead the strain relaxed.
Yanci, dressed in her new black, regarded
herself in the pier glass, and then wept
because she seemed to herself very sad and
beautiful. She went downstairs and tried
to read a moving-picture magazine, hoping
that she would not be alone in the house
when the winter dark came down just after
four.

This afternoon Mrs. Oral had said *carpe
diem* to the maid, and Yanci was just starting for the kitchen to see whether she had
yet gone when the reconnected bell rang
suddenly through the house. Yanci started.
She waited a minute, then went to the
door. It was Scott Kimberly.

"I was just going to inquire for you," he
said.

"Oh! I'm much better, thank you," she
responded with the quiet dignity that
seemed suited to her rôle.

They stood there in the hall awkwardly,
each reconstructing the half-facetious, half-
sentimental occasion on which they had
last met. It seemed such an irreverent
prelude to such a somber disaster. There
was no common ground for them now, no
gap that could be bridged by a slight reference to their mutual past, and there was
no foundation on which he could adequately pretend to share her sorrow.

"Won't you come in?" she said, biting
her lip nervously. He followed her to the
sitting room and sat beside her on the
lounge. In another minute, simply because
he was there and alive and friendly, she was
crying on his shoulder.

"There, there!" he said, putting his arm
behind her and patting her shoulder idiotically. "There, there, there!"

He was wise enough to attribute no ulterior significance to her action. She was
overstrained with grief and loneliness and
sentiment; almost any shoulder would have
done as well. For all the biological thrill
to either of them he might have been a
hundred years old. In a minute she sat up.

"I beg your pardon," she murmured
brokenly. "But it's—it's so dismal in this
house to-day."

"I know just how you feel, Yanci."

"Did I—did I—get—tears on your coat?"

In tribute to the tenseness of the incident they both laughed hysterically, and
with the laughter she momentarily recovered her propriety.

"I don't know why I should have chosen
you to collapse on," she wailed. "I really
don't just go round doing it in-indiscrimi-
nately on anyone who comes in."

"I consider it a—a compliment," he responded soberly, "and I can understand
the state you're in." Then, after a pause,
"Have you any plans?"

She shook her head.

"Va-vague ones," she muttered betwee[n]
little gasps. "I thought I'd go down an[d]
stay with my aunt in Chicago a while."

"I should think that'd be best—mue[h]
the best thing." Then, because he coul[d]
think of nothing else to say, he adde[d]
"Yes, very much the best thing."

"What are you doing—here in town?
she inquired, taking in her breath and littl[e]
gasps and dabbing at her eyes with a han[d]
kerchief.

"Oh, I'm here with—with the Rogerse[s]
I've been here."

"Hunting?"

"No, I've just been here."

He did not tell her that he had staye[d]
over on her account. She might think
fresh.

"I see," she said. She didn't see.

"I want to know if there's any possib[le]
thing I can do for you, Yanci. Perhaps g[o]
downtown for you, or do some errands
anything. Maybe you'd like to bundle u[p]
and get a bit of air. I could take you out
drive in your car some night, and no on[e]
would see you."

He clipped his last word short as the i[m]
advertency of this suggestion dawned o[n]
him. They stared at each other with horr[or]
in their eyes.

"Oh, no, thank you!" she cried. "I real[ly]
don't want to drive."

To his relief the outer door opened a[nd]
an elderly lady came in. It was Mrs. Or[al.]
Scott rose immediately and moved bac[k]
ward toward the door.

"If you're sure there isn't anything [I]
can do——"

Yanci introduced him to Mrs. Oral; th[en]
leaving the elder woman by the fire walk[ed]
with him to the door. An idea had su[d-]
denly occurred to her.

"Wait a minute."

She ran up the front stairs and return[ed]
immediately with a slip of pink paper [in]
her hand.

"Here's something I wish you'd do," [she]
said. "Take this to the First Natio[nal]
Bank and have it cashed for me. You c[an]
leave the money here for me any time."

Scott took out his wallet and opened [it.]

"Suppose I cash it for you now," he s[ug-]
gested.

"Oh, there's no hurry."

"But I may as well." He drew out th[e]
new one-hundred-dollar bills and gave
them to her.

"That's awfully sweet of you," s[aid]
Yanci.

"Not at all. May I come in and see y[ou]
next time I come West?"

"I wish you would."

"Then I will. I'm going East to-nigh[t.]"

The door shut him out into the snow[y]
dusk and Yanci returned to Mrs. Or[al.]
Mrs. Oral had come to discuss plans.

"And now, my dear, just what do y[ou]
plan to do? We ought to have some p[lan]
to go by, and I thought I'd find out if y[ou]
had any definite plan in your mind."

Yanci tried to think. She seemed to b[e]
self to be horribly alone in the world.

"I haven't heard from my aunt. I wi[re]
her again this morning. She may be [in]
Florida."

"In that case you'd go there?"

"I suppose so."

"Would you close this house?"

"I suppose so."

Mrs. Oral glanced around with pl[a]
practicality. It occurred to her that
Yanci gave the house up she might lik[e]
for herself.

"And now," she continued, "do [you]
know where you stand financially?"

"All right, I guess," answered Yanc[i]
differently; and then with a rush of se[nti-]
ment, "There was enough for t-two; th[ere]
ought to be enough for o-one."

"I didn't mean that," said Mrs. O[ral.]
"I mean, do you know the details?"

"No."

"Well, I thought you didn't know [the]
details. And I thought you ought to k[now]
all the details—have a detailed accou[nt of]
what and where your money is. So I c[an call]
up Mr. Haedge, who knew your father [very]
well personally, to come up this after[noon]
and glance through his papers. He [was]
going to stop in your father's bank, too[, by]
the way, and get all the details there[, so you]
don't believe your father left any will."

Details! Details! Details!

"Thank you," said Yanci. "That'll b[e]
nice."

Mrs. Oral gave three or four vigo[rous]
nods that were like heavy periods. T[hen]
she got up.

(Continued on Page 89)

(Continued from Page 86)

"And now if Hilma's gone out I'll make you some tea. Would you like some tea?"

"Sort of."

"All right, I'll make you some ni-ice tea." Tea! Tea! Tea!

Mr. Haedge, who came from one of the best Swedish families in town, arrived to see Yanci at five o'clock. He greeted her unreally; said that he had been several times to inquire for her; had organized the pallbearers and would now find out how he stood in no time. Did she have any idea whether or not there was a will? No? Well, there probably wasn't one.

There was one. He found it almost at once in Mr. Bowman's desk—but he worked there until eleven o'clock that night before he found much else. Next morning he arrived at eight, went down to the bank at ten, then to a certain brokerage firm, and came back to Yanci's house at noon. He had known Tom Bowman for some years, but he was utterly astounded when he discovered the condition in which that handsome gallant had left his affairs.

He consulted Mrs. Oral, and that afternoon he informed a frightened Yanci in measured language that she was practically penniless. In the midst of the conversation a telegram from Chicago told her that her aunt had sailed the week previous for a trip through the Orient and was not expected back until late spring.

The beautiful Yanci, so profuse, so debonair, so careless with her gorgeous adjectives, had no adjectives for this calamity. She crept upstairs like a hurt child and sat before a mirror, brushing her luxurious hair to comfort herself. One hundred and fifty strokes she gave it, as it said in the treatment, and then a hundred and fifty more—she was too distraught to stop the nervous motion. She brushed it until her arm ached, then she changed arms and went on brushing.

The maid found her next morning, asleep, sprawled across the toilet things on the dresser in a room that was heavy and sweet with the scent of spilled perfume.

(TO BE CONCLUDED)

DEBTOR'S COWARDICE

(Continued from Page 23)

...e facts. When I was married I had ...ve dollars and a job. At the end of the ...rst year we were in debt and there was a ...aby coming. I increased my earnings by ...aking on extra work, but the expenses ...ways kept a little ahead. The cost of the ...aby's birth swelled the total in red, and ...e went into our second year of married ...fe owing between five and six hundred ...ollars. By working very hard and economizing as much as it was possible for us to ...e paid some of the old bills then, but ...the end of the year we were almost a ...ousand dollars behind. Now we have ...een married ten years, and our total in...btedness, in spite of the fact that we have ...ade payments on earlier accounts when...er we could, runs into something like ...ve thousand dollars. This means that we ...ve spent more than we have taken in, ...ar by year, at the rate of at least six or ...ven hundred dollars in each twelve months. ...here is something wrong with a system ...at gives a young family that sort of ...cord, and I have been trying to determine what it is.

What did the money go for? Well, doc...rs and hospitals first; bad investments ...cond; extravagance and wasteful buying ...ird; losses caused by carelessness fourth; ...ally by our effort to keep up somewhat ...th appearances and to do what other ...ople of our incomes do—in short, speak...broadly, for the unduly heavy expense ...being average Americans.

I feel worse and do less about my bills ...o doctors than about any of the others, ...d I have been trying to determine why ...is is, because I know that it is a common ...perience. Perhaps it is mainly because ...ctors are easy creditors. You must have ...em, and according to their ethical re...irements they must come at your call, ...ether you pay them or not. Perhaps it is ...because most doctors' bills—after you ...well—seem exorbitant; perhaps because ...a doctor has no recourse except to sue, ...d it is only in cases where large sums ...involved that he cares to do this. On ...other hand, a doctor becomes, in the ...y nature of the case, more or less your ...rsonal friend. That, I am sure, is what ...kes us feel so badly about owing them. ...rsonally I like most of the men we have ...t about us professionally, and occa...ally I make up my mind to let everyone ...wait, and pay the doctors and dentists ...d surgeons and specialists first. Then I ...out their bills and total them up and ...ange my mind. The whole sum is too ...midable.

...had investments in my case do not mean ...sing stocks or money loaned to plausible ...ends for their enterprises, or speculation ...perpetual-motion machines or wave mo... ...or in the streets of dead Spaniards. ...ved in the West when I was younger ...g enough to see the inside of all the fake ...ck and promotion enterprises known to ...n, and I am gun-shy. My bad invest...ats have all been good investments that ...e been lost because I could not keep up ...ments. They include a small ranch, ...houses and lots, an automobile, a horse, ...quite a number of smaller things such ...phonographs, cameras, patented ma...es for lightening my wife's work, and ...n.

I am handing myself the worst of it, perhaps, in the bulk of this article, and I want to hand myself the best of it when I can. It is only fair to say—and I think a great many men in my own predicament could honestly make the same claim—that a lot of our money has gone in an effort to make my wife and children happier, to give them more of the things I see other men giving their families. It is a weakness, perhaps, but it is at least partially pardonable. The automobile we tried to buy was contracted for because my wife was much happier and physically better with it. I think, as a matter of fact, that the possession of one at a certain period when she needed to get away from the tedium and trying work of the house and to get the children outside and give them a good time without taxing herself, actually saved her health if not her life. So I have no particular apologies to offer for the attempt to purchase that car, even though we had to give it up in the end, and lost our investment in it.

My efforts to get a home were laudable, I am sure, but I went at it in the wrong way. I used poor judgment in buying. I bought once when we were compelled to move away before the house was ours, and in the case of the chicken ranch, any man with any business discretion would have known that it would not pay out. But I had no business discretion, and more than eighteen hundred dollars was swept away.

Our third drain resulted from extravagance and wasteful buying, which are not the same thing. By extravagance, in the first place, I do not mean high living, or even living beyond our means. We dress modestly enough, and our house—we are buying again on the partial-payment plan—is neither costly itself nor expensively furnished. Once in a while, to be sure, there has been a dress suit or a dinner gown or a dancing frock or a pair of shoes that were extravagant for us. In the aggregate the amount we have spent for pleasure has been too high, not because we have had too much pleasure, but because we doubt if that is possible, but because we have gone too high for it. Dress-circle seats instead of seats in the balcony or gallery; high-priced picture shows—of which we are both very fond—when we might have gone to the neighborhood theater; and the best cafés when we should have been in the little Italian or French places on the North Side—all these have contributed. We bought one another Christmas presents costing fifty dollars each when we should have exchanged handkerchiefs and stockings, I suppose. When we had a party we usually went to a good place—which meant a place, as it seems to mean all over America, where a good stiff price is charged for everything.

But wasteful buying was our worst offense. My wife takes some of the responsibility here. She had had no experience in keeping a house on small means, and during the first years she bought very wastefully, not through carelessness or extravagant notions, but because she didn't know how. Our grocery bills were scandalous. We had canned and glassed foods that cost enough in themselves to have furnished the whole

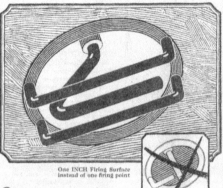

THE POPULAR GIRL

VI

By F. Scott Fitzgerald

ILLUSTRATED BY
CHARLES D. MITCHELL

She Went Up to Her Room in the Most Fashionable Hotel in New York and Ate Her Bun

TO BE precise, as Mr. Haedge was to a depressing degree, Tom Bowman left a bank balance that was more than ample—that is to say, more than ample to supply the post-mortem requirements of his own person. There was also twenty years' worth of furniture, a temperamental roadster with asthmatic cylinders and two one-thousand-dollar bonds of a chain of jewelry stores which yielded 7.5 per cent interest. Unfortunately these were not known in the bond market.

When the car and the furniture had been sold and the stucco bungalow sublet, Yanci contemplated her resources with dismay. She had a bank balance of almost a thousand dollars. If she invested this she would increase her total income to about fifteen dollars a month. This, as Mrs. Oral cheerfully observed, would pay for the boarding-house room she had taken for Yanci as long as Yanci lived. Yanci was so encouraged by this news that she burst into tears.

So she acted as any beautiful girl would have acted in this emergency. With rare decision she told Mr. Haedge that she would leave her thousand dollars in a checking account, and then she walked out of his office and across the street to a beauty parlor to have her hair waved. This raised her morale astonishingly. Indeed, she moved that very day out of the boarding house and into a small room at the best hotel in town. If she must sink into poverty she would at least do so in the grand manner.

Sewed into the lining of her best mourning hat were the three new one-hundred-dollar bills, her father's last present. In such a way, she did not know, unless perhaps because they had come to her under cheerful auspices and might through some gayety inherent in their crisp and virgin paper buy happier things than solitary meals and narrow hotel beds. They were hope and youth and luck and beauty; they began, somehow, to stand for all the things she had lost in that November night when Tom Bowman, having led her recklessly into space, had lunged off himself, leaving her to find the way back alone.

Yanci remained at the Hiawatha Hotel for three months, and she found that after the first visits of condolence her friends had happier things to do with their time than to spend it in her company. Jerry O'Rourke came to see her one day with a wild Celtic light in his eyes, and demanded that she marry him immediately. When she asked for time to consider he walked out in a rage. She heard later that he had been offered a position in Chicago and had left the same night.

She considered, frightened and uncertain. She had heard of people sinking out of place, out of life. Her father had once told her of a man in his class at college who had become a worker around saloons, polishing brass rails for the price of a can of beer; and she knew also that there were girls in this city with whose mothers her own mother had played as a little girl, but who were poor now and had sown common; who worked in stores and had married into the proletariat. But that such a fate should threaten her—how absurd! Why, she knew everyone! She had been invited everywhere; her great-grandfather had been governor of one of the Southern States!

She had written to her aunt in India and again in China, receiving no answer. She concluded that her aunt's itinerary had changed, and this was confirmed when a post card arrived from Honolulu which showed no knowledge of Tom Bowman's death, but announced that she was going with a party to the east coast of Africa. This was a last straw. The languorous and lackadaisical Yanci was now in earnest at last.

"Why not go to work for a while?" suggested Mr. Haedge with some irritation. "Lots of nice girls are nowadays, just for something to occupy themselves with. There's Elsie Prendergast, who does society news on the *Bulletin*, and that Semple girl ——"

"I can't," said Yanci shortly with a glitter of tears in her eyes. "I'm going East in February."

"East? Oh, you're going to visit someone?"

She nodded.

"Yes, I'm going to visit," she lied, "so it'd hardly be worth while to go to work." She could have wept, but she managed a haughty look. "I'd like to try reporting sometime, though, just for the fun of it."

"Yes, it's quite a lot of fun," agreed Mr. Haedge with some irony. "Still, I suppose there's no hurry about it. You must have plenty of that thousand dollars left."

"Oh, plenty!"

There were a few hundred, she knew.

"Well, then I suppose a good rest, a change of scene would be the best thing for you."

"Yes," answered Yanci. Her lips were trembling and she rose, scarcely able to control herself. Mr. Haedge seemed so impersonally cold. "That's why I'm going. A good rest is what I need."

"I think you're wise."

What Mr. Haedge would have thought had he seen the dozen drafts she wrote that night of a certain letter is problematical. Here are two of the earlier ones. The bracketed words are proposed substitutions:

Dear Scott: Not having seen you since that day I was such a silly ass and wept on your coat, I thought I'd write and tell you that I'm coming East pretty soon and would like you to have lunch [dinner] with me or something. I have been living in a room [suite] at the Hiawatha Hotel, intending to meet my aunt, with whom I am going to live [stay], and who is coming back from China this month [spring]. Meanwhile I have a lot of invitations to visit, etc., in the East, and I thought I would do it now. So I'd like to see you——

This draft ended here and went into the wastebasket. After an hour's work she produced the following:

My dear Mr. Kimberly: I have often [sometimes] wondered how you've been since I saw you. I am coming East next month before going to visit my aunt in Chicago, and you must come and see me. I have been going out very little, but my physician advises me that I need a change, so I expect to shock the proprieties by some very gay visits in the East ——

Finally in despondent abandon she wrote a simple note without explanation or subterfuge, tore it up and went to bed. Next morning she identified it in the wastebasket, decided it was the best one after all and sent him a fair copy. It ran:

Dear Scott: Just a line to tell you I will beat the Ritz-Carlton Hotel from February seventh, probably for ten days. If you'll phone me some rainy afternoon I'll invite you to tea.
Sincerely,
YANCI BOWMAN.

VII

YANCI was going to the Ritz for no more reason than that she had once told Scott Kimberly that she always went there. When she reached New York—a cold New York, a strangely menacing New York, quite different from the gay city of theaters and hotel-corridor rendezvous that she had known—there was exactly two hundred dollars in her purse.

It had taken a large part of her bank account to live, and she had at last broken into her sacred three hundred dollars to substitute pretty and delicate quarter-mourning clothes for the heavy black she had laid away.

Walking into the hotel at the moment when its exquisitely dressed patrons were assembling for luncheon, it drained at her confidence to appear bored and at ease. Surely the clerks at the desk knew the contents of her pocketbook. She fancied even that the foreign labels she had steamed from an old trunk of her father's and pasted on her suitcase. This last thought horrified her. Perhaps the very hotels and steamers so grandly named had long since been out of commission!

As she stood drumming her fingers on the desk she was wondering whether if she were refused admittance she could muster a casual smile and stroll out coolly enough to deceive two richly dressed women standing near. It had not taken long for the confidence of twenty years to evaporate. Three months without security had made an ineffaceable mark on Yanci's soul.

"Twenty-four sixty-two," said the clerk callously.

Her heart settled back into place as she followed the bell boy to the elevator, meanwhile casting a nonchalant glance at the two fashionable women as she passed them. Were their skirts long or short?—longer, she noticed.

She wondered how much the skirt of her new walking suit could be let out.

At luncheon her spirits soared. The head waiter bowed to her. The light rattle of conversation, the subdued hum of the music soothed her. She ordered supreme of melon, eggs Susette and an artichoke, and signed her room number to the check with scarcely a glance at it as it lay beside her plate. Up in her room, with the telephone directory open on the bed before her, she tried to locate her scattered metropolitan acquaintances. Yet even as the phone numbers, with their supercilious tags, Plaza, Circle and Rhinelander, stared out at her, she could feel a cold wind blow at her unstable confidence. These girls, acquaintances of school, of a summer, of a house party, even of a week-end at a college prom—what claim or attraction could she, poor and friendless, exercise over them? They had their loves, their dates, their week's gayety planned in advance. They would almost resent her inconvenient memory.

Nevertheless, she called four girls. One of them was out, one at Palm Beach, one in California. The only one to whom she talked said in a hearty voice that she was in bed with grippe, but would phone Yanci as soon as she felt well enough to go out. Then Yanci gave up the girls. She would have to create the illusion of a good time in some other manner. The illusion must be created—that was part of her plan.

She looked at her watch and found that it was three o'clock. Scott Kimberly should have phoned before this, or at least sent some word. Still, he was probably busy—at a club, she thought vaguely, or else buying some neckties. He would probably call at four.

Yanci was well aware that she must work quickly. She had figured to a nicety that one hundred and fifty dollars carefully expended would carry her through two weeks, no more. The idea of failure, the fear that at the end of that time she would be friendless and penniless had not begun to bother her.

It was not the first time that for amusement, for a coveted invitation or for curiosity she had deliberately set out to capture a man; but it was the first time she had laid her plans with necessity and desperation pressing in on her.

One of her strongest cards had always been her background, the impression she gave that she was popular and desired and happy. This she must create now, and apparently out of nothing. Scott must somehow be brought to think that a fair portion of New York was at her feet.

At four she went over to Park Avenue, where the sun was out walking and the February day was fresh and odorous of spring and the high apartments of her desire lined the street with radiant whiteness. Here she would live on a gay schedule of pleasure. In these smart not-to-be-entered-without-a-card women's shops she would spend the morning hours acquiring and acquiring, ceaselessly and without thought of expense; in these restaurants she would lunch at noon in company with other fashionable women, orchid-adorned always, and perhaps bearing an absurdly dwarfed Pomeranian in her sleek arms.

In the summer—well, she would go to Tuxedo, perhaps to an immaculate house perched high on a fashionable eminence, where she would emerge to visit a world of teas and balls, of horse shows and polo. Between the halves of the polo game the players would cluster around her in their white suits and helmets, admiringly, and when she swept away, bound for some new delight, she would be followed by the eyes of many envious but intimidated women.

Every other summer they would, of course, go abroad. She began to plan a typical year, distributing a few months here and a few months there until she—and Scott Kimberly, by implication—would become the very auguries of the season, shifting with the slightest stirring of the social barometer from rusticity to urbanity, from palm to pine.

She had two weeks, no more, in which to attain to this position. In an ecstasy of determined emotion she lifted up her head toward the tallest of the tall white apartments.

"It will be too marvelous!" she said to herself.

For almost the first time in her life her words were not too exaggerated to express the wonder shining in her eyes.

VIII

ABOUT five o'clock she hurried back to the hotel, demanding feverishly at the desk if there had been a telephone message for her. To her profound disappointment there was nothing. A minute after she had entered her room the phone rang.

"This is Scott Kimberly."

At the words a call to battle echoed in her heart.

"Oh, how do you do?"

Her tone implied that she had almost forgotten him. It was not frigid—it was merely casual.

As she answered the inevitable question as to the hour when she had arrived a warm glow spread over her. Now that, from a personification of all the riches and pleasure she craved, he had materialized as merely a male voice over the telephone, her confidence became strengthened. Male voices were male voices. They could be managed; they could be made to intone syllables of which the minds behind them had no approval. Male voices could be made sad or tender or despairing at her will. She rejoiced. The soft clay was ready to her hand.

"Won't you take dinner with me to-night?" Scott was suggesting.

"Why"—perhaps not, she thought; let him think of her to-night—"I don't believe I'll be able to," she said. "I've got an engagement for dinner and the theater. I'm terribly sorry."

Her voice did not sound sorry—it sounded polite. Then as though a happy thought had occurred to her as to a time and place where she could work him into her list of dates, "I'll tell you: Why don't you come around here this afternoon and have tea with me?"

He would be there immediately. He had been playing squash and as soon as he took a plunge he would arrive. Yanci hung up the phone and turned with a quiet efficiency to the mirror, too tense to smile.

She regarded her lustrous eyes and dusky hair in critical approval. Then she took a lavender tea gown from her trunk and began to dress.

She let him wait seven minutes in the lobby before she appeared; then she approached him with a friendly, lazy smile.

"How do you do?" she murmured. "It's marvelous to see you again. How are you?" And, with a long sigh, "I'm frightfully tired. I've been on the go ever since I got here this morning; shopping and then tearing off to

luncheon and a matinée. I've bought everything I saw. I don't know how I'm going to pay for it all."

She remembered vividly that when they had first met she had told him, without expecting to be believed, how unpopular she was. She could not risk such a remark now, even in jest. He must think that she had been on the go every minute of the day.

They took a table and were served with olive sandwiches and tea. He was so good-looking, she thought, and marvelously dressed. His gray eyes regarded her with interest from under immaculate ash-blond hair. She wondered how he passed his days, how he liked her costume, what he was thinking of at that moment.

"How long will you be here?" he asked.

"Well, two weeks, off and on. I'm going down to Princeton for the February prom and then up to a house party in Westchester County for a few days. Are you shocked at me for going out so soon? Father would have wanted me to, you know. He was very modern in all his ideas."

She had debated this remark on the train. She was not going to a house party. She was not invited to the Princeton prom. Such things, nevertheless, were necessary to create the illusion. That was everything—the illusion.

"And then," she continued, smiling, "two of my old beaux are in town, which makes it nice for me."

She saw Scott blink and she knew that he appreciated the significance of this.

"What are your plans for this winter?" he demanded. "Are you going back West?"

"No. You see, my aunt returns from India this week. She's going to open her Florida house, and we'll stay there until the middle of March. Then we'll come up to Hot Springs and we may go to Europe for the summer."

This was all the sheerest fiction. Her first letter to her aunt, which had given the bare details of Tom Bowman's death, had at last reached its destination. Her aunt had replied with a note of conventional sympathy and the announcement that she would be back in America within two years if she didn't decide to live in Italy.

"But you'll let me see something of you while you're here," urged Scott, after attending to this impressive program. "If you can't take dinner with me to-night, how about Wednesday—that's the day after to-morrow?"

"Wednesday? Let's see." Yanci's brow was knit with imitation thought. "I think I have a date for Wednesday but I don't know for certain. How about phoning me to-morrow, and I'll let you know? Because I want to go with you, only I think I've made an engagement."

"Very well, I'll phone you."

"Do—about ten."

(Continued on Page 105)

The Floor Manager Was Sorry, But the Lady Really Must Have Left it at Home. There Was No Fifty-Dollar Bill in the Cash Drawer

THE POPULAR GIRL

(Continued from Page 19)

"Try to be able to—then or any time."

"I'll tell you—if I can't go to dinner with you Wednesday I can go to lunch surely."

"All right," he agreed. "And we'll go to a matinée."

They danced several times. Never by word or sign did Yanci betray more than the most cursory interest in him until just at the end, when she offered him her hand to say good-by.

"Good-by, Scott."

For just the fraction of a second—not long enough for him to be sure it had happened at all, but just enough so that he would be reminded, however faintly, of that night on the Mississippi boulevard—she looked into his eyes. Then she turned quickly and hurried away.

She took her dinner in a little tea room around the corner. It was an economical dinner which cost a dollar and a half. There was no date concerned in it at all, and no man—except an elderly person in spats who tried to speak to her as she came out the door.

IX

SITTING alone in one of the magnificent moving-picture theaters—a luxury which she thought she could afford—Yanci watched Mae Murray swirl through splendidly imagined vistas, and meanwhile considered the progress of the first day. In retrospect it was a distinct success. She had given the correct impression both as to her material prosperity and as to her attitude toward Scott himself. It seemed best to avoid evening dates. Let him have the evenings to himself, to think of her, to imagine her with other men, even to spend a few lonely hours in his apartment, considering how much more cheerful it might be if — Let time and absence work for her.

Engrossed for a while in the moving picture, she calculated the cost of the apartment in which its heroine endured her movie wrongs. She admired its slender Italian table, occupying only one side of the large dining room and flanked by a long bench which gave it an air of medieval luxury. She rejoiced in the beauty of Mae Murray's clothes and furs, her gorgeous hats, her short-seeming French shoes. Then after a moment her mind returned to her own drama; she wondered if Scott were already engaged, and her heart dipped at the thought. Yet it was unlikely. He had been too quick to phone her on her arrival, too lavish with his time, too responsive that afternoon.

After the picture she returned to the Ritz, where she slept deeply and happily for almost the first time in three months. The atmosphere around her no longer seemed cold. Even the floor clerk had smiled kindly and admiringly when Yanci asked for her key.

Next morning at ten Scott phoned. Yanci, who had been up for hours, pretended to be drowsy from her dissipation of the night before.

No, she could not take dinner with him on Wednesday. She was terribly sorry; she had an engagement, as she had feared. But he could have luncheon and go to a matinée if he would get her back in time for tea.

She spent the day roving the streets. On top of a bus, though not on the front seat, where Scott might possibly spy her, she sailed out Riverside Drive and back along Fifth Avenue just at the winter twilight, and her feeling for New York and its gorgeous splendors deepened and redoubled. Here she must live and be rich, be nodded to by the traffic policemen at the corners as she sat in her limousine—with a small dog—and here she must stroll on Sunday and from a stylish church, with Scott, handsome in his cutaway and tall hat, walking devotedly at her side.

At luncheon on Wednesday she described to Scott's benefit a fanciful two plays. She told of a motoring trip up the Hudson and gave him her opinion of two plays she had seen with—it was implied—adoring gentlemen beside her. She had read up very carefully on the plays in the morning paper and chosen two concerning which she could garner the most information.

"Oh," he said in dismay, "you've seen *Dulcy?* I have two seats for it—but you won't want to go again."

"Oh, no, I don't mind," she protested truthfully. "You see, we went late, and anyway I adored it."

But he wouldn't hear of her sitting through it again—besides, he had seen it himself. It was a play Yanci was mad to see, but she was compelled to watch him while he exchanged the tickets for others, and for the poor seats available at the last moment. The game seemed difficult at times.

"By the way," he said afterward as they drove back to the hotel in a taxi, "you'll be going down to the Princeton prom tomorrow, won't you?"

She started. She had not realized that it would be so soon or that he would know of it.

"Yes," she answered coolly. "I'm going down to-morrow afternoon."

"On the 2:20, I suppose," Scott commented; and then, "Are you going to meet the boy who's taking you down—at Princeton?"

For an instant she was off her guard.

"Yes, he'll meet the train."

"Then I'll take you to the station," proposed Scott. "There'll be a crowd, and you may have trouble getting a porter."

She could think of nothing to say, no valid objection to make. She wished she had said that she was going by automobile, but she could conceive of no graceful and plausible way of amending her first admission.

"That's mighty sweet of you."

"You'll be at the Ritz when you come back?"

"Oh, yes," she answered. "I'm going to keep my rooms."

Her bedroom was the smallest and least expensive in the hotel.

She concluded to let him put her on the train for Princeton; in fact, she saw no alternative. Next day as she packed her suitcase after luncheon the situation had taken such hold of her imagination that she filled it with the very things she would have chosen had she really been going to the prom. Her intention was to get out at the first stop and take the train back to New York.

Scott called for her at half past one and they took a taxi to the Pennsylvania Station. The train was crowded as he had expected, but he found her a seat and stowed her grip in the rack overhead.

"I'll call you Friday to see how you've behaved," he said.

"All right. I'll be good."

Their eyes met and in an instant, with an inexplicable, only half-conscious rush of emotion, they were in perfect communion. When Yanci came back, the glance seemed to say, ah, then —

A voice startled her ear:

"Why, Yanci!"

Yanci looked around. To her horror she recognized a girl named Ellen Harley, one of those to whom she had phoned upon her arrival.

"Well, Yanci Bowman! You're the last person I ever expected to see. How are you?"

Yanci introduced Scott. Her heart was beating violently.

"Are you coming to the prom? How perfectly slick!" cried Ellen. "Can I sit here with you? I've been wanting to see you. Who are you going with?"

"No one you know."

"Maybe I do."

Her words, falling like sharp claws on Yanci's sensitive soul, were interrupted by an unintelligible outburst from the conductor. Scott bowed to Ellen, cast at Yanci one level glance and then hurried off.

The train started. As Ellen arranged her grip and threw off her fur coat Yanci looked around her. The car was gay with girls whose excited chatter filled the damp, rubbery air like smoke. Here and there sat a chaperon, a mass of decaying rock in a field of flowers, predicting with a mute and somber fatality the end of all gayety and all youth. How many times had Yanci herself been one of such a crowd, careless and happy, dreaming of the men she would meet, of the battered hacks waiting at the station, the snow-covered campus, the big open fires in the clubhouses, and the imported orchestra beating out defiant melody against the approach of morning.

And now—she was an intruder, uninvited, undesired. At the Ritz on the day of her arrival, she felt that any instant her mask would be torn from her and she would be exposed as a pretender to the game of all the car.

Bam-Bee-No
THE NATIONAL GAME

JUST OUT

Play Real Baseball
at Home or Club

Here's a landslide of sport for those who like that grand old game of Baseball, Bam-Bee-No, a real baseball game for home or club. Played on any table, anywhere. Exactly the same as baseball—all the tight pinches, strikes, balls, singles, doubles, triples, homers—everything that the pop bottles and rah checks. Fun! Thrills! Man, Man! You'll get your money's worth every time you play. Just the thing for these days. You don't need to wager to make it exciting.

Two or More Can Play
Great Sport for Young or Old

Bam-Bee-No can be played by two or more—the more the merrier Makes racket forget about the office of shop. Takes grandfather back to his boyhood days. Even mother will play it by the hour. And the young folks—they'll play Bam-Bee-No in their dreams. (Not for tots.) Just the game to turn the dragging party into a screaming success. Finest game out for men's and boys' clubs, lodges, Y.M.C.A's, K. of C's, Boy Scout Troops, etc. Get started! Be the first in your neighborhood or organization to introduce this riot of excitement. See what a hit you make!

Order Bam-Bee-No now
Start playing right away

Get in the game! Play ball! All you need is the Bam-Bee-No outfit, with the Book of Plays that covers every combination known to baseball. Any table is a ball-park when you have Bam-Bee-No. Nothing complicated. You'll catch on in a minute. Enjoyment starts with the first roll of the Bam-Bee-No outfit. Try it out—if you don't think it's the biggest bundle of enjoyment you ever had for the price, we'll refund your money. Order now! (Canada and west of Rockies, $2.25.)

Babe Ruth says: "I've played the baseball game which you have doped out and certainly think you have hit on a popular idea."

Joe Vila, Sport Editor of the New York Sun, says: "I've played your baseball game and found it one of the most interesting novelties I've ever seen."

Special Trial Offer Buy a Bam-Bee-No outfit today. Have a game with the family or choose up sides with your friends. Play three games. If you're not satisfied, return the outfit and we'll refund your money. Descriptive folder free.

The Bambeeno Sales Co.
402 Madison Ave., Toledo, Ohio

Dealers: Bam-Bee-No is a quick and sure seller in Department Stores, Drug Stores, Cigar Stores, Novelty Stores, Sporting Goods Stores and departments. Write or wire at once for attractive proposition.

$2.00 (Canada and West of Rockies $2.25)   Folder FREE

106   THE SATURDAY EVENING POST   *February 18, 1922*

"Tell me everything!" Ellen was saying. "Tell me what you've been doing. I didn't see you at any of the football games last fall."

This was by way of letting Yanci know that she had attended them herself.

The conductor was bellowing from the rear of the car, "Manhattan Transfer next stop!"

Yanci's cheeks burned with shame. She wondered what she had best do—meditating a confession, deciding against it, answering Ellen's chatter in frightened monosyllables—then, as with an ominous thunder of brakes the speed of the train began to slacken, she sprang on a despairing impulse to her feet.

"My heavens!" she cried. "I've forgotten my shoes! I've got to go back and get them."

Ellen reacted to this with annoying efficiency.

"I'll take your suitcase," she said quickly, "and you can call for it. I'll be at the Charter Club."

"No!" Yanci almost shrieked. "It's got my dress in it!"

Ignoring the lack of logic in her own remark, she swung the suitcase off the rack with what seemed to her a superhuman effort and went reeling down the aisle, stared at curiously by the arrogant eyes of many girls. When she reached the platform just as the train came to a stop she felt weak and shaken. She stood on the hard cement which marks the quaint old village of Manhattan Transfer and tears were streaming down her cheeks as she watched the unfeeling cars speed off to Princeton with their burden of happy youth.

After half an hour's wait Yanci got on a train and returned to New York. In thirty minutes she had lost the confidence that a week had gained for her. She came back to her little room and lay down quietly upon the bed.

x

BY FRIDAY Yanci's spirits had partly recovered from their chill depression. Scott's voice over the telephone in midmorning was like a tonic, and she told him of the delights of Princeton with convincing enthusiasm, drawing vicariously upon a prom she had attended there two years before. He was anxious to see her, he said. Would she come to dinner and the theater that night? Yanci considered, greatly tempted. Dinner—she had been economizing on meals, and a gorgeous dinner in some extravagant show place followed by a musical comedy appealed to her starved fancy, indeed; but instinct told her that the time was not yet right. Let him wait. Let him dream a little more, a little longer.

"I'm too tired, Scott," she said with an air of extreme frankness; "that's the whole truth of the matter. I've been out every night since I've been here, and I'm really half dead. I'll rest up on this house party over the week-end and then I'll go to dinner with you any day you want me."

There was a minute's silence while she held the phone expectantly.

"Lot of resting up you'll do on a house party," he replied; "and, anyway, next week is so far off. I'm awfully anxious to see you, Yanci."

"So am I, Scott."

She allowed the faintest caress to linger on his name. When she had hung up she felt happy again. Despite her humiliation on the train her plan had been a success. The illusion was still intact; it was nearly complete. And in three meetings and a dozen telephone calls she had managed to create a tenser atmosphere between them than if he had seen her constantly in the moods and avowals and beguilement of an out-and-out flirtation.

When Monday came she paid her first week's hotel bill. The size of it did not alarm her—she was prepared for that—but the shock of seeing so much money go, of realizing that there remained only one hundred and twenty dollars of her father's present, gave her a peculiar sinking sensation in the pit of her stomach. She decided to bring guile to bear immediately, to tantalize Scott by a carefully planned incident, and then at the end of the week to show him simply and definitely that she loved him.

As a decoy for Scott's tantalization she located by telephone a certain Jimmy Long, a handsome boy with whom she had played as a little girl and who had recently come to New York to work. Jimmy Long was deftly maneuvered into asking her to go to

a matinée with him on Wednesday afternoon. He was to meet her in the lobby at two.

On Wednesday she lunched with Scott. His eyes followed her every motion, and knowing this she felt a great rush of tenderness toward him. Desiring at first only what he represented, she had begun half unconsciously to desire him also. Nevertheless, she did not permit herself the slightest relaxation on that account. The time was too short and the odds too great. That she was beginning to love him only fortified her resolve.

"Where are you going this afternoon?" he demanded.

"To a matinée—with an annoying man."

"Why is he annoying?"

"Because he wants me to marry him and I don't believe I want to."

There was just the faintest emphasis on the word "believe." The implication was that she was not sure—that is, not quite.

"Don't marry him."

"I won't—probably."

"Yanci," he said in a low voice, "do you remember a night on that boulevard ——"

She changed the subject. It was noon and the room was full of sunlight. It was not quite the place, the time. When he spoke she must have every aspect of the situation in control. He must say only what she wanted said; nothing else would do.

"It's five minutes to two," she told him looking at her wrist watch. "We'd better go. I've got to keep my date."

"Do you want to go?"

"No," she answered simply.

This seemed to satisfy him, and they walked out to the lobby. Then Yanci caught sight of a man waiting there, obviously ill at ease and dressed as no habitué of the Ritz ever was. The man was Jimmy Long, and not since a favored beau of his Western city. And now—his hat was green actually! His coat, seasons old, was quite evidently the product of a well-known ready-made concern. His shoes, long and narrow, turned up at the toes. From head to foot everything that could possibly be wrong about him was wrong. He was embarrassed by instinct only, unconscious of his *gaucherie*, an obscene specter, a Nemesis, a horror.

"Hello, Yanci!" he cried, starting toward her with evident relief.

With a heroic effort Yanci turned to Scott, trying to hold his glance to herself. In the very act of turning she noticed the impeccability of Scott's coat, his tie.

"Thanks for luncheon," she said with radiant smile. "See you to-morrow."

Then she dived rather than ran for Jimmy Long, disposed of his outstretched hand and bundled him bumping through the revolving door with only a quick "Let's hurry!" to appease his somewhat sulky astonishment.

The incident worried her. She consoled herself by remembering that Scott had had only a momentary glance at the man, and that he had probably been looking at her anyhow. Nevertheless, she was horrified and it is to be doubted whether Jimmy Long enjoyed her company enough to compensate him for the cut-price, twentieth row tickets he had obtained at Black's Drug Store.

But if Jimmy as a decoy had proved a lamentable failure, an occurrence of Thursday offered her considerable satisfaction and paid tribute to her quickness of mind. She had invented an engagement for luncheon, and Scott was going to meet her two o'clock to take her to the Hippodrome. She lunched alone somewhat impatiently in the Ritz dining room and sauntered out almost side by side with a good-looking young man who had been at the table next to her. She expected to meet Scott in the outer lobby, but as she reached the entrance to the restaurant she saw him standing not far away.

On a lightning impulse she turned to the good-looking man abreast of her, bowed sweetly and said in an audible, friendly voice, "Well, I'll see you later."

Then before he could even register astonishment she faced about quickly and joined Scott.

"Who was that?" he asked, frowning.

"Isn't he darling-looking?"

"If you like that sort of looks."

Scott's tone implied that the gentleman referred to was effete and overdressed. Yanci laughed, impersonally admiring the skillfulness of her ruse.

It was in preparation for that all-important Saturday night that on Thursday she went

(Continued on Page 109)

(Continued from Page 106)

to a shop on Forty-second Street to buy me long gloves. She made her purchase d handed the clerk a fifty-dollar bill so at her lightened pocketbook would feel avier with the change she could put in. o her surprise the clerk tendered her the ckage and a twenty-five-cent piece.

"Is there anything else?"

"The rest of my change."

"You've got it. You gave me five dollo-s. Four-seventy-five for the gloves leaves enty-five cents."

"I gave you fifty dollars."

"You must be mistaken."

Yanci searched her purse.

"I gave you fifty!" she repeated franally.

"No, ma'am, I saw it myself."

They glared at each other in hot iritran. A cash girl was called to testify, then a floor manager; a small crowd gathered.

"Why, I'm perfectly sure!" cried Yanci, o angry tears trembling in her eyes. "m positive!"

The floor manager was sorry, but the ly really must have left it at home. ere was no fifty-dollar bill in the cash awer. The bottom was creaking out of nci's rickety world.

"If you'll leave your address," said the or manager, "I'll let you know if any-ng turns up."

"Oh, you damn fools!" cried Yanci, ng control. "I'll get the police!"

And weeping like a child she left the p. Outside, helplessness overpowered . How could she prove anything? It after six and the store was closing even she left it. Whichever employe had the y-dollar bill would be on her way home w before the police could arrive, and why uld the New York police believe her, even give her fair play?

n despair she returned to the Ritz, ere she searched through her trunk the bill with hopeless and mechanical tures. It was not there. She had known uld not be there. She gathered every ny together and found that she had -one dollars and thirty cents. Telening the office, she asked that her bill ade out up to the following noon—she too dispirited to think of leaving before .

he waited in her room, not daring even end for ice water. Then the phone rang she heard the room clerk's voice, cheerand metallic.

Miss Bowman?"

Yes."

Your bill, including to-night, is ex-act-ly -one twenty."

Fifty-one twenty?" Her voice was bling.

Yes, ma'am."

Thank you very much."

reathless, she sat there beside the tele-ne, too frightened now to cry. She had cents left in the world!

x1

RIDAY. She had scarcely slept. There ere dark rings under her eyes, and a hot bath followed by a cold one d to arouse her from a despairing argy. She had never fully realized t it would mean to be without money ew York; her determination and vital-seemed to have vanished at last with fifty-dollar bill. There was no help for w—she must attain her desire to-day ever.

he was to meet Scott at the Plaza for She wondered—was it her imagina-or had his manner been consciously the afternoon before? For the first in several days she had needed to

make no effort to keep the conversation from growing sentimental. Suppose he had decided that it must come to nothing—that she was too extravagant, too frivolous. A hundred eventualities presented themselves to her during the morning—a dreary morning, broken only by her purchase of a ten-cent bun at a grocery store.

It was her first food in twenty hours, but she self-consciously pretended to the grocer to be having an amusing and facetious time in buying one bun. She even asked to see his grapes, but told him, after looking at them appraisingly—and hungrily—that she didn't think she'd buy any. They didn't look ripe to her, she said. The store was full of prosperous women who, with thumb and first finger joined and held high in front of them, were inspecting food. Yanci would have liked to ask one of them for a bunch of grapes. Instead she went up to her room in the hotel and ate her bun.

When four o'clock came she found that she was thinking about the sand-wiches she would have for tea than of what else must occur there, and as she walked slowly up Fifth Avenue toward the Plaza she felt a sudden faintness which she took several deep breaths of air to overcome. She wondered vaguely where the bread line was. That was where people in her condition should go—but where was it? How did one find out? She imagined fantastically that it was in the phone book under B, or perhaps under N, for New York Bread Line.

She reached the Plaza. Scott's figure, as he stood waiting for her in the crowded lobby, was a personification of solidity and hope.

"Let's hurry!" she cried with a tortured smile. "I feel rather punk and I want some tea."

She ate a club sandwich, some chocolate ice cream and six tea biscuits. She could have eaten much more, but she dared not. The eventuality of her hunger having been disposed of, she must turn at bay now and face this business of life, represented by the handsome young man who sat opposite watching her with some emotion whose import she could not determine just behind his level eyes.

But the words, the glance, subtle, pervasive and sweet, that she had planned, failed somehow to come.

"Oh, Scott," she said in a low voice, "I'm so tired."

"Tired of what?" he asked coolly.

"Of—everything."

There was a silence.

"I'm afraid," she said uncertainly— "I'm afraid I won't be able to keep that date with you to-morrow."

There was no pretense in her voice now. The emotion was apparent in the waver of each word, without intention or control.

"I'm going away."

"Are you? Where?"

His tone showed a strong interest, but she winced as she saw that that was all.

"My aunt's come back. She wants me to join her in Florida right away."

"Isn't this rather unexpected?"

"Yes."

"You'll be coming back soon?" he said after a moment.

"I don't think so. I think we'll go to Europe from—from New Orleans."

"Oh!"

Again there was a pause. It lengthened. In the shadow of a moment it would become awkward, she knew. She had lost—well? Yet, she would go on to the end.

"Will you miss me?"

"Yes."

One word. She caught his eyes, wondered for a moment if she saw more there than

Number

442

—one of the twelve
most popular pens
in the world

No. 442, the Jackson, a
Falcon - shaped stub, leads
all other stub pens in popularity. It carries a gener-
ous supply of ink, glides
smoothly over the paper
with little effort, and is an
easy pen to use.

Choose from the dealer's
display case, order by number for safety's sake and
buy by the box—it is red.

**The Esterbrook Pen
Mfg. Co.**
72-100 Delaware Ave.
Camden, N. J.

Canadian Agents: Brown Bros., Ltd.
Toronto, Canada

Send 15c
for samples of the
twelve most popular
pens in the little
red box.

Esterbrook

---

that kindly interest; then she dropped her
own again.

"I like it—here at the Plaza," she heard
herself saying.

They spoke of things like that. Afterwards she could never remember what they
said. They spoke—even of the tea, of the
thaw that was ended and the cold coming
down outside. She was sick at heart and
she seemed to herself very old. She rose
at last.

"I've got to tear," she said. "I'm going
out to dinner."

To the last she would keep on—the illusion, that was the important thing. To
hold her proud lies inviolate—there was
only a moment now. They walked toward
the door.

"Put me in a taxi," she said quietly. "I
don't feel equal to walking."

He helped her in. They shook hands.

"Good-by, Scott," she said.

"Good-by, Yanci," he answered slowly.

"You've been awfully nice to me. I'll
always remember what a good time you
helped to give me this two weeks."

"The pleasure was mine. Shall I tell the
driver the Ritz?"

"No. Just tell him to drive out Fifth.
I'll tap on the glass when I want him to
stop."

Out Fifth! He would think, perhaps,
that she was dining on Fifth. What an appropriate finish that would be! She wondered if he were impressed. She could not
see his face clearly, because the air was
dark with the snow and her own eyes were
blurred by tears.

"Good-by," he said simply.

He seemed to realize that any pretense
of sorrow on his part would be transparent.
She knew that he did not want her.

The door slammed, the car started,
skidding in the snowy street.

Yanci leaned back dismally in the corner.
Try as she might, she could not see where
she had failed or what it was that had
changed her attitude toward her. For the
first time in her life she had obstinately
offered herself to a man—and he had not
wanted her. The precariousness of her
position paled beside the tragedy of her
defeat.

She let the car go on—the cold air was
what she needed, of course. Ten minutes

had slipped away drearily before she
realized that she had not a penny with
which to pay the driver.

"It doesn't matter," she thought.
"They'll just send me to jail, and that's a
place to sleep."

She began thinking of the taxi driver.

"He'll be mad when he finds out, poor
man. Maybe he's very poor, and he'll have
to pay the fare*himself.* With a vague
sentimentality she began to cry.

"Poor taxi man," she was saying half
aloud. "Oh, people have such a hard time—
such a hard time!"

She rapped on the window and,when the
car drew up at a curb she got out. She was
at the end of Fifth Avenue and it was dark
and cold.

"Send for the police!" she cried in a
quick low voice. "I haven't any money!"

The taxi man scowled down at her.

"Then what'd you get in for?"

She had not noticed that another car
had stopped about twenty-five feet behind
them. She heard running footsteps in the
snow and then a voice at her elbow.

"It's all right," someone was saying to
the taxi man. "I've got it right here."

A bill was passed up. Yanci slumped
sideways against Scott's overcoat.

Scott knew—he knew because he had
gone to Princeton to surprise her, because
the stranger she had spoken to in the Ritz
had been his best friend, because the check
of her father's for three hundred dollars
had been returned to him marked "No
funds." Scott knew—he had known for
days.

But he said nothing; only stood there
holding her with one arm as her taxi drove
away.

"Oh, it's you," said Yanci faintly.
"Lucky you came along. I left my purse
back at the Ritz, like an awful fool. I do
such ridiculous things——"

Scott laughed with some enjoyment.
There was a light snow falling, and lest she
should slip in the damp he picked her up
and carried her back toward his waiting
taxi.

"Such ridiculous things," she repeated.

"Go to the Ritz first," he said to the
driver. "I want to get a trunk."

(THE END)

THE SATURDAY EVENING POST

(More Than Two Million and a Quarter Weekly)

Table of Contents

February 18, 1922

Cover Design by Norman Rockwell

Appendix Two
ILLUSTRATIONS

HEAD AND SHOULDERS

"I Hope I Haven't Given
You the Impression
That I Consider Kissing Intrinsically Irrational"

"What Do They Expect for a Hundred a Week—Perpetual Motion?" She Grumbled to Herself in the Wings

"I Know," Agreed Marcia, Nodding—"Your Name's Horace. I Just Call You Omar Because You Remind Me of a Smoked Cigarette"

MYRA MEETS HIS FAMILY

"Dearest, Dearest!" He Cried. "I Shouldn't Have Told You! I Shouldn't Have Told You!"

"As for You, My Exquisite Young Lady, You'd Better Understand That the Best Thing You Can Do is to Decide to Settle Down Right Here. This is My Home, and I Mean to Keep it So!"

"Myra, I've Done a Ghastly Thing — to You, to Me, to Us. I Haven't a Word to Say in Favor of Myself"

THE CAMEL'S BACK

A Little Man Who Knew It All Persuaded Perry to Superman Her, to Tell Her She'd Have to Marry Him at Once or Call it Off Forever. This is Some Stunt

"You 'Fraid of Me?" Said Betty. "Don't Be. You See I'm a Snake Charmer, But I'm Pretty Good at Camels Too"

"Julius Cæsar," Announced Perry, Turning Round From the Mirror.
"Man of Iron Will and Stern 'Termination"

BERNICE BOBS HER HAIR

*He Wondered Idly Whether She Was a Poor Conversationalist Because She Got
No Attention or Got No Attention Because She Was a Poor Conversationalist*

Bob 211

"Well," said Marjorie, "No Girl Can Permanently Bolster Up a Lame-Duck Visitor, Because These Days it's Every Girl for Herself"

ICE PALACE

*Swathed in Furs Sally Carrol Put in a Morning
Tobogganing on the Country-Club Hill*

They Passed Through the Gateway and Followed a Path That Led Through a Wavy Valley of Graves

"I Told You I Wouldn't Want to Tie My Life to Any of the Boys That are Round Tarleton Now, But I Never Made Any Sweepin' Generalities"

OFF SHORE PIRATES

*Her Feet, in Blue Satin Slippers Which Swung Nonchalantly
From Her Toes, Were Perched on the Arm of a Settee*

"Go on," She Urged. "Lie to Me by the Moonlight. Do a Fabulous Story"

"Is it a Proposal of Marriage? Extra! Ardita Farnam Becomes Pirate's Bride. Society Girl Kidnaped by Ragtime Bank Robber"

POPULAR GIRL PART I

"Who Was the Gentleman With the Invisible Tie?" Scott Asked. "Is His Personality as Diverting as His Haberdashery?"

She Was Overstrained With
Grief and Loneliness; Almost
Any Shoulder Would Have
Done as Well

The Maid Found Her
Next Morning, Asleep,
Sprawled Across the
Toilet Things on the
Dresser in a Room
That Was Heavy and
Sweet With the Scent
of Spilled Perfume

POPULAR GIRL PART II

She Went Up to Her Room in the Most Fashionable Hotel in New York and Ate Her Bun

The Floor Manager Was Sorry, But the Lady Really Must Have Left it at Home. There Was No Fifty-Dollar Bill in the Cash Drawer